MW01036206

ARACHNOID

MICHAEL COLE

SEVERED PRESS
HOBART TASMANIA

ARACHNOID

CHAPTER 1

Sweaty palms gripped the steering wheel. The bearded figure watched the winding road, his eyes fixed on the distance. His throat was tight, his heartrate gradually rising. His eyes only left the pavement to check on the LED clock on the console. Seven-oh-two. It had officially been twenty-four hours since Bob Graf should've arrived at the lab with the shipment. Instead, there was no arrival. No phone call. No email. No text. No word from the lab in Allegan County, aside from the call stating that the delivery was en route.

"Maybe he's not here. Maybe he went to Iron County."

Dr. Myles Bower watched the trees pass by his passenger side window, not even bothering to give his assistant eye contact.

"Why would he do that?"

"I don't know, Doc," Alex said. "Maybe he discovered what it is. Maybe word got out about Dr. Perez."

"He's here. Somewhere. We'd know if Graf jumped ship."

"How, exactly?"

"If he took it to the authorities, we would've been alerted by now."

"It's only been twenty-four hours. Perhaps the police are getting a warrant together."

"Alex, I'm getting tired of explaining this. He doesn't even know what's in that container. I've used Bob Graf for several jobs. He's delivered specimens and equipment for me on multiple occasions. Most of the time, he didn't know what he was shipping, but he's not the type to give a shit. That's why I hired him. He knows all he has to do is deliver and not ask questions."

"Except he *didn't* deliver it. If he had, then it'd be in our lab right now. Now here we are, driving the very route we instructed him to follow."

Myles did his best to not appear worried, hence his deliberate lack of eye contact. It didn't make sense for Bob Graf, the trucker, to ditch the job, especially since the last text update stated he was nearing Wells Township, located at the southern border. Why would he drive the entire length of Michigan just to disappear in the last couple hours of travel?

Alex Fincher looked up to the sky. It had been a sunny day up until roughly thirty minutes ago. A shadowy overcast had taken over most of Marquette County, offering its usual promise of rain. The visibility was decent for now. It was only seven in the evening, and despite the trees blocking out the sun's rays, light was still plentiful. It was late September, and sunset wouldn't occur until a few minutes past eight.

The Sandusky Road was a stretch of pavement running from Lake Superior to Delta County. Much of that passageway was surrounded by dense woods and state parks. Some of the leaves had already begun changing into shades of red and brown for the fall. As with much of the UP, Marquette County was made up of dense woods. One could travel miles up here without seeing a single house. It reminded him of old westerns he used to watch, when characters described their neighbors *only* living forty miles apart. In the two hours they'd been on the road, Alex and Myles had only seen a dozen other vehicles so far.

The clouds continued rolling from the south, like spirits casting an evil spell over the Chevy Colorado truck below. The steady breeze that pushed them kept the tree branches in constant movement.

"Maybe we should give Mr. Jedlinsky another phone call," Alex said.

"And tell him what?"

"He should know what's going on."

Myles finally turned his head. "Not until we know ourselves." His stern voice was enough for Alex to know not to broach the subject again. Myles was always paranoid about having his funding cut, and the Jedlinsky Corporation was notorious for slashing funds and shredding contracts. Myles was not going to risk them dumping his project, and his fortune along with it.

"There's a hundred explanations as to why Bob hasn't turned up yet," he said.

Alex scoffed. He was surprised the rationalizations didn't start sooner.

"Maybe he stopped at a bar and had too many," he quipped. Myles' lack of amusement was evident in his wrinkled brow. Alex noticed the forefinger tapping incessantly against the doctor's knee, and the nervous ticks in his left eyelid. It wasn't the ticks themselves Alex saw, but the constant blinking Myles did to rid himself of them.

"I've seen trucks stuck on the highway for hours, waiting for repairs. He probably blew a tire or had some sort of engine trouble."

"And he didn't notify us?"

"You know how cell reception can be with these woods all around," Myles said.

"He wouldn't use a cell phone to call for repairs. He'd use the radio," Alex said. Myles squinted his left eye. He didn't even get the luxury of believing his own explanation for a second before his assistant shot it down.

Alex shook his head. Myles Bower was a brilliant geneticist, but perhaps he had spent too much time in the lab. When Alex first took the job, he couldn't help but find it odd that, considering the breakthroughs he'd had, Myles wasn't working for the government or the CDC, or some other advanced research facility where six, or even seven, figures would be guaranteed.

It only took a little bit of reflection to fill in the gaps. He thought of his own history. Four years in Jackson State Prison for armed robbery, illegal possession of a firearm, grand theft auto, and assault. Those days were behind him now. He took up college courses, intending to become a veterinarian assistant. Despite getting the degree and passing all certificate programs, his troubled past always came up when applying for jobs. Then came this offer from a genetics firm—at least, he was told it was a firm. In actuality, it was a privately owned lab, funded by Jedlinsky Corp, whom he'd never heard of prior to the job offer. When looking into their history, Alex found a dozen government investigations, five subpoenas to testify before Congress, and allegations of illicit overseas deals with military regimes.

Alex had found himself torn between his conscience and the basic need for income. Nobody would give him a chance, and his bank account was dry. Thus, he became the type of employee Myles preferred—somebody who did what he was told, and didn't ask too many questions.

Being the glass-half-full kind of guy, he tried to look to the future. That tactic showed hopes of promise after a few years, once the doctor finally found success in his bizarre experiments. After thirty-one failed embryos, A-32 was born. It was a miracle. The potential for medicine research was off the charts with this particular project. It survived every injection they administered, producing what would be the ultimate antivenom.

It wasn't exactly what Alex had in mind when he trained to be a veterinary assistant. He always thought of tending to dogs and cats, maybe horses and cows—certainly not *that* thing. But even then, the needs of a paycheck and promise of a pension prompted him to keep going. He tended to the horrific creation, while constantly reminding himself it was going to change the world.

Then, along with Bob Graf, it had suddenly vanished. Now Alex had no choice but to drive south on Sandusky Road, hoping to figure out what had happened to the truck and its precious cargo. He watched the outstretched shadows from the trees. That hour of sunlight would dwindle fast, and knowing Myles, they were going to be out all night looking for this guy.

"We could simply call the State Police and ask if he's been seen. We have the truck and plate—"

"Goddamnit, Alex, we're not getting third parties involved. Especially state-run. No, we're doing this ourselves."

"They don't know what's in the container. They won't have any reason to look," Alex said.

"They *will* inspect, because that's what they do," Myles replied. "Keep your foot on the gas pedal. There's hardly anybody driving in this area. If Bob broke down out here, he'll stick out like a sore thumb."

Alex clamped his jaw shut. The doctor was clearly on edge, and his suggestions were clearly not helping. There was clearly no chance of him convincing Myles to call off the search. Thus, there was nothing else to do but prepare himself for a long night of driving.

****

It was nearing eight and the sky was turning a dark shade of grey. They arrived at the gas station in Wells Township, where Bob stated he was in his last update. They checked the couple of motels in the area in the unlikely event that Bob decided to spend a day in town. It was unlikely that Bob would do such a thing, but it was worth checking since they hadn't found his truck on the way down. Maybe Bob stopped to get gas, met some woman, and decided to hook up for the night. The search in the Township lasted five minutes. The container truck would've stuck out like a sore thumb in any of those parking lots.

"Where the hell is he?" Myles said.

"Maybe we should try his phone again," Alex suggested. Myles lifted his smartphone and dialed the number, only to receive a dial tone.

"Nothing." He tucked the phone away and stared through the windshield. The veins in his neck looked as though they were about to burst. Alex looked away, resisting the urge to ask "what now?" Instead, he drove around the small town, passing a few neighborhoods, still finding no sign of Bob Graf.

With nothing spoken by Myles, Alex took the initiative to return to Sandusky Road, where he headed back north. It was dark now. With no other cars on the road, he flashed his high beams. More than once, that saved him from colliding into a deer. Anybody who lived in Michigan knew how deer loved to cross the roads at night.

The stench of sweat filled the truck. The dilemma of what to do next was like a storm raging in the doctor's mind. He was caught between trying to figure out what happened to the shipment, while also determining what to tell Mr. Jedlinsky.

Better yet—*when* would he tell Mr. Jedlinsky? He could already envision how that conversation would play out. The fat, bald CEO would smash his fist against his agarwood desk and chastise Myles for the funds wasted. He then would likely seize the lab and all available data, then likely blacklist Myles, making him more unemployable than he already was.

The thought again made Alex think of the unasked questions he never dared to ask. It was evident that Jedlinsky wanted Myles for the same reason Myles hired him. The only difference was that Myles contained a valuable skillset, but there were other genetic researchers all over the world. Jedlinsky would find one for the right price.

Of course, that was all speculation in Alex's mind. Speculation that added up perfectly, hence Myles' increasing irate demeanor. He was shifting in his seat, while scrolling through the contacts in his phone.

After twenty minutes of travel, he finally worked up the courage to talk.

"Would Jedlinsky allow us time to create another specimen?"

Myles glared at him. "Where has your head been at the last two years?"

Alex nodded. "Good point."

Myles finally sank. "I'm fucked. He'll confiscate everything. He'll accuse me of selling the project out to some other corporation."

"You think that's where Bob took it?"

"That *has* to be the case," Myles said.

"Who?"

"I don't know. There are all sorts of Institutions specializing in genetic engineering all over the country, let alone the world. One of them could've somehow gotten word on our project and paid him off to ship it to them. But *I'm* the one who hired the guy. Jedlinsky knows that, and he'll pin it on me."

"You said he doesn't know what it is, though."

"No, but if someone else figured it out, it wouldn't matter. How they discovered it, I have no idea. Maybe they hacked our computers. Maybe they've been spying on us. Maybe they've been talking to *you.*"

Alex's fingers tightened around the steering wheel. The doc couldn't be serious with that insinuation, could he?

"Maybe Perez got word out before… you know…"

"Maybe, maybe not," Myles said. His eyes were fixed on the assistant now. Alex could see their glow in his peripheral vision, reflecting the light from his smartphone.

Each heartbeat was like a hammer in Alex's chest. He dreaded this drive from the start, but he didn't anticipate the bizarre turn it had taken. It was the trick from Myles' normally mild-manner behavior. He was well-spoken. Polite even, until shit hit the fan.

Alex found himself at a crossroads. He was innocent in these accusations, but it was clear Myles wouldn't believe that. And judging by his discovery of Dr. Perez's gold wristwatch found in the specimen's paddock, it was clear he had no qualms about disposing of people he couldn't trust.

"Get that thought out of your head, Doc," Alex said. Despite their tight grip, his hands felt loose on the wheel. The perspiration from his palms glistened over the rubber.

Myles straightened himself in his seat. He seemed to be deep in thought while watching the road. Alex kept an eye on him, while considering his options. The hairs on the back of his neck were on end. Myles' fingers coiled like talons, while his lip quivered. It was an odd, yet nerve-wracking sight. It almost seemed as though the Doc would either violently snap at any moment, or throw himself into a fetal position and burst into tears like a mentally disturbed child.

Instead, his eyes widened. He leaned forward, propping his hands on the dashboard. He pointed through the windshield, then spoke as rapidly as though he had just downed four coffees simultaneously.

"Stop-stop-stop-stop!" He was already looking behind them.

Alex stomped on the brakes, the forward momentum nearly putting his forehead through the steering wheel. Myles was already out of the truck and jogging several yards back. He had a flashlight in hand, which he aimed at the pavement.

"Look at this," he said, scanning the light over a series of long semi-circles.

"Tread marks?" Alex asked.

"Fresh ones too," Myles said. He seemed relieved, yet increasingly tense all at once. He walked along the road, following the treads. They went from one side of the road to the other. He followed them past their pickup and stared ahead. The high beams illuminated a zigzagging trail of tire treads.

"Jesus, whoever this was, they were all over the road," Alex said.

"*Who* exactly do you think this was?" Myles snapped.

"Doc, no offense, but Bob Graf was not the only truck driver in existence. I'm sure others take this path to get to one of the townships up north."

"Within the past twenty-four hours?" Myles said. He spoke like it was a gotcha moment.

Alex raised his eyebrows. "Uh—yes." He was getting a headache. Either Myles was losing his mind or just didn't do well under pressure—or both. The only other time Alex ever saw his behavior so erratic was when the specimen fell ill. And, of course, when Dr. Perez threatened to quit the experiment and report him.

Unfortunately, there was nothing he could do but humor the doc. He also realized he *wanted* this trail to be a clue to Bob's whereabouts, as it would direct the paranoid suspicion away from him.

Myles did have a point: the tread marks were all over the place. If only they'd caught it on their way to town, they'd have the advantage of a little daylight to examine it.

"Whoever this was, it looks like they've lost complete control over the vehicle," Alex said.

"Or was under some kind of duress," Myles replied.

"Losing control would do that," Alex said.

"Yeah—but *what* made him lose control?" Myles walked along the side of the road for a couple hundred yards. The trail kept going, causing a few marks in the grass where it went off the road. They could see dirt on the road where it angled back.

Myles hurried back to the truck. "Let's follow this trail."

Alex got into the driver's seat and slowly accelerated north, keeping the brights on. The treads continued in their wide arcs. Every couple hundred feet, there were tread marks in the grass where he started angling off.

After five hundred feet, it angled off to the side, right into a narrow pathway in the forest. Myles was out of the truck before Alex even brought it to a stop.

"Doc, wait up!" He parked the truck and ran after the doctor. He stood at the tree line, immediately noticing the several pieces of wood lying in the dirt. They were fragments of two pieces of wood, which judging by the screws, were constructed into a cross-shaped sign which read *Private Property.* The pathway itself was a foot trail. The treads had ripped up the dirt, as well as the vegetation on the edges. Low hanging branches were torn from the surrounding trees and spread all over the dirt.

Tiny particles of light reflected back at them. Myles knelt down and ran his fingers through the mess. Windshield fragments pricked his fingertips. He stood up and aimed his light deep into the woods. The wind, like a haunting spirit, swayed the branches back and forth. They were like claws reaching down at his head, barely out of reach as he passed under them. The trail bent to a slight left, the treads following it for a hundred feet or so.

"Doc?" Alex said. His eyes widened. There it was, the container truck with the yellow label *B.G. Shipping.* The cargo doors had been busted open, the edges frayed where the latch had been.

"Oh, no," Myles muttered. "It got out." He hurried around the driver's side window. The windshield was gone, the glass edges stained with blood. It was at least a day old. The hood and top of the cab were covered in deep grooves.

At that moment, it became abundantly clear what had happened.

"It broke through the doors, climbed over the top, and started busting through the glass to get at Bob," Alex said. He shone his light at the busted trail behind him. "He must've seen the trail entrance. In desperation, he tried to drive through it in hopes of knocking the specimen off with the low canopy."

"It's loose. It's somewhere out here," Myles said.

Alex began shining his light into the canopy. "It could be anywhere. Doc we need to—where are you going?"

Myles pressed several yards into the trail. "I need to get a clue to its location."

"We HAVE a clue!" Alex replied, pointing around at the surrounding woods. Myles continued onward. Alex groaned. These woods were the last place he wanted to be right now. Yet, he didn't want to risk Myles' wrath by retreating back to the road. How would he explain this to Jedlinsky? A man like Myles Bower had worth. But Alex Fincher? People like him were a dime a dozen. They'd probably make him disappear just for being a loose end. In addition, he couldn't simply cut ties and quit, despite wanting to. He would easily be tracked down, especially when he inevitably ran out of money and would begin applying for credit cards and loans just to live. And he didn't have the know-how to live off the grid. He was too dependent on the internet and the resources it provided.

Myles stopped to glance back at him. "Come on!"

Alex swallowed. He was angry, not at the doctor, but at his twenty-two year old self. Had he not been so stupid back then…

He started into the woods, immediately jumping at the crack of a twig under his foot.

The two men continued on for several yards.

"There should be a property somewhere behind these woods," Myles stated.

"Yeah, and considering that private property sign we saw back there, they might not be too pleased to see us. Especially at night," Alex said.

"You don't find it interesting that they didn't report Bob's truck? You'd think they would've heard it and called the police."

Alex nodded. It was a fair point; one that made him want to get out of these woods even more.

After several dozen yards, they noticed a clearing up ahead. They found the residence, which was surrounded by half-an-acre of open space. After panning their lights through the surrounding trees, they rushed for the property.

Alex stopped immediately upon seeing the house. "Oh, good heavens…"

Myles sucked a breath through his nose. Again, he was tense, yet relieved all at once. "It's here."

"Doc?" Alex started backing away, unable to take his eyes off of the wall of white coating the two-story building.

"Okay, good. We know where it's hiding out. Let's go back. I know exactly who to call," Myles said. "Whoever lived here won't be blowing the whistle on us."

"Are you sick?" Alex spoke in a sharp whisper. He whipped his light around. The thing could be anywhere. The branches moved, as though deliberately mimicking the motion of frolicking legs.

He moved his light back to the house. There was no movement in the coating, except swaying caused by the wind. It had a smooth white texture, except for one funnel shape near the back porch. It was about six feet in height, strung up about a foot off the ground. It was pulsing.

Alex then saw the hand protruding from the side, the fingers slowly coiling, then opening back up.

To hell with the job. To hell with the experiment. To hell with Dr. Bower.

Myles saw his expression. "Alex, I wouldn't. Remember, it can—"

Alex turned on his heel and started sprinting for the truck. Immediately, the trees played their tricks on him. He jumped at the swaying of a long, leafless branch. He continued dashing along the trail.

His foot caught the edge of a root, sending him crashing face-down into the dirt. His flashlight hit the ground and shattered, before bouncing behind a series of bushes. Its white glow vanished, coating Alex in thick darkness. He pushed himself up, enduring the pain of a cracked rib which immediately squeezed his right side. He continued for another fifty feet, then shrieked as the tip of a branch caught his shoulder. His imagination went wild, making him believe it was the leg of the specimen reaching out for him. The presence of the bark and a few leaves didn't matter to his panicked mind. He darted off the trail to the left, winding between several trees.

He looked down to dig out his smartphone. He pulled it from his pocket and flashed its light. He looked up and aimed it ahead.

He screamed and dug his feet into the ground. It was too late. He plowed directly into the wall of white silk. It instantly clung to his skin and clothes like glue. He thrashed his arms and legs, shaking the silky net. Its wet texture moistened his face. His phone dropped from his hand, only to get snagged along a section of net parallel to his waist.

Alex tilted his head back. He could see the glint of the doctor's flashlight moving about like a firefly in the distance.

"Doc! DOOOC!"

He felt a vibration in the net. Alex froze, thinking it was merely the wind, or maybe an involuntary twitch from his own body. That comforting lie didn't even last five seconds. Another vibration shook the web, followed by another. There was a sense of stretching. The net, as well as Alex, was being hoisted into the trees.

He looked up and screamed.

Pincers, like those on a crab, reached down and seized him. The mandibles unveiled, revealing two fleshy pedipalps, each of which contained eighteen-inch curved fangs.

The creature turned its body to adjust. Alex looked back up, just in time to see the abdomen cocking back. He screamed as he saw the rigid barb protruding from its end. Like a third fang, it began oozing venom from its tip.

"NO! NOOOO!" Alex screamed.

Myles spotted the light, which came from the same direction as the screams. He ran into the woods, only to stop after a few steps. There it was, perched twenty-feet high in the trees. Alex thrashed like a fish as he was hoisted toward its abdomen. It wasn't his assistant he was focused on, however.

The specimen itself looked healthy. Aside from a few abrasions, it appeared to have come out of the crash uninjured.

Alex looked back, his cheek stretching as it pulled against the web. "DOC!"

Myles shrugged. "I warned you. It makes multiple traps."

The assistant's eyes went back up to the creature. He could only see its front legs as it positioned itself over him. Then, its abdomen slammed down like a cellar door, jabbing the stinger between the shoulder blades. Alex convulsed, foaming at the mouth. His fingers coiled as every muscle tightened into a knot. Immediately, there was sensation of spinning as the arachnoid proceeded to secure its prize in a cocoon.

Myles only had a minute before it would turn its interest on him. He found the trail and ran back to the road. Luckily, they had left the truck engine running. He threw himself into the driver's seat and floored the accelerator.

A sigh of relief escaped his lungs.

He had a definitive location on the project. The web traps confirmed that it would remain in that area until all available food ran out. He already knew who to call. First, he had to get back to his lab.

Meanwhile, the specimen would be safe in the forest. After all, it had enough food to tide it over.

CHAPTER 2

Kira Brine rolled her window down and took in the cool morning air. She was an autumn girl, and the changing of leaves and changing of temperature triggered a giddiness that no other time of year brought. Summer was okay, but the bugs and heat proved a nuisance. Spring was often too wet. But fall was just perfect.

"Girl, roll that damn thing up! I'm freezing!" Laurie complained.

Kira glanced over at her best friend. She had a fleece blanket wrapped around her sweater. She pulled her knees up to her chest and hugged them.

"Oh, goof grief," Kira said. In the thirteen years since meeting in their junior year of high school, nothing had changed. Laurie considered herself the outspoken type, something Kira jokingly referred to as a whiner. "You'd think we were driving into Antarctica."

"You'd probably like it there," Laurie said.

"Actually, I probably would," Kira replied. "No people. Just the wildlife…such as this." She slowed the car to a stop as a family of deer galloped across the road. Kira smiled, watching them disappear into the trees. Laurie smiled too, only because she was amused by Kira's fascination with nature…and general dislike of people.

"For an isolationist, you'll be hanging with an awfully large crowd."

"Six people isn't large."

"For you it is."

Kira shrugged. "Maybe, but that's kinda the price I have to pay to get my cottage restored. I'm no handy-woman. If I tried to get it done myself, I'd likely cause more damage than repairs."

"Repairs, huh? That why you 'hired' Marshall to help?"

Kira rolled her eyes. *Not this again.* Then again, she didn't know why she was surprised—she KNEW the bitch would bring this up. Time to play stupid.

"Well, obviously. Marshall's great at this stuff. He knows more about construction and roofing than your average contractor. I'm not worried about him ripping me off. On that note, that was another factor that played into my decision; he was willing to work for cheap."

"Yeah? Why do you think that is?"

Kira sighed. "Oh, stop it."

"He's still got a thing for you." Laurie was giggling now.

"Oh, boy. Heeeere we go."

"And I'm willing to bet you still have a thing for him. Why else would you have hired him…in this remote cabin, a hundred miles away from civilization."

"Uh, didn't I just explain to you? Like I have a million other times?"

"You fed me some bullshit," Laurie said. "You're like a politician at a press conference. You give a roundabout so-called answer to any tough question thrown your way."

"You'd certainly pass for what qualifies as journalists nowadays," Kira retorted. "And, for the record, we won't be *alone* in this 'remote' cabin. There's you, Tyler, and Sue. And by the way, it's a cottage."

"Oh. Well, excuuuuse me," Laurie said. "And 'by the way' Tyler and Sue will be sleeping in their camper. I'll have the guest bedroom. Not much to keep Mr. Fix-it from sneaking upstairs and doing a little maintenance."

"God, Laurie!"

The brunette smiled. "I'm not gonna stop pressing the issue. I've always sensed unresolved issues between you two."

Kira shook her head. "You also sensed chemistry between you and Dustin Lynch."

"Haven't yet proved that wasn't real," Laurie joked.

Kira smiled. For the next several seconds, she drove in silence, hoping Laurie would give up her crusade. In that time, she could feel her friend's gaze burning into her temple.

"It's been four years."

"Yeah? And?"

"For fuck sake. I swear, when I turn eighty, you'll still be hounding me about this."

"Because I know I'm right," Laurie said.

"I'm starting to wish he and I broke up in a screaming match or something. You'd probably be convinced we're not right for each other." Kira inhaled deeply. "It was actually the healthiest breakup I've ever had. We realized we had different lifestyles. We—"

Laurie snorted. "And I was seriously about to drop the subject until you spouted that BS."

"Wha—? What do you mean?"

"'We realized we had different lifestyles,'…uh, you mean *you* had a different lifestyle!" Laurie laughed. "And the 'healthy breakup' you're referring to? You think I've forgotten you traveling to your dad's private island in Lake Huron, and breaking up with Marshall by TEXT?! I'm actually shocked *he* handled it as well as he did, all things considered."

Kira shrugged. "Alright. Fine. Shouldn't this prove to you we aren't meant to be a thing?"

"Maybe…aside from the fact that you haven't had a real relationship since."

"I've dated…"

"I said RELATIONSHIP. Going out to dinner once every few months is not a relationship. Barely even a date."

Kira groaned. "Keep it up, and I'll roll the window down again."

"Hey, this is what you get for having me get up at five! Who do you think you are? My dad?!"

I would've hired him instead if not for his arthritis. Kira watched the trees while she sped fifteen miles over the limit over an empty road. Every road sign she passed was thirty years old at least. Several were rusted to the point of obscurity. Some even had bullet holes in them. It was like living in Texas. It all served as a reminder that the police hardly came up this way, unless they were called by one of the dozen residents that lived over here. Most of these places were private cabin properties or cottages, such as the one she was driving to.

Despite her dislike for hot weather, she would've preferred to get these repairs done in the summer. In fact, that would've been preferable, that way it was done in time for fall. Unfortunately, she hadn't come out to the cottage all summer. Only three weeks ago, when she made her first visit in a year, did she notice the mold growing in the south wall, the shingles falling apart, and issues with the plumbing.

Kira checked the clock. They had another twenty minutes, roughly, before finally arriving at the cottage. Sue had texted her around six-thirty, stating they had just departed. Considering they had another half-hour further to travel, it would be two hours at least before they arrived. Nothing from Marshall so far.

Guy was never great with communicating. Hell, I wonder if he's even on his way yet... She heard her phone vibrate in the cupholder. After reading the caller ID, she was relieved she didn't voice her thoughts out loud.

"Could you answer that for me?"

Laurie glanced at the phone. Immediately, her face lit up with joy.

"Oh, absolutely!"

Alarm bells went off in Kira's mind. "Wait, never-mind! Give that back!"

Laurie already had the phone in her hand. "Kira's phone! Hey, Marshall. Yeah, she's driving. We were just talking about you, actually..."

With one hand on the wheel, Kira lunged for the phone. "Give that back!" Laurie laughed, deliberately leaning right, just out of reach.

"Uh-huh! Oh, yeah!" She looked over at Kira, studying her.

"Uh-huh...you're already there. Sweet!... We're almost there. We're on Dray Street, maybe eighteen minutes away." She nodded, then looked over at Kira, who stared back with a 'don't you even think about it' expression. Laurie's smile widened. "She's wearing her hair down, wearing those same style boots you bought her...no, not the same ones, but the same brand. I think you got her hooked. Same denim jacket, though."

"For fuck sake, Laurie!"

"What's that? Oh, that was just her saying she can't wait to get there. Once she saw your name on the phone, she was all like 'Ahh! It's Marshall!'"

"Alright, give me the phone." Both girls cackled as Kira lunged for the device. Laurie hugged the window, trying to keep it out of reach, while still attempting to talk to Marshall.

"What the hell's going on over there?!"

"Just girl stuff! Hmmm, that sounded a bit lesbo." She laughed again as Kira continued to reach, while trying to keep her eyes on the road. Her hand accidentally found its way to Laurie's right breast. "Whoa, Kira! Maybe I wasn't too far off with that statement!"

"Just give me the damn—WHOA!!" She straightened her posture and stomped on the brake, nearly throwing Laurie into the console. From out of the woods on the left, another family of deer darted across the road. Unlike the others, this group didn't take their time. They ran with the determination of a zebra fleeing a cheetah. Kira caught her breath. "Whew!"

She could hear Marshall's voice through the speaker. *"You sure everything's alright over there?"*

It took Laurie a moment to answer. "Yeah. Your girlfriend just can't drive."

Kira's eyes flared again. "I'm gonna kill you! Tell him we'll be there soon. He can park his trailer in the north yard."

Laurie smiled as Marshall spoke.

"What'd she say?"

"She says she wants you in her pants. Also, that we'll be there soon... Mmhmm... yep." She chuckled, then glanced at Kira's wide-eyed expression. "Yep, she said the north yard. Not the *only* thing she said, believe me. Alright, we'll see you shortly. Bye." She hung up and made an obnoxious smile at Kira.

"Oh...my...god. I'm never inviting you anywhere ever again, as long as I live."

"The way you drive, that might not be very long," Laurie said. She tossed the phone onto Kira's lap.

"Not my fault a stampede of deer decided to run out after us." Kira leaned back in her seat. "What the hell was up with them, anyway?"

"Hey, *you're* the nature girl," Laurie said. "Maybe they're trying to keep you out of their lake water. Can't say I blame them. God, I already miss my hot tub."

"It's sixty degrees out," Kira said.

"Cold enough for me!" Laurie said.

"Well, get used to it, girlfriend." Kira eased on the accelerator. "We've got a week of fun ahead of us."

"Oh, someone's gonna be having fun alright," Laurie said.

"Jesus!" Kira mimicked a slapping motion. "I swear, you're worse than the jocks at U of M. By the way, I'm so going to kill you for your stunt."

"Hey, you're not even paying me for this week of torture. I deserve to have a little fun."

"I've bought you lunch."

"Oh, wow, geez. Panera chicken tortellini. That 'bowl' portion that oughta be a friggin' shot glass. Totally worth a week in the cold." She stuck her tongue out at Kira, who rolled her eyes.

"Sixty degrees is NOT cold. And there's plenty of ways to warm up."

Laurie scoffed. "Says the one who's gonna get laid."

Kira went to smack her again, deliberately falling short. She shook her head and smiled. "You bitch." Laurie laughed, then shrieked as Kira rolled the window back down.

"Hey!!!"

"Yeah, that's what you get."

CHAPTER 3

Marshall Creed towed his horse trailer along the tree line on the north side of the property, then parked. He stepped out of his truck and gazed at Kira Brine's private cottage. The property was approximately an acre wide, with a small hill on the south side. The cottage faced east toward a small lake. It was a tranquil little body of water, appearing to be a little over a thousand feet wide. About thirty feet from the southwest corner of the cottage was a propane tank.

After fixing his flannel shirt, which had gotten partially untucked in the ride over, he walked over to the cottage. He took the liberty of checking the propane valve. It was full. Kira had the good sense of having it checked by a company, likely every three months.

He walked to the front of the cottage, seeing a pleasant-looking cement patio. Centered in the twelve-by-twelve block of space was a round table, two chairs, and a charcoal grill.

Marshall couldn't help but grin. Nothing had changed since he last saw this place. It had been a little over four years. The white paint of the cottage had started fading then, and it looked way worse now. The siding definitely needed replacing near the back. Some of the plaster had been ripped, revealing the support beams underneath. Termites had gotten into the structure. Although Kira had stated she had an exterminator smoke them out, he felt the need to check for himself. He'd hate to install new bones for the house, only for them to be eaten out.

He pulled a small flashlight from his keyring and shone it through the opening. The light found the hundreds of tunnels the little bastards had carved for themselves. Little brown bodies littered the inner wall and insulation. They were dead alright. He backed away to take another look at the roof.

"God, I hope there isn't rain damage or mold. I can't be here longer than a week. The Stuart Raabe job starts next Monday." The front door was locked, so he'd have to wait for Kira to get here before inspecting any further.

That led to another smile. He could tell by the phone conversation that Laurie was badgering her, and probably had been since Kira dumped him. Oh, the dumping by text message. Not necessarily the best way she could've handled it, but it wasn't like Marshall didn't see the writing on the wall. She had grown distant in the last year of their relationship, constantly wanting to travel while he was tied down with work. She was a free spirit who enjoyed her solitary lifestyle. They remained friends, though mainly through social media and the occasional text on holidays or birthdays. On *Facebook*, she'd often like his post, as he would for hers. There was definitely no animosity between them. Sure, Marshall could have stirred some up by the insensitive handling of their separation. However, one thing he had learned in his thirty-one years of life was that grudges and anger were like headlights draining a battery once the car was parked. They didn't do any good. Best to shut them off, or you'll never get to your next destination.

Once Marshall accepted the 'it is what it is' attitude, his life took off. His construction business grew. What started as a three-person crew had grown to ten, and showed no signs of slowing down. The current project would be finished by the upcoming Wednesday, which he trusted his crew to finish without him so he could help Kira.

He was a little surprised she asked him for a helping hand. Then again, he wasn't *too* surprised. Going the cheapest method was par for the course when it came to Kira Brine. When traveling, she didn't spend too much money on fancy hotels, because she had little intention of spending time in them. She wanted to be out hiking and enjoying all the other festivities of wherever it was she visited…as long as it didn't involve too many people.

Marshall gazed at the lake. There was a wooden dock protruding twenty feet out, with an aluminum boat moored on one side, and a paddle boat on the other. Both were covered in tarps to help protect them from the elements.

Immediately, he was tempted to cast a line out.

"Damn. Should've gotten here earlier," he said to himself.

He glanced back at his trailer. He had used it all of his life at horse shows and county fair events. He had retrofitted the dressing room, clearing out most of the equestrian gear to allow space for sleep. He had a folding cot ready to be set up, as well as a couple of books, and a laptop with a few DVDs in the event of a rainy day. Other than that, the only personal entertainment he brought were his fishing poles—something he was hoping to put to use in his spare time.

Well…I have ten minutes at least…

"Screw it." He went to the trailer and put together a rig. He had bait in his cooler. He stuck a nightcrawler onto a string of hooks, then clamped a weight. With long strides, he hustled to the edge of the dock. The memories of quiet vacations with Kira returned. He recalled all the good spots where the fish usually bit. The lily pads still bunched up on each side of the dock, just as they always had. Sixty feet out to the right was a bend where he remembered catching a few seventeen-inch bass.

He cocked the rod back then launched the rig like a catapult. It plopped dead center of the bend and sank. Right away, a breeze threatened to put his line into the weeds.

"Oh no you don't," he muttered. He swung the pole to the left, keeping the line from arching around the lily pads. He felt the string tug against his finger. The blood rush began. The line tugged back again. He yanked back on the rod. The hook was set in the fish's jaw. It started to run, threatening to pull Marshall off the dock. He dug his heels in and let the fish wear itself out. Definitely a bass. He pulled it to the left and reeled in a few feet of line. The bass jumped and plunged again.

Marshall watched the pole bend as the fish tried going deep. Once again, he waited for it to wear itself down.

Car tires on gravel drew his attention to the driveway. His heart fluttered, seeing the white Toyota and the two women inside. Kira parked beside the cottage and switched off the engine. Right away, they both stepped out.

Kira's almond hair was twelve-inches longer than she used to wear it. In the past, she preferred the tomboy-ish short cut. Now, it was down to her shoulders. She had also gotten a few new tattoos since their breakup. Her shoulders were completely visible, minus the thin straps of her tank top. They revealed sketches of ocean waves and sea life swimming along the surface. Four years ago, she just had a few sharks on her forearm. Now, by the looks of it, she had completed her design of an entire ecosystem residing on her upper shoulder and chest. The left shoulder wasn't as heavily tattooed, but it was clear by the design of ocean waves and a few other creatures that she intended to complete another sleeve.

She waved at him, and he back at her, almost forgetting about the fish fighting to escape him.

First thing's first.

"Hey! Just one minute!" He proceeded to reel in the exhausted catch.

Laurie stepped out of the car and smiled at Kira's annoyed expression. She was straightening her hair back behind her shoulders, while watching her ex fish on the dock. She wasn't annoyed at him or his activities, rather, the inevitable tension that Laurie was trying to brew between them.

"It's not happening," she replied.

"Uh-huh," Laurie said. Kira proceeded to watch her ex relish in his glory on the dock. A part of her hated herself for hiring him. Her stone-faced expression failed to hide the obvious reminiscing of old memories of them fishing on the lake, paddle boating, as well as a few other activities shared during the warmer days.

Marshall hauled his fish from the water, clutched it by the lower jaw, and held it up for the ladies to see. Laurie proceeded to clap.

"Woohoo! Nice one!"

Kira simply gave a thumbs up. She glanced at his horse trailer, only to feel another flood of memories. She had attended several of his shows, and rode on several trails with him. Through social media, she heard that his quarter horse, Beau, had to be put down over a year ago. One of the perks of living alone was that nobody was there to witness her cry. Both for the loss of a great horse, and friend, as well as sorrow for Marshall's heartbreak at the time. Now, his trailer was mainly used for hauling supplies and equipment. The thought was somewhat depressing. She couldn't deny the brief ping of excitement she felt when she saw the trailer, only to remember it no longer carried a horse inside.

She sighed.

"What's wrong?" Laurie asked.

"What?" Kira whipped around, as though caught doing something illegal. "Oh…nothing." She turned toward the dock. Marshall was still admiring his catch. "Hey! Either get its number, or toss it back."

Marshall chuckled. He gave the fish a final glance. "It's your lucky day." He tossed it back into the lake and secured his hooks before walking back up the shore.

Laurie pointed at the flannel shirt and jeans. "See? He dresses appropriately for the weather!" A breeze made her cringe, as though it took pleasure in making her point.

"You're such a wuss," Kira said.

"Some things never change," Marshall said.

"Only the truth," Kira replied.

"Yeah—" he looked at the cottage, "the *truth* is, judging by those shingles, you might have more than termite damage in there. Mind letting me in so we can get a look."

The first millisecond of that sentence, she was relieved he wasn't taking the bait set up by Laurie during the phone conversation. Now, on the other hand, that relief turned into a worse dread than dealing with old wounds.

She fumbled for her keys. "What kind of damage?"

"Hopefully nothing. Worst case scenario, mold damage. Rain could easily get through those patches in the roof. Haven't you noticed that before?"

"I did say it needed new roofing," she said.

"You implied the shingles were old and needed replacing. Haven't you noticed any rain leakage?"

"I haven't been here most of the year," she replied. "Not since early March, at least." She isolated the key to the door and let them in. She hit the switch, illuminating a large, round living room area. To the left was a kitchen area. Between them was a hallway that led to the bathroom and one of the spare bedrooms, where most of the termite damage was located. To the left was a stairway leading upstairs to the master bedroom and second guest room.

Marshall remembered the layout. The only major change were the curtains and the rug. It used to be made of bear skin—a gift from him, no less. Now, it was just some generic plush rug.

What a shame. He forced it from his mind and continued upstairs. He checked the master bedroom, which lined up with some of the damaged sections of roof. No water stains in the ceiling tile. Good sign. He proceeded to the bathroom. Small water stain, but nothing too serious. Likely wouldn't need anything more than ceiling tile replacement, which wasn't the end of the world.

Next was the guest bedroom.

"Oh, boy."

"What?" Kira said. She looked up, her eyes wide. There were large wet stains on the ceiling. Marshall stood up on the bed and pushed the tile apart. He tried to look up, but couldn't get high enough.

"Gonna grab a ladder out of my trailer. Hang on."

"Okay…" Kira said. Even despite getting a discount price by hiring Marshall, the cost of the supplies was hitting her savings account hard. The thought of more repairs sent ripples through her tough-girl facade.

She looked out the window and saw Marshall open the back of his trailer. He stepped in, then emerged with a small folding ladder. She cursed under her breath, dreading the results of this inspection. Her throat tightened with the sound of footsteps on the stairs. Even Laurie knew better than to make quips at the moment. She stood out of the way as Marshall returned with the stepladder.

"Okay, I'm back." He set it up behind the bed and climbed through the ceiling. He pulled a flashlight from his toolbelt, also obtained during his run to the trailer, and shone it up into the ceiling. He winced, then stepped back down. "Oh boy. You got mold up there."

"Oh…fuuuck," Kira groaned. Marshall examined it further, panning his light back and forth. Kira felt beads of sweat forming under her tank top. "How bad is it?"

"Oh…man."

"Huh?"

"Not good…" Marshall lowered himself down the ladder, his face rife with disgust. He shook his head and exhaled sharply.

Kira felt her blood pressure spike. If a construction expert like Marshall Creed was showing such apprehension, then it HAD to be bad.

"Oh God…" she muttered. She covered her mouth, unsure if she would cry when the bad news was finally delivered. Whenever he finally spouted it out. *What's the damn holdup?!*

Marshall looked at her and shook his head, his lips scrunching.

Finally, her reaction to the worst case scenario broke through. "Oh my God?! I'm gonna need a whole new roof! I can't fucking believe this—"

Suddenly, Marshall smiled.

Kira glared at him. "What's that about?!"

"Just messing with you," he said.

"Huh?!"

"There's just a little bit of damage as far as I can see," he said, shining his light into the ceiling once more. "One of the rafters looks a little shitty, so I'll have to replace that. I'll also have to lay down some new decking, as well as replace the felt underlayment, which we were planning on anyway."

Kira released an extended sigh of relief. She then playfully grimaced at Marshall.

"You asshole."

He chuckled. "Sorry. You were getting so damn tense, I couldn't help myself."

Laurie broke out into laughter, then pointed at Kira. "Ohhhh my God. You should've seen the look on your face."

Kira glared at her. "Yeah, you laugh now. Just wait till you're sleeping in one of these guest rooms with the ceiling or walls torn free."

Laurie's grin vanished.

"Oh, don't be mean," Marshall said. "The couch in the living room extends into a bed. And it's arguably more comfortable than this cheap ass bed."

"Well, shit then!" Laurie said. "I'm gonna go grab my belongings...and make sure we have plenty of firewood handy." She clicked her tongue at the former couple then hurried into the hall and down the steps.

Marshall chuckled. "She's still a wuss when it comes to the weather, huh?"

Kira nodded. "Some things never change."

"She'll appreciate it once we get to work. Better to hammer nails now than in ninety-five degree heat."

"Speaking of which, how much is this extra labor gonna cost me?" Kira asked.

Marshall blew raspberries, then held his hands up in a 'whatever' pose.

"Don't worry about it."

"Huh?"

"It's not too much extra work. I have the parts left over from another job I finished two weeks ago. I can apply them here."

"Oh, thank God," Kira said. She immediately felt selfish. "You sure you don't want anything in return?"

"Nah."

"Well...thank you." Kira smiled awkwardly. Despite her relief, she couldn't overcome the awkward feeling of being in a room alone with Marshall. They'd had a few in-person interactions over the years, but always in group settings. The part that made it awkward was how much she realized she liked it—like there was a piece of her that was missing and suddenly it was right in front of her.

Marshall continued examining the ceiling to make sure he hadn't missed any other signs of damage. He rubbed his freshly shaved jaw, then turned back toward her. There was that look in his eye; the look which usually meant he had something up his sleeve.

Her heart bounced. Was he going to make a move? The stage was set, thanks to Laurie. He tucked the flashlight into his toolbelt, then rolled back the cuffs of his sleeves. He stepped toward her.

Kira suppressed the urge to step toward him, but not the words that escaped her throat. "What's on your mind?"

Marshall continued walking…around her, toward the door. He glanced back at her on his way out. "Hmm? Oh, I figure I might as well get started. Best to start with the roof. I'd like to get that done as soon as possible, just in case the weather were to surprise us with some rain."

"Oh…great," Kira muttered. She hoped he didn't pick up on the frustration behind her words.

"I thought Tyler and Sue were coming?" he said.

"They are," Kira said. She realized she was speaking in a low mumble. "They texted me and said they were running a couple hours behind. They'll probably get here close to noon."

"I see. Oh well. Might as well get started anyway." He proceeded down the steps, leaving a disappointed Kira alone in the guest room. Disappointment piled upon disappointment, leaving her frustrated and confused. She *didn't* want to rekindle anything—at least, that's what she convinced herself. She certainly put a lot of effort in convincing herself of that. She didn't want him to make a move. Yet, she was disappointed he didn't. And she was disappointed that she felt disappointed. They weren't right for each other. She was certain of it. She liked being by herself most of the time, save for hanging out with Laurie. She didn't need to cling to a man.

"Damn you, Laurie," she muttered. The consequence of her phone stunt was worse than Kira ever imagined. The damned brunette actually SET THE EXPECTATION that Marshall would do something.

"Hey! Kira! You having a hot date up there, or what?!"

Speaking of Laurie…

Kira rolled her eyes. "I'm coming!" She trotted down the steps into the living room. Laurie had her stuff by the sofa. She winked and clicked her tongue at Kira, who pointed her finger at her. "Not another word."

"Hey, I wasn't going to say anything," she said, following it up with a giggle. "Except *you're the* one who invited him. I'm just trying to help you cut through the bullshit and get the ball rolling again."

"Shh! Shut up. He might hear you," Kira said.

"He's by his trailer. Besides, who says that would be a bad thing?"

"I swear, I'm gonna drag you up here in the middle of winter," Kira said.

"Dunno." Laurie shrugged. "You'll probably be too busy, making up for lost time up here with Mr. Fix-it."

"Oh my God, you're not gonna let this go," Kira said.

"Nope!"

Kira couldn't help but let her gruff exterior break for a laugh. "I don't know what I'm gonna do with you. Except put you to work. Come on, we have stuff to do."

Laurie followed her out the door. "I better get something more out of this than a dinky ass portion of Panera tortellini. And Tyler and Sue better hurry their asses up."

CHAPTER 4

Sue Howard shook in her seat. With the idiotic pace Tyler was driving, she felt the RV would tip at any point. It didn't help that the road was barely wide enough for motorbike riding, and here they were trying to pass through in something the size of a tank. The trees were scraping the roof of the vehicle, the leaves tearing against the windows and windshield. She could see the edge of a small branch protruding over the top edge of the front passenger side window. It had been there for a half hour, meaning it was caught on the skylight rim.

"Seriously, Tyler, is there not a better route to take than this skinny ass road?!" Her live-in boyfriend shrugged his shoulders then shook his head. Sue watched the dirt road ahead. It felt as though the forest was closing in on them. The irresponsible speed in which Tyler was driving didn't help.

"I'm with her," Chris Kalb said. Tyler looked in the rear-view mirror, seeing the twenty-nine year old landscaper clinging to his seat.

"This is the fastest, most direct route," Tyler said.

"We're not home delivering pizzas," Sue replied.

"No, but we are running late," Tyler said.

Sue groaned. "Thanks to you and..." She stopped, not wanting to make Chris feel guilty. She couldn't blame him, after all. He was under the assumption that everyone was aware of his involvement in the project. The guy was trying to make a turnaround, and she couldn't blame him for that. Still, she wasn't looking forward to Laurie's reaction.

She had her phone in her lap. Four times, she tried to give a heads-up in the form of a text, but she could never manage to hit *send.* Maybe she's over it. Maybe she knows Chris is turning his life around and is trying to do better. It's hard enough for ex-cons to get back on their feet to begin with. Having the stigma of friends and family only makes it harder. Right?

Then again, I'm not the one who had valuables stolen by her ex-boyfriend... Sue closed her eyes. The dread of anticipating Laurie's reaction had her on edge. No wonder she was so agitated with Tyler's driving. Unfortunately, she couldn't chastise him without Chris overhearing. She felt like a World War 2 bomber carrying a heavy load of high explosives that would go off as soon as they reached their target. Unlike some of those planes, there'd be no chance of escaping the blast.

She fixed her hoodie and dug her pale hands into the pockets. She glanced at the mirror and noticed Chris staring out the side window. It was obvious by his sour expression that the 'and' of her previous statement made its stinging impact. Now, not only was she anxious, but she felt guilty as well. And with all the work she had committed to, she would soon add soreness to that list of grievances.

"What a way to spend my weeks' vacation," she muttered.

"I can think of worse ways to spend it," Tyler replied.

"I only get a week in a year," Sue said.

"Yeah. So do I. What's your point?"

"You never said how much your friend is paying you for this," Chris said. Sue scowled, but not at Chris. It was Tyler who made the arrangement to split their earnings with him, without her consideration. He thought he was doing a good deed by adding manpower to Kira's project without upping her costs.

"Your cut will be two hundred," he said. Chris nodded.

Sue couldn't help but watch him in the mirror. It was obvious he was hoping for more, but at least had the self-awareness to understand it was better than he was getting lately. Nobody would hire him, nor would anyone do business with his new landscaping company. Some anonymous source on the internet had already tarnished his name. Sue wasn't completely sure who it was, but did have her suspicions. If those were true, sadly, she couldn't really hold it against the perpetrator.

Tyler followed the road to the left. Each shake of the RV wreaked havoc on Sue's anxious state of mind. She felt like a caged animal being prodded by a dozen sticks before eventually being sent to the slaughterhouse.

"It'll be nice to see Marshall again," Tyler said. That managed to bring a smile to Sue's face.

"Yes indeed," she replied.

"Old friend?" Chris asked.

"Yes, but a little more complicated than that," Sue replied.

"He and Kira were a thing back in the day," Tyler said.

"*Were?*"

"We have a feeling that's gonna change," Tyler said. "I think she regrets dumping him. It's obvious to us that her bringing him on to restore her cottage is a subconscious attempt to hook back up."

"Oh really?" Chris said. He cracked a grin. "Is it one of those situations where it's obvious to everyone except the person making the moves?"

"Definitely," Tyler replied.

Now, Sue's smile became truly genuine. "We've been giving her some shit for it."

"Oh, not as much as Laurie is. I guarantee it!" Tyler said.

Chris cocked his head back. "Wait—Laurie?"

Sue's smile folded upside down into a scowl. Tyler could feel the heat from her gaze. Had her temper been any hotter, the whole RV would erupt into flames. *Oh, shit.*

"Laurie Yarbrough?" Chris said. His voice trembled.

"Y-yes…" Tyler said, his voice barely above a whisper.

"You didn't tell him?!" Sue's voice rang his ears in the confined space of the RV.

Tyler cringed. "I forgot all about that."

"Oh my God! You're such an idiot," Sue said.

"She's *actually* gonna be there?" Chris said. He hoped by some miracle they were playing some horrible joke on him. Their lack of response, and Sue's chastisement of Tyler, indicated the opposite. His stomach felt like he had an ulcer on the verge of perforating. "You can't be serious."

"You are TOTALLY sleeping outside while we're up here," Sue said.

"You'd miss me," Tyler replied.

"Don't bet on it, mister."

Chris dug his face into his palms. "This can't be happening."

"Relax, man. She's probably over you by now," Tyler said.

"Ugh!" Sue ran her fingers through her dark hair. "Yeah, she's *totally* over him. Not like she has anything else to be pissed about."

"Can we not talk about that?" Chris said.

"It was just a breakup…right?" Tyler glanced back at Chris. "Didn't you guys…" Then it dawned on him. "Ohhhhhh…"

Chris was on the verge of panic. "You've got to take me back."

"Yeeeeaaah…we're almost there, actually," Tyler said.

"I don't care. Laurie doesn't want *anything* to do with me. Does she know I'm coming?"

"Yeah…no."

"Jesus, dude! Are you TRYING to get me killed?" Chris exclaimed. His face was red. "Please, I'm begging you. Take me back. I would've never come up here if I'd known she would be there."

"Relax," Tyler said. The RV hit a bump, rocking all three passengers.

Now Sue's face was turning red. "Tyler?" She spoke calmly, then exploded. "Are you making it your mission to piss me off?! Watch where you're going, please."

"It's fine, babe." He glanced back at Chris again. "Sorry buddy. It takes a lot of gas to fill this baby up. Plus, I'm cramped as hell. We've been on the road for five hours. You'll just have to survive."

"Easy for you to say."

"It's been eight years. I'm sure she's over it."

"Dude, I stole her mom's wedding ring," Chris said. "Her mom gave it to her before she died. It was passed down in her family for three generations before her."

Tyler's eyes widened. "Ohhhh…"

"Yeah, 'oh'," Sue replied.

"I just thought it was a bad breakup before the…you know," Tyler mumbled. Chris put his head down again.

Sue eyed her phone. "Maybe we should go back."

"Wha—We're a half hour away!"

"I can tell them I'm carsick and not capable of spending a week in a camper."

"Balderdash!"

"*Balderdash*? What, are we a hundred years old now?"

Tyler chuckled. "Insulting the English language…and my driving, is not a successful method of changing my mind." He glanced back at Chris again. "Sorry, buddy. I'll vouch for you when we get there—"

"Tyler, WATCH WHERE YOU'RE GOING!" Sue screamed. Tyler whipped back just in time to see the road bend to the left… and the tree that was directly in his way.

He shrieked and hit the brakes, while cutting the wheel to the left. The RV whipped to the side, kicking up dust and sticks. He avoided the tree, but went too far left, putting him in the path of another tree on the opposite side of the road. He cut to the right, avoiding impact, but not enough to straighten the vehicle's path. It plowed into the woods, and settled halfway down a small hill.

Tyler let out a sharp exhale. "That was too close."

"Too late to insult your driving?" Sue snarled.

"Or your clever route?" Chris added.

"Yeah! Saved a bunch of time, didn't we?" Sue said.

"Alright! Alright! Alright!" Tyler said, waving his hand as though batting flies. He put the RV in reverse, cocked his head to watch his progress through the window, and eased on the accelerator. Tires spun uselessly against dirt. The RV rocked back, only to settle once again in place. Tyler smiled nervously. Over the years, he had gotten used to Sue's angry stares. But this time, those eyes seemed a little bit more threatening than usual. He smiled nervously. "You're pretty."

"Ugh!" Sue snapped her head back, then stepped out of the RV. She walked around the front. The front tires were caught in mud. "Nice going."

Chris and Tyler stepped out.

"I don't suppose we can push it out…" Chris said.

"Yeah, good luck," Tyler replied. He got on his hands and knees and inspected the RV's underside. "Everything looks fine. No damage. Just stuck."

"Well, I feel soooo much better," Sue said.

"Relax! We just need a little help getting pulled out. Just call Kira."

"She drives a *car*!" Sue said.

"No shit. But doesn't Marshall have a truck? That's all we need."

"Assuming he has something to tow us out with," Sue said. She dug her phone out.

Chris was ready to pull his hair out. "So much for turning around."

Sue walked further down the road until she finally got a signal. She found Kira on her contact list and hit *send.*

"Hey! It's Sue... Yeah, we're on our way…in a sense. I have a question: does Marshall have a towing strap or bar?... We ran off the road a little bit…. Uh-huh… Yes, Tyler's magnificent driving skills… Funny you ask, we're on the Ranch Trail… Yes-yes, I know, I told him it was a stupid idea too, but you know how he is about routes… Oh, thank God. Thank you… Yep, we'll see you when you get here." She hung up and walked back to the others. "They're on their way."

Tyler was using a branch to try and dig some of the mud from around the tires. "You know, I might be able to pull this off myself."

Sue pointed a finger at him. "Don't even think about it, mister!"

"I'm just saying—"

"Your clever ideas have got us in enough trouble."

Chris leaned against the rear bumper. He was tapping his foot incessantly on the ground.

"Maybe I should just hang in there while we back it out."

"Not gonna change anything. They're gonna find out you're with us one way or another. Might as well face the music," Tyler said.

"Great. Are there any graveyards nearby? I think they'll be getting a new resident soon."

"I can think of someone who could use a spot," Sue said.

Tyler shrugged and pointed back at her. "My loving girlfriend, ladies and gentlemen!" Her glare didn't waver. Tyler swallowed, then edged back toward the RV. "I think I'll just wait inside until they get here."

CHAPTER 5

"How the hell did they manage to do that?" Marshall said. He uncoupled the towing lever from the trailer and tossed it into the bed of his pickup.

Kira held her hands up in surrender. "Hey, you remember Tyler."

"He's made goofy decisions, but this is a new one for him," Marshall said. He opened the driver's side door. "You said Ranch Road?"

"Yes," Kira said.

"Okay. I know where it is. I'll be back in an hour, roughly."

"Wait! You going by yourself?" Laurie said.

Marshall stuck his head back out. "Yes. Not my first rodeo."

"Oh, come on! We can't pass up this opportunity to poke fun at Tyler and Sue." Laurie grabbed Kira by the shoulders and thrust her toward the truck. "Let's go."

"I thought you'd spent enough time in a vehicle," Kira said.

"Gimme a break. I gotta see this."

Kira rolled her eyes. "Fine. I'll sit in the—" Before she could say 'back seat' Laurie rushed into the truck and sat in the back. She leaned against the side and stretched her legs across the seat.

"I'm sure you don't mind, do ya?" she said to Marshall.

"Nah, it's nothing but country out there. Not much to worry about, except deer."

"Unless you're Tyler Paul," Kira said. She climbed in. Apparently, her new thing was shooting 'I'm-gonna-kill-you' looks at Laurie. She certainly didn't waste the opportunity while she climbed into the passenger seat. *Clearly trying to keep Marshall and I in close proximity.* She buckled up. "Let's go."

****

They followed Dray Street south for fifteen long miles before it intersected with Maple Stone Road. They took a right and followed that road southeast, passing Sandusky Road, and continuing into a stretch of woods, where they took a left turn at Ranch Road. They followed the winding pathway for a couple of miles, jolting back and forth with each bump in the road.

"There they are," Marshall said. Up ahead was the RV's rear bumper sticking out of the tree line. Sue was standing by a tree with her arms crossed. She gave a mild wave and a half-assed smile. They couldn't see Tyler anywhere. Judging by the look on Sue's face, Marshall guessed he was probably hiding in the RV.

"Ohhhh, boy, she looks pissed!" he said. He parked the truck around the bend, then aligned the tailgate with the bumper. Kira and Laurie both got out to help him gauge the distance.

"Great start to your day, huh?!" Laurie said.

"You're telling me," Sue said.

Kira waved Marshall on. "Just a little more." She held her hand up. "Okay! I think right there should do it."

Marshall stepped out. "How the hell did you guys manage to pull this off?"

"You can thank Tyler for that one," Sue replied.

"For picking a road like this to bring a camper through, no shit. You scraped the hell out of the sidings. But how the hell did you run off the road?" He glanced back at the trail. "The way the tread marks are, you'd think you were driving on ice."

"Oh, we were talking, and the idiot looked back to say something to—" Sue stopped. Her irritated expression faded, and suddenly she was nervous. She glanced over at Laurie, then looked away.

"What?" Laurie said. She lined up the dots in her mind. *'The idiot looked BACK to say something to—' Who?* Whoever it was, it had something to do with her, and it wasn't positive, judging by that look. "What's going on? Who'd you bring?"

"Wait? You invited someone else?" Kira said.

"TYLER did," Sue replied defensively.

Kira laughed. "Sue, it's fine! I really don't care. I'm assuming whoever it is, they will be sleeping in your camper. You probably should've said something first."

"Yeeaah, about that…"

Laurie laughed. "What? Did you bring *Jason Voorhees* with you? Who's so bad that you're afraid to mention?"

The side door opened up. Tyler popped his head out first. He grinned obnoxiously and waved. The third occupant finally stepped out. Laurie's upbeat expression vanished the instant she recognized the curly brown hair, Greek nose, and razor wire tattoo on the left wrist, slightly faded after ten years.

"What?!" Laurie looked back at Sue, then again at Chris. "What is he doing here?"

"You can thank Tyler for that one," Sue said.

"Is that like your motto?" Tyler replied.

"YES, actually! I swear it's gonna be engraved on my tombstone at this rate."

"Better make your arrangements now," Laurie snapped. "Seriously, what's he doing here?"

Chris held his hands up in defense. "Laurie, I didn't know you'd be here."

"Holy hell!" Marshall exclaimed. "What is going on?!"

"Someone's about to get killed, that's what," Laurie said.

"I vote Tyler," Sue said.

"Holy crap!" Tyler exclaimed. "Totally not getting laid tonight."

"Hell no. Not ever again, the way I'm feeling right now."

Laurie pointed a finger at Chris. "I said if you ever came near me again, I'd kill you. And I didn't mean it as, 'oh, ha-ha, I'm gonna kill you' funny like. No, I meant I will cleave your fucking skull."

Marshall stepped between them. "Okay! This went from zero-to-a-hundred in no time flat!"

Kira put her hands on Laurie's shoulders. She was near tears at this point.

"It's alright. Just wait in the truck." Laurie nodded then walked off. Kira turned toward Tyler. "No offense, Chris, but what were y'all thinking?"

"He honestly didn't know she'd be here," Sue said. "I'll vouch for him."

"Let's back up for a sec. How the hell did this happen?" Kira said.

"It was a last minute decision, made by someone I know." Sue pointed her elbow at Tyler.

"Hey, if you practiced a little communication, I wouldn't have gone through with it," Tyler argued.

"You're gonna lecture *me* about communication, when you didn't even tell me we were picking Chris up?!"

"Holy God Al'mighty! I didn't know the whole ordeal. I just knew they went out for about four months and broke up. It's been eight years. I didn't think it'd be that big of a deal. I didn't know about the rest."

Marshall leaned toward Kira. "What's the rest?" She rubbed her forehead, then led him by the arm around the bend, so they could speak privately.

To Chris, it didn't matter. It was obvious what she was going to tell him.

Great. Last thing I need is the stigma of another stranger. Now he'll think I'm untrustworthy from here on out.

"Spit it out," Marshall said to Kira.

She leaned against a tree. Her hands and knees were somewhat twitchy from the unexpected outburst.

"His name is Chris Kalb. As you gathered by what Tyler and Sue were saying, he and Laurie dated several years back."

"Water not quite under the bridge?"

"No, but it's a little more complicated than that. Chris, at least at that time, didn't hang around with the best crowd. Nor was he a particularly productive member of society. He drank…a lot. Smoked weed with his friends. Nearly got Laurie hooked on the shit. She didn't even know of the meth until later. Unfortunately, since Chris was not one to get a job, he had to get money to pay for all that crap. So, he pawned items, including some of hers."

"I see," Marshall said. It was all starting to come together now. "So, he stole some of her stuff and pawned it off. No wonder she's pissed."

"It's worse. One of those items was a wedding ring given by her mom before she died, which was passed down from *her* mom, who also had it passed down from her mom, and so forth. Three or four generations, I think. We still don't know where it ended up."

"Oh, lovely," Marshall said. "You keep indicating 'back at that time'. What changed? Did he get caught?"

"Yes, but not for that. He and his buddies decided to rob a bank. It didn't go well, and a guard was shot and killed. By one of his *buddies*, not Chris. A few days later, he turned himself in. Did six years, one on probation, is now a free man."

"And you all remained friends with this guy?!"

"Sue and I have known him since high school. He wasn't always that bad. Just got mixed up with the wrong crowd. Sue and Tyler touched base with him, claimed he made a big change. Trying to start up a business, from what I hear. We went out to dinner a couple of times, and Tyler insisted on bringing him along. Of course, all the drama with Laurie happened before he and Sue hooked up."

"And your impression of him is…?"

"He seems fine now. Definitely *looks* cleaner than he did before. More well-spoken. He took some classes in prison, from what I understand."

"I'm not so much worried about him, but do I have to worry about my shit while we're cooped up at your cottage?"

"No, no. Considering he's riding with Tyler and Sue, it's not like he has a getaway vehicle," she said. "Honestly, I think he carries a lot of guilt."

"Well, if he was involved in a robbery that got somebody killed, he should," Marshall said. "He waited three days before turning himself in. Are we *sure* it was one of his buddies that killed the guard? What'd the security footage show?"

Kira looked away. "They were all wearing masks. All three of them had nine-millimeters." He could tell by the way she spoke that she had her own suspicions on the matter.

"Kira, I can handle this project myself," he said. "You're not obligated to let this guy hang around your property. I would say you're obligated to chew out Tyler and Sue for their poor judgement on the matter."

"Yeah, no shit," she replied. She thought about it for a moment. "If you're uncomfortable, I can send them away."

"Kira, you know him. I don't. If *you* are comfortable with it, then I'm fine with it. It's your place. I'll work one way or another. I'll even have a beer with the guy, if you think he's alright."

A warm feeling filled Kira's chest. He remembered she was a big advocate of felons turning their lives around in a positive way. Her first two years in college were in social work, before she changed to go into private business. Still, it was a matter she felt strongly about. Now, she had to decide whether she wanted to live up to that sentiment. Clearly, Marshall trusted her judgement.

"It's fine. He'll be fine. I promise. We'll probably just have to keep him and Laurie apart."

"Easier said than done. It's not THAT big of a property."

"I think it'll be good. Maybe this'll be a way for them to bury their grievances. I'll talk to Laurie and see what she thinks. Meanwhile, why don't we get back to hauling their trailer out of the woods?"

"Sounds good to me!" They walked to the vehicles together. "This week certainly promises not to be boring."

"I'll drink to that," Kira said.

CHAPTER 6

"I don't want to talk to that prick."

Ethan Fekete was ready to throw his phone out the window. When the recruitment liaison, Largo, appeared on his phone, he expected another business proposition with the Chinese genetics lab in Guangzhou. Three times so far they'd hired him to collect rare species for their bio experiments. Ethan's philosophy was simple: have enough zeroes on the paycheck. He was a master of not caring, so long as he benefited from it. The last assignment sent him into the north Atlantic, where he had to catch a rare twenty-two foot great white shark. Alive. Why they needed it? He didn't know. And because the money was right, he didn't care.

But then, there were those who Ethan wanted to avoid at all costs.

"Dr. Bower is promising a handsome fee," Largo said.

"And?" Ethan's words had a hiss to them. His left leg pulsed as he recalled the memories of the last job, which nearly claimed his life. The brace around the knee suddenly felt as though it was constricting him like a python.

"Apparently, it's a time sensitive offer."

"Meaning he's lost something," Ethan muttered.

"Y-yes."

"He seems to be making a habit of engineering animals he can't control. That's *his* problem."

"This is what you do, Ethan. You hunt exotic creatures. This is nothing new to you. You've traveled all over the globe. You've been exposed to venomous snakes and bugs in the Amazon and Asia rainforests. You've been to islands across the Pacific and down the South American Coast."

"You're not impressing me by reading back my resume," Ethan said.

"I'm just saying, this assignment is easy. Literally here at home. Well, relatively speaking. You'll have to fly out to Michigan."

"Michigan?!"

"That's where he says the target is located. He even has equipment available for transporting it, but he needs somebody

to help track it down and capture it. Specifically, someone who understands the importance of being a team player."

"What the hell did he lose in Michigan?"

"That's hush-hush. He'll only give that info to you."

"What's he offering?"

"One-hundred grand."

Ethan spat. "Ha!"

"For a local job that shouldn't even take a day, it's fairly reasonable, Ethan."

"Not for *him*," Ethan replied. He stomped his way through his mansion, dripping suds on the floor. His bath-towel threatened to come loose from the half-ass knot at his left hip. The brace whined as he walked, irritating him further. He passed a mirror on his way to his office. His malformed calf and thigh gave his left leg a shriveled appearance. The surgical scars would forever remind him of the last job he took for Dr. Myles Bower.

"We can negotiate a higher price, but right now, he's requesting a Skype interview within the next five minutes. As far as I'm concerned, it's relatively easy money."

"I recall you saying the same thing about the last job," Ethan barked. He could hear Largo groaning.

"I've had enough of this, Ethan. You gonna take the call or not? I've got other clients who might actually take him up on the offer..."

Ethan grimaced. There was a part of him that wanted to say no. He hated Dr. Bower for what his experiments had done to him. The last job had essentially ruined his hunting career. He remembered the intense pain in his leg when the stinger pierced his thigh. Within an hour, his leg had turned black. Had he arrived at the Jedlinsky Medical Center twenty-minutes later, the venom would have certainly led to amputation, and possibly death. Despite the medical breakthroughs, the muscle tissue in his thigh and calf couldn't be saved.

The muscle wasn't the only thing lost.

Almost immediately, the job offers stopped coming in. Most clients couldn't see past the injury. Once in a while, a few jobs slipped through the cracks, but they were relatively simple assignments with meager pay. Collecting specimens, transporting them, sometimes the jobs were simply consultations.

Ethan Fekete could still shoot a pigeon out of the sky from a hundred yards out, track a cheetah over a hundred miles across the African plains, wrestle a crocodile into submission, and drive the rarest of snakes from their burrows. With the brace, he could even sprint—though not as fast, and with great pain in the remaining muscle. But Ethan was no stranger to pain, and as long as he had the brace on his leg, he was the same effective killing machine as before. But his clients didn't see it. They only saw a crippled man in his late forties. All of his triumphs and accomplishments were in the past now, obscured by the curtain of time. All because of Dr. Myles Bower and his crazy genetic experiments. Not to mention his pathetic inability to relay important need-to-know information on the specimens.

The idea that Dr. Bower had lost another project actually gave Ethan a sense of joy. He had a little understanding of Mr. Jedlinsky's personality. If you did right by him, he treated you well. You screw up, and you're way past fucked. When Myles lost his last project, he made the decision to keep Jedlinsky out of the loop, likely out of fear of backlash. However, the news eventually reached his desk after the specimens killed a staff member during transit. From what Ethan heard, Myles tried to bribe the other men in charge of shipping to bury the incident, but they wouldn't go for it. Ethan didn't know the details of what went down, but he understood men like Jedlinsky. The only reason Myles was still operating, let alone even alive, was that the specimen produced results. Vaccines were produced from the specimen's venom and were in the process of undergoing a patent. Results produced big bucks, and people who produced big bucks were allowed to stay in the club—as long as they didn't cause more problems than what they were worth.

This was the second time Myles lost an experiment the second that Ethan was aware of. The mention of a time-sensitive matter was the indicator that the clever doctor was crossing that line into the status of 'more trouble than he was worth.' The thought made Ethan smile.

Good. Let the bastard get what he deserved. The only shitty aspect to this is that I won't be there to see the prick get drawn and quartered.

It was a safe bet to believe Bower couldn't afford any other mercenary, hence he was contacting Ethan Fekete, who hadn't had a decent job in two years. Not only that, but Bower also knew of Ethan's hatred of him, or at least he should've known. If so, he was hiring a guy who was as likely to kill him as his own experiments were.

Anger and joy fought for dominance in his mind, both out of disdain for the doc. The temptation to let the guy rot in his despair was almost too much to resist. Unfortunately, he couldn't get his father's voice out of his head.

"Only a fool makes any decision in the height of emotion."

Ethan took a breath. The suds continued sliding down his chest. He embraced the chill of the air, which contrasted sharply to the warm water of the hot tube he stepped out of to take the call. He focused on that chill, as it helped him to temper his rage.

"Ethan? You still there?"

He rolled his eyes. Largo was a reliable man, but his voice was like a prick in his ear sometimes.

"FINE! Give him my info. Tell him to make it quick."

"Got it. It'll feel good to get back to work."

A thousand responses rolled through Ethan's mind, all of which contained some unpleasant mention of fornication. However, in this business, it was important to keep good relations with the recruitment liaison. He simply hung up.

He stepped in his office. Before taking a seat at his desk, he glanced about at the various trophies taken from his many travels. High up on the north wall were a series of claws. Shaped like an eagle's talon, they were taken from a large *Architeuthis Dux*, which appeared along the shores of Washington. On the corner of the wall were a series of great white and tiger shark jaws. Next were those of several species of crocodiles, as well as the jaws of an eighteen-foot anaconda. Stuffed lions and tigers occupied the lower sections of the walls, serving as a visual document of his travels. In his younger days, he had a storage room filled with trophies taken from wildebeests, rhinoceroses, elephants, and many other herbivorous animals. As the years went on, the thrill of hunting those particular creatures faded, no matter how exotic. It got to the point where he only wanted to hunt animals that could hunt him back. There was no greater triumph than being locked in an embrace with an eleven foot crocodile, which was keen on twisting his body into a mangled distortion. He could feel the pull of his bowie knife after twisting it in the creature's throat.

The memory came to an abrupt stop. His leg throbbed incessantly, tormenting his mind, as though intentionally reminding him that his best days were behind him.

He sank in his office chair and turned on the monitor. The computer came to life with a blue-white glow, which turned to a screensaver of the Amazon River. He activated Skype and waited for the incoming call. There was no point in getting dressed. His soaks in the hot tub were one of the few things that made his leg feel better, and Myles Bower was interrupting his peace. Let the bastard see him in nothing other than a bath towel. Ethan didn't care. He reached into a drawer and found a cigar. He bit the end off, lit the tip, then took the first draw.

****

Myles Bower opened his cabinet and found his Jim Beam. He pulled it down and reached for a glass. Any glass, it didn't matter. He just needed to quell his nerves. Only now, it was hitting him that he was about to speak to Ethan Fekete—a man who would probably kill him for free at this point. Myles filled the glass halfway than sat at the monitor. The man named Largo was setting up the call for them. A text came in at the lower left corner of the screen.

"Linking feed…"

Myles took a sip, winced from the burn, then took another. He wasn't much of a drinker. It was mainly on site for when Jedlinksy or his representatives visited. They were all fans of scotch and bourbon.

The image turned to black. Two seconds later, the black vanished, and he was looking into a room lined with trophies. Staring back at him was the slayer of all those beasts, with a look in his eyes that suggested that Myles was his next target.

Myles winced again, but not from the whiskey. The tan-skinned, dark haired man on the screen leaned back in his seat and puffed his cigar. Pink lines stretched across his chest, a reminder of a lion who thought it could get the better of him in Kenya. The skin on his upper right bicep was a completely different shade than the rest of his body, thanks to the jaws of a Komodo dragon—or rather, the resulting infection.

An untrained mind would think that a Komodo's venom would be the worst thing Ethan Fekete endured in his many years of hunting. The reality of that matter was obscured beneath the bottom screen frame—something Myles was thankful for, considering the fact that Ethan wasn't dressed.

"Good morning, Mr. Fekete. Good to see you again." He waited for a response, but Ethan offered none. The awkward silence, along with the unblinking stare, proved more insufferable than the chastisement he anticipated. "You doing well since we last met?" He quickly took another drink of his bourbon.

Ethan leaned forward, his pale left eye centered on the monitor.

"And I thought you couldn't get more pathetic."

"Pardon?" Myles felt the jitters consume him. The fluid swirled in his glass.

Ethan pointed. "Drinking bourbon in a wine glass? Doctor, it's almost as if you're actively trying to add to the reasons you should be drawn and quartered."

"I had to act quick and…" Myles zipped his lips, realizing he was about to verbally admit that he was freaked out of his mind and needed a quick drink. Then again, that ship had sailed as soon as Ethan laid eyes on him. He set the drink down and straightened his posture. "Mr. Fekete, I appreciate you taking the time to talk—"

"Will you just cut to the chase?" Smoke puffed with each word. Ethan leaned to the right. As he did, part of the towel peeled back, revealing his thigh. Or rather, what was left of it. "Meanwhile, someone in this conversation has to drink properly." He straightened, holding a bottle of Michter's Celebration Sour Mash Whiskey and a skull-sculpted glass. He drew on his cigar, then drank the whiskey, then planted the cigar back between his teeth. His eyes narrowed at the camera. "Well?"

Myles cleared his throat. "Mr. Fekete, I have a proposition for you. My company has an asset out of containment, and I believe you are the man to help us reacquire it."

Ethan snickered. "*Your* company? Funny, I remember this spiel from three years ago. Funny how the actual people running the company aren't making these calls, but the genetic engineer they've *contracted.*"

Myles fought to maintain a confident demeanor, while simultaneously clutching the arm of his chair as though he was undergoing a flight landing during high turbulence.

"So, Doc, what'd you lose? Another oversized snake?"

"A snake? No. That project is at the Jedlinsky lab and is undergoing the vaccine trials." He cleared his throat, then suddenly leaned forward, as though he suddenly remembered something he wanted to add. "Thanks to you. And Bryce. How is she, by the way?"

"Answer the goddamned question, won't you Doc? I thought you were in a hurry."

"My apologies." Myles could sense how fast he spoke. It was like he was hopped up on caffeine. He wanted to control it, but couldn't. "This project has nothing to do with the snake genus. This is a member of the arachnid order."

"An arachnid? You mean a spider?"

"For simplicity sake, let's say yes."

"Doc, when you say simplicity, I think complexity. You've called me to hunt this thing. WHAT exactly is it?"

"It's…" Myles rubbed his forehead. "It's hard to explain via Skype. I have the models in my lab here in Michigan."

Ethan downed his whiskey, then belched. "Doc, I don't know how you've made it this far in life being such a pussy, and for beating around the bush as much as you do. I've seen politicians give straighter answers. I don't give a shit about the data. How big is this thing? How does it feed?"

"It's a combination of certain species. I've crossed the genes between the deathstalker scorpion and the brown widow spider."

Ethan stared at the screen. "Doc, you're fucked up, you know that?"

"It was part of our methods of creating antivenom," Myles said. "You see, the brown widow's venom is deadly, but their transfer is insufficient compared to black widows. So, we combined its genes with that of the scorpion, whose venom is severe, though not enough to kill most adults."

"So, this thing is part-scorpion, part spider?"

"I simply call it an arachnoid."

"And your cover story is to create antivenoms?"

"That is the official plan," Myles said.

"Right." Ethan took another drink of his whiskey. "Because, clearly, you needed to make a giant spider to make an antivenom."

"We've been injecting various venoms into its bloodstream to create antibodies."

"Or to strengthen the toxicity of its venom," Ethan replied. "Doc, I see right through you. Sure, maybe there's some medical stuff that might come out of this project, but I'm willing to bet my right calf muscle that Jedlinsky has a contract with someone else regarding this experiment." A minute of silence passed. Ethan grinned at Myles' speechlessness. Clearly, he was under strict instructions to tell nobody about this specimen without the authorization of Jedlinsky.

"I'm willing to pay a hundred-grand upfront," he said.

"Oh, right. I don't suppose Largo warned you about the fee."

"What about it? It's a simple job, Mr. Fekete. Stateside. Twenty-four hours. I'm providing supplies and equipment. A hundred-thousand is more than generous—"

Ethan raised his shrunken left leg, putting the muscles...or lack thereof, in plain sight. Myles winced, then quickly fixed his expression.

"Generous, right?" Ethan said. He dropped his foot to the floor. "You understand the pain from a muscle constantly trying to heal itself, even though most of it is not there? It is not something simply cured by a nightly dose of Tylenol, let me assure you."

Myles looked over at his whiskey. "I understand our last mission didn't go as planned..."

"Would've been just fine had you been upfront with me sooner," Ethan said. "You told me you lost an eighteen-foot snake. You warned me that it was a constrictor. You DID NOT state that it was also a venomous species, nor did you state that it was pregnant with live young—who were equally venomous."

"Mr. Fekete, I was under the impression that the specimen had over a week to go before giving birth."

"Oh, for fuck sake. You're so full of shit, Bower," Ethan said. "'Oh, I was under the impression.' Give me a break, you were the geneticist in charge of developing the fucking thing. And because of that..." Ethan felt his leg, remembering the hot sensation of miniature fangs piercing his flesh, and the intense burning that followed. It was like molten lava was flowing under his skin. He had the mother tranquilized and ready for pickup. Little did he know she was guarding a nest.

Myles was gripping the chair again. Unfortunately, he didn't have much more than a hundred grand in his account. Much of his funds went to a cleanup crew. At least, that's how he referred to them. There needed to be some sort of story for Dr. Perez's sudden disappearance. His mind raced.

How can I up the fee?

He thought of contacting Jedlinsky. He could come up with a lie that he needed additional construction for the barn, where he was storing livestock intended to be fed to the specimen. Or perhaps he could state he needed additional equipment for the lab.

Then reality hit. Jedlinsky wouldn't transfer funds. He'd simply request a list of the items, and purchase them directly, then have them shipped to the facility.

Ethan gnawed on his cigar, smiling at the doctor's forlorn expression. It was obvious that Myles was far up shit creek with no way out. Ethan got exactly what he wanted: to see the growing desperation of a man he despised.

"What's the matter, Doc? It almost looks like you're going to cry." He chuckled, watching the beads of perspiration drip from Myles' shaking face.

"Ethan...I need your help. If I don't get this thing back, it's over for me."

Ethan slammed a fist on his desk. "Good! Now you know what it feels like to have your livelihood destroyed. I hope Jedlinsky burns you slow. Maybe he'll toss one of those baby snakes at your leg; that way you can feel your muscles rotting under the skin."

****

Bryce Fekete leaned her head back, submerging her scalp in the bathwater. With Ethan out of the tub, she had enough space to lay flat if she so chose. Her arms waded back and forth, brushing the suds over her soft flesh. She was staring straight up at the ceiling, almost completely submerged now. The water was at her chin and brow, leaving the suntan flesh of her face untouched.

The sound of a thud made her lean up. Ethan was raising his voice. It was a stark contrast to the tone used when answering Largo's call. It had been a while since they'd embarked on a good hunt. The past three years had been frustrating for both of them. A year of physical therapy, a now-lifetime of pain for Ethan, and a frustration from lack of travel.

Strands of brown hair stuck to Bryce's neck and shoulders as she rolled herself onto her knees. She leaned over the tub to listen through the open door. Judging by the direction Ethan's voice was coming from, he had to be in his office. Whom he was talking to, she wasn't sure. However, he had been gone for several minutes now. Usually, his phone and Skype conversations were short and to the point. The fact that it even went on for this long meant that there was an issue with negotiation, or that Ethan had a personal beef with the client. Whatever the matter was, it certainly didn't sound like it was leading to a deal.

Was he seriously turning down a job? After all of his complaints about being overlooked due to his injury?

No fucking way. It's been WAY too long since I've gotten to shoot something.

The conversation sounded as though it would end any moment. Bryce hauled herself out of the tub and marched into the hallway. Dripping wet, she proceeded to the end of the corridor and took a right turn. Bare feet touched wooden stairs, which led to another small hallway. At the end of the twelve-foot passage was Ethan's office.

She could hear the voice on the computer.

"Mr. Fekete, I can probably negotiate a higher sum from the company to transfer into your account upon completion of the assignment."

"Ha!" Ethan replied. "Good luck. At this point, you'd be lucky to get stale coffee from Jedlinsky, once he finds out you lost another specimen."

"But sir, I'm begging you. Nobody else can catch the arachnoid."

"Because they're too expensive. Just like me."

"But sir, due to the lack of work, a hundred grand has to be sufficient."

"I'm doing just fine. I've scaled down a bit, but I've made a good living, and up until I met you, I haven't been stuck at home wasting money on streaming services and online shopping. My savings will last."

"For how long? You have a large house, Mr. Fekete. Clearly, it must require significant funds just to maintain."

"Nice try, short round. You know? You can talk tough, but you're not very convincing when you look like you're two seconds away from shitting your pants. Sorry, you'll have to hunt your bug on your own. Wave your hundred grand at Jedlinsky's goons when they pay you a visit."

Bryce's eyes widened. A hundred grand? An arachnid. *Noid?* Whatever the difference, it sounded intriguing. She stormed into the office.

"Hold on!"

Ethan spun in his chair to see his wife standing in the doorway, stark naked.

"Water getting cold?"

Bryce looked at the man on the computer, who stood wide eyed at her figure. She didn't care about his gaze; just about who he was. This was the man who engineered a giant snake, lost it in Columbia, and recruited them to hunt it down. Her thoughts weren't on Ethan's devastating injury that resulted from the assignment. That was in the past. She needed a good hunt, and considering who it was on that computer screen, this was bound to be a good hunt. "You're turning down a job? What are you doing? An arachnid? Where is it?"

"Uh…" It took a moment for his mind to take its focus from her nakedness and take in her question. "Michigan. Marquette County in the upper peninsula. We have a private facility in a small area called Pettengill."

"Nothing that matters to us," Ethan said, glaring at his wife. He glanced back at Myles. "Good luck with Jedlinsky." He killed the call.

"HEY!" Bryce stepped forward, but the screen was already black. She slapped her husband on the chest. "You bastard. Why'd you do that?"

Ethan scoffed. "You're kidding, right?" He refilled his whiskey glass and marched into the hall. The smell of tobacco, and her rampaging mood, triggered a desire in Bryce to smoke as well. She grabbed a cigar and lighter from the desk, quickly filled a whiskey glass, then stormed after Ethan. Thick beads of water ran down her skin as she followed him down the hall. She lit the cigar and took a long draw.

"You've been bellyaching about being overlooked for jobs, and suddenly, you're turning down the best offer we've had since…" She pointed at his leg.

Ethan stopped and looked at her.

"You've got to be shitting me. You saw who that bastard was."

"Yes, I did. What about it?"

"This is the best gift I could've ever received. That dumb fuck has lost a SECOND genetically engineered specimen. Apparently, he's not as good at keeping his pets under control as he is at growing them. Considering he 'forgot' to address the pregnancy issue of the last one, I'm more than happy to let the Jedlinsky Corporation feed him to their zoo of genetic freaks."

"What if he hires someone else?"

Ethan proceeded up the small flight of stairs. "He doesn't have enough money for anyone else worth their salt. Not enough to keep them quiet, at least. Either he'll try to capture the thing himself, which I suspect he won't bother doing, or he'll have to confess to Jedlinsky. Either way, he's fucked."

He proceeded to the opposite end of the hallway, which led into a staircase lobby. In the center was a large wooden cabinet, storing more whiskey. Ethan took the liberty of refilling his glass, then proceeded upstairs. Bryce drew on her cigar, then followed him.

"Ethan, I want you to call him back."

He reached the next floor then glanced back at her, his face displaying disgust. "I'm not calling that idiot back. Let him rot."

Bryce reached the top stair. Her cigar wobbled between her teeth as she spoke.

"We've been stuck in this house for three years," she said.

Ethan looked around him. "You're complaining?"

"About the house? No. But the life we have compared to before is different."

"We travel some."

"I'm not talking about going to the beach," Bryce said. "We need this. We haven't had a significant hunt in years."

"I'll schedule us a trip to Kenya."

Bryce waved her hand. "Old news."

"Plenty of crocs to get in Asia."

"You know we can't keep spending our funds like that," she replied. "We used to get *paid* to do this stuff. Not anymore."

"So what? We'll write a book, then."

Bryce removed her cigar from her mouth then pressed her body to his. Her forehead aligned with his nose, allowing him to look straight down into her blue eyes.

"We haven't had a thrilling hunt since the snake. It's an itch I've been needing to scratch badly." She put her hands on his waist, her thumbs brushing his skin.

"No," Ethan said. He broke away from her and started marching for the bedroom. "You'd be disappointed anyway. We wouldn't be killing the thing. He needs it captured alive."

"I can settle for that," Bryce said. She noticed the tremor in his upper body, which usually happened when he was screaming internally. She smiled. It was obvious he knew he was losing the argument. Still, he was too stubborn to concede.

That only spurred Bryce to act further. Ethan only needed a little 'encouragement' to seal the deal. It was obvious he was aware of that too, judging by the way he was going for the drawer.

Getting dressed? I don't think so!

She pressed herself to his back, reached around his waist, and slipped a hand under his towel. Ethan tilted his head back toward her. He knew what she was doing, yet he couldn't bring himself to stop her. He inhaled slowly, relishing the sensation of her hand on his manhood.

"Let's go to Michigan," she whispered in his ear, her tongue flicking on his neck like a snake's.

"No," Ethan said. Bryce smiled and gently started to bite at his shoulder. Sure, he had said the word, but she could sense the conflict in his voice, not to mention the intensified breathing. She felt powerful in moments like these. Even after being married for twelve years, he was unable to resist her body. She pulled at the knot in his towel, dropping it to the floor. She spun him around to face her, then pressed her mouth to his.

With his physical reaction intensifying below, she pulled away. She placed both hands on his face.

"Call him back. Take the job."

Ethan exhaled sharply through his nose. Better. She was making progress. Thirty seconds ago, it would've been another outright 'no'.

She leaned back onto the bed, raised her arms behind her head, then raised her right knee. Ethan felt himself leaning over the bed, ready to crawl over her. There wasn't even conscious effort involved. It was automatic, as though he was a machine being piloted by someone else. The tattoos of a black anaconda swirling up her thigh toward her pelvic region seemed to taunt him to go through with her wishes.

Like a cobra, Bryce suddenly leaned up and pulled him over her. He went to make the final move, only to feel both of her knees pressing into his hips, blocking access.

Licking her lips, Bryce leaned up toward him. Her smile was a combination of feminine and sinister. Ethan was breathing heavily now, frustrated by the obstruction, as well as his defeat in the argument.

"So, what do you say?" she said.

"I hate you," he groaned.

Bryce laughed, then spread her knees. "No you don't." She laughed with a high-pitched shriek as Ethan's powerful hands grabbed her by the hips. In one powerful motion, he spun her onto her stomach. He had become a lustful and vengeful beast. Bryce's hands clawed the bedsheets and her mouth gaped open. Her laughs turned into sensuous gasps of air as his body rammed against hers.

She had won.

CHAPTER 7

It took every ounce of self-control Laurie could muster not to slam the cottage door shut behind her. The only reason she didn't was out of respect for Kira's property. Had it been her own, or anyone else's for that matter, she would've slammed it shut with enough force to break the window.

She sat on the sofa, crossed her arms, and stared at the fireplace. Two seconds later, the door opened again. Kira stepped inside. She stood in the middle of the living room and looked at her best friend.

"You could've said no."

Laurie leaned her head back. "You said you were fine with him coming here. It's *your* cottage. What am I supposed to say?"

"You could have spoken your mind," Kira replied. "I would've listened."

"I don't know. The fact that you would even *consider* letting that fucktard stay here speaks volumes in itself."

With a sigh, Kira sat down next to her. She clasped her hands, then twiddled her thumbs while thinking of what to say.

"Look...I think he's changed. For the better. Tyler and Sue are obviously comfortable with him being in their RV..."

"How would you know? You hang with us the least. You're always out, doing your own thing, visiting places, recording your audiobooks, doing business..."

"Don't change the subject," Kira said. "Fact is, he's here now. Sending them back would mean forcing Tyler and Sue to drive three-hundred something miles back the way they came."

"That's on *them* for bringing that guy," Laurie said.

"Well, that ship has sailed. I asked you back at Ranch Road while Marshall was towing them out. You said okay, and now you're acting pissed."

"I relented because I still have some modicum of consideration for Tyler and Sue. Unlike them for me," Laurie said. "Plus, sending them back would mean a five hour fight. By the time we get home next weekend, we'd probably learn that Tyler was dead." Finally, a smile broke. "See? I'm a good person. I saved a life today."

Kira chuckled. She looked over her shoulder through the window. She could see Marshall and Chris hauling supplies from his trailer. Further to the left, she could see the rear of the camper. Sue and Tyler were out of sight, but their bickering could still be heard.

"Well...I wouldn't get too far ahead of yourself." She stood up and went for the door.

Laurie stretched, then swung herself across the couch. She shut her eyes and pretended to go to sleep. "Can't we just take the first day and relax? I feel like we've been on the road for a hundred years."

"I won't stop you," Kira said. "But you know Marshall. He's got that 'the sooner we start, the sooner we get finished' attitude."

"Men," Laurie moaned.

Kira stepped outside and walked for the trailer. Marshall already had two stepladders set up at the northwest corner of the house. It was nearing two in the afternoon, and the tree standing a few yards from that provided a perfect amount of shade. Not that it was hot to begin with. The temperature had risen to sixty-five degrees and was holding steady.

Marshall loaded his toolbelt with a hammer, nails, and scrapers. He had his gloves on and was walking toward the ladder when he saw Kira.

"Hey!"

"Hey," she replied. She looked at the roof, then back at him. "So, what can I do to help?"

"Well, we can rip off some roof shingles. There's tools and some spare belts in the dressing room," he replied.

Kira tied her hair into a knot, then cleaned her glasses.

"Whatever you say, foreman." She proceeded into the trailer. The tools and supplies were located in the back of the room behind the cot. She felt the nylon material. *That can't be too comfortable.* She forced the feelings of sympathy aside then moved for the tool bag near the back. She tightened the brown leather belt around her waist, then loaded the pouch with a scraper, a hammer, and a box of nails. She searched for an extra set of gloves, which she finally found atop a large plastic case.

What the hell's in here?

Her first instinct was to not touch the case, but curiosity got the better of her. It was unlatched, after all. She lifted the top and saw the steel barrel of a twelve-gauge shotgun.

She chuckled. Guns didn't intimidate her. She shot them all of her life. The fact that Marshall felt he needed one here in the middle of nowhere was what she found amusing.

"Need help in there?" he called out.

"No, I'm good." Kira stepped out and jogged to the ladder. Chris was standing near the tree, holding a heavy-duty trash bag to collect the scraps tossed by the workers above.

"Hey," he said, reaching out to Kira. He then pointed his thumb toward the living room window. "Listen, I SWEAR I had no clue she was gonna be here."

"I know. This is a case of *them* dropping the ball," Kira whispered back. She tilted her head in the direction of the RV. "Hey, I'm not gonna talk down to you like you're a child. You're here with us. I trust you. Sue and Tyler obviously trust you. I spoke with Marshall and he trusts my judgement on you."

"He knows about…the, uh, you know?"

"Thanks to that little explosion back at the road, I was obligated to say something to him," she said. Chris nodded. Her reasoning made sense. He hated being a person that people had to be warned about. It was humiliating, and worse, made him question if he could pick up the pieces to his life. He would be forever connected to the murder of that guard, even if he wasn't the one who squeezed the trigger. It also didn't help that *that* aspect wasn't completely proven to the public, either.

"I understand," he said.

Kira tapped him on the shoulder. "She'll loosen up. In the meantime, cheer up. The group as a whole is good with you, dude. Let's get some work done, and who knows? Maybe we'll all have a little fun in the process."

Both of them glanced at the RV as a verbally beaten Tyler stepped out of the driver's side.

"You're totally on my shit list," said an angry Sue Howard from somewhere inside the vehicle.

"Story of my life, babe," he replied. He shut the door and smiled at the two people watching him. "Just expressing our loving feelings for each other."

"You two ought to star in your own sitcom," Chris said.

"You guys *sure* you're alright?" Kira asked.

"Oh, you know Sue. She'll spend all day yelling at me. But at night, she's all like 'come over here, you bad boy.'"

The RV window opened. "I heard that, you asshole! By the way, fat chance!" She slammed the window shut.

Tyler bit his lip. "Tonight might be the exception."

"I would hope so, if I'm gonna be sleeping in there," Chris said.

"Fair point. Kira, mind if I use the facilities?"

Kira snorted. "Dude, we're all here for a week. You seriously assumed I wasn't gonna let you use it without permission?"

"Everyone's making fair points today," Tyler said. He squeezed between her and Chris and disappeared into the cottage.

Chris rolled his eyes. "Gonna be a long week sleeping in the same confined space as them two."

Kira sniggered. She thought for a moment, debated the new idea in her mind, then discarded her concerns. "Listen, if you can handle the cold, there's a spare bedroom on the ground floor."

"I thought Laurie was gonna use that?"

"She's opting for the couch in the living room so she can have the fireplace."

"Oh! Well, uh… what about Marshall?"

Kira stood silent. Once again, her mind was at war with itself. *No, you bitch, you weren't hoping to invite Marshall upstairs.*

"Uh, I think he's content with his setup in his trailer," she replied.

"Oh!" Chris smiled. "On that note, thank you very much. I appreciate it."

"Not a problem, dude." She stepped aboard the ladder and started to climb. She stopped halfway up, noticing the trash bag in Chris' hands. "Hey, you might wanna get a heavy duty bag. Some of these tiles might have nails sticking out of them. They'll rip right through that sucker."

Chris nodded. "As Tyler would say, fair point. Unfortunately, this is all we packed."

"It's alright. Laurie and I brought a few boxes. They're in the cottage, under the sink." She started to step off the ladder. "Oh, crap. She's in there… I'll go get them. Might be best if you two keep your distance."

"No, no. I can do it," Chris said.

Kira winced, then shook her head. "I don't know if that's a good idea…"

"Don't see what difference it'll make, especially if we intend to sleep under the same roof."

"I know. It's just that she's still a little worked up from the revelation of, well, your presence."

"I'm not gonna start anything, I promise. But I can't feel like I'm walking on eggshells here. We've only been here twenty minutes and I already feel like a walking time bomb. Unless you think *she's* gonna go off on me?"

"No. I don't think so," Kira said. "She's in her mood right now, but she's already agreed to let it go."

"Alright. Then I'll be right back." He trotted off to the front door. Kira proceeded up the ladder. She was surprised Marshall hadn't called down to ask what was taking her so long. The answer then became obvious when she heard him talking on the phone.

"Yep, I'm just getting started... The drive wasn't too bad. No traffic issues for once. Saw a backup on I-96 southbound. Looks like it was due to construction. Hopefully, that'll be cleared up when I head back... Oh, really? That sounds fun... Sure. When I get back, we'll get tickets..."

Kira stood at the top of the ladder, frozen in a trance, watching her ex on the phone. His back was turned. He looked as though he was smiling. There was an upbeat tone to his voice. Then again, he always sounded upbeat. However, it triggered a temptation to eavesdrop.

She stepped onto the roof. Though she couldn't make out the words, she could hear the voice on the receiver. It was definitely female. Kira's heart thumped in that exact rhythm she felt whenever she was about to get into an argument. Her blood pressure skyrocketed. She felt as if she had walked in on a cheating boyfriend. Except he wasn't cheating, nor was he her boyfriend. The emotional and rational forces in her mind were at war again.

I hate myself.

"Right... Okay..." Marshall turned and saw Kira standing there. He squinted, noticing her pissed-off expression. She snapped into reality, then forced a smile.

"Sorry, Tyler's pissing me off," she lied. Marshall nodded, his phone still pressed to his ear. He raised a finger.

"Just one sec," he mouthed. He then rolled his eyes. Twice, he opened his mouth to speak, but the person on the other end wouldn't let up. Finally, he got his chance. "Not sure about Saturday, because that's when I'm coming back. Not sure what time I'll be leaving, and there's that thing I said about traffic. Sunday for sure… Oh, hell yeah, *Bob Evans* sounds great!"

Though he didn't see it, that look had returned to Kira's eyes.

"Okay, babe. I've gotta go. Gotta get started before the boss rips me a new one."

This time, Kira could make out the words, and the giggle. *"You ARE the boss!"*

"True that. But the client outranks me," he said. "…Yep… Talk to you later. Mmhmm, bye." He lowered the phone to end the call. As he did, Kira got a glimpse of the name on the top screen. *Amanda.* First name only—not a good sign. The worse sign was that she felt jealous.

Marshall tucked his phone away and turned toward Kira. "Sorry about that."

"New client?" Kira said, barely disguising the disappointment in her voice.

"Something like that," he replied.

"Take all your clients to *Bob Evans*?" she asked. Marshall couldn't tell if she was being silly or truly interrogating him. He decided to treat it as the former, though he suspected the latter.

"Good place for discussing contracts. Plus, I love their pot roast hash."

"I remember," Kira said. She was staring off into the distance. The silence was broken by the tearing of a roof tile.

"You alright?" Marshall asked.

Kira jolted, snapping once again into reality. "Uh, yeah! Was just thinking of—uh… Oh, shit! I almost stepped on a nail."

"Be careful there," Marshall said. He tossed the old shingle to the ground. Kira turned away and started working another old shingle loose with the hammer. It split down the middle, much to her frustration. She tore the fragment off, tossed it to the grass, and worked on the other half.

****

Chris hesitated before grasping the door handle. The take-charge tenacity he felt moments ago had suddenly vanished, and now, he was a jittery load of nerves. He reminded himself that all he had to do was grab the bags and leave. No words needed to be spoken. He squeezed his eyes shut, took a deep breath, then went in.

Laurie was seated on the left side. He turned his head just enough to see her in his peripheral vision. The way she sat up was enough to convey what she was likely thinking. Chris turned to the right and went to the kitchen.

Under the sink, Kira had said. He knelt down, opened the cabinet, then saw a variety of kitchen items, mainly sprays, a dry rack, spare trash can...and plastic bags. He grabbed the box, then quickly hurried out the door, keeping his gaze away from Laurie. Once outside he heard the shingles pelting the ground. He pulled a bag from the box, only to immediately notice its white color. He read the label. *Tall kitchen drawstring bags.*

"Fuuuck!" he muttered. Wrong ones. He turned around and hurried back. He would be quicker this time...and pay a little better attention to what he was going inside for. He stepped through the open doorway...right into Laurie.

"Hey!" she exclaimed, staggering backwards as his weight collided with hers.

"Oh, shit! My bad..."

"The hell are you doing?!" she snapped. Chris immediately knew he had entered a battle he had no way of winning. Best to end it quick.

"Sorry," he said. "I just grabbed the wrong thing. Was just coming back to get the right trash bags."

"Yeah? Well remember to close the cabinets this time," she retorted. Chris looked at the open cabinet under the sink. In his rush, he hadn't even bothered to shut it.

"Fine," he said. He went to the sink, replaced the bags, then dug around for the heavy duty ones.

"The hell are you even doing? Sorting through Kira's stuff while she's up on the roof?"

Chris exhaled through his nose. He let himself tense for five seconds, then released. Arguing wouldn't help. Being the ex-con, there was little he could say that didn't make him look bad.

"I'm helping them with the roof. I just grabbed the wrong set of bags. Now, if I could only find the heavy duty ones..."

"They're on the right," she said. Chris looked. Had he not been on edge, he would've noticed them sooner.

He snatched them up, made sure to close the cabinets, since apparently that was a big deal to Laurie, then started toward the door.

"Thanks," he said, raising the box. It was meant to be genuine, but the shade of red that passed over her face indicated she took it as sarcasm.

"You're a piece of shit, you know that?"

A dozen rude replies went through Chris' mind before he settled on, "I spent eight years dwelling on that."

"Yeah? So, where the hell is my mother's ring?"

Chris looked up to the heavens. *Didn't take long for that to come up.* The floodgates had opened. Laurie was on the assault, despite her promises to Kira. As it turned out, promises were a poor barrier to emotions pent up over the course of eight years.

"There's nothing I can tell you that'll bring you comfort," Chris said. "I'm sorry—that's all I can say. I wish I could take it all back."

That wasn't enough for Laurie. She stepped closer, speaking through clenched teeth. "Where. Is. *IT?*"

Once again, Chris found himself in the 'damned if you do, damned if you don't' position. Not answering would make it look like he had something to hide, and that he wasn't repentant. Yet, the actual answer would not satisfy her either. If anything, it would piss her off more.

"You know the history of that ring and what it meant to my family."

"Yes…I remember."

"Where is it? I want it back."

"I don't know. I sold it eight years ago. Don't have a clue where it ended up. At this point, it could be in another country for all I know."

Her hand found his face. In the following instant, Chris' gentle expression turned into a seething, wrinkled, wide-eyed aberration of its former self. Veins swelled in his forehead. His teeth were clenched. Only a modicum of self-control kept him from yelling at her, and even that was at risk of slipping away.

"WHOA!"

Chris and Laurie turned and saw a bewildered Tyler in the hallway. Both hands were up, his posture like someone ready to hurtle himself between two brawlers. His attention was mainly fixed on Chris.

Judging by sound of a flushing toilet behind him, Chris suspected that he had missed everything leading up to the incident…and his first impression of it was the sight of an enraged Chris Kalb sizing up Laurie.

"What's going on here? Everything alright?"

Chris relaxed his posture. "Yes."

"You sure…because you looked like you were about to hulk out just then," Tyler said.

Chris couldn't believe it. This chain of events was so stacked against him, he wondered if some evil mastermind was at work.

"No. It's fine." He went back outside.

Tyler eased up. "Whew! What the hell happened there?"

If looks could kill, the one Laurie gave Tyler would've ruptured his skull. "'What happened?!' Oh, I don't know. Maybe the fact that you brought my criminal ex-boyfriend here. And now I have to spend a week with him."

"Hey now." Tyler raised his hands again. "It wasn't my fault."

"Your fault? Who brought him here?"

Tyler grinned nervously. "In fairness, I didn't know about the ring-stealing thing. That was new information to me."

"Dude, you're as oblivious as a frog in boiling water."

Tyler shrugged his shoulders. "Well…depends on how fast you crank up the heat. If it's TOO hot, the frog will just leap out and—"

"Ugh!" Laurie pushed past him and went for the bathroom, only to step out again. "Jesus, Tyler! What did you do in there?!"

He shrugged again. "Well, I had a lot of coffee on the way up, and—"

"I wasn't looking for a literal answer!"

"Oh—right! Sorry, I, uh…Oh, look at that! Marshall and Kira are tearing up the roof. I better get out there and help them out. See ya!" He rushed out the door, letting it slam shut on its own.

Laurie put her hands over her face. "I can't believe I'm stuck up here with these clowns."

CHAPTER 8

The afternoon sun had begun its arch down the western sky. The hours dragged on for Patrick Ruffing, who stared nervously at his phone. Six texts and three phone calls to his father had gone unanswered. It wasn't completely abnormal for Mr. Ruffing to miss a text or a call, but this many, over the course of several hours without answering, was far beyond normal.

Patrick's girlfriend, Audrey Couture, shivered in the breeze. Through the course of the day, she watched Patrick's concern for his dad intensify. That morning, when he didn't answer Patrick's call to confirm they were still on for breakfast, it was simply a case of 'Oh, Dad probably just had his phone on vibrate.' Later, when he didn't arrive at *Char Roy's Diner* in Wells Township, was when Patrick started getting nervous. Three of those six texts were sent there.

Still, it was chalked up to 'Oh, Dad was probably just busy. There's work in the backyard that needs to be done, and he's got a lot to do with his hardware shop. He probably just forgot.'

At least, that's what Patrick tried to convince himself. Forgetting meeting for breakfast, he could understand. But they were supposed to head for golf afterward—and that was at Dad's request. He was an avid golf lover and was always bugging other people to go to the course with him. Patrick enjoyed golf well enough. He wasn't an enthusiast, but it was a relaxing way to pass the time and talk bullshit with his father.

As Patrick neared the age of thirty, he had started to appreciate the time one had to spend with his parents, especially after Mom died three years prior. His siblings all lived in other areas in the country. Only Patrick stayed behind, partly because he wasn't the type who cared for traveling and preferred the familiar, low populated region of the UP. Also, there was Audrey.

The two of them met the basic rules for a successful relationship: the more in common you have, the more likely you will succeed. It was something Robert enjoyed throwing in the faces of naysayers, who always fed him the 'opposites attract' garbage. He'd retort, 'yeah, they may attract, but they never last.' And it was true.

She was a salon owner. Despite being located in a tiny town in Delta County, her business did fairly well. Like him, she enjoyed the vast woods that northern Michigan provided. And outside of work, she enjoyed peace and quiet. Occasionally, she enjoyed a trip or two just for a brief change of scenery, but overall, she liked it here. Patrick managed an electronics store in Munising Township in Burt County. Not a glamorous job, and a bit of a drive from where they lived, but it paid enough.

His mind briefly fixated on his route to work. Not because he was scheduled to work, but because of the drive time. It took forty-five minutes to go from home to Munising Township…slightly less than the time it would take to drive to Pettengill.

If I can drive near an hour to work every day, I can do it once to check on Dad.

Patrick looked at his phone. It was after four now. His seventh text had gone unanswered.

Dad. Everything good over there?

It was getting difficult for him to focus on anything. As far as he knew, his Dad had regular checkups every six months. A little build-up in his valves, but nothing alarming, even for a sixty year old. His blood pressure was a little high, but not necessarily anything to lose sleep over, especially since Dad adjusted his diet. None of this changed the fact that he was not returning Patrick's calls, and that he was a sixty year old man living alone, with very few neighbors.

There was only one thing Patrick hadn't tried yet.

He dialed the number to his Dad's hardware shop. He was about to breathe a sigh of relief when the call was answered.

"Ruffing Hardware. Can I help you?"

That millisecond of relief vanished, adding frustration to the anxiety. It was Harvey, Dad's employee.

"Hey, Harvey. It's Patrick. Is my Dad at the shop today?"

"No." Harvey sounded confused. *"I thought he was supposed to be with you today. He mentioned it to me yesterday."*

"He did?"

"Yeah. I figured that's where he's been, because I tried calling him to ask about a receipt issue, but he wouldn't answer. I assumed he was busy with you."

"He was supposed to…" Patrick's voice faded. Now this was getting legitimately scary. It wasn't just a question of his mind fixating on the worst-case scenario. Something wasn't adding up and Patrick didn't like it. "Thanks, Harvey. Call me back if you hear from him, please."

"No problem."

Patrick stuffed his phone into his pocket then hurried into the house for his car keys. Audrey spun in her computer chair to look at him.

"What's going on?" she asked.

"I'm gonna go check on Dad," Patrick said. He went into the bedroom, found his keys, wallet, and a ballcap, then started heading out.

"He still hasn't texted?" Patrick shook his head. He brushed his curled, brown hair back, then pressed the cap over his head. "I texted Brandon and Stacie. Neither of them say they've heard from him today. And I just spoke with Howard at his store. Nothing."

Audrey shut the computer down. "I'll head with you."

Patrick shrugged. "It's probably nothing." Audrey threw a jacket on and slipped into her brown knee-high boots.

"Probably. If so, I wouldn't mind a drive. My brain's rotted out from online shopping anyway." She managed to disguise her concern a little better than Patrick. Still, there was no denying that there was cause for concern. Mr. Ruffing enjoyed their get-togethers. Considering he lived alone and the other kids were out of town, all he had was the shop, Patrick, and maybe a few other friends scattered across the county. And he was not one to simply let calls and texts go unanswered all day. If he was busy, he'd simply text that just to end the barrage of messages.

Patrick locked the door behind them then got into his car. It would be about fifty minutes before they got to his Dad's house. Knowing how heavy his foot was on the accelerator, they'd probably get there in forty.

****

Audrey hated the silence. Patrick was usually a chatty guy, but it was hard for him to discuss grocery lists or tell stories of annoying customers at work when he was this anxious. He had his phone propped up in a small storage compartment in front of the center console. The screen was faced upward, in case his Dad finally responded. Three times, his eyes played tricks on him. The first was when a friend messaged him a gif about some stupid political nonsense. The second and third times were simple reflections caused by streetlamps or the position of the sun, causing the screen to appear as though it lit up.

He kept his eyes on the clock. They only had about seven minutes to go.

"I'm sure he's fine," Audrey said.

"I know," Patrick said.

"He's probably working in the backyard. Or maybe doing some stuff on one of the trails. There's always crap coming down from the trees."

"Maybe," Patrick said.

Audrey touched his arm. "Remember two years ago? That tree fell over and he forgot to call you on your birthday? It's not TOO out of the realm of possibility that he's dealing with something similar, especially if he forgot to take his phone out there with him."

Patrick nodded. He almost forgot about that, probably because he was busy with a hundred other things on his birthday. Most of it involving copious amounts of alcohol, which led to vigorous activity between him and his girlfriend. Even now, he couldn't help but smile at the memories, at least, those that survived the hangover.

"What are you thinking about?" Audrey asked.

"Nothing."

"Uh-huh. I see that smile."

It was wider now. Patrick glanced over at his girlfriend. Oh, how good the last five years had been. Definitely a keeper. Their personalities meshed well, and the physical attraction never wavered. In fact, he actually found her more desirable now than when they first met. Her hair was really short in those days. It was still short now, hanging just below her ears—still enough to maintain that tomboy look, but not the crewcut it used to be. Part of it was motivated by a simple desire for change, though it was also partly due to stupid assumptions that she was a lesbian.

Patrick squeezed her hand, then focused on his driving. Not that there was much to worry about out here. The road was so wide and so straight, he could cruise it with his eyes shut. After a minute, they found the first traffic sign for miles.

He turned north onto Dray Street. Almost there.

"It's coming up on five. Maybe he'll be putting something on the grill," Audrey said.

"He better be. Tell you what, he's gonna serve us something for missing our dates and scaring the hell out of me like this,"

Patrick said. Audrey leaned over the center console and gave him a kiss on the cheek. He smiled. "Love you too." She nipped at his earlobe. Patrick chuckled. "Not sure if Dad wants us doing *that* on his property. That might seal the deal on the heart attack."

"I'm just doing what I can to put you at ease," she said. She kissed his temple. "Who knows, if you're really feeling adventurous, we can pull over somewhere and—" She suddenly pulled away. "Hey, stop for a sec!"

Patrick smiled again. "I like what you're thinking, but we're almost there—"

"No, STOP! There's a car off the road!" Patrick hit the brakes. Audrey opened the skylight and stuck her head out to look at the trees further back. "Oh my God."

Patrick looked over his right shoulder, then gasped at the sight of the overturned SUV propped against the trees. He put the car in reverse and backtracked several meters. He could hear the crunching of debris under his tires—something which didn't register the first time due to him being fixated on Audrey's actions.

He pulled over to the side and parked. He got out of the vehicle and rushed to the SUV.

"Is there anyone inside?" Audrey asked.

"No. Jesus, the windshield's busted. The door's barely hanging on. This thing looks like it flipped over twice before ending up here. The hood's been ripped to shreds. Look like something took giant metal cutters to it."

He looked around for any signs of the driver. He took a few steps into the road, cupped his hands over his mouth, and shouted "Hello?!" His voice carried into the trees, lost with the eerie whistle of the wind.

Audrey peered into the SUV, cupping a hand over her mouth. The front tires were flat, the grill and bumper in shambles, and there was a smell of gas.

"Where do you think he is?" Audrey asked.

"I don't know. Maybe somebody came by and picked him up. Maybe he made a phone call."

"And no tow truck came? Even all the way out here?" she asked. She peered into the truck again. "And why would he leave his phone in here?"

Patrick looked and saw the device near the gas pedal. "That's a good point. Judging by this wreckage, he probably got his bell rung pretty good. I don't see him anywhere, so maybe a State Trooper or some resident came by and found him."

Audrey pointed at the grass. "What the hell is all this?"

"Well, babe, debris tends to scatter when there's been an accident. Probably just a case of some idiot driving at night with no headlights. Or drunk."

"No, I mean *this*."

"Careful." Patrick knelt by her. "Don't pick up the pieces. You'll cut your hand wide open—"

What she held up wasn't metal or glass. It almost resembled a tangled up piece of curtain, though very stringy. Pieces of windshield were caught up in the tiny threads that made up the rope. It stretched as she raised it from the ground.

Audrey looked at Patrick, whose eyes were fixed on the rope, but not the section held in her hands. Rather, he was looking at the continuation, which appeared to go all the way into the woods.

Much of it was clinging to the pieces of bumper and the grill. The strands twisted around the fragments where they clung. The white rope extended all the way up the hill, there it was somewhat coiled. The end was frizzy, like a busted cable.

"Hang on a sec." He jogged back up to the road and looked to the other side. There was another section of white stringy substance along the pavement. It was coiled up along the side of the road, like an outstretched wire that had been snapped. The rope continued several meters into the woods, where it appeared to be attached to a couple of trees.

"Jesus. Whatever it is, it looks like it was strung across the road. Looks like this vehicle came by, hit this thing stretched across, and—" He blew a puff of air, mimicking an explosion with his hands.

"What the hell is it?" Audrey said.

"I don't know."

Audrey tried to drop it, only to realize it was clinging to her skin and sleeves.

"Fuck! It's sticky!"

"Hang on," Patrick said. He went over to his girlfriend, who was restlessly attempting to free herself. "Hang on. Kneel down. Press the stuff to the ground. Just watch out for the glass shards."

Audrey grimaced as she knelt down. Her hands were practically cuffed to the bizarre substance. She pressed it down to the grass. Patrick stepped on the rope on each side, pressing it to the ground with his weight. He grabbed Audrey under her arms. Pressing with their feet, they pulled at once, slowly prying her hands from the substance.

"Ow!" she exclaimed.

"Just hang on. We're almost there," Patrick said.

"OW!" Audrey was near tears. "It feels like my skin's coming off." The substance stretched three feet off the ground, forming a white silky curtain. Even now, it clung to her hands relentlessly, as though fused with her skin. "What is this shit?!"

Even Patrick's concern was plain on his face. He shook his head. "I'm not sure. It almost looks like…" he eyed the stringy texture as it stretched, "…a spider web."

"Don't put that thought in my mind," Audrey said.

"Yeah, like there's a giant spider big enough to do this," Patrick said. He tried to crack a smile at his own joke, but it turned to a grimace. This stuff, whatever it was, was not letting her go. He pulled a folding knife from his back pocket and attempted to saw the blade against the strings. He only managed to cut through a few strands before the knife was packed with the substance. He managed to pull it back and try again. A few more strands broke free. "Okay, pull again, because this stuff's packing against the edge."

Audrey pulled back on the substance. It stretched further, demanding to maintain its grip. Audrey took several steps back. Finally, bit by bit, the stuff came free. She shook her hands, relieved to no longer be attached to the strange rope.

"Finally!"

Patrick was trying to free his knife from the stuff. "Holy crap! This stuff sticks to you instantly. It really does remind me of—oh, SHIT!"

"What's the matter?" Audrey asked.

Patrick lifted his left foot, lifting a strand of the stuff from the ground. Both of his boots were caught along the soles. In his attempt to free his girlfriend, he'd ended up getting *himself* stuck to the stuff.

"Son of a bitch," he muttered. He tried pulling away. Each movement sent ripples of vibration down the length of the rope. He tried cutting away at it, but at this point, there was so much gook on the blade, the edge could not reach the target.

"Here, let me," Audrey said. She took the knife and scraped it against a shard of windshield glass protruding from the frame.

The stuff bunched, but refused to come free. Making matters more difficult, the strands still attached to her palms made it difficult to maneuver the knife. The handle was now stuck to her hand. "My God!" She was scared and frustrated. This bizarre material had created a domino effect of problems within a few short minutes.

Patrick went from nervous to pissed off. He hadn't forgotten his concern for his father. Somehow, the discovery of this wreckage, along with this stuff, had worsened his concern for Dad's wellbeing. Now, he was practically stuck to the grass. He fell on his rear and pulled against the strand. Each movement shook the long white rope. Like soundwaves, the ripples traveled far into the forest, where the trap was secured to a large pine tree. From there, the ripples traveled along thin lines, which connected the trap to another tree. From there, the vibrations traveled down another wire to the next tree, then to the next. Like phone lines, the wires continued for nearly a mile north, where they connected to a large funnel, hidden deep within the woods.

****

Vibrations tickled the hairs on its carapace. Its legs uncoiled from beneath its underside, stretching the walls of its hideout. Its brain switched on and, like a computer, immediately worked on analyzing the sensations traveling through its web. There was no question that prey had been snagged in one of its traps. It hesitated, but only to discern from which direction the signals were coming from.

The pings continued. They were coming from the space between the trees, where it had caught the large, inedible creature. This whole area seemed rife with prey. The arachnoid didn't feel any sense of triumph, as it had no such concept. Nor did it experience the joy in hunting, as it didn't experience joy at all. It only knew of its existence and the perpetual needs of its body. Consideration for others didn't exist. Such an outlook required critical thought, something else the arachnoid was not capable of—beyond what it took to trap, hunt, and kill. It didn't see the creatures in its traps as living things, beyond the fact that they were made of flesh and, more to its interest, blood. As far as it was concerned, the rest of the world existed to serve its purpose.

It had been dark when it last fed. The temperature here was far lower than what it was accustomed to. Its body was working strenuously. It was cold-blooded, and it was not accustomed to the sluggishness it experienced. It was not a heavily active creature to begin with. Chasing prey, especially at its size, required tremendous energy. It could run in short bursts, traveling a hundred feet in a few short moments. Its legs were strong and spring-like, the hydraulic musculature capable of drawing up enough power to launch it for several meters. But only when the need arose. It was a trapper, as the method best served its needs.

Right now, its need was to feed.

The arachnoid emerged from its funnel. The human habitat had nothing more to offer. The vessel embalmed in the webbing was nothing more than a dry shell, completely void of fluid. It had finished draining the other two when the sun began to rise.

It waited, allowing for its body to adjust to the temperature, and its eyes to the light. It then crawled over the funnel, allowing its hairs to feel the cross section of web wires that stretched all over the forest. Like a calculator performing basic math, it confirmed the direction from where these vibrations originated. It turned southeast and followed the trail set by itself. It was a longer distance, but despite its sluggish nature, the arachnoid managed to travel at great speed. Its front legs stretched over two meters with each step. Like oars on a Viking ship, they carried its bulk across the landscape.

Glands within its abdomen swelled. Beads of venom dripped from the tip of its stinger. They were full and ready to commit to their purpose. Its front arms were tucked under its head, ready to lash out at any moment.

There was movement all around. The natural wildlife within these woods fled east as they detected the huge beast. Had it not already had prey snagged in its trap, it would have chosen a target and pursued. Instead, the beast chose to conserve its energy. The distance to the trap was taxing enough in this temperature. Soon, there would be warmth. It would soon feel the sensation of blood entering its body. It would feed, then return to its slumber.

To feed, it must kill.

As it approached the destination, it picked up sounds. There was vibration along the ground, consistently coming from one specific location. It found the pine tree where its trap originated.

The thick web rope was wiggling. The creature bound at its end was struggling ferociously at this point.

It was close enough to the road now to see the clearing. It spotted movement on the grass. The terror the smaller creature experienced only ensured the arachnoid that it was thoroughly trapped. Its arms quivered. They were seconds from serving their purpose, as was its jagged stinger.

The arachnoid advanced.

****

They could hear rustling within the trees. Twigs snapped and bushes wavered. Audrey shrieked. She staggered from the trees then fell over. The deer stopped less than a yard away from her.

It was the third one that had come racing out, the predecessors having arrived thirty seconds earlier. It darted across the road and disappeared into the woods.

Patrick caught his breath. For a second, it looked as though his girlfriend was about to be trampled before his very eyes. Audrey stood up, the knife still glued to her hand. Before either of them could say anything, they looked to the north. Other animals were escaping the trees. They saw a couple of deer, as well as a few other creatures. Several birds were taking to the sky.

"What's going on?" Audrey said.

"I don't know, but I don't like it," Patrick said. He tugged at the snag. "Come on, help me get out of this."

"Just take off your boots," Audrey said. Patrick pulled a couple more times, then relaxed himself. He hated the idea of being barefoot, but then again, at least he wouldn't be bound to this rope. He reached for his laces to undo them.

The sound of something heavy scraping the ground caught his attention. It didn't sound like running feet. He looked to the woods. He saw the infinite number of trees. In that maze was a mountainous object. In the shade, it looked like a large rock. He froze, his eyes locked on the thing.

That was not there before...

Audrey stood by him. She saw it too.

The 'rock' shifted. There was movement on both sides, semi-circular, frolicking like the legs of an insect...

...or an arachnid.

The light hit the beast, revealing its dark grey color. Eight black eyes emerged between the trees, attached to a twelve-foot

71

bulk. Pedipalps huddled under those eyes, taunting them with thin black fangs. Its feet hit the earth like enormous drums. Each step resulted in an audible *thump*.

Audrey screamed. She pulled at his shoulders, only to reel backward out of fright when it closed in.

Patrick didn't scream, though only due to the paralyzing fear. He stared, mistrusting his senses, until the beast scurried toward him. Only when its crab-like arms reached out did he finally scream.

He tried scurrying backward, but the net held him in place. His scream amplified, as did Audrey's, when the pincer clamped down on his ankle. Bone snapped instantly, the claw's razor edge slicing the skin and drawing blood. The other pincer clamped down on his other leg, slicing his thigh muscle. Patrick clawed at the ground, unable to outmuscle the pull. He rolled to his right shoulder and reached for Audrey. She was up on the hill, her hands cupped over her face while she stared wide-eyed at the event. She was caught in that impossible dilemma of choosing to save herself or her lover. Her love for Patrick kept her from running, but her fear of bugs and spiders…especially this giant one, kept her from rushing to his aid. All she could was stand and scream.

Patrick saw the creature's shadow encompass him. When he looked back, it was propped up on its hind legs, allowing its bulky abdomen to fold under its body. From a large pore in the carapace, a rigid object protruded. Years of *National Geographic* flashed in his mind. He had seen enough stingers from wasps, scorpions, bees, ants, and so many others to know exactly what this creature was about to do.

"NO!" As if every muscle in his body came to life, determined to flee the carnivore, he spasmed. But the strength of the claws kept him pinned. The abdomen ached under the creature's body, and at an agonizingly slow pace, it was lowered to his. He saw yellow fluid beading from its tip. His brain went into overdrive. Adrenaline spiked to intense levels. Yet, he could not move. "NOOO! N—"

The stinger plunged.

Audrey cried his name. She stepped forward, then back again. The stinger had struck his abdomen. Immediately, Patrick tensed. It looked as though he was shocked by a high voltage wire. His fingers coiled, then bent backward to their max limit.

White foam spilled through the corners of his clamped jaw. His eyes were wide, as though the creature had possessed him.

It released its grip, leaving a limp Patrick on the ground.

When it turned toward Audrey, the instinct for self-preservation finally overpowered her love for Patrick. Its claws were now raised over its head, its abdomen raised high. Audrey spun on her heel and sprinted for the car. The engine was running, the door left open. She threw herself inside and slammed her foot on the gas pedal. The engine roared, but the vehicle didn't move. Screaming, she continued to tap it, then realized that she hadn't put the car in drive. She shifted the lever.

The earth drummed. A shadow overtook the vehicle. Audrey screamed as the window shattered. Pincers sliced thin grooves into the frame, shifting the car to the left. She floored the accelerator.

The arachnoid flailed its legs. Its carapace scraped against the pavement as it clung to the fleeing victim. The car dragged from the intense weight, but kept going. She floored the pedal, pushing the engine to the max. She looked to the left, only to see if it was still holding on. Not only was it holding on, but it had also pressed its face right up to the broken window. Round, bulging eyes…deep black abysses with no soul, stared at her.

Audrey screamed incoherently, simultaneously begging God to save her, while also telling the spider to go away. As though it comprehended human language, let alone compassion.

With the pavement scraping away at its abdomen, the arachnoid clawed at the vehicle with its legs, securing a grip on the trunk and skylight. It lifted over the vehicle, then leaned over the windshield. Its claws pierced the glass like pickaxes. Glass fragments cut Audrey's face. Screaming, she leaned back and forth as the pincers reached in, swerving the car all over the road. They clicked as they snipped at her face, the tips within inches.

The wind assaulted her eyes. She couldn't hold still even for a split second. Panic flooded every rational thought and calculation. Sanity was out the window. She simply screamed, while keeping her foot pressed to the pedal. Then came the sensation of falling. The car teetered to the right, then slipped down a small hill. Right as she realized what was happening, the car struck a tree, faceplanting her against the steering wheel. Next came the airbag. Rather than cushion the impact, it only served as a second blow, knocking her back against the seat.

Audrey was caught on the verge of blacking out. She drifted in and out. It was like being in a different realm. Time hardly seemed to move. There was a feeling of weightlessness. She saw various shades of light, ranging from gold to purple. The purple shifted to red. Then she felt warmth and wetness.

She was bleeding from her nose and forehead. Somehow, the sensation of blood brought her nearer to reality. She looked straight ahead. The creature was not there. She only saw the base of the tree which she struck. The car wasn't shaking anymore. She tried looking back, but her blurry vision obscured anything more than a few feet away. Regardless, there was no sign that the thing was perched up top. Her head was throbbing, as though her skull was threatening to cave in. Her hands stuck to the wheel. After pulling them loose, she pushed the car door open and stepped out, only for her legs to give way. She fell forward and crawled away.

It took sheer force to scale the small hill. There was no drumming noise, no hisses, only the sound of rustling leaves high above. Blood smeared against the grass. The throbbing intensified. Audrey didn't have any sense of direction at this point. Even her memory had gone fuzzy. There was only the sensation of overwhelming terror and the need to run from something.

She rolled onto her side, enough so she could look back. Even though she had glanced at the wreck moments prior, it was the first time her brain was registering it for what it was. It was Patrick's car…but there was no Patrick.

Then it all came back to her: the webbing on the ground, the sticky stuff on her hands, the SUV wreck, Patrick stuck in the rope—web; the stinger; the claws…

The arachnoid.

Now, she was truly awake. When the huge shadow overtook her, she wished she wasn't.

The beast stood over her, having fallen off the car when it rolled off the hilltop. For a creature as patient as it, a minor delay meant nothing. Its stinger was poised, as were its claws, which snapped to action. Audrey felt the serrated edges fasten over her shoulders, keeping her in place. She wiggled and whimpered, squeezed her eyes shut, then shrieked. The stinger struck her thigh. That was the first muscle to stiffen. Next was the lower legs, then the abdominal muscles, then those in her arms and back.

The terror and nausea never subsided. She could still feel the pincers on her body, and the sensation of being lifted. She could curl her fingers somewhat. Her heart still beat, though faintly. Once again, she was back in a world between consciousness and unconsciousness. The only difference was that the sense of terror didn't subside, especially when she felt a wet silky substance being weaved over her body.

The same stuff she'd found on the road.

CHAPTER 9

Ethan Fekete growled under his breath as he watched the hills of the Michigan Upper Peninsula pass underneath his window. The closer their private plane got to their destination, the grumpier he felt. He still preferred to let Myles Bower suffer the wrath of the company.

He could feel his wife's hand on his thigh. It had been there for most of the ride. Occasionally, her foot rubbed against his shin, as though to remind him of the act that changed his mind. She was giddy, clearly eager to embark on a new hunt. There was no thrill like hunting something that could hunt you back. Bryce wanted nothing less. The closer they got to the airfield, the wider her smile became.

"This is ridiculous," Ethan said.

"Lighten up, darling," she replied, squeezing his thigh. "You had the chance to object."

"I *did* object," he said. Bryce chuckled. Her hand left his leg, only to caress her other love. In her lap was the stock of her long range 500 FPS Titan Crossbow. She wore a Beretta on each hip and had her rifle in storage. Those would only be used if necessary, as this was a trip to capture the trophy alive. Still, that did not eliminate the thrill of an impending hunt. And who knows? Perhaps she would be able to sever a foot or fang from the arachnoid as a trophy.

The plane set down at a private airfield near Lake Superior. From there, a private car awaited the two hunters. The driver, given implicit instructions to get them to the facility as soon as possible, plowed through a few red lights until he was on a long stretch of pavement which led deeper into Michigan. From there on, they were surrounded by thick woods. Driving twenty miles over the limit, the normally forty-minute trip was complete in a half-hour.

They came across a gap between the trees. A long stretch of pavement led them to a gate. With a swipe of a card, the gate opened, then shut again once the car was through. For a few moments, they were surrounded by trees as they followed the path. After two hundred feet, the woods spaced out. They were in a vast yard with a pond in the center. Further back was an enormous two-story building. Judging by the design, it seemed almost a cross between a hospital and a private mansion. There were two balconies on the upper levels overlooking the vast lawn. There were a few hired guards patrolling the gates, most of which looked bored out of their minds. It was clear this was a place where nothing took place, yet, judging by the automatic weapons and high-tech equipment, they were guarding something of great importance. Or at least, they thought they were.

Ethan smirked, then leaned to whisper in his wife's ear. "These guys are Jedlinsky's employees, not Dr. Bower's."

She chuckled and nodded. The car pulled up to the front doors. Before they stepped out, those doors opened. Out came a short, dark haired, man. His cheekbones were reminiscent of his Ukrainian mother, while the rest of his features were clearly passed down by his father, whom Ethan heard was from China. Ethan was tempted to make the stereotypical 'short Asian' joke. The doctor was five-foot-six at best, and maybe a hundred and sixty pounds soaking wet. His wife read his mind and elbowed him in the ribs.

"Ow. What was that for?"

"Don't be rude."

He sneered. "I think you're a little too nice to this fucker. One thing's for sure—you seem to be quick to forget he caused this." He rubbed his injured leg.

She leaned over. "Once this hunt is done, and the money has come through, I'll knee him in the nuts for you," she whispered, then licked his lips. "Then, maybe, we'll stick a knife in his leg as payback for his fuckup. But, *for now*, I want to hunt this big ass spider. And I don't want you ruining my fun."

Ethan rolled his eyes and stepped out of the vehicle. Myles smiled and stepped down the concrete steps.

"Excellent! Welcome, Mr. and Mrs. Fekete." His smile wavered into an awkward expression when he saw Bryce. The image of her naked body was burned into his brain, making this meeting slightly uncomfortable. The awkwardness elevated when Ethan's coldblooded stare pierced him. "Please allow me to take you inside and brief you."

One of the security guards stepped up and reached for Ethan's briefcase.

"Pardon me, but I need to check this."

"No!" Myles snapped. He eased up. "Excuse me, I guess you didn't receive the memo. These people are associates of Jedlinsky. They're here on classified business. Let them through."

"Headquarters specifically states that all newcomers HAVE to go through a check…"

"I know what the protocol is," Myles stated. "I've already cleared them. Now, step aside."

"I'll have to get on the phone with Jedlinsky's office," the guard said.

"Feel free. Just consider the fact that we're about to start a private conference with him. It's up to you to decide if you want to interrupt that or not."

Judging by the way the guard looked away, Myles' obvious bluff seemed to work. He retracted his hand from the briefcase then backed away.

"My apologies."

"Now, we have things to do," Myles said. He led the two hunters into the building. They stepped into a vast lobby full of lavish furniture, a large fireplace, rec area, television, and private dining.

"Is this a lab or a five-star resort?" Bryce asked.

"Jedlinsky treats his employees well," Myles replied.

"As long as they deliver the goods, right?" Ethan said. He was grinning ear to ear.

More than ever, Myles wanted this job done and over with. Still, he couldn't afford to go to war with Ethan. If anything, it made him appreciate the missus all the more for keeping the vile hunter under control.

He turned to look at her. "May I offer you a coffee?"

"No thanks," Bryce said. Myles turned to Ethan, who simply shook his head. They passed through the lobby to the back door. With his key swipe, Myles led them through a series of labs. Glass aquariums lined the walls, holding spiders and insects obtained from all over the globe. Dead specimens were preserved in jars, their abdomens split open as though they had undergone an autopsy.

Ethan snorted. "'No animals were harmed in the making of this lab.'"

"To create, one often must destroy," Myles said. He led them into the next room. This one was larger, with a high ceiling.

Judging by the view outside the windows, they were in the back of the building. But it wasn't the window they were fixated on—

On the right side was a large glass pen, roughly fifty-feet long, and thirty-feet high. Inside were large, artificial tree branches, canopy, and a pond on the far left. Nothing moved inside the pen.

"I'm assuming this is where you mean to hold your pet?" Bryce asked.

"That's right," Myles said, proudly.

"How the hell do you plan on getting it inside? Lead it by a leash?" Ethan said.

Myles hesitated to respond. "That wouldn't be wise." He cleared his throat and pointed at the ceiling. "The canopy opens up. We have a crane in the back that we'll use to lift the specimen, which'll be contained in a net. We'll lower it in, close the canopy, and the creature will be mine to present to the company."

"Yeah? When do your overlords arrive?" Ethan said.

Myles was trying not to cringe. "In two days." He cleared his throat and straightened his posture to appear more authoritarian. "With that in mind, let's get down to business."

"Please," Bryce said. "What exactly *is* this arachnoid thing?"

"We've been working with splicing genes from various species of animals," Myles said. "We started with plants, then proceeded to move on to insects and reptiles."

Ethan's leg pulsed. *Yeah, I'm aware.*

"The idea was to develop new pharmaceutical drugs and vaccines using the herbs obtained from the plants and venom in the animals."

"But why the cross-splicing? And increase in size?" Bryce asked. Myles stuttered.

"Uh, well—it's hard to extract significant blood samples and venom from normal-sized species. So, we have to increase their physiology in order to create the various antivenoms."

"But how does splicing of DNA apply to that?" Bryce said.

Ethan was rolling his eyes. "Let me save the doctor from straining himself, babe. They've got more contracts than just with pharmaceutical companies. There's only ONE other industry that rivals those corporations—and that's weapon manufacturers and dealers." He saw Myles' face wrinkle with objection. "Oh, give me a break, Doc. Don't feed me some scientific bullshit about how making a scorpion-spider helps develop medicines. The company has more contracts than just with drug pushers. I bet there's whole nations involved. Hell, maybe even the good ol' U.S. of A."

"Mr. Fekete, this corporation—"

"Doc, your secret is safe with us," Bryce said. "I just want to hunt this fucking thing. Clearly, we're on a tight schedule, so can we get to it?"

Myles was somewhat more relaxed. "Follow me." He led them to the west side of the building. They went up a stairwell and into a conference room, fitting with Myles' story about having a conference call with Jedlinsky.

He lit up a projector and got on the computer. The files were already pulled up and in order.

"This is A-32," he stated.

"Sounds like a battery," Ethan quipped. Myles ignored the statement and projected the image of a newly hatched arachnid hybrid. It was roughly the size of a football at birth, its carapace clearly soft and vulnerable. It was bright white in color, except for its eight black eyes. Its forearms were tucked under its head, almost invisible due to the transparent state of its body. At this stage, it almost resembled a cuttlefish more than an arachnid.

The next image showed the creature at two weeks old. Now, it had obtained its full color and had a body size matching a desktop monitor. Myles shuffled through a few more images and videos, which displayed the creature spinning its web.

"Pay attention to this video here," Myles said. "This'll display its feeding habits."

They watched as a pig was lured into its chamber. The camera was fixed on the clueless pig, which proceeded to walk toward its doom. It oinked and hobbled around, looking for vegetation to scavenge. The camera panned upward at the large funnel-shaped nest high above. The specimen's legs were protruding from the opening.

Ethan and Bryce waited, expecting to see the beast spring from its lair and attack. Instead, it simply waited.

Ethan leaned his chair back. "Boring." They continued to watch as the pig wandered around the lure. "Jesus wept! Clearly, this is some rampaging beast you've created, Doc. Won't even bother to catch a pig."

"Just watch."

"I AM! This works better than Benadryl. THERE'S your pitch to the pharmaceutical companies! 'We've got spider video

SO BORING it'll work better than sleeping pills!'" Bryce started to laugh. Even *she* wasn't coming to Myles' defense on this one.

Finally, the pig wandered close to the web. It tried to step away, only for one of its hooves to be caught in the strands along the ground. It squealed and tried pulling away. The thread pulled at the main body of web, sending vibrations all the way up to the arachnoid.

The funnel rippled as the legs came to life. The arachnoid emerged from its funnel and gazed down at its prize. At this stage of its life, it was roughly six feet in length, its legs expanding seven feet on each side. The pig panicked as the predator moved down along its web. The pincers expanded.

The creature moved fairly slow at first. Suddenly, after closing within fifteen feet, it closed the distance in a blur of motion. Suddenly, the pig was in its grasp. The abdomen folded under its body and sank its stinger into its victim, paralyzing it. Next came the procedure of cocooning the still-twitching prize.

"Interesting," Ethan said. To Myles' surprise, he didn't appear to be sarcastic. "How big is it now?"

"Twelve feet in length," Myles replied.

"I anticipated it would have a big tail, like a scorpion," Bryce said.

"No. As you can see, the abdomen is a little more elongated, somewhat like that of a scorpion, but still spider-like. It allows the body a little flexibility to bend the abdomen underneath so it can sting its prey."

"Does it always hunt like this?" Bryce asked. "What is the likeliness that we might have to chase it down?"

"Better yet, what's the likeliness that it'll try to chase *us* down?" Ethan added.

"Out in the wild, there is a possibility. It's hungry and living in lower temperatures than it's used to," Myles said. "That said, based on what I've observed, it's still using the same hunting methods."

"Which is?"

"Establishing a territory, weaving a main lair, then setting up various traps all around it for unsuspecting prey to stumble across," Myles said. "It will go after prey if they're close enough, or if it's hungry enough. But typically, it likes to rest and let the traps do most of the work."

"So, you've engineered the world's laziest spider," Bryce said.

Myles smirked. "Have you ever seen a spider web? What is it you think they do? They wait for unsuspecting victims to come by and get trapped. For A-32, we ought to be able to find it slumbering in its lair. Before it even notices us, we should be able to tranq it."

Bryce crossed her arms. "Well, that's disappointing. Might as well shoot fish in a barrel."

Ethan, on the other hand, was fairly relieved. The easier it was to track the thing, the sooner the job would get done. At least the hundred grand would provide a little beer money.

"How do we tranq it?" Bryce asked.

Myles opened up one of the large briefcases on the end of the table. Inside were several black arrows, loaded with glass vials containing tranquilizer fluid. Wires and tubes connected the vial to the neck of the arrow.

"Once the tip punches through the carapace, the fluid is injected into the bloodstream. As you said, fish in a barrel. This'll be the easiest hunt of your life."

Once again, Bryce failed to hide her disappointment.

"I thought we'd be tracking this thing through the woods."

"Believe me, you don't want that scenario," Myles said. "And you DEFINITELY don't want to be caught in its web."

"Is its venom fatal?"

"No. Just paralyzes your skeletal muscular system and slows the cardiac process, but not enough to keep the heart from beating entirely. It prefers warm, fresh blood. It's not clear whether consciousness is lost or not. One way or another though, you get caught by this thing, you'll live long enough to feel your blood get vacuumed out." He made a slurping noise.

Bryce's eyes widened. The sense of thrill was returning.

"Where the hell is it?" she asked.

"Twenty-two miles south of here, on a property off a main road called Sandusky."

"A property?"

"The truck crashed along a private trail in the woods. The specimen made a nest around the resident's house and made lunch of the owner. Once the thing is captured, we'll have to do a little extra work to erase that evidence."

Bryce spun in her seat, directing a questionable stare at him.

"Erase evidence?"

"He's already dead," Myles said. "We just need to eliminate any trace of its lair. I saw a propane grill there. I think it's safe to assume an 'accident' could have taken place while Mr. What's-His-Name was cooking burgers."

"Yeah, because outdoor grills frequently result in house fires," Ethan remarked.

"You know what I mean!" Myles said. "Look, it's a simple extra task. Not like I'm asking you to kill anybody."

"Yeah. You're not paying me enough," Ethan said. He stood up and inspected the arrows. "How many of these should it take to put the thing down?"

"One should make it sluggish. Two will knock it out for sure. I have a truck in the garage. There's a forklift in the container to haul it aboard. I can operate that, though I might need your help with positioning its body onto the lift."

"As long as I get some fragment of it to hang on our wall," Bryce said.

Myles opened his mouth to protest, but quickly relented. "Fine."

"You sure your security boys won't question why a truck is leaving, only to suddenly return with your pet?"

"That's a problem I'm willing to deal with," Myles said. "Right now, I need to get that specimen back asap."

Bryce stood up, walked around the table to the arrows, and picked one up. She took her crossbow from its case and loaded one of the arrows. It fit perfectly. She smiled, then looked at Myles.

"I'm ready to go when you are."

It was exactly what the doctor wanted to hear.

"Give me five minutes to get changed. I'll meet you at the garage."

CHAPTER 10

The arachnoid moved east. During its chase, it had been taken a significant distance from its established lair. Once again, it was in new territory. Its memory was short, and its simple brain could not yet comprehend the sense of direction. It was not accustomed to this world, and while its natural instincts had gotten it far, it was still a stranger in a strange land. To it, the forest was nothing but an endless maze—though one full of prey. It did not feel fear, but there was an urgency to create a new nest and protect itself from the decreasing temperatures.

With its cocooned victim clutched in its pedipalps, the hybrid continued into the woods. New vibrations tickled the hairs on its legs. Deer and other critters retreated as soon as they sensed its presence. Unfortunately, it did not have any traps to snare them in as of yet. It would have to establish a new lair, as well as another series of traps.

It turned to the north, where it discovered a small creek. It lowered its mouth to drink, but the tiny stream was too thin for its fangs to absorb without taking in too much sediment. It needed a larger body of water to properly hydrate itself. It followed the creek further north. After a hundred meters, it stopped. Its hairs felt vibration, from two sources, each coming from the same general direction. It froze. Several seconds passed before it spotted movement coming from the right. One critter was small, hardly larger than any of its feet. It was a furry critter, leaping through the brush, while another, larger mammal pursued it.

The fox was closing in on the jackrabbit. Even for the injury in its hind leg, its victim was maintaining a good pace. The fox's initial attack had failed. Had the fox been less clumsy, it would've had a simple task of springing from the underground tunnel, seizing the meal, then returning. It should've been an easy task, since the jackrabbit made the error of wandering too close to its den. Unfortunately, the fox had not timed its ambush right, nor did it secure a firm hold on the rabbit with its jaws. It was not a total loss, as its teeth had sunk deep into its hind leg. Gradually, the jackrabbit was slowing, and the fox was fully rested and spry. The distance was closing. With each added foot, the predator salivated.

Out of desperation, the jackrabbit took a wide left turn. The fox followed. Drips of saliva jetted between its bared teeth. It was not trailing at seven feet. It only needed to narrow the gap a little more before it could close it completely with a bounding leap.

Within seconds, the necessary distance was closed. The fox made its leap. Its jaws closed down.

Dirt and grass filled its mouth. The fox spat the soot and looked back. It had leapt right over the rabbit, which had stopped in its tracks. Its ears were up. Despite its pursuer being within striking range, the rabbit suddenly seemed oblivious to its presence. It looked up, slightly to the left, then turned and darted the other way.

The fox turned around, ready to follow, only to stagger to the side when it noticed movement on its right side. Huge legs vaulted, lifting an enormous shape. Huge mandibles quivered. Large, armored claws extended. The fox had lived in the woods for five years, and never once had it seen a fiend like this. Instinct rang every alarm bell in its brain. The fox had no comprehension of what this thing was, but it knew a predator when it saw one.

Had it not been for the fallen tree in-between them, the arachnoid would have been on top of the fox in less than a second. By the time it scaled the thick branches, the prize had fled into the woods. The arachnoid's brain made a split-second decision on whether or not to pursue.

Hunger dictated its actions. The enormous beast shot after the furry critter, shredding bushes and fallen branches with each rapid swing of its legs.

The fox could sense that the distance was quickly closing. It had now taken the role of the rabbit. Fortunately, there was luck in its favor. Its den was nearby. The fox knew the layout of this section of woods. It took a right turn, then lunged between a thick pairing of trees. The arachnoid came to the barrier, unable to squeeze between the thick branches, which forced it to scurry around.

With several meters of distance added to its retreat, the fox had the advantage. Weaving between the various obstacles in the woods, it found the hillside where its den was hidden. Already, the huge creature was gaining distance. It could hear its feet thumping against the earth.

The fox spotted its tunnel and dove inside.

The arachnoid closed in on the hill. Like magic, the fox had disappeared. The spider stood, poised for a strike. Its feet could sense vibration coming from below. The fox was still there, hidden under the ground.

For several minutes, the beast waited. The vibrations continued. The fox was not going anywhere. Had there been another way out, the vibrations would have stopped.

The arachnoid went right to work. It leaned forward and cocked its rear legs toward the pore in its abdomen. In circular motions, they pulled thick strands of white webbing and laid them along the hill. It moved around the den, coating the earth around it. It did not lay any silk over the entrance aside from the edges. As soon as the task was complete, the arachnoid moved away. The trap was set. There was nothing left to do but wait. And with no concept of time, patience was the arachnoid's forte.

In the meantime, there was other work to be done.

The pair of trees used by the fox to delay its advance would now serve a purpose for the arachnoid. The arching of thick branches overhead provided a perfect base for securing its funnel. With the human prize still clutched in its pedipalps, the creature climbed the trunks. At thirty feet, it reached the branches. They crossed each other and curved down, resembling a roof awning. For the next hour, it weaved a thick web casing. With thread after thread, the funnel had a wall as sturdy as concrete, yet soft as fleece. From there, it strung a web which stretched all the way to the ground.

The arachnoid was growing fatigued. The chase on the road and the recent one in the forest, along with the taxing effect of producing web demanded much from its body. Still, there was more to be done before it could rest. It needed to set its traps—all this work would be for nothing without the ability to snag prey.

First, it secured the cocoon in the web, then proceeded to connect a thread from the funnel to the trap at the fox den. Any vibration caused by struggling prey would alert the predator. Once the wire was set, the creature proceeded north, with silk trailing from its abdomen.

The breeze carried moisture, signaling the presence of water. The arachnoid turned eastward and continued on a path which led it to a shoreline. For the first time in its life, it discovered a body of water larger than itself. The beast stood firm, still hidden a few yards behind the tree line. Though large, and having never been defeated in its lifetime, it still had the built-in instinct of caution. Its DNA roots did not adjust for its size. It still had a sense of self-preservation, as other predators could be lurking about.

Several minutes passed. The creature saw nothing but clear air and rippling water. Finally, it moved in on the shore and drank. Its range of hearing instantly expanded, as there were less obstacles out here to muffle sounds. After satiating its thirst, it turned north again, alarmed at various vibrations further up the shoreline. The shore curved to the right, and was not as spacious. They were lined with thick trees, making travel difficult. Its eyesight blurred after thirty meters. Still, it could sense activity somewhere to the north—and it was enough to interest it.

After laying a trap near the shoreline where it drank, the creature moved north, staying within the cover of the trees. The commotion intensified as it neared. Soon, the hairs on its legs detected vibrations. Slowly, it advanced, during which it monitored the signals. They didn't vary much during the time of travel, meaning the sources were centralized in one main location.

This location was close to the shore. The creature slowed as it spotted a clearing several meters ahead. The trees ended at top of a small hill. Its sensory receptors went into overdrive. There was an abundance of prey here, and judging by the signals, they were oblivious to its presence.

It crouched a few feet from the edge of the clearing and watched. It spotted a large area, with numerous humans moving about. There were three mechanical beasts in which these biped creatures traveled on. They were in place, not making the rumbling vibrations from when in motion. The humans were moving on and around a large nest, similar to the one it had cocooned the previous night.

Immediately, the creature considered its options. It could attack or it could wait. Considering the state of its body, it would lose most, if not all, of the potential prey in a direct assault. It had food waiting at its web, which would help it endure the night.

The best results would require its signature hunting method.

The arachnoid slowly backed out of sight, then proceeded to thread long sticky strands of web along the ground.

CHAPTER 11

By six-thirty, Tyler and Chris were dragging their feet. Most of the roof tiles had been removed, as had several sections of roof decking. Even Kira was finally feeling the fatigue of a five-hour drive followed by several hours of work. The only one who seemed unfazed was Marshall.

Sue was on the ground, using a magnet to pluck screws, staples, and other metal debris from the grass. Only Laurie refused to be seen. The argument between her and Chris could be heard throughout the property, and it had left an awkward tone on the group. Occasionally, Marshall and Tyler would initiate some kind of small talk, but still, the uncomfortable tension would not cease.

Most of the roof had been cleared and Marshall had successfully removed the rotten sections of decking. He and Kira could see down into the guest bedroom now, which was peppered with residue.

"Lovely," Kira said.

"Nothing a vacuum cleaner can't take care of," Marshall replied.

"You're one to talk. Considering you never use one."

"Never really had to since Riley died."

Kira looked over at him, shocked at the news. A year and a half before their breakup, Marshall had gotten a German shepherd puppy, who shed so much she wondered if the thing would go bald. Thus, dog hair took over his house. Kira's housecleaning instincts would always kick in when she went over to his place, as Marshall had gotten lazy at cleaning up the clumps of fur.

"Wait—Riley died?"

"Yeah," Marshall said. He spoke in a neutral tone of voice in a vain attempt to act as though he wasn't bothered. But Kira remembered clear as day how attached he was to that puppy.

"What happened? When?!"

"About a year ago, roughly. Liver failure. Poor fella started losing weight. Had no appetite. By the time I realized something was off, he was too far gone." Marshall pried a piece of rotten roof decking free. "Gosh, you're lucky we caught this in time, or else this whole room would be caked with mold."

"What's next?" Chris called up from the ground. Kira and Marshall glanced down at them. Sue and Tyler looked zombified, leaning against a tree. Their sweaty faces were peppered with dirt and slivers of residue.

Tyler raised his hand. "More specifically, when do we call it a day?"

Marshall checked his watch. "What? You guys a bunch of pussies? We still have plenty of daylight left."

"Says you," Sue muttered.

"I'm beat," Tyler said.

"Aren't you used to working late?" Marshall said. "I recall hearing you brag about the tips you'd make from those pizza deliveries."

"Driving around a town I've memorized since I was two is one thing," Tyler said. "Hammer and nails, that's something else entirely."

"I don't recall you even picking up a hammer," Sue said.

"Shh! You're not helping. We need a united front on this," he whispered. For once, Sue agreed with him.

"I'm starving," she said to Kira.

"I've brought burgers!" Tyler said. The two people on the roof remained silent. "Oh! And brats! And smore-makings."

They heard the cottage door open.

"Did I hear the word 'smores'?" Laurie said.

"Yes, you did!" Tyler exclaimed. He was like a politician trying to gain as many votes as possible.

Kira chuckled. Clearly, it was three-to-two so far, with only one member yet to cast his vote.

"What about you, Chris?"

"Hmm?" He seemed surprised to be asked, and simultaneously hesitant to answer. It was clear he didn't want to step on anyone's toes, even on an issue as inconsequential as this. The poor guy had not gotten out of the shadow of guilt for the brief chaos caused by his very presence.

"Yeah, man? What say you?" Tyler said.

Chris faked a chuckle. "Whatever you all want."

Kira groaned. It became clear that this would go on forever unless she took a definitive stance. While she hated the idea of leaving the roof practically torn open, there was a reason they planned a whole week for this. Besides, they were making extremely good progress. At this rate, they'd be done by

Wednesday…maybe even Tuesday, considering Marshall's work ethic, leaving Thursday and Friday free for pure relaxation.

"Alright, I suppose we can call it quits," she said.

"Bunch of sissies," Marshall joked.

"Hey, we're not the ones trying to impress somebody," Laurie said.

Kira wanted to facepalm herself. *She is REALLY going all out.*

"Wait, what?" Tyler said.

Sue pointed up at them. "Are you guys getting back togeth—"

"Hell no!"

Marshall and Kira's simultaneous replies surprised even themselves. Laurie cracked up laughing.

"I'm so convinced."

Kira stammered. "I—you—we—where's that damn tarp?!"

"Got it here," Marshall said. He picked it up and started unfolding it. He walked along the planks, carefully avoiding the gap where they had torn the section of decking free, then handed one side to Kira.

"You know, I'm sure in some foreign country, a man handing a woman a tarp is a symbol of proposal," Laurie said.

"Oh, for godsake," Kira said. *At least she's back to being her usual self.* They secured the tarp over the roof, then climbed down the ladder. Kira smirked at Laurie. "By the way, I'm leaving the windows open all night."

"Yeah—I don't think so," Laurie retorted.

"Whew! Speaking of which, it's getting chilly," Sue said.

"*Getting* chilly? You're acting like it just started," Laurie said.

"It's not so bad," Marshall said.

"Especially when you're working," Tyler added.

"Weren't you just complaining about working?"

"About working. Not the temperature. Honestly, I think it feels great!"

"Oh, you're all freaks," Laurie groaned.

"Perfect temperature for fishing," Marshall added. "With that in mind—" He marched toward his trailer then snatched up his fishing rod.

"Where you going?" Laurie said.

"I'm commandeering a vessel," Marshall replied.

"But we're making dinner," Tyler said.

"Knowing you, I have a good hour before the fire is even set," Marshall replied.

Tyler shrugged. "Another fair point."

"I'll get wood," Chris said. He immediately walked for the woods. Kira followed him with her eyes. She then looked at Laurie, whose facial expression briefly returned to fiery contempt when she looked at him.

Kira tapped her on the shoulder. "Can you help me cut some produce for the burgers?"

Laurie rolled her eyes. She recognized the lie, but went along with it anyway. "Sure."

They walked into the cottage. The door hadn't even shut when Kira turned around to face her.

"Listen, is it *really* necessary for you to be this angry?"

"Ex-CUSE me?!"

"Shhh!" Kira carefully raised her hands to signal they lower their voices. Last thing the group needed was to overhear another argument.

"Don't shush me. We've already had this conversation," Laurie said.

"Listen, I'm not saying you have to like that Chris is here, but my God! You couldn't make this whole thing more awkward if you tried."

"You're just made because I'm calling you out for your attempts to hook up with Marshall."

"I'm not trying to hook up with Marshall. And quit changing the subject," Kira said. "Everyone here is worried you guys are gonna blow up at each other. I'm BEGGING you, don't let this get out of hand. Or else, it's gonna be a long week."

Laurie crossed her arms. "You seem to have a lot of faith in that guy."

Kira threw her head back in frustration. "I told you, he seems to have changed for the better."

"You know, they never determined which of those bank robbers killed that guard." She clicked her tongue. "Might've been him."

"He's also the only one who turned himself in," Kira retorted. "What's wrong with you?" Laurie scoffed. Kira closed her eyes. "Okay, that was a stupid question. Yes—he stole the ring and other shit. I guess all I'm asking is for you to TRY and get along with him while we're here. You don't even have to initiate any unnecessary conversation with him. Just don't blow up like you did earlier. It's like you're walking around with a lit fuse, and the rest of us are afraid you'll detonate any time."

Laurie sniggered. "I'd say you have it coming." She then sighed. "Alright-alright. I'm sorry...ish." Kira smiled and they hugged.

"You're not mad at me, right?"

Laurie looked out through the window at Marshall, who was loading her boat up with fishing gear. "No, but I am gonna get back at you again." She went for the door. Realizing what her friend was looking at, Kira pointed a finger.

"Oh, don't you even fucking think about it..."

"Hey, Marshall?"

He turned to look back. "Yeah?"

"Kira's talking about how she misses fishing, but she's too shy to ask if she can go out on the boat with you."

Kira cringed. "I swear, I'm bringing ALL of your ex-boyfriends next time you come up here."

"Tell her to come aboard, then," Marshall replied.

Laurie giggled.

"You're dead!" Kira said.

Marshall cupped his hand around his ear. "What'd she say?"

"She's jumping with excitement," Laurie said. "Give her a sec. She's on her way." She shut the door and turned toward Kira, who stood, fists on her hips, face scrunched with anger—or rather, the illusion of anger. "Nice try. I see through the bullshit act."

"Stop trying to make this happen."

"I've barely put any effort into it."

"Good, because it's wasted effort," Kira said.

"Oh, Kira. Ye of little faith."

"Ye of common sense. He's not gonna go for it. He has a girlfriend!"

Laurie's eyebrows lifted. "Really?"

"Yes."

"How do you know this?"

"I saw him on the phone when I went up on the roof," Kira said.

"Yeah? So?"

"I saw the contact name. Some bitch named Amanda." Kira watched as Laurie shook with laughter. "What?"

"I love how your whole argument has gone from 'I'm not interested in rekindling' to 'Nothing can happen. He's unavailable—supposedly.'"

"He *isn't* available…and I'm not interested. Give it a rest."

"Yeah, I don't see you refusing to get your fishing rod," Laurie said.

"I have *you* to blame for that," Kira said. "He's expecting me now. I'm *obligated*."

"Uh-huh. Looks to me like you're going out with the "unavailable" guy," Laurie said.

"Oh…my…god. He's not—he's…I swear you're insane."

They looked to the window as Marshall's voice echoed from outside. "Hey! You making an Italian sub in there, or something?"

"She's coming!" Laurie replied.

Kira started marching to the back room, stopping briefly to point at Laurie. "It's only fishing."

"Some people call it that."

"Jesus Christ. You don't give in. He's attached."

"Oh yeah. Amanda, right?" Laurie said. "Well…she should've come up here then."

"Laurie!"

"Relax. Take it from me; sometimes it's fun to be 'the other woman.'"

Kira smiled and shook her head. "You were always a whore."

"I'll remember that when I'm cupping my ears tonight while trying to sleep." She pointed at the ceiling, then mimicked the sound of a creaking spring.

Kira shook her head, then walked into the back room.

Five minutes later, she stepped back out. She had a flannel jacket on, had her fishing pole and tacklebox in hand, and a ball cap on her head. Laurie was outside by now. Kira was grateful for this, as she was bracing for a remark regarding the tacklebox, which was a gift from Marshall back in the day.

Then she realized Laurie was at the dock handing something to Marshall.

"What is she doing?" Kira stepped through the door and went for the dock. Laurie was handing Marshall a six pack of beer. "Did you take that from my fridge?!"

Laurie smiled. "Maybe. Whatcha gonna do about it?"

Kira passed her on the dock and handed her gear to Marshall. "God, I hope we get a frost tonight."

"Wow, Kira. You get awfully testy when you don't get flung."

Marshall smirked. Kira pointed at him. "What's that look for?"

"Nothing."

"Riiiight. I need a cigarette."

"Before you light up, you have fuel on hand? This motor's looking a little empty," Marshall said.

"Yeah. There's a full can in the storage room at the back of the cottage."

"Just needed to say storage room. I remember where it is," Marshall said. He got out and headed for the cottage. As he approached, he couldn't help but notice Tyler snooping around his trailer. "You lost?"

"No…just, uh, realized we forgot to pack water," Tyler said.

Sue was seated near the firepit. She leaned her head back and groaned. "Tyler, I swear you need to go on assisted living."

"I'm so in love with you," Tyler said with a smirk.

"Oh, knock it off with that shit."

Marshall snorted. "There's a full pack in the dressing room. Help yourself."

"Thanks!" Tyler quickly disappeared into the trailer. Marshall went into the cottage, found the gas can, then stepped back out. Tyler emerged from the trailer.

"Whoa, man! Planning on doing some deer hunting?"

Marshall shot him a glance. "Beg your pardon?"

"Saw the shotgun case in there," Tyler said.

"Well, yeah. There's bears up here, genius," Marshall replied.

"Hmm, fair enough. I thought you were afraid of some *Deliverance* action."

"Nah. We'd just throw you to the rednecks, which would buy the rest of us time to escape," Marshall retorted.

"I'm down for that," Sue added.

"Funny," Tyler said. "Good to have friends."

"There might be something to that," Chris said. He was walking back from the woods with armfuls of wood.

Tyler gulped. "The bears or the rednecks?"

Chris glanced at the woods. "Dunno. All I can say is that I heard something moving around back there."

"Probably some deer," Marshall remarked.

"What's the holdup, *Ahab*?" Kira shouted.

"Gotta go. If I find out anyone touches that shotgun, they're gonna find it shoved up their ass," Marshall said. He started for the lake.

"What if a bear comes?" Tyler said.

"Same game-plan as for dealing with the rednecks," Marshall replied.

"I'll certify that!" Sue said, raising a beer.

"Should we be on *Dr. Phil* or something?" Tyler quipped.

Marshall refilled the outboard motor, then handed the can to Laurie. "Mind taking this back?"

"You're gonna make me carry this heavy thing?"

"I'm sure you can muster the girl power," he replied. Laurie lifted the can.

"Hmm, not that bad actually." She clicked her tongue as Marshall untied the mooring line and shoved the boat away. "Have fun."

Already, Kira had a beer open, while giving Laurie the evil eye.

"It's not happening," she mouthed.

"Yeah, sure," Laurie mouthed back. She smiled ear-to-ear as she walked back, impressed at herself for the clever scheme she had pulled off. Her plan was working perfectly.

That smile faded somewhat when she saw Chris by the firepit. She sucked in a breath.

Just behave. You promised Kira you wouldn't start anything.

"Fuck, this is gonna be a long night," she muttered.

CHAPTER 12

Myles Bower could feel his palms sweat as they approached the destination. The truck engine roared like a hungry beast as he drove down Sandusky. He was quickly getting déjà vu from the previous evening. Every tree, every pothole, every road sign seemed so familiar. It was a good thing, because he couldn't afford to waste time remembering where they found the wreck. It was getting late into the evening and the remaining daylight was dwindling fast.

Cigar smoke filled the vehicle. Both Ethan and Bryce had one clenched between their teeth. The latter stroked her crossbow as though it was her lover. She watched the windows, appearing as though contemplating a drive-by shooting of any wandering critter she noticed.

"We're almost there," Myles said.

"You sure we didn't pass it? I've seen at least three trails on the way up here," Ethan said.

"Trust me, I know where it is," Myles said.

Ethan glared at him, the cigar rolling to the corner of his mouth. "You don't seem very confident."

"I *saw* it with my own two eyes. It's there. Trust me."

"Why the nerves, then?"

The jittering of the doctor's wrists and elbows intensified with the observation.

"I just want this thing caught and this job done," he said. "Fair enough?"

"Sounds like there's a lot of money at stake," Ethan said. Myles scowled. The hunter was speaking like someone contemplating renegotiation.

"Yes, money for very powerful people," he said.

"Big Pharma would certainly hate to have word of this thing get out," Ethan said.

Myles swallowed. "Yes."

"And whatever weapons manufacturer Jedlinsky has contracts with?"

"Perhaps."

"Oh, Ethan. Leave him alone," Bryce said.

"Hang on, babe. Just getting a better sense of the importance of this project," Ethan said.

"I already explained it," Myles said.

"Except I'm curious of a little detail you might've left out," Ethan said. "You were worried about the bug wandering around in this temperature. I also noticed the little hot spring in its little cave back in your mansion. Clearly, you're not worried about this thing dying in the current temperature. So, if that's the case, why do I sense a degree of unease?"

Myles shook his head. "No. I don't understand what you're—"

Ethan patted his brace. "How stupid do you think I am?"

Myles felt his throat dry up. He hoped Bryce would rein Ethan in, but she didn't, which implied she was curious of the answer as well. Myles was at a standstill. Would the truth affect whether they would continue the job? It's not like they signed a contract. They could depart at any point, and Myles would be powerless to stop them.

He saw the skid marks up ahead. "We're here." He parked the truck along the side of the road and got out. There were no signs of any vehicles approaching. At this time of day, in an area as sparsely populated as this, the odds were pretty good they could load the specimen unseen.

He crossed the road into and pointed at the trail entrance. With sunlight at his aide, he could see the glass and other debris all over the ground.

Ethan stepped beside him. He had a high-powered rifle in hand, locked and loaded.

"Don't forget you're to take it alive," Myles said.

"That's the plan. But don't think I won't blow that thing's head off if this gets out of hand. I'm not sure how much I trust your tranquilizer."

"It'll work," Myles said.

"Yeah? Wasn't it sedated during the trip?"

Myles exhaled slowly through his nostrils. "The driver probably stopped off at some point. Gave it a few extra hours to wake up." Finally, he worked up the courage to look Ethan in the eye. "If you had all of these questions and concerns, why weren't they addressed earlier?"

The answer to the question joined them, crossbow in hand.

"What are we waiting for, boys?"

Ethan slung his rifle over his shoulder and shouldered his crossbow. The arrow was loaded, the vial of drugs ready to be injected. He pointed into the woods.

"Lead the way, Doc."

Myles took the first step. He contemplated arguing that *they* should go first, considering they had the weapons. All he had was a briefcase filled with additional tranquilizers should he believe more needed to be applied after the specimen's capture. It was just another way for Ethan to mess with him. It worked. Myles felt like bait for his own hunt as he pressed into the trail.

Immediately, as though deliberately to mess with his mind, a breeze swept through. Branches wobbled. Leaves spiraled down all around him. Myles shuddered.

They came to the truck.

Ethan inspected the back doors, which had clearly been forced open. "Jesus. Your bug managed to break through this? What's to keep it from breaking out of that tin can we rode down here in?"

"It won't wake up in time. Plus, the locks on our truck are much sturdier," Myles replied.

"You boys mind keeping your voices down?" Bryce said. She was watching the trees. "Okay, Doc. You said that you saw it in these woods. Lead the way."

Myles led them down the trail, then found the scuff marks where Alex Fincher had taken his stumble. He pointed south into the woods.

"It had a web down this way," he said.

Ethan gave a hand signal to Bryce, instructing her to take the right. They pressed further in. Crossbows aimed high at the trees, while their eyes cautiously watched the world around them. A creature as stealthy as the doctor described could ambush them at any point.

Bryce whistled, getting Ethan's attention. She pointed at something further up, left of his trajectory.

There it was: a giant spider web, stretching at least twenty-feet from the ground to a couple of branches up in the trees. Sections of it were torn near the bottom, where unlucky creatures wandering by were caught and snatched by the inhabitant. There was no funnel in the trees, nor were there any cocoons secured in the web.

Ethan and Bryce slowly closed in. Fingers rested on their triggers, ready to send drug-filled arrows into anything that moved.

"I don't see it," Ethan said. He kept his eye down the sights of his weapon as he panned it along the trees.

"It's not here," Myles said. "Let's head further east. It had spun a web at the house. It's probably there."

"It better be," Ethan said.

"Oh, quit being such a pussy, darling," Bryce said. He glared at her. She shook her head at him. "This is the most alive I've felt in forever. Aside from…you know." She winked.

"More than one beast in these woods," Ethan said.

They followed the trail to the private residence, stopping briefly to gaze at the huge funnel of white that encased the house.

"Jesus," Ethan said.

Myles pointed at the trees over to the right. "Look!" The hunters followed his finger and saw the thick funnel weaved in the branches. The entrance faced away from them, making it impossible to see its occupant. Even with the funnel in sight, Ethan was cautious. He constantly watched the trees and the web-encased house as he crossed the yard. There was about thirty feet of lawn between the south porch and the web. He signaled to his wife, instructing her to keep her bow pointed at the funnel, while he watched the house.

They advanced, with Myles lagging a couple of yards behind. He stopped, seeing's Ethan's flabbergasted expression. The hunter lowered his crossbow a few inches as he took in the sight of the cocooned corpses hanging on the side of the building.

Beads of sweat trickled down the doctor's face. There were two humans, both shriveled into skeletal husks. The skin was as dry and flaky as leaves shed in the autumn. The hair, what remained on the scalps, was wiry and white. The eyes had shrunk into the sockets, and the skin hugged the skull like a tight latex glove.

"Holy hell, Doc," Ethan muttered.

Myles didn't respond. The briefcase trembled in his grip. His bowels threatened to humiliate him, forcing him to squeeze his buttocks. The realization struck, and he was suddenly aware of the danger they were in. The arachnoid was a trapper, but it was perfectly capable of springing from its hideout and paralyzing them all. These bodies were a simple reminder of the risks involved. He had seen the feeding process. The last place he ever wanted to be was wrapped in a cocoon and drained of all fluids—alive. He'd rather be condemned as a witch and burned at the stake during the Salem Witch Trials.

Ethan circled around the east side of the house, then gave a thumbs-up. No spider around the corner. If it was here, it was in that funnel. Like a military unit, the two hunters prepped for their assault. They could just see the edge of the funnel opening from where they stood.

Crossbows aimed high, Ethan tapped his wife on the shoulder. *You ready?* She nodded. He counted down with his fingers. *Three...two...one...*

They sprinted the short distance, then turned on their heels, ready to fire up into the lair. Ethan tensed, his finger pressing the trigger halfway before he released. There was nothing inside but white silk and brown residue. The funnel was empty.

Myles joined them, then dropped his jaw at the unexpected revelation. There was no specimen. The hunters immediately went to work combing the area for any trace. The creature was not resting on the house, nor did it appear to be in any of the trees. There were no other funnels in sight.

After checking the north side of the property, Ethan lowered his weapon and marched straight toward Myles.

"I don't see any bug, Doc."

Myles stammered. "It's clearly been here recently."

"Yeah? Then where is it now?" Ethan said.

"You're the tracker."

"It's your pet. You said it'd be here."

"We don't know yet that it's gone," Myles said.

"He's right," Bryce said.

"You're not his mommy," Ethan said. "You don't need to come to his rescue every single time."

"You're not his father. You don't need to get on his case at every turn," she replied. "Besides, we have a trail." She pointed at a thin white thread that ran from the web connected to the funnel.

"It's a link to a trap," Myles said.

"Beg your pardon?" Ethan said.

"It spins several webs as traps. When prey gets caught and struggles, the vibration travels along the thread and alerts the arachnoid."

"A dinner bell of sorts," Bryce said.

"Exactly."

"This thread appears to head this way." She pointed southeast.

"It might be down there," Myles said. Ethan snorted, registering the hopefulness in the doctor's voice.

"If it went this way to get dinner, it's likely we'll encounter it on its way back," he said.

"Good," Bryce said. She took the first step into the woods. "What are we waiting for?"

Ethan's leg throbbed. Only thanks to the brace was he able to keep up with his wife. Still, his mind was semi-distracted by a desire for effective painkillers. Since those weren't available, he had to focus on the positives. Catching this spider-thing would put his wife in an extremely good mood. Her good mood almost always led to good things. And he *never* grew tired of that.

Sooner we catch this bug, the sooner we can return to the hot tub.

****

As Ethan led the way, he couldn't help but notice the activity in the woods. In the twenty minutes since leaving the property, they had seen several deer and other critters wandering about. Either the natural inhabitants of the area were not aware of the new predator in their midst, or there was no longer a threat for them to be wary of. Considering the way they retreated at the first sight of the humans, it seemed extremely unlikely that a twelve-foot monstrosity could have recently wandered through the area.

Ethan's sixth sense started to tingle. Somehow, he could sense that the objective was no longer here. Still, he couldn't leave any stone unturned. They proceeded carefully, watching the world around them. The damn deer, especially ones galloping in the distance, were playing tricks on their eyes. Adding to the problem was dusk. There wasn't much sunlight left, and not even an experienced hunter such as Ethan was going to stalk a creature such as this in the dead of night, where it had all of the advantage. Spiders and insects did not depend upon sight as humans did, and Ethan was aware of this. With each foot added to their journey, the likeliness that they would have to postpone the hunt increased. Of course, this would lead to objections by Myles, which Ethan would promptly shoot down.

Then there was Bryce, who was as gung-ho as she ever was about this hunt. She would probably express a desire to continue the search, even with no moon to cover them.

Ethan's blood pressure added to his leg pain. He forced the inevitable debate from his mind and focused on the task at hand. Maybe, just maybe, the creature would be at the end of this trail. However, he couldn't deny that all the signs indicated that the creature had moved on.

They stopped when they came to a sheet of webbing strung around the trunk of a fallen tree and the surrounding bushes. For the next several minutes, the hunters inspected the area with caution, making sure the creature was not hiding in the web or the nearby trees.

Finally, Bryce picked up a large section of branch and tossed it into the web. The trap bounced and wobbled like a trampoline. The hunters crouched, ready for its creator to scurry out with a vengeance. Instead, nothing happened.

"It's not here," Bryce said. Ethan inspected the ground and found a white web strand leading from the trap to the east. He could see an abundance of sunlight up ahead.

"Looks like there's a clearing. A road, maybe," he said.

"We still have a lead. Let's go," Myles said. They proceeded in single file. Bryce stopped, but only to inspect the ground. There were grooves in the soil.

"Not deer hooves. Certainly doesn't resemble anything caused by your typical woodland critter," she said. She looked back at Myles, who inspected the grooves. They were single, curved lines in the ground, spaced several feet apart from each other.

"Yep, that's it."

"These are only a few hours old. They're going this way." Bryce stood up and led them towards the clearing. "There's a road up here."

"Dray Street," Myles said.

"Careful. Watch for any funnels in the web. Or movement in general," Ethan said.

Bryce watched the trees as she went. When her eyes finally leveled back to the road up ahead, she noticed the large mass a little to the left past the trees. She shook, took aim, and fired her crossbow. Next came the sound of a metallic thud. She lowered the weapon and squinted. "What the—?"

The group stepped onto the grassy hill between the trees and the road.

"Nice, babe. You killed an SUV," Ethan said. He circled the vehicle, pointing out the web on the hood and windshield. "Looks like your bug tried taking this for a spin."

"Don't think so," Myles said.

"Well, something tells me this wreck is not the result of texting and driving. More like—" He circled around back and saw the body lying in the grass. "Whoa!" The others hurried to see. It was a male, mid-to-upper twenties. He bled from the ankle and abdomen, where he had suffered a single puncture wound. "Looks like your pet's been making the rounds, Doc."

Myles cursed under his breath and approached the body. The victim was somewhat pale, eyes partly closed, fingers moving ever so slightly.

"Is he still alive?" Bryce said.

Myles checked for a pulse. After several seconds, he felt the slight throb in the victim's neck. His mind soared in search of options. Can't have witnesses…and he did not have the funds to pay the Feketes to dispose of people.

He cleared his throat. "No."

"Wait-wait-wait," Ethan said. "Back at your mansion, you said its venom would only paralyze its victims. You made a big speech about how we don't want to be caught by it, because then we'd be cocooned and sucked dry like those man-bags we saw there at the house."

"Well—clearly he was left behind," Myles said. "A-32 would cocoon him if he was worth saving for food. It left him behind. Thus, his blood isn't so fresh anymore."

"It wasn't long ago," Bryce said. "These marks are only a few hours old."

"And I doubt he was the same guy driving the vehicle," Ethan said.

"How do you know that?" Myles said.

"Basic science—DOC! Anyone involved in a wreck this bad is gonna be roughed up a bit. This guy looks clean—aside from being impaled. And dead. Not to mention his foot looks like it's caught in part of the web, as though he wandered up on it."

"Well, he didn't walk here. Unless—" Bryce sprinted up the hill, avoiding fragments of bumper and large glass shards. "Holy shit. You see this, Ethan?" Her husband came up to the road and looked at the large, thick strand of web.

"Looks like it set a trap," he said.

"For vehicles? Is it *that* smart?"

"Ask him." Ethan pointed his thumb back at Myles, who remained crouched by the 'dead' victim.

"It probably saw a clearing and decided to set a trap for prey wandering at night," he said. He stepped halfway up the hill, high enough to see across the road. "The web goes all the way into the woods. It might be back there."

Ethan sighed. Somehow, he didn't think so, but it would be worth a look regardless.

"Let's find out." He and Bryce followed the web toward the tree line.

Myles waited until they were past the cement before he returned to the body. He froze briefly after seeing the victim. The eyes moved slightly, as did the jaw. The tongue flickered and the lips quivered.

"He—eell---p…"

"Shhh!" Myles cupped a hand over his mouth. He opened his briefcase. "Just be quiet. I have something here that'll help you." He withdrew a vial and a syringe, then briefly stood up to make sure the hunters weren't watching. He loaded the syringe with tranquilizer.

The victim's eyes widened. Whatever that green fluid was, an entire vial of it seemed like too much. He shook, moving his arms a few inches, and groaned.

"Just relax," Myles said. He pressed the needle into his arm. The victim gasped for breath, then shook. His throat tightened and his heartbeat accelerated briefly before slowing again. Consciousness quickly faded, sparing him the effects of the overdose killing his internal organs and respiratory system.

Myles exhaled, then quickly secured the vial in his briefcase. He stood up as he heard the hunters returning.

"Any luck?" he asked.

"No. It's not here," Ethan said. He stopped in the middle of the road. "We have skid marks here."

Myles quickly ran onto the road to look. Black marks moved side to side, all over the road, going north for at least a half-mile.

"There was probably someone else. They stopped to inspect the wreck. They got out to inspect the SUV, one got caught, which alerted the arachnoid. It attacked, got him, then maybe…MAYBE…it attacked the vehicle. The other person probably drove off with the specimen on top of the car!"

"Can't imagine they'd get far with that thing on them," Bryce said.

"They would if they were flooring the pedal. The thing was probably fighting to hold on as much as it was trying to get its meal."

"So, if it's not here because of that, then it didn't abandon that guy because he was damaged goods," Bryce said, pointing back at the victim. "So, he might be alive."

Myles stuttered. "No-no-no. I already checked. He's dead." Both hunters stared at him questioningly. "Don't believe me? Check him yourself."

Ethan went ahead and did so. No pulse. But only a fool would miss the obvious needle puncture in his right arm.

He looked back at Myles, holding his gaze for several seconds. "Yeah, he's dead."

Myles fixed his shirt. Little wet spots where he sweated began to soak through, despite the temperature only being fifty-seven degrees and dropping.

"Alright then! Let's head up this way. We might yet find it before nightfall."

"We better," Ethan said. He looked at the sky. "Because we have another hour at best."

"Let's quit wasting time then," Myles said. "Right, Bryce?"

She chuckled, watching his jittery body language. "Sure you're alright, Doc?"

"Just eager to get my experiment back in the lab. Is that such a bad thing?" Myles replied.

"Don't get too worked up. You'll spring a leak," Ethan said. He started walking up the road. "Let's stick to the trees in case anyone comes by."

"Fine with me," Myles said. He spoke as though he had consumed a half-dozen sugar pills. "After you."

CHAPTER 13

Kira yanked the fishing rod back as soon as she felt the tug on her line. She cranked the reel, only to realize the lure was weightless.

"Damn it!"

"Missed again?" Marshall said.

"Yeeeeess."

"Don't you remember what I taught ya? Gotta wait just the right amount of time. Sometimes, they test the lure before they commit to running off with it."

Kira reeled her lure in, confirming that the nightcrawler was gone. "Bastard managed to take my bait too."

"That, or it fell off, considering how hard you yanked," Marshall said.

Kira stuck her tongue out at him and cracked open a beer. "I know something that needs yanking."

"I bet you do," Marshall said, chuckling. He lit a cigar and cast a line. Kira squeezed her eyes shut.

"Wait…NO! I didn't mean *that!*" She groaned. Smelling the tobacco smoke, she decided to light up a cig, then drained half of her bottle. It was her second, and at this rate, she'd be halfway down the third by her next cast. She was falling RIGHT into Laurie's trap and she knew it. *So, why am I not stopping myself?*

"So, what did you mean?" Marshall said. He pulled the cigar from his lips, as it threatened to fall into the water thanks to his uncontrollable snickering. Kira fixed her glasses. Not that there was anything wrong with them, but she needed something—anything, to allow her to delay her response.

"Fuck, I don't know. I'm half drunk. Leave me alone."

"Half drunk? You're not even passed two beers!"

"Oh, shut up."

"As you wish! I'm too busy to talk to you anyway," Marshall said. Kira finally looked back at him.

"Oh, is that right?"

"Yeah, because…fish on!"

She scowled as the pole bent toward the water. The line quivered, then zagged back and forth as the fish attempted to flee the strange force pulling it to the surface. Some things don't change. He was always showing her up when they fished together…way back. Days she had thrown away, because she was convinced she was better off alone. There was no tragedy in her past. She had nothing to grieve. No betrayals to lament over. No bitter enemies. She genuinely just liked being alone for the most part. Or so she thought.

The line started coming toward her end of the boat. She smirked, then reached for her tacklebox. Marshall's eyebrows stretched high when he saw the pliers in her hand. That smirk turned to a full grin as she pretended to reach for his line.

"Don't you even THINK about it!"

Chuckling, she withdrew. "Nah, I wouldn't. Or would I?" The fish jumped, splashing her face with water. "Blech!"

"That's what you get!" Marshall said.

Kira pulled her glasses off. This time, they REALLY needed to be cleaned. When she placed them back over her eyes, she saw Marshall raise the sixteen-inch bass out of the water.

She leaned toward it. "What was that for, you little bastard. I was about to cut you loose."

Marshall pried the hook loose, then held the fish toward her. He opened and shut its mouth with his finger, while talking in a cartoonish voice.

"Sorry, lady! But I think you're full of shit!"

Tremors of contained laughter shook Kira. "In that case, I look forward to eating your sorry ass."

"You wouldn't do that! You think I'm too cute!"

"Yeah, not so much!"

"I'm calling you out! How 'bout a big kiss!" Marshall leaned forward and extended the fish to her lips, making kissing sounds. Kira laughed and fell back against the gunwale, waving her hand about.

"Get that thing off me, you dick!"

After a few added seconds of pestering her, Marshall pulled the fish away. He gave it a quick glance. "Go find your girlfriend and make a bunch of little fish." He tossed it back into the water.

Kira straightened herself in her seat. "Surprised you didn't keep it."

"Eh, don't feel like keeping it in a live-basket. And with all the work we have yet to do, I can't be sure if I'll get around to cleaning it for the next few days. If we pull this off by Wednesday, maybe we'll come out again and catch enough for a fish fry."

"We?"

Marshall shrugged. "Or just me. Probably wouldn't make a difference either way, considering you can't seem to catch shit." He leaned back to dodge a slap on the shoulder.

Kira shook her head. "What am I going to do with you?" Then, in the blink of an eye, the warm and blissful feeling she experienced began to evaporate. Sure, their banter was joyous, but the likeliness of it leading to a second chance between them was slim. Marshall was attached, and contrary to what Laurie told her to do, she wasn't the type to steal someone who was already attached, no matter how bitter she felt about it. To top it off, Marshall wasn't the cheating type.

Unfortunately. She wasn't either, but at this stage, a move by him would set her over the edge. But that wouldn't happen. They were just friends, fishing together, resting in preparation for another hard day's work. That smile, which came so naturally, was now a struggle to maintain.

It was at this point when she realized she was no longer at war with herself. For as long as she remembered, she suppressed the desire to recoup her relationship with him, convincing herself of the lie that they had opposite goals and lifestyles. Perhaps it was partially true at the time—and only for the time. Marshall was raking in a lot of money now and had plenty of employees to conduct the labor should he not be available. Had they stayed together, he'd be able to go on a large percentage of their getaways. Instead, she tossed that all away, because of some stupid desire to see the country and get away from the rest of society.

His phone buzzed. His face became animated when he saw the contact name on the screen, and he quickly answered it.

"Hey! Awe, calling to wish me goodnight? It's only eight! You know me… Oh, yeah, we're done for the day… Yeah, it's going very well…"

Kira reached for her cigarettes. This could not be happening. A phone call from Amanda? Really?! Right after she finally acknowledged the truth, which she had avoided forever. It was like she had taken a punch to the gut. And to make it worse, Marshall was bouncing in his seat like a puppy, clearly ecstatic to take the call. Either it was a new relationship and he was lost in that bliss, or they had been together for a while and it was working out fabulously. Either way, it didn't look good for Kira.

Time for that third beer.

"Fucking bitch," she mumbled under breath. She removed the cap. *Bottoms up.*

"Munn Ice Arena? Yeah, sure... Probably not this weekend, because I'll just be coming back. Next Saturday then?... Sounds great..."

Kira faced away from him. *That bitch!* Skating was probably the ONE date, other than the occasional movie and going out to eat, where she didn't mind being around a bunch of other people. And at Munn Ice Arena?! The place Marshall used to take her? Unbelievable!

That beer was quickly half-drained.

Marshall continued bantering with Amanda. "Oh, really? Twin Lake? A discount, huh? Three-twenty-five for the whole week? Sounds nice, but I've already taken a week off. I really shouldn't—... November, huh?... Hmmm, that might be just long enough for me not to seem too irresponsible... Where's that at?... Oh, Lake Station?! I know where that is... Yeah, the leaves should be gorgeous by the lake."

Kira almost dropped her beer. *Yeah, you know where that is...because I wanted to take us there! Leaves by the lake?! That was MY rationale.*

"Yeah... uh-huh... Gosh, are you *that* bored without me? You're coming up with date after date..."

Kira drew on her cigarette. "Yeah, for real. Get a life."

Marshall chuckled. "Alright-alright-alright! Tone it down, I'm not alone. Whew!" Though he couldn't see it, the cigarette carton was crunching in Kira's fist. God only knew what Amanda was putting in his ear. He nodded along and listened for a few moments. "Alright, I'll call you back in the morning... Yes, I'll take you out when we get back. *Bob Evans,* right?... Oh, sure! *Amigo Hideaway.* Gosh, I've really gotten you hooked on that place."

This time, Kira did drop her beer. *Amigo Hideaway*, the Mexican-themed restaurant where they went out constantly. What the hell was going on here? Was he deliberately naming all of their previous dates out loud to get back at her? Was he using their relationship as a playbook for this new hoe? Every damn thing he named, the Munn Ice Arena, the cabin at Twin Lake— specifically in November, *Amigo Hideaway.* One after the other, all the things that were unique to them, they were planning. With her sitting right next to him, no less!

Kira spun around. She'd had enough. *If he resents me, fine! But this bullshit has gone on long enough and—okay, what's with that shit-eating grin on his face?*

He was looking at her, while nodding along with whatever Amanda was saying on the phone. What followed were a series of "Yeahs" "Uh-huhs" and "Yeps", with Marshall seeming giddier with each one. But it wasn't the giddiness of someone lovestruck, rather, it was that of someone who had a scheme.

Kira thought of the conversation she had just overheard. He mentioned all of their dates out loud conveniently. Had Amanda said, 'Let's go to Amigo Hideaway" wouldn't he had just said, "Sure. Gosh, I've really gotten you hooked on that place."? Then there was the oddity that EVERY DATE mentioned was specific stuff they used to do together.

Then there was that smug grin on his face as he watched her.

He nodded. "Uh-huh. Yeah, I think so."

'Think so' what?! Some other date? Think you'll get back on Saturday...alive? Kira looked to the west at the shore. She could see the firepit, and three people sitting around it. Three...not four. Where the hell was Laurie?

Then it hit.

Kira's jaw dropped. She looked back at Marshall, who looked as though he was about to explode with laughter. She lunged for him.

"Give me that fucking phone!"

Marshall leaned back. "Why? Wouldn't it be awkward for my date to speak with my ex?"

"I'll make it awkward for you!"

Finally, Marshall's laughter broke free as Kira practically threw herself over him. They wrestled for the device for a few seconds before she freed it from his grip. Sure, the contact name read *Amanda*, but she knew that was bullshit.

"LAURIE?!"

"Laurie... I don't know any Laurie. I'm Amanda!"

"Sure, and I'm *Shania Twain!*" The laughter on the other end of the line exposed what tiny bit remained of Laurie's cover. Kira slapped herself on the forehead, absorbing the titanic prank that was just played on her. "Oh my God! I'm gonna KILL YOU!"

She was grateful nobody else was on the lake, as her voice echoed far and wide. She held the phone out so Marshall could have the pleasure of hearing the laughter through the receiver.

He couldn't even sit up straight at this point, as he was still cackling up a storm of his own.

Kira shook her head. Several times, she tried to speak, but couldn't come up with any words. She was truly, exceptionally, dumbfounded.

Finally, Marshall took the phone. "I think we've been made."

"Looks like it. Alright, cowboy. I'll leave you to the rest." The screen lit up as she hung up.

Kira crossed her arms. "Interesting name change!"

"Hey, you believed it," Marshall said.

Kira bit her lip, shook her head, then punched him in the shoulder. Finally, she laughed. "You son of a bitch!" She threw herself on him, pretending to strangle him. Marshall fell back against the bow, wrapping his arms around his 'attacker' as she maintained her hold on him. Finally, their lips met, tongues entwined, and their hands caressed each other's bodies, rocking the boat side to side with their vigorous activity.

"I hate you!" She managed to say between kisses.

"Yeah? Keep punishing me then."

"Gladly." She wrapped her arms around his head and pressed her mouth to his.

CHAPTER 14

Sue cocooned herself in her fleece blanket. The late evening chill was really starting to have some bite. She regretted leaving her beanie back at home, though she did remember the fleece socks and several hoodies. The bluish white light reflected against her pale face as she scrolled through her *Facebook* home page, liking and commenting on the various posts she saw. In her peripheral vision, she saw the spark of a flame, followed by Tyler explaining "Aw, come on!" when the breeze blew out the match. After what felt like the fiftieth try, a flame finally took hold in the fireplace.

Sue looked up from her phone. "Oh, look at that! You actually managed to get the flame going. For a second, I thought I was gonna have to rub two sticks together."

Tyler smiled. "And your dad wonders why I haven't popped the question yet."

"What makes him think I'd even say 'yes'?"

Tyler sank into the chair beside her and opened the cooler with his foot. "I don't know. My rugged handsomeness? The zeroes in my bank account?"

"What zeroes? Aside from the singular one I usually see whenever I check in?"

Chris took a seat across the firepit, chuckling as he cracked open a beer. "I was afraid she was gonna say something about the handsomeness."

"Oh, we're just getting started," Sue said. She leaned toward the fire, which was gradually getting larger. As she held her hands to it, she glanced over to Chris, who was putting something in his pocket. "Wait a sec…was that a lighter?"

Chris cleared his throat. "No."

"Let me see that!"

Chris grinned. "I don't know what you're talking about."

"I appreciate you covering for Tyler, but frankly, you suck at it," Sue said. "Come on, let's see it."

Chris looked at Tyler and shrugged. "Sorry buddy." He held the lighter out.

"Look at that!" Sue said, turning to face her boyfriend. "You've been wasting matches since the Stone Age and it turns out you weren't the one to even get the fire going."

"Like you were a big help," he retorted. "You look like you've been dropped off in Antarctica. I don't even think it's that bad out."

"You and Marshall, I swear you guys are weird. Chris, back me up here. Don't you consider this freezing cold?"

Chris shook his head. "Nah."

Sue tightened her blanket then hung her head down. "I give up."

"You and Laurie. I swear," Tyler said. He looked over at the cottage. "Speaking of which, is she ever gonna come out of there?"

"She said she had to make a call," Sue said. "Probably figured it was a lot warmer in there."

"Well, for what it's worth, back in Cooper State Prison, I spent at least an hour a day outside. Didn't matter if it was zero degrees out with high wind. So, you could argue I acclimated to it."

"There, see? That makes sense. Tyler, give me a beer," Sue said.

"I could give you more than that," he said.

"Not a chance," she replied, looking away.

"What? NO! I mean…that too…but I was referring to these!" Tyler reached into the cooler and pulled out bottles of rum, vodka, followed by cases of soda. "There's also strawberry margaritas for anyone here that needs the fruity taste."

"Great. You couldn't remember water—a basic necessity, but God forbid we don't have booze," Sue said.

"How do you think our relationship has managed to last this long?" Tyler replied.

"Because I'm so pretty," she replied.

Tyler considered his options for replying. Sarcasm, or go with the flow. The wink in his girlfriend's eye pushed him toward the latter.

"Well, OBVIOUSLY!" He leaned in toward her with a kiss, immediately overdoing it by working his way down her neck, sparking laughter from her.

"Stop it," she said.

"I just can't get anything right according to you. Guess I'll have to try harder." He practically rolled off of his chair onto hers, teetering it to the side. Chris sipped his beer for the next several seconds, realizing the make-out was going to continue longer than initially expected.

"You know, I thought part of the idea of starting this fire was to get some dinner going?"

"Hold your horses." Tyler's voice was muffled by Sue's mouth against his.

Chris stood up. "Gotta take a piss anyway." Tyler and Sue didn't even seem to notice as he headed over to the cottage. There was the usual hesitation before going through the door. He opened it, made sure Laurie wasn't there to freak out, then proceeded to the bathroom. After relieving himself, he wandered to the guest bedroom area. There was a granola bar in his bag which would serve to tide him over until the next Ice Age, which was when dinner would likely be served at this rate.

He noticed the window was shut. Immediately, he rolled his eyes. There was only ONE person sleeping in this cottage who was hyper-sensitive about the autumn chill. He cracked it open a few inches, as the chill usually helped him sleep, as long as he could bundle up in his blankets.

He stepped away, only to stop and face the window again. There it was, the same rustling sound he heard before. He opened the window the rest of the way and stuck his head out. Something moved up around the tree. It was so quick, he couldn't identify it.

"What the hell is moving around out there?" he said to himself. He stepped out through the back door and headed up to the tree line. He heard it again. Unfortunately, the back porch light could not reach the woods, and he didn't have a flashlight other than the one on his iPhone to see ahead. He blasted it into the trees, the white glow reflecting off a few trees.

Something shifted to the east. He panned the light to the left, catching only a brief glimpse of something falling off the tree. He walked along the tree line. Again, he saw something. It was up on the tree, then suddenly, it fell off.

"What the hell am I looking at?" The bushes rustled. When Chris froze, he was at the front of the cottage. He held his phone high to get the light over the bushes.

Two green reflections stared back at him. They were like tiny dots in the dark of the woods, less than two inches apart from each other. Then he heard the growl.

A dozen curses fled his tongue as he realized he was looking at a fully grown cougar. It reared its head up, exposing its frown fur to the light, then bared its fangs.

Chris backtracked several steps, spun on his heel, and went to sprint… only to run straight into Laurie who was standing up from the front porch chairs. She screamed, the collision knocking her several feet back. As soon as she hit the ground, she pounded her fists.

"You fucking prick!"

Sue broke away from Tyler. "Oh, Jesus, babe!" She pointed to the front corner of the cottage. Tyler turned just in time to see Laurie hit the ground. Judging by the way she fell, she had clearly taken a hard blow which knocked her a yard-and-a-half backward. Already, she was springing to her feet, ready to take a swing at a flabbergasted-looking Chris.

"Oh, shit! Shit's going down!" he said. They sprang from the chair and raced toward the incident. By now, Laurie was springing to her feet and throwing a fist at Chris.

He dodged the first two swings, holding his hands out to grab her. "Hey-hey! Stop—" The third one clocked his chin, knocking him to the right. "Goddamnit! Stop, Laurie!" Another blow struck him in the ribs. This time, his temper snapped. He reached out and grabbed her arm, eyes blaring. "Bitch! Fucking stop!"

"Hey-hey-hey-hey!" Tyler shouted. He threw himself in-between them.

"You saw it!" Laurie said. Chris' grip loosened and she yanked her arm away, then pointed a finger in his face. "This guy's fucking insane. INSANE!"

"Would you all shut the fuck up?!" Chris said. He glanced back over his shoulder at the woods.

"Laurie, you alright?" Sue said.

"Chris, man? What's wrong with you?" Tyler said. "I know you two can't stand each other, but if I knew it'd get THIS out of hand—"

"What? No! There's something…something back there!"

****

The sounds of distant shouting caused Marshall and Kira to perk up. All four of their friends were gathered by the front porch, and their tones and body language radiated of drama.

"What the hell's going on over there?" Kira said.

"I have no idea, but it's clearly not anything good." Kira sat at the bow while Marshall started the motor. He pushed it to third gear, speeding them toward the dock. As they got closer, the sounds of argument became clearer. It looked like Tyler and Sue were forcing themselves between Laurie and Chris.

Kira pressed her palm to her forehead. "Oh, God!"

"Something tells me those two are at it again," Marshall said.

"Goddamnit," Kira muttered. "Alright, let's figure out what's going on."

"At this rate, one of those two is gonna have to leave," Marshall said.

"Yeah, I'm realizing that now," Kira said. "We're not even through the first night yet, and they're at each other's throats."

Marshall brought the boat along the dock and secured it. Immediately, he and Kira climbed out and ran up to the group. Chris and Laurie were shouting at each other, their words blurred together, while Sue and Tyler were yelling for them to knock it off.

Marshall raised his hands. "WHOA!" All eyes turned toward him. The commotion settled, for the most part, at least. Chris turned, keeping an eye on the woods as he paced. Laurie's hair was practically as frizzled as a wild mustang that needed a comb and a brush. There was dirt all over the back of her sweater, and a little bit on her jeans. Clearly, she had fallen pretty hard.

"Everybody relax!" Kira said. She then pointed at Laurie and Chris. "You guys, separate right now. Chris, you go that way toward the trees…"

"No fucking way!" he said.

"Chris! I own this place. I swear, I'm about to kick you out."

Chris waved his hands, "No, that's not what I mean—"

"*About to*? We watched him throw her to the ground," Sue interrupted.

"What?! NO!"

"We saw it, dude," Tyler said.

"God-fucking-damn it! I didn't throw her. I never ATTACKED her!" Chris pointed at the woods. "There's a big-ass CAT in there. A cougar, or mountain lion, whichever. I saw it rear up, I turned and ran, and didn't know she was standing right there."

Laurie gazed into the woods. "I don't see anything."

"Probably ran off," Marshall said. "They don't typically care to attack people. They'll snarl, but they won't make a move, typically."

"Wait? You're buying into this story?" Laurie said.

Marshall looked at Kira. "You wanna talk to her?" She nodded then put a hand on Laurie's shoulder.

"Come on. Let's go this way." They walked toward Marshall's horse trailer.

Marshall let a few seconds pass by in silence while the others blew off steam. "Cougar? Where was it?"

Chris looked over at him, making sure he wasn't being sarcastic. "Maybe a couple dozen feet into the woods, that way." He pointed toward a series of bushes. Marshall stepped to the tree line.

"Well, it's LONG gone now," he said.

"Listen, man. I swear, that's what happened."

"I believe you," Marshall said. Sue and Tyler shook their heads. Chris noticed this, then shuddered in frustration.

"Sorry man," Tyler said. "I can't deny we saw what we saw." Chris looked around.

"What are you doing?" Sue asked.

"Looking for my phone. You'll see that the flashlight's on and…There it is!" His excitement ended instantaneously. The phone had hit the concrete patio and broke the flashlight lens. "Fuck."

"Hey, man, we're not trying to throw you under the bus…"

Chris turned around, ready to yell back, but had a smidge of self-control holding him back.

Marshall stepped between them. "Please! Let's not start another fight." Tyler and Sue stepped back. Marshall rubbed his stomach. "Listen, guys, despite what just happened, I'm freaking starving. How's the food situation?"

"Got hot dogs and smoked sausage in the cooler," Tyler said.

"Amen. Let's break it out," Marshal said. Tyler and Sue nodded, then returned to the fireplace. The latter looked back at him.

"There's booze too."

"Good. I think we all need it," Marshall said. He took a breath, then looked at Chris, who sank into the patio chair. "You alright?"

"She got me pretty good," Chris said, rubbing his jaw.

"Looks like you got her pretty good too," Marshall replied. Chris tensed.

"I didn't assault her. I went into my room in the cottage. Someone, probably Laurie had been in there to shut the window. So I opened it…"

"Wait a sec: you specifically think *Laurie* was in your room?"

"Yeah. Considering she was the one complaining about the cold air." Chris realized how he sounded. "No, I did not have a beef with her for that! I was just stating that I think she closed my window. The point I was getting at was that I opened it, then heard something in the woods. I went to check to see what it was. Moved around this way where I showed you. Saw the cougar. I freaked out, turned and ran—smack dab into Laurie. I didn't even know she was there, until…" He mimicked a collision with his hands.

Marshall nodded. "I see." He let out a sharp exhale as he thought of how to articulate his next suggestion. "Listen, about that room Laurie was offering you—"

"Oh yeah, no arguments there," Chris said. "Probably best we not be under the same roof. Wouldn't be so bad if the upstairs one was available, but, well you know how it is." Chris scratched his chin. "I guess it's back to the trailer. Though those two aren't gonna be happy to see me either."

"Tell you what," Marshall said, "I don't know if you have a spare mattress or something, but you can have my room in the horse trailer. Not the Five Seasons, but—"

"Oh, man, I appreciate it, dude," Chris said. "And no, it's no problem. Trust me, I've slept on worse."

"I bet. Alright then, let me arrange some stuff and move some things out of there," Marshall said. Chris realized what he was talking about. Once again, the frustration was threatening to billow.

"I'm not gonna touch your shotgun, man."

"I believe you," Marshall said, "but I still don't know you. Not well, at least. Even if I did, it wouldn't matter. That thing stays with me. Listen, man, I hate to use the word 'relax' because it tends to have the opposite effect in these situations, but *try* to relax. Let's get through the night, and maybe tomorrow will be better."

Chris sighed. "Yeah. Sounds good man." He gazed into the woods. "You ARE sure about that cougar, right? You think it ran off?"

Marshall nodded. "Yeah. If nothing else, the commotion definitely scared it off. Still, doesn't hurt to be careful."

CHAPTER 15

The hundred-and-eighty pound cat leapt from the tree it was perched on. It had escaped one potential threat, only to stumble on another. It was not the first time it had encountered humans. On two occasions, it was driven off by a loud crack of sound. The second of which brought pain, as though that sound had somehow grazed its upper shoulder, drawing blood. The injury had long since healed, but the sense of caution remained. Humans were dangerous and not worth hunting.

Yet, there was something worse in these woods. The cougar had seen the predator lurking about in the daylight. It was large, with legs similar to the daddy long legs scurrying about in the grass. The cougar's natural instincts warned it to keep a distance. It had witnessed the creature chase a fox into its den, which indicated it was capable of quick bursts of speed, of which the cougar would not be able to escape. Its best bet was to hide, especially after the predator began lurking into its usual territory.

Night had fallen. The cougar's trained eyes were extremely adept to hunting at night, which was when it preferred to hunt. It could see every little critter scurrying in the grass, their size providing natural invulnerability to the new inhabitant. There was no significant movement to be seen in the nearby woods. All of the deer had vacated the area, as had the coyotes and wolves that typically lurked around. There was an unusual silence, aside from those made by the birds flocking overhead. It was likely gone.

The cougar chose to rely on this possibility, as it did not want to remain close to the humans. Some sort of conflict was starting to take place near their den. Either they were fighting amongst themselves, or simply getting riled up by its presence. Either way, the cat was not interested in finding out which.

It hit the ground, looked about, then proceeded to venture southwest, carefully watching for any sign of the strange predator. Considering it had been moving about during the day, there was the likeliness that it was not a nighttime hunter like itself. As it moved, it stuck close to the trees. The cougar, a creature that preferred to ambush prey, was not an adept runner. A long chase would exhaust it quickly, thus its best chance of survival would be to climb out of the creature's reach, should it ever appear. Considering it had not witnessed the thing climb a tree, it assumed it was incapable of doing so.

The cat stopped. It saw movement up ahead. It crouched, studying the phenomenon behind the security of a bush. It was a hundred yards away. These were not the movements of a wandering predator, or even a nocturnal creature on the hunt. In fact, it was much smaller than itself. These were struggling movements, as though whatever caused them was locked in combat. Yet, the cat could only see one moving body.

Its determination to flee was overtaken by the overwhelming need to feed. It had not eaten for three days and its body was demanding sustenance. The animal in the distance flopped like a fish out of water, unable to free itself from some unseen force. With its interest piqued, the cat took several steps closer, keeping crouched to avoid being seen.

It was a racoon. It was trying to run, but could only make a few steps before being flung backward. Its hind right leg was caught in some sort of white mesh strung between the trees. The cat studied the strange substance from a distance. Likely something discarded by the humans. Throughout the cougar's life, it had seen all sorts of debris, including soda cans, plastic bags, boots, articles of clothing, and fishing gear abandoned in the woods. During one of the cougar's first hunts, it had stumbled upon an abandoned fishing net and had gotten its claw caught in it. The net was already hung up on a bush, where its owner had likely tossed it, causing the branches to get intertwined with the mesh. Thus, when the cougar got caught, it was essentially stuck to the bush. It took an hour to free itself from the bizarre contraption. While this white weaving was different in appearance, the racoon appeared to be caught in a similar manner. Except this mesh was far larger than the small net the cougar had encountered. However, it still looked like something humans would leave behind. And this time, it would play to the cat's benefit, as it resulted in easy prey.

The cougar emerged from hiding. The racoon stopped its struggle, only to double its efforts in the next moment after spotting the approaching cat. It reached back and nipped at the sticky substance on its leg, only for one of its whiskers to get stuck. The racoon yanked its head back, squealing as the whisker tore free.

The tiny speck of blood elevated the cat's interest. It would kill this critter, then carry it off to somewhere safe. It had the best of both worlds—it had food, and would be well hidden from the strange being that was lurking behind those trees somewhere.

The raccoon snarled, baring needle-like teeth. The efforts went unnoticed. The cat was just a couple of yards away. When the raccoon recognized the pouncing position, it went haywire, snarling and nipping at the air, while rolling back and forth, still desperate to free itself from this snare.

The cougar pounced. Its front claw slammed the raccoon's head to the earth, pinning it there while it sank its teeth into its throat. The raccoon juddered, its legs tensing, while its jaw snapped at the grass. Its body shuddered as life fled, then went limp. The cat lifted its head, licking the blood on its teeth. This was one of the easiest kills it had ever experienced. Quick; efficient; complete. Now to scoop it up and carry it somewhere safer to feed.

There was only one problem.

The cat lifted its paw, only to realize the white substance stretched with the movement. Just like the net, the cat was snagged. It tugged repeatedly, shaking the entire net, and the white wire that connected it to several other trees in the woods.

For several minutes the cat fought against the trap. Unlike the fishing net, which had gotten strung around its paw and nails, this strange material seemed to stick directly to its fur. Only when the cougar twisted and turned did the web start to wrap around its foot. It tried to claw at it with its other front paw, only for that one to get stuck as well. Snarling and hissing, the cat frantically fought to free itself. Its motions became increasingly erratic. Interest in its meal vanished as panic took over. No matter how it pulled, the stuff held on. The cougar wrestled with the net, oblivious to the immense shape that approached from the south. Only when it heard the rustling of leaves did the cougar realize its dilemma had taken a turn for the worst.

The arachnoid was already on approach, as it had detected the faint vibrations of struggling prey. While on route to inspect the trap it had set, the vibrations grew more rapid and intense.

Its stinger dripped venom as it discovered the cougar struggling in the bloodstained web it had strung. It was snarling intensely, a sound that had no meaning to the much larger creature. There was no sense of fear, nor was there a sense of risk when it approached. The arachnoid moved in like a machine, extending its pincers towards its victim.

The cougar bit at the air and tried to slash its claws, only for both of its paws to lift eighteen inches from the web. It tried backing away, only achieving a similar minute distance. It tugged and tugged, then reeled backwards to avoid the claws, which was only successful in getting its entire right side stuck to the web.

Its snarl turned into a squeal as razor-edge pincers closed over its shoulder and hind legs. The arachnoid plunged its stinger through the hip bone, inducing paralysis. The predator waited until the prey was motionless. It then drew its pincers to its pedipalps. From a pore in-between them came a tongue-like organ, which oozed a watery fluid over the appendages. Freshly coated in this substance, the claws were lowered to the cat. Spreading the fluid over the web, it came loose, allowing the arachnoid to pull the victim free without ravaging its flesh too badly.

Next came the cocooning process. With its hind legs, the creature weaved several thick strands of web over the cougar. Each second brought four-to-six strands. The beast weaved, its legs moving in a circular pattern, until the prey was fully encased. Only a small opening in the cocoon remained; a pore for it to draw blood from. That time would come soon enough. For now, the catch would be stored near the main web, as the arachnid had recently fed on the victim it caught by the road.

The hairs on its legs detected vibration. It placed the cocoon on the ground, then walked to the north. It came near the large clearing again. There was an orange light in the middle of it. Those biped creatures were moving about, still oblivious to its presence.

Again, it felt a temptation to attack. Like a heavenly force coming to their rescue, a breeze swept by, bringing with it an icy chill. The arachnoid tensed. The temperature had dropped fifteen degrees since sunset, resulting in lethargy. It took the creature twice as long to move from its funnel to the trap than it did in the daytime. In such a state, it would not be able to chase these other creatures down. Yet, it didn't want to abandon the prospect of losing the blood source.

The humans were moving about regularly—thus, it was likely that one of them would wander into the woods.

The arachnoid waited. It watched.

CHAPTER 16

"Here. Why don't you have one of these?"

Laurie leaned against the side of Marshall's horse trailer. They were on the left side, which faced away from the yard toward the north side of the woods. She stared at the trees, then at the Budweiser in Kira's hand. Begrudgingly, she took it. Looking at Kira's empty hands, she smirked.

"You're not having one?"

"I've already had three. Thanks to *you*," she replied.

Laurie started to laugh. "Oh, man. We had such fun planning that. That was why I took a seat on the porch afterwards. I wanted to see if I could see your boat rocking back and forth, if you know what I mean."

"You're nuts, you know that?" Kira said. "Plus, it's too cold to do... *that*. Even for me."

"That hickey on your neck suggests otherwise," Laurie said. Kira felt her neck, then rolled her eyes.

"Well, I guess we'll never know, considering we had to rush back here to make sure nobody was getting killed." She watched Laurie's smile vanish. "So, what happened?"

Laurie took a slug of her beer, then looked back at her. "You the camp counselor or something?"

"I'm just trying to get to the bottom of this," Kira said. "Listen, I'll admit, maybe it was a bad call to let Chris stay here. I'm realizing that now. I didn't want to send Sue and Tyler all the way back." Laurie glared at her. Kira could read the expression in her eyes. "Yes, I know, it's Tyler's own fault. And Sue's too. They brought it on themselves for bringing him here without telling me."

"Damn right they did."

"So, what exactly happened? Did he attack you? You guys get into another argument?"

Laurie squeezed the neck of the beer bottle, then took another drink. She needed several seconds to overcome the temptation to lie. All she had to do was say 'Chris came after me and knocked me to the ground.' It'd be the easiest thing to do; everyone in the group clearly was on her side, including Tyler and Sue. However, despite how badly she wanted to, she couldn't bring herself to do it. She hated his guts, no doubt, but that stupid conscience of hers wouldn't allow such a lie to be told. They'd certainly turn him in to the Sheriff's station for sure.

Laurie moaned. "It was just something that got out of hand. I saw him wandering by the trees. His back was to me, so he didn't know I was there. Still, I didn't feel like staring at him, so I got up to walk to the campfire. That's when he ran into me."

"So, it was an accident?" Kira said.

Once again, Laurie fought back the temptation to lie. "Yes. I got knocked over, by HIM of all people. I lost my shit, went after him, and you know the rest."

"I see," Kira said. "I appreciate you telling me the truth."

"You'd know if I was lying anyway," Laurie said.

"Maybe." Kira smiled. "Listen, clearly it's not working out having you two around each other. So, I'll let you be in charge. You want me to tell Sue and Tyler to drive him back tomorrow? Just say the word and I'll talk with them."

Laurie thought for a moment. "I'd hate to make them do that."

"Their own fault."

"Fair point. Still, they came up to help. Their intentions are good…"

"I'm paying them each five-hundred bucks," Kira added.

"That's true. They're not as good of friends as I am…who works for free…and got your boy toy back."

Kira rolled her eyes, then grinned. "You haven't worked *at all* so far!"

"Eh. There's that." She sighed. "Let's see how it goes tomorrow. Maybe I can control my attitude a little better."

"You sure? I'm a little worried. I had faith in the beginning, but now it feels like the situation's turning into a ticking time bomb," Kira said. "Who's to say *he's* not gonna be confrontational, considering everything that just happened?"

Laurie snorted. "The way you talk, it almost sounds like you're thinking about that bank robbery thing. I thought you were convinced he didn't kill that guard?"

"Well, I am, but…"

"But there's that tiny part of you that wonders, right?"

"Eh…" Kira shrugged. "Clearly YOU don't truly believe so, or else you'd never have said yes to him coming here in the first place. Nor would Sue and Tyler, if they thought he was a murderer. And no, I don't believe it. He just made a lot of bad decisions mixed with a little bad luck. Don't forget, he turned himself in."

"I know," Laurie said.

"So, what's the verdict? Because I'm hungry and it's making me pissy."

Laurie cracked a smile. "The real reason you're pissy is because your little grope-fest out there got interrupted." Kira rolled her eyes. Laurie pointed. "Ah-ha, you're not fooling anyone." They heard movement on the other side of the trailer. The two women stepped around the back and found Marshall unloading stuff out of the dressing room. "Speak of the devil."

"You all good there, Laurie?" He watched Kira's facial expression. "Or do you go by Amanda?"

"I actually like that name!" Laurie said. She watched him as he hauled a few items out of the trailer. "Moving in?"

"In a sense," Marshall said. He locked the shotgun case in his truck, then brushed his hands. "Making space, rather. Chris and I arranged for him to sleep in here instead of the cottage. Just helping to maintain the peace."

"What about Tyler's trailer?" Laurie said.

Marshall glanced over at the couple. They were snuggling by the fire, exchanging kisses on the lips and neck. In their hands were margarita glasses, which seemed to have successfully dulled the jitters caused by the recent tension.

"Probably best to let them have their privacy."

"Where do *you* plan on sleeping?" Laurie said, smirking. Kira punched her shoulder.

"Don't know what I'll do with you," she said.

Laurie giggled. "Might as well put your stuff upstairs, sailor. In the meantime, I'll have to sleep with my headphones on."

"Before *anything* happens, I need to freaking eat," Kira said. She looked over at Sue and Tyler. "How the hell do they go from nearly killing each other to having glued faces?"

"Don't know, but looking at it makes me want to turn green," Laurie said. "HEY! YOU GUYS!" Tyler and Sue broke apart and turned toward her. "Where's the food?!"

"Do I look like a chef? Grab a dog and a stick and roast it yourself!" Tyler replied. He leaned over and held up a few metal prongs.

"They drove all the way over here with *those*? Surprised Sue hasn't impaled Tyler yet," Marshall said.

"Give it time. She'll be her usual self by morning," Kira said. They shared a laugh as they took seats by the fire.

"Don't forget," Marshall said to the group, "work starts at six tomorrow."

The group replied with a unanimous "Ugh!"

"No way in hell!" Sue said.

"I'll be too drunk," Tyler replied.

"Likewise," Laurie said.

"Sooner we get started, the sooner we'll be done," Marshall said.

"Yeah—I'm not starting before sunrise," Sue said.

"Kira, it's all on you girl! Do what you have to do to get him to sleep in," Laurie said. The group laughed.

Tyler stopped suddenly then stared across the firepit. Only now did it register that Kira was sitting on Marshall's lap.

"Wait a sec? Are you guys…?"

Laurie shook with barely containable laughter. "Just wait till you hear this story."

CHAPTER 17

The engine was still warm when they found the car. Ethan Fekete lifted his hand from the hood. Bryce shone a light over the open driver's side door, while Myles was studying the grooves on the trunk and top of the vehicle.

"We were right. It went after this vehicle. The driver floored the gas pedal, took it a mile up the road, then crashed here."

"She crashed here, but it doesn't look like this door was ripped open," Ethan said. "Handle and latch works just fine, and there's no grooves on the door. Looks to me like she bolted."

"Something as big as your pet would leave obvious marks if it went on a chase," Bryce said. She shone her flashlight over the grass. "I don't see any signs of such an occurrence."

"Wait! Just wait a second," Myles said. He walked up to Bryce. "I thought you wanted a unique hunt."

"I do, but it's clear you can't tell us where your bug is," she replied. "Not to mention, it's killed at least three people, and maybe a fourth. Assuming she wasn't picked up by somebody."

"I doubt it," Ethan said. "She'd go straight to the cops. They might not believe a story about a big spider, but they would be interested in these crashes, which in turn would lead to an investigation."

"Yeah! See?" Myles said.

"Unless she was picked up RECENTLY," Ethan added.

Myles shrank. His hands were still jittery from 'examining' the victim on the roadside. This hunt was not going at all as planned. He was certain they'd be back at the lab by now, and that the hunters would be on a plane heading back home. And the clock was ticking.

Bryce searched along the roadside. "Got something over here." The two men quickly accompanied her. Centered in her flashlight beam were several marks in the ground, reminiscent of the arachnoid tracks.

Myles smiled. "It WAS here. Must've fallen off a little ways back before the person crashed. They came over here, probably disoriented, and A-32 intercepted."

Ethan and Bryce couldn't help but glance at each other. The idiot was 'happy' that his pet stung and cocooned a human being, and that they were cocooned somewhere in these woods. Maybe still alive, even.

Bryce walked further north several yards past the crash site. "There's tracks here. It hangs a right." She followed them up to the tree line. "It went this way."

"*Away* from its nest?" Ethan said.

"It doesn't have a sense of the geography," Myles explained. "As far as it knows, its lair might as well be a hundred miles away. So, it went this way to search for a place to make a new one." He took a step into the woods. "Come on! Let's go!"

Ethan grabbed him by the back of his shirt collar and yanked him back. "You insane?"

"I want you to do the job I hired you for," Myles hissed.

"Yeah, hunting an oversized bug in the dead of night, without a precise location to its whereabouts? Not smart."

"I thought you were the best in the business," Myles said. "You afraid of a little nightfall?"

"When it benefits the thing I'm hunting? Yeah," Ethan said. "We're talking about something that can climb trees, has patience that no other living creature possesses, and can possibly blend into its environment, especially at night. No, going after it at this point means we may as well offer ourselves up to it on a platter."

Myles whipped to the left to look at Bryce. Clearly, she would be the voice of reason. After all, her very purpose for coming here was for an exciting hunt. He could see in her eyes that she was conflicted. That triggered a sense of hope, which evaporated when she eventually shook her head.

"He's right," she said. "We'll wait till dawn."

"You've GOT to be kidding me," Myles said. "We're SO CLOSE! We could probably find it within the next half hour!"

"Or we could stumble on one of its traps," Ethan said. "Wandering in the woods at night, the web would blend right in. And judging by what we've seen, we get caught in its traps, then it's game over."

"Agreed," Bryce said.

"Unbelievable," Myles said. He shrieked as Bryce grabbed him by the shirt and yanked him forward, her grip tightening the fabric around his throat.

"Listen, weasel, I'm a daredevil, but I'm not stupid. It's not a simple matter of us stalking it and it stalking us at the same time. It's likely got several traps laid out by now. I'm eager to shoot it, but I'm willing to recognize when I'm outmatched. Right now, until we have the benefit of sunlight, we're outmatched." She let him go.

Myles rubbed his throat. Arguing would only result in further escalation, which in turn, would likely lead to him absorbing a few blows. Considering the way Ethan was favoring his injured leg, he was just waiting for a good excuse to drive a fist into Myles' gut.

"Fine! What should we do, then?"

"We wait," Ethan said.

"Here?"

"In the truck, genius," Bryce said. "We'll head back and bring the truck up in here. In the meantime, we'll use the forklift to hide the wreckage behind the trees. We're lucky enough as it is that nobody has reported it already."

"It's Dray Street. It dead ends about three miles north of here. From this point onward, there's not much on this road except for a couple of residential properties. Whether or not they get many visitors, I couldn't tell ya," Myles said.

"Well, at least two of them are late for dinner," Bryce said.

"In a sense," Ethan added.

"Only other property along this road that I know of is a cottage down by a private lake. Other than that, this area's dead, except in hunting season, which has yet to start."

"Unless they're somebody who doesn't believe in following the rules," Ethan said, cocking his head in the direction of the SUV further south. "Alright. Enough chit-chat. Let's get to the truck and bring it around. Who knows? Maybe we'll get lucky and your pet will come out at night to string a web across the road."

"I get first dibs on shooting it," Bryce said.

"Whatever you want, babe." Ethan smacked her on the ass as they started the trip back to the truck.

"I want a lot of things," Bryce said. She winked and clicked her tongue. "I'm not feeling particularly sleepy, either."

Myles swallowed. *Are they being serious?*

"Hope the container's warm enough for you, Doc," Ethan said. "That's where you're sleeping."

Myles lagged behind. What could he say to that? He couldn't believe it. *I'm the client? Yet, somehow, I get to call NONE of the shots.* Then again, considering their outrageous lifestyle, those two were going to do whatever they wanted regardless of whether he was there or not. *Truck container it is.*

CHAPTER 18

Tyler and Sue, half drunk, and spilling mustard from their hot dog buns, folded over with laughter as Laurie finished explaining what she called her 'love doctor' scheme.

Kira had an arm around Marshall's neck as they listened to the story. Sitting on him, she bounced with his laughter. She leaned back and put an arm around his neck.

"I ought to strangle you, you know?"

"I'd still say it was worth it," Marshall replied.

"How the hell did you guys plot this thing without her knowing?" Sue asked.

"Oh, it was easy. I found his number, and we simply communicated it once we found out she was looking for help fixing this place up." Laurie looked over at Kira. "Don't worry. There was only A LITTLE inappropriate texting between us."

"I'm sure there was," Kira replied. *Slut. Wouldn't be surprised if you considered attempting to get a quick lay before setting us up.*

Tyler pressed a smoked sausage over a prong, then held it to the flame. While it blackened, he glanced about.

"Where's Chris?"

"Light's on in the cottage. I think he's keeping to himself after…well, the thing," Marshall said. The mood quickly went from upbeat back to awkward.

Sue watched as her hubby's food started to turn crisp. "Uh, babe. You like your sausage black?"

"No, but I hear that's how *you* prefer it," Laurie said.

"Oh, Jesus, Laurie," Kira said. The others proceeded to laugh. "You guys are weird."

"Hey, I'm the only one not getting laid tonight. Let me at least have this," Laurie joked.

"Never confirmed the case with this guy," Sue said, pointing at Tyler. He then handed her another drink.

"Night's still young," he replied. He pointed at Laurie. "And technically, you're wrong. You're not the only one. Chris isn't getting any either." That joke failed to garner any laughs. Tyler took immediate notice of the awkward silence, as though a ghostly entity had crept into the group. "Oh, hey! Look at that! My food's overcooked! And, uh, babe? You gonna take this?"

Sue faked reluctance as she took the margarita. "I know what you're doing, mister."

"We all do," Kira said.

"Too bad it's working," Tyler replied. "There's more for you guys as well."

"Oh, I'm alright. I had enough while we were out fishing," Kira said. She took a closer look at the collection of rum sticking out of Tyler's cooler. "Is that *El Dorado?*"

"Twelve," Tyler said. He held it up.

Kira crumpled her lips, trying to resist. "Okay, I'll have a little of that."

Tyler grinned. "Let me fix that up for ya."

Laurie raised her hand. "I'll take a glass of that too. What about you, Marshall?"

"Don't be the oddball who doesn't drink, foreman," Tyler said.

Marshall shrugged. "Alright. I'll take one."

Tyler pulled out the plastic cups. Not the most ideal for drinking good rum, but then again, who really cared at this point? He passed the cups along and the group drank around the fire, exchanging stories, which grew more slurred as the evening went on.

****

It was nearing eleven when the group finally broke up. The fire was still going, courtesy of Tyler for tossing logs on it, even while the others were stating they were ready to call it a night. Not that it was any loss. There was nothing around the firepit to spread the flames. It would serve as a flickering nightlight before finally fizzling out over the next few hours.

Sue and Tyler were practically hanging off of each other as they returned to the RV. Tyler waved to the crowd, like a politician during a campaign.

"Alright, y'all! See you in the morning. Or at noon. At SOME point, tomorrow."

Sue tugged on his arm. "Come on, sailor."

"You don't have to tell me twice," he said.

Marshall chuckled as he watched them disappear into the RV. "Come morning, she'll find something to be pissed off at him for."

"It'll probably have something to do with getting her boozed up," Laurie said. She stood up, then wobbled. "Whoa! Speaking of which!"

"Take it easy there," Kira said. She clung to Marshall as they stood up. She held on to her plastic cup. No matter how drunk she was, she wasn't going to allow littering on her yard.

"Come on, babe," Marshall said. He put an arm around her waist and led her into the cottage.

She pressed against him and smiled. "Mmmm. You're warm."

"Just the booze," he replied.

"No, it's not," she said. They went inside. They stopped for a moment, expecting to see Chris there. Marshall looked back at his trailer and saw that the dressing room door was open a crack. He had shut it after he finished clearing it out. They were all so preoccupied with eating and drinking that they never noticed him cross the lawn.

"I'm starting up the fireplace," Laurie said. "Gotta have something cozy to stare at while I doze off."

"You know you can sleep in the spare bedroom," Kira said.

"Yeah, no thanks. This extended sofa is MUCH more comfortable. Plus…the fireplace."

Marshall looked at Kira. "I thought the spare bedroom was mine." She shook her head, grabbed him by the shirt, and led him up the steps.

"Yeah, you're not fooling anyone," she said. Without saying anything further to Laurie, they disappeared up the stairway.

Laurie giggled, proud of the result of her handiwork. She changed into some sweats and kept her hoodie on, then proceeded to light a fire, before snuggling on the couch with some fleece blankets.

Already, she could hear the creaking from upstairs. She reached into her bag and pulled out some headphones. She lay back, watched the fireplace, and waited for the booze to send her into a deep sleep.

CHAPTER 19

Laurie leaned up on the sofa. She was tired, dehydrated, and frustrated. Sleep showed no signs of coming. Any other time rum entered the equation, she would be out like a light. But tonight, nothing short of two Benadryl tablets seemed to be capable of doing the trick. Unfortunately, she didn't bring any, and she wasn't going upstairs to ask Kira if she had any. One thing she did need was water.

She got up, used the restroom, then dug into the fridge for a water bottle. Immediately, she downed half of it—a sign that her body really needed it. As she returned to the sofa, she considered throwing another log in the fireplace, only to realize the only wood in the cottage was already burning. She'd have to go outside to get more.

That's when she realized the fire outside was still burning. After two hours? It should have died out by now. She gazed out the window, realizing somebody was sitting by the fire.

Chris.

Oh, great. Laurie sank into the couch. She crossed her feet and stared at the dying flame inside the fireplace, trying to force several thoughts from her mind. A draft came through the window, making her snuggle tighter with her blankets. She groaned. She couldn't be wider awake now, especially with the guilt she now felt. Her natural instinct screamed at her, telling her she was right for hating Chris, that he absolutely deserved for his life to be a living hell. Then there was the more rational, compassionate side of her. It was the 'angel and devil on the shoulders' scenario.

Another draft came through. She began to wonder if Chris couldn't sleep because it was so freezing cold in that trailer. Was there a space heater in there? Marshall seemed like the kind of guy that could sleep in a thin sleeping bag in the Arctic. But Chris? He did mention he could tolerate the weather, but that was during daytime. She doubted that even in prison he was accustomed to sleeping in cold temperatures. Especially these days, when prisoners were given better living conditions than people in nursing homes.

She laid her head back. Every attempt to force him from her mind only resulted in her dwelling on the subject even harder.

Finally, the self-reflection set in. Laurie faced the facts: clearly, the guy had no intention of starting trouble. She admitted to Kira, and subsequently, *herself*, that the incident where he knocked her down was clearly an accident. Also, she had to acknowledge that every unpleasant encounter was initiated, or at least spurred on, by her behavior and attitude.

There was much anger still. She wasn't sure if she could forgive him for the wrongdoings of the past. Then again, maybe that was the problem. Perhaps she just needed to let go. To make peace.

She looked out the window again. He was still seated by the firepit, having a beer while roasting a hot dog over the fire. *Did he not eat while he was inside?* Laurie went into the kitchen and checked the trash can. Nothing in there that wasn't already present. By the looks of it, he wasn't the type to simply help himself to Kira's canned goods and lunch meats. Another indicator of improved character. Went from stealing jewelry and rings to not even taking a slice of bread.

Now she was feeling *really* guilty. Her conscience ate at her, reminding her that it was her fault he was sleeping out in the cold, practically.

"Ugh. It was much simpler just hating the guy," she said to herself. She took a breath, let the anxiety of talking to him wear itself out, then stepped outside.

Chris was facing the lake, watching it and the fire at once. He heard the door open, then looked away when he recognized Laurie.

"Oh, for fuck sake." Though under his breath, she still heard it. By the way he shifted, he was clearly about to stand up and walk off.

"Relax," Laurie calmly said, raising her palms. "I come in peace."

Chris relaxed somewhat, though was still a little on edge. Laurie took a seat across the firepit.

"Can't sleep?" he asked. He wasn't sure what else to say. He definitely didn't want to bring up old wounds.

"Unfortunately, no," she replied. "How's the jaw?"

Chris shrugged. "I've had worse."

"Oh! Mocking me, I see," Laurie said, hoping the sarcasm didn't go unnoticed.

"First day in the yard, I took a slug from a three-hundred-pound ex-college football player," Chris said.

She nodded. "I see your point." She smiled nervously. Silence took over as both of them tried to think of where to direct the conversation. *When in doubt, get right to the point.* "Listen dude, it's freezing out here."

"It's not too bad," Chris said.

"Gosh, you're crazy," she said. That sparked a smile. "But no, seriously, you CAN'T be comfortable sleeping in that smelly horse trailer."

"Marshall has it pretty clean, actually," he replied.

"Clean? Maybe. Comfortable? I highly doubt it. And don't give me this bullshit about how anything's better than a prison bunk."

"Anything IS better than a prison bunk," Chris said. "It's in *prison.*"

Laurie could sense his guard was high.

"Listen, man. Go ahead and grab your stuff and bunk in the spare bedroom."

Chris shook his head. "I'm not sure if that's a good idea. Kira might not—"

"Listen, she'll be cool with it as long as she knows I'm cool with it," Laurie said. "Which I am. Look, I might not have—okay, definitely not 'might'- I *clearly* did not react well to you being here. I was on a knife's edge since we towed the RV out, and overreacted to simple things."

"Seriously, Laurie, if I knew you were gonna be here, I'd—"

"I know, I know," she said. "Shitty circumstances. Not really your fault. I get it. The clumsiness didn't help, particularly sprinting full speed into me." She smiled to show she wasn't being too serious with that statement. Finally, Chris smirked.

"Well… there *was* a pretty pissed-off looking cougar back there."

They shared a laugh.

"Hey, since I'm on a roll, I'm gonna get this out of the way," Laurie said. "I'm letting you off the hook for the ring thing. Yeah, it was a shitty thing for you to do, but it was eight or nine years ago. And I like to think you aren't the same person today. Kira doesn't think so. Nor do Sue and Tyler. Despite their quirks, I don't think they'd associate themselves with an ex-con unless he was making sincere efforts of improving his life."

Chris nodded. "I appreciate you saying that."

"And, that said, I'll throw in an apology for hitting you. The slaps too when we bumped into each other in the cottage earlier."

"Eh, I had that coming. Just took eight years or so to get there." Chris finished his beer and set it down beside his seat. "Listen, if I could take it back, I would. I truly wish I could track down that ring. To say it was a shitty thing to do is an understatement. I could monologue about it all night, but to sum it up; I'm sorry."

Laurie nodded. It was what she needed to hear. She believed him. Though she had only been around him a day, there were several indicators that he was on the straight and narrow. His demeanor was different. His appearance was cleaner. He definitely was not on drugs. He was much more articulate and actually had consideration for others. How she hooked up with him in the first place was beyond her. But it was in the past now. Time to move forward, finally.

"Thank you," she said. A breeze swept over them. She shivered. "Okay, I hate to cut this short suddenly, but I'm going back where it's warm. You need help getting anything out of the trailer?"

"I just have a few items, enough to get me through the night," Chris said. "Most of my belongings are in the RV and, well…" He glanced at it and made a disgusted face.

"Yeah, I don't blame you for not wanting to go in there," Laurie said. "Don't mind me. I'll be getting new wood for the fireplace and…" She looked around. "Aw, hell."

"What's the matter?"

"Looks like Tyler used up all the firewood that was over here," she said. "It doesn't look like there's any left on the main stack."

Chris smiled. "Give me a sec. There's a dead tree a few yards back there that's already been cut up into sections."

"Good ol' Kira. Gotta do it herself. Lumberjack girl. No wonder she likes showing off her arms," Laurie said.

"I'll take care of it. Hopefully I won't wake anyone up going in and out in the middle of the night."

"Believe me. Considering the booze in their systems, and recent 'physical exertions', they'd sleep through an F5 tornado at this point," Laurie said.

"Good for them. I suppose I'll get started then." Chris went to the trailer, retrieved a small bag of personal items and clothes, then carried them to the cottage. He set them down on the living room table, then quickly stepped back outside. He stopped a few inches from the trees. "Crap."

"Something wrong?"

"I forgot the light on my phone doesn't work," he said. Laurie dug into her pocket.

"Here, I've got mine. Best two of us go in at the same time anyway, since we've already seen a cougar in there."

"Marshall says they're unlikely to go after us," Chris said.

"Yeah, but I don't see Marshall volunteering to get close to one. Come on, I'm getting chilly." She turned on the iPhone's flashlight and proceeded into the woods, watching carefully for any cats.

The trees shook, causing her to jolt. Leaves rained down around them. This damned time of year. Laurie didn't understand how so many people loved it. She constantly fantasized about moving further south where snow almost didn't exist. California, that was her dream. If only they didn't tax everyone to oblivion down there.

"You alright?" Chris said. He was right behind her.

"Just the breeze," she replied. She held the light forward. "Ah-ha. There's the log pile."

The light struck the fallen tree. It had been chopped up into sections, with the stump used as a platform. The wood was well over a year old and had dried out. Laying across the stump was an axe that Kira had used for slicing it up. Laurie walked over to it and picked it up by the handle. "Geez. Girl thinks she's a dude." She dropped the axe.

Chris walked to the log pile and scooped up an armful. "How much do you think you'll need?"

"That should do it."

"Sounds good," Chris said. He started walking back. Laurie looked down at the remaining logs.

On second thought, maybe a couple more should do it. She leaned down to scoop a couple of them up.

Chris stopped and looked back at her. "Gosh, you plan on being up all night watching the fireplace?"

"At this rate, I'm not gonna be asleep for another couple hours at least. I'd have to down two more cups of that rum at this point—which, honestly doesn't sound too bad—"

Several leaves rained down around her. They heard the brushing of branches overhead. Laurie froze. There was no wind to cause that. Chris had the same nervous feeling.

Laurie aimed the light into the tree above her. She saw several barren branches, curling about, descending down from the canopy. Only when she saw the huge bulk in-between them did she realize they weren't branches. Pedipalps dripped slime on her face in the split-second the thing dropped down on her. It was a thing of nightmares. It was crustacean. Insectoid.

Arachnoid.

The impact hit the earth with a sound of thunder. Laurie was driven face-first into the log pile, sending wedges scattering everywhere. The phone bounced off into the distance, the residual light creating a silhouette of flailing legs and clamping claws.

There was a grinding sound of a struggle as Laurie was violently pulled to the side, driving her against the dirt. There was a second sound of thunder as her scalp struck the edge of the stump. She raised her head and screamed. That scream abruptly intensified, propelled by a new piercing pain, then suddenly, she went quiet.

Chris shrieked. He took a step forward and reached out, only to immediately stop and backtrack. He saw the silhouette swiftly turn toward him. He spun on his heels and ran. Never in his life had he pushed his legs so hard. He had fled cops, violent inmates, drug dealers, and crime scenes. None of those instances compared to this. He could hear the nightmare tearing the woods apart behind him.

He emerged from the trees with a bounding leap. He could sense the beast behind him, but had no way of gauging its distance. He looked back, seeing nothing but trees and night air.

The next step stopped abruptly, as though his foot had struck a concrete ledge in the ground. Catapulted by momentum, Chris fell forward. Instantly, upon hitting the lawn, his world went black.

CHAPTER 20

For the seventh time, Myles Bower woke up. And for the seventh time, he checked the door to see if dawn had finally come. The steel floor of the container was NOT built for sleeping in, and he did not think far enough ahead to bring a mattress. The sight of the rising sun brought relief—relief that they could finally resume the hunt. And, more specific to his aching back, relief that he didn't have to lie in this container any longer.

He could hear the hunters moving around outside. When Myles stepped out, he saw Ethan standing by the side of the road, gnawing on jerky. Bryce was somewhere in the woods, out of sight.

Ethan gazed at the doc. "'Bout time you woke up. I was about to pound on that door."

"Where's your wife?"

"Taking care of business. You'd rather she squat here on the side of the road?"

"No, thank you." *Knowing how nonchalant you guys are, I'm shocked she isn't.* He rubbed his eyes. "Damn it. I wish I packed coffee."

"Way ahead of you, *Frankenstein,*" Ethan said. He held out a small bag. Inside were coffee beans.

Myles shook his head. "I'm good. But thanks."

Ethan tossed a bean into his mouth and munched on it. "Sorry. They don't come with mocha flavored cream."

"Toss me one, darling," Bryce said. She stepped from the trees and held out her hand, like a baseball catcher. Ethan tossed her one, which she proceeded to crunch between her teeth. Myles winced, much to Bryce's amusement. "Alright there, sport?"

"I'm good."

"Good. I'm ready to carry on whenever you two are," Bryce said.

"Let's go."

Right then, Myles registered the fullness in his bladder. "Give me just a minute." He hurried off to the other side of the road.

Ethan turned to his wife and chuckled. "Little peashooter's gotta get his load off."

"Since we're alone for a few minutes…" Bryce stepped up to him and nipped at his neck.

"You've been awfully frisky lately," he said.

"You know this stuff gets me going," she replied. She leaned back. "If it's too much for you to handle…"

He grabbed her by the waist and pulled her in for a kiss. "Never." They made out for another minute until the sound of Myles' footsteps ended the little event. Ethan brushed a few strands of hair behind his wife's ear. "Wanna go to South America after this? I hear there's been several fatalities in northern Argentina. Jaguars down there are getting increasingly vicious. Maybe they're starting to see people as a source of red meat."

Bryce groped his crotch. "I think that sounds lovely." She pulled him in for a ravenous kiss, which concluded with her teeth lightly clenching his lip.

Myles cleared his throat. Bryce maintained her grip for a few more seconds, then unslung her crossbow. "You finally ready, Doc? Or should we fix ya up some pancakes and eggs first?"

"Let's finish this job, and I'll personally treat you to brunch," Myles said.

"Plane ride will do," Ethan said. He slung his rifle strap over his right shoulder, checked the vial on his crossbow arrow, then studied the ground. "Trail leads this way. Let's go find your pet."

Myles followed them into the woods. As he did, he felt his phone vibrate. He had entered a tiny signal hotspot, where the device received a dozen messages and two voicemails at once. He recognized the security staff supervisor's number, as well as that of Jedlinsky's office line.

He started to sweat. Clearly, the two of them had exchanged words. Suspicion would only elevate the longer he remained out of the lab. He could try and make some sort of excuse, but nothing short of reporting the specimen's arrival at the lab would suffice.

The sooner we catch this thing, the better.

CHAPTER 21

Even in the abyss of deep sleep, Marshall could feel Kira's wet lips press against his. He awoke to the sensation of skin and fleece covers pressing against his body. Slowly, she started to mount him, ready to start the day off with a 'bang'.

"Well, good morning there," he said.

"Hi," she said, smiling. She brushed her hair back, then leaned down over him. She folded her arms around his head and pressed her forehead to his. "Sleep well?"

"Oh yeah." He looked at the sunlight streaming through the window. "Jesus. How late did I sleep in?"

"You're seriously thinking about the *time* right now?"

Marshall took the hint and gazed down at her neckline and chest. Everything was how he remembered it from years back, except for the added design of her tattoo sleeve.

"No." He proceeded to kiss her neck, then, much to her delight, flipped her onto her back. The joys of lovemaking only lasted a few more seconds, however. He swung himself off the bed and pulled on a pair of pants.

"Uh, excuse me? Where do you think you're going?" she said.

"Relax, I'll be right back. Even your sexy ass doesn't detract from the fact that my bladder is on the verge of bursting."

Kira grinned. "Alright. I suppose I'll let you off the hook."

Marshall took a left down the hall, where the guest bedroom and restroom were located adjacent to one another. As he relieved himself, he could hear movement through the cracked bathroom window. Then he heard Tyler and Sue. He couldn't make out the words, but he recognized the tone. After finishing, he peered out the window. Chris was face-down in the grass, with a panicked Tyler and Sue at his side.

"Jesus!" He hurried back into the bedroom and found the rest of his clothes. Kira leaned back, alarmed by his frantic movements.

"What's wrong?"

"Chris is lying unconscious outside." As he got dressed, he could hear the front door open.

"Guys!" Sue called.

"I saw it. We'll be right down," Marshall called back. He buttoned his shirt and slipped his boots on. Kira quickly went to her drawer and pulled out a pair of jeans and a plaid shirt.

"Is he hurt?"

"We'll find out in a minute," Marshall said, tucking his shirt in. "Definitely looks like he took a bad fall." He went down the steps and saw Sue standing at the door. She was glancing through the downstairs hallway and around the living room.

Chris' belongings were on the floor. Sue raised an eyebrow and looked up at Marshall. "Is Laurie upstairs?"

Marshall shook his head. "I assumed she was out there with you guys."

"No." She looked at the floor again. "Why is Chris' stuff in here?"

"I don't know. He was supposed to be sleeping in my trailer," Marshall said.

Kira came down the steps and saw the belongings. It was immediately clear she was wondering the same thing they were.

The three of them stepped outside. Tyler was kneeling by Chris, acting as though afraid to touch him. Marshall knelt beside him.

"He's still breathing. That's a good thing." Marshall leaned to look at Chris' face, which was cocked to the left. There was dirt and purple bruising all over his brow.

"Looks like he tripped over here," Tyler said, pointing to a crease in a small mound in the lawn. "Probably just took a bad step, and had an even worse landing."

Marshall studied the ground. It was firm. "I don't know if he'd make a little crater like that just from a bad step. He had to have been running." He then shook Chris' shoulders. "Hey, bud! Wake up." Chris stirred somewhat.

Kira approached with a water bottle. Marshall took it and poured a little over Chris' face. That did the trick. Chris opened his eyes, and winced. Then, all of a sudden, as though struck by a bolt of lightning, he sprang from the ground screaming. He turned toward the trees, eyes wide as though he'd seen a demon.

"Whoa!" Tyler said.

"Relax, man!" Kira said. "You're alright. You just took a fall."

"Got your bell rung in the process," Marshall added. Their words didn't appear to register. Chris continued backing up, as though some masked killer was approaching him.

Marshall held his arms to the side, stopping the others from approaching Chris.

"Hey, man." He waved a hand. "It's just us."

Chris kept his eyes on the trees. Kira followed his gaze. From where she stood, she couldn't see anything too out of the ordinary.

Tyler decided to take a step forward, which caused Chris to jolt. He sidestepped, accidently plowing into the tree near the northwest corner of the cottage. He yelped, stumbled, and ultimately fell to the ground.

The others rushed to his side.

"Chris?!" Kira said. "Snap out of it, man!"

He leaned up. "I—I'm alright." Marshall and Kira helped him to his feet. The fall seemed to help snap him into reality. Still, he looked horrified.

"What the hell happened? Tyler and Sue found you lying face-down. Looks like you took a tumble," Marshall said.

"You've cut yourself pretty bad," Tyler said.

The memory of impact shook Chris' mind. It all raced back to him: the shape; Laurie's scream; the sound of heavy feet thumping the ground; the feeling of terror, tripping over the ground.

Someone touched his shoulder. Chris screamed and jumped back. He looked behind him, then back to the south woods.

Marshall and Kira shared a glance, their eyes expressing the same concern. *Something happened last night.* They needed to approach this delicately. Clearly, Chris was on edge, ready to snap. He was under a ton of duress, meaning they'd have to work slowly and patiently in order to figure out what happened.

Sue, unfortunately, didn't share that sentiment.

"Chris, what happened last night?"

Chris shook again, as though the words physically struck him. "What? I—I don't know! It happened so fast…"

"Where's Laurie?"

He gasped. "Laurie." His eyes went back to the trees. "She's—"

"Oh, fuck," Tyler mumbled. He took Marshall by the shoulder and led him a few steps back. "I think we have a problem here."

"No shit."

"No, I mean—" Tyler sighed. "Obviously those two have been going at it since we got here. You think maybe they had a spat while we were sleeping?"

"No! That's not what happened!" Chris shouted. Tyler swallowed. He obviously had not lowered his voice well enough.

"Let's take this slowly," Marshall said.

"No, we need to get to the bottom of this," Sue said. "Chris. Something obviously happened last night. Laurie's not here. She's not in the house. Not in any of the trailers. The boats and vehicles are all here. And we found *you* lying in the dirt. What fucking happened?"

"We—" Chris stammered.

"*We* what?" Sue said.

"Sue, hold on," Marshall said.

She whipped toward him. "We can't hold on. Something happened. And clearly, he's doesn't want to tell us." She looked back at Chris. "Was it too cold out here? Let me guess? You decided to move into the cottage. Laurie woke up, got pissed off, probably told you to fuck off. You took it outside, and out into the woods? That what happened?!"

"Holy shit, Laurie! You're not helping," Kira said.

"I didn't do anything!" Chris exclaimed.

"Alright, alright, alright!" Marshall said, holding his hands up again, offering peace. "We believe you. Just tell us what happened."

Chris ran a hand through his hair. He started to say something, then stopped suddenly. He winced, his eyes glued to the trees. "You won't believe me."

"Yes, we will," Kira said.

"You'll think I'm insane."

Now, even Marshall was struggling to maintain a calm demeanor. These non-specific, vague phrases used by Chris, along with the hesitation and panic leading up to it, and Laurie's disappearance, all pointed to the possibility that something drastic happened while they slept.

"No, we won't, Chris," Marshall said. "You keep looking at the woods. Did something happen there?" Chris nodded. "Nice and slow. Just take us through what happened. Did you and Laurie get into a fight?"

"No. I sat by the fire after you guys turned in. She came out around midnight or so. We made amends. And—"

"She visited *you*?" Sue said. "How does that explain why your stuff is in the cottage?"

"Sue, stop," Marshall whispered. "Chris, keep going."

"She said she felt bad about me sleeping in the trailer!" Chris said, defensively. "She told me she was okay with me sleeping in the guest room, and that Kira would be alright with it."

"Alright," Marshall said, calmly. "What happened after that?"

"She needed firewood. She had trouble sleeping, and wanted to keep the fireplace going in the living room. I offered to help her collect some. So, we went into the woods and…it all happened so fast."

Hearts started drumming. Breathing intensified. Every member of the group was on pins and needles.

"What happened so fast?" Marshall said.

"We were getting the wood…" Chris' voice trailed off. "Then, something came after us. Dropped down from the tree…"

Kira cupped her mouth. "Oh, Jesus." She looked at Marshall. "The cougar?"

"Was that what it was, Chris?"

"No. It was dark, I couldn't see what it was."

"You couldn't see, but you know it wasn't the cougar?" Tyler said.

"I'm telling you there's something out there!" Chris shouted.

Marshall marched to his truck and grabbed his shotgun out of the case. He loaded eight shells into it, strung the ammo belt over his regular belt, then headed for the south tree line.

"Let's go take a look," Marshall said. "How far back did it happen, Chris?"

"By the log pile."

Everyone followed him, including Chris. He hesitated, but quickly caught up. Every person he got close to was quick to make some extra distance. Yet, each one of them glanced his way every few moments, as though keeping tabs on him while they investigated.

Marshall took the lead, immediately seeing the log wedges scattered all over the ground. As they approached the stump and log pile, they saw all kinds of abrasions on the ground. Clearly, a violent struggle had occurred. He saw Kira cup a hand over her mouth. She was looking at the stump.

"Oh, Christ," Marshall muttered. The edge of the stump was smeared with blood and strands of hair. He knelt down beside it, seeing tiny dried-up flakes on the stump and surrounding soil. He looked away and took a breath to control the gag reflex. "Skin."

"Where—where is she?" Sue said. She had gone from angry to the brink of tears.

Marshall continued looking about. After five minutes, he shook his head. Laurie wasn't here. What alarmed him even more than that was the blood on the stump.

"She was clearly driven down to the ground and dragged about. I doubt a cougar would slam her head against the stump like this."

"Look here," Kira said. She walked over to some bushes over on the left side, crouched down, and held up a smartphone. "It's Laurie's." She studied the abrasions on the case. "Looks like it got flung."

All eyes went to Chris. He started backing away.

"Don't fucking look at me like that."

"This was no cougar. No claw marks on the ground. No paw prints. There's these abrasions," Marshall leaned down to point out strange grooves in the soil. "But nothing a cougar or even a bear would make."

"I didn't *say* it was a cougar. Maybe a bear," Chris said.

"Would a bear smash her skull against the stump?" Tyler said.

"Not likely. On top of that, there's hardly been any recorded instances of black bear attacks. It's so freaking rare," Marshall said. "And there's nothing else in these woods that would carry a person off like this."

"Looks like someone wrestled her to the ground, bashed her head in, then carried her off," Sue said. She looked at Chris. Marshall turned to her, ready to tell her to shut up.

But the damage was done.

Chris backtracked out of the woods.

"Chris! Wait!" Marshall said. They ran out after him. Chris froze, remembering Marshall had a shotgun. It wasn't held in any threatening manner, but at this point, he wasn't ready to test him.

"I didn't kill her!" he said.

"Never said you did."

"Then who did?" Sue said.

"Sue, please stop," Kira snapped.

"It was…some animal!" Chris shouted. "It had huge legs that sprawled out like…" he held his hands out, "like, I don't know, a spider or something!"

The group stood silently.

Sue rubbed a hand over her face. "Oh my God." Her expression was a combination of someone on the verge of hysterical sobbing and laughter. Not the laughter of someone who found this situation funny, but rather that when all sanity was lost.

She then looked back at him. "Chris? Are you back to using drugs?"

He almost jumped. "NO!"

Even Kira was nodding. *That would explain a lot.*

"His bag is in the trailer. We could check," Tyler said.

"We're not checking anything," Marshall announced. "Not by ourselves, at least."

"What do you mean?" Chris asked. He backed up further, ending up near the firepit. His heart was racing, his hair now soaked in sweat.

"We're gonna have to call the Sheriff's department and get somebody out here," Marshall said.

"The cops?!"

"Chris, this has to be investigated," Kira said.

"I can't be here when they get here," Chris said. He turned back and forth, looking as though he was gonna take off running. "I can't! I just can't!"

"Why not?" Sue said. "If you didn't do anything, why are you   so   fearful?"

"Sue!" Marshall said.

"Because I'm an ex-con! They'll automatically assume I'm guilty!"

"No, they won't," Kira said.

"Yes, they will! That guard that died, he was an ex-cop! I can't be here! They'll automatically assume I killed her!"

"If you leave, it'll just look worse," Marshall said.

"And the longer we wait, the worse it looks for all of us," Kira added. She pulled out her phone. "I'll make the call."

"Wait! Not yet!"

"Sorry, Chris," she said. She began dialing.

Chris looked to the ground. Near his foot was the prong for roasting hot dogs. He snatched it up, then lunged for the nearest person, which was Sue. She screamed, tried to flee, but could not escape his grasp. He locked an arm around her neck and held her in front of him, while pressing the tip of the prong to her neck.

"Chris! What the fuck!" Kira shouted.

"Let her go!" Tyler said.

"Stay back!" Chris growled. He nodded toward Marshall. "Drop that gun!"

"Chris, this won't end well."

"Just drop it!"

Marshall held his left hand out, signaling compliance, while he slowly lowered the weapon to the ground.

"Alright. Everyone get your phones out. Right now! SLOW!"

"Do as he says," Marshall said. He slowly reached into his pocket and retrieved his phone.

"Hold them up. Make sure I can see the screen. I'm aware of the little SOS tricks they install into these things," Chris said. Kira and Marshall held their phones high. Tyler hesitated, distracted by his girlfriend's sobbing, as well as the blood trickling down her neck.

"Dude, you're digging the prong into her skin."

"Tyler, get your phone out," Marshall said. Tyler relented. He reached into his back pocket and held his phone high.

"Alright, keep them up," Chris said.

Sue squeezed her eyes shut. "Please let me go."

"Shut up!" Chris said. "I'm not going back to prison. You guys clearly are ready to feed me to the cops. You think I killed Laurie, and they will too. I'm NOT going back. You have no idea what it's like! You don't know what it's like to be ganged up on, beaten to a pulp, and fucked up the ass by a dozen inmates!" He inhaled deeply, his arm tensing around Sue's throat, causing her to gag.

"Loosen up, man," Marshall said.

"Back up," Chris said. "Keep those phones high. Back up to the lake!" Slowly, they all moved toward the lake. Tyler was the slowest. His feet felt like they were filled with cement. He didn't want to back up, but spring forward and knock this prick to the ground. This guy, who he had faith in. Whom he befriended DESPITE his criminal and drug background. Who everyone believed had turned a corner in his life, now held a pointed object at his girlfriend's neck.

Chris followed them, pushing Sue along with his body. They stopped at the lake. There, the three group members awaited Chris' next instruction.

"You gonna make us swim?" Kira said.

"Toss your phones into the water," he demanded. Sue let out a cry as the prong sank another millimeter.

Marshall tossed his phone in first. Then Tyler, who never took his eyes off his terrified girlfriend. The phones hit the water and sank to the depths, the electronics shorting out, rendering the devices no more advanced than the pebbles they landed beside.

Kira threw her phone into the water, then raised her hands. "Alright. We did what you wanted."

"You think I'm stupid?" Chris said.

"What?! No, of course not," Kira replied.

"I saw you pick up Laurie's phone. It's in your back pocket. Pull it out and throw it into the lake!" He tightened his grip on Sue's neck, resulting in another scream, which came out more as a gag. Kira didn't waste time. She carefully reached back, pulled the phone out, then flung it back into the water.

"Alright. It's done."

"Almost," Chris said. He removed the prong from Sue's neck and held it in his other hand, which was still locked over her throat. He tapped around her pants in search of her phone. "Stop your whining." He found the phone, forced it from her jeans, then launched it as far as he could.

Tyler, seeing the moment of vulnerability, took a step forward.

"AH-AH!" Chris fixed his posture and took the prong back in his right hand. He raised it high, like Zeus about to hurl a lightning bolt. Tyler stopped. His hands came up. This guy was seriously about to ram those prods into her jugular.

"Chris?" Marshall said. He was shaking his head. "I understand where you're coming from. But you're not doing yourself any favors."

"Let her go," Kira said. "She didn't do anything to you."

"She thinks I killed Laurie," Chris said.

"Did you?" Marshall said.

"NO!"

"You think you're gonna convince us by holding a sharp object to her neck?" Marshall said.

Chris stared at him, his teeth clenched. Only now was it starting to sink in. By giving in to panic, he had practically removed all doubt of his guilt—for a crime he didn't commit. He was creating the very scenario he wanted to avoid.

"There's something in the woods," he said. His voice was soft. He took several deep breaths, as if winding down from a long marathon run. "I didn't kill her. I swear. I—"

He looked at the blood seeping from Sue's neck, then his arm locked around her. He could feel her rapid heartbeat and saw the tears streaming down her face. It dawned on him what kind of horrible act he was committing.

The prong fell from his hand. His hand fell from her neck, freeing her. Sue dashed for Tyler, throwing her arms around him while sobbing.

Chris backed up, horrified by what he had done, then fell back on his buttocks. He stared into the distance, his jaw trembling. For a moment, it looked as though he was lost in some sort of trance.

Marshall and Kira approached, the latter taking the prong and tossing it to the side.

"You alright, Sue?" Marshall asked.

"What the hell do you think?" she snapped. "That psycho tried to kill me!"

"Shhh!" Marshall waved his hand, warning her to calm down. *Last thing we need is to trigger another outburst.* He knelt by Chris. "You alright, man?" Chris nodded. "I need you to listen very carefully. You listening?"

"Yes." It was barely audible.

"We're going to get the police here. We HAVE to find out what happened to Laurie. This means there'll be a lot of people out here. It also means they will probably see you as a suspect, at least initially. Do NOT resist when that happens. If you're innocent, they will find out. We'll get to the bottom of what happened."

"You've got to believe me, man. There's something out there. I saw it. There's something out there."

"Marshall?"

He looked up and saw Kira standing near the firepit. He joined her, glancing back to keep an eye on Chris. While he was there, he scooped up his shotgun.

"You okay?" he asked.

Kira nodded. "There's no landline in the cottage. Since we don't have phones, we're gonna have to go TO the Sheriff's station."

Tyler and Sue quickly joined them.

"No way we're all going together. Not with *him* in the vehicle with us," Tyler said.

"You doing alright, Sue?" Marshall asked. She shook her head, still clinging to Tyler. Her injury was minimal. The prong barely broke the skin. However, the trauma would last the remainder of the day. Being in close proximity to Chris would not help matters.

"Only way I'd be comfortable is you holding that shotgun to him," she said.

"Police might not take too kindly to that when we arrive at the station," Kira said.

"No, they wouldn't," Marshall said.

"And we can't call to warn them ahead of time," Tyler said. "Our phones are in the lake and Chris' is broken."

"Then one of us is gonna have to go to the station," Kira said.

"We'll volunteer," Tyler said. He looked at Marshall. "Probably best for you to remain here. I think you're the most suitable to handle that guy if things get out of hand. Besides, if I stay here alone with him, *I'll* probably end up being arrested."

"Alright," Marshall replied.

Kira dug into her jeans pocket and handed him her car keys. "Go ahead and take my car, that way you don't have to steer that big ass RV up the driveway. You'll get there faster, too."

"Sounds good," Tyler said. He glanced at Chris, who was still seated by the lakeside, then leaned toward Marshall. "What do you think happened?"

"I don't know. He's clearly under duress, and in some sort of shock. Something bad went down, that's for sure. Either he did it himself, or he witnessed something horrible. I'll leave it up to the detectives to figure out."

"Can we get started, please?" Sue asked. "I just want to get the hell out of here."

CHAPTER 22

In the few minutes that followed, Kira and Marshall applied some gauze to Sue's neck. She took a shot of rum to help calm her nerves. It seemed to help somewhat. What didn't help was Tyler's attempt at humor.

"Only nine-thirty. Starting early, girl." That earned him glares from her, Kira, *and* Marshall. He cleared his throat. "Not that I'm judging…"

"Let's just get out of here, please," Sue said. They gathered by Kira's car.

"You guys sure you'll be alright?" Tyler asked. Their eyes kept going towards Chris, who was now seated near one of the firepits. He appeared exhausted, not displaying any threatening mannerisms. If anything, he looked as though near the point of breaking down into tears.

Marshall gripped his shotgun by the frame, keeping the muzzle pointed at the dirt.

"We'll be fine. Get Sue's neck checked, will ya?"

"You betcha," Tyler said. He opened the passenger door for his girlfriend, then went around to the other side. "Keep an ear out for their sirens. I'll warn them of your, uh, preemptive measures so they don't draw on you." He nodded at the weapon.

"I'll set it down once I hear them approach," Marshall said. He took a step back. "Alright, go on."

Tyler started the engine and took the car in a U-turn, then carefully accelerated up the long, winding driveway.

Marshall watched as the taillights dimmed around the first bend, then looked over at Kira. Her eyes were welling up at this point. It was now starting to hit her that her best friend was likely dead somewhere in the woods. He walked over and gave her a hug.

"I can't believe this is happening," she said. Her voice broke, but she kept from crying.

"I know. It'll be okay," he said. "Tyler and Sue are getting help. All we have to do is wait."

****

Sue pressed her hand to her wound, clenching her teeth at the sting from the disinfectant Kira applied. Her heart raced as recent events replayed in her mind. Her fear turned to anger. In her mind, there was no doubt that bastard Chris killed Laurie and hid her body out of sight. She probably landed a blow to Chris' forehead, maybe with a log wedge, hence the bruising. The thought made her sick. She couldn't believe they actually befriended a homicidal maniac. He probably *did* kill that bank guard. With that in mind, she wondered if he turned himself in to make it seem like he was innocent in the matter. Perhaps that's what he was attempting now. Was that the plan? Let her go, allow them to bring the cops here, in hopes that it would improve his image?

Either way, she was fuming with hatred. Getting the cops here would be the ultimate payback, and she couldn't wait to see it play out. Her face stiffened as Tyler eased on the brakes.

"The *one* time I want you to floor the pedal, and you drive like a freaking wuss," she said.

"I'd rather not crash," he said.

"Oh, NOW you want to drive carefully…when you're in a car built for speed. But when we're in a sixteen-foot RV—"

"We don't own the car," Tyler said.

"Put your foot to the damn lever, or *I* will," she said.

"Christ…" Tyler cleared the bend and accelerated. There was a hundred feet of space before the road bent again to the left. Once they cleared that, they'd be on Dray Street. He made the turn. "Alright, here we—WHAT THE FUCK?!"

He slammed on the brakes, but it was too late. Less than two meters ahead was a long, rope-like material that stretched across the driveway. Tyler only had enough time to grab his girlfriend and pull her head down before the car made impact. The material, taut as cable, struck the windshield, shattering it, then snapped like a rubber band. The car whipped to the left and plowed into a tree, the thunderous impact sending a resounding echo through the woods.

****

Marshall, Kira, and Chris turned to the west, startled by the sound.

"What the hell just happened?" Marshall said. Chris leapt to his feet.

"They crashed," he mumbled.

"Fucking Tyler," Kira mumbled. "Can't drive for the life of him."

"Come on, let's make sure they're not hurt," Marshall said.

"Wait," Chris said. "You don't know what's out there!" His warning went unnoticed as Kira and Marshall sprinted up the driveway. Chris remained, conflicted between his own well-being, and the good-natured drive to help his friends, whom he had done wrong.

The thought of being by himself made his throat tighten. Perhaps there was safety in numbers. And IF that thing was real, he'd want to be near the guy with the shotgun.

Chris groaned, then forced himself to sprint after the others.

****

Smoke rose high from the engine. Tyler lifted his head off of the steering wheel. Blood trickled from his brow. Glass from the windshield had cut his face. But he wasn't concerned about his well-being as much as he was for Sue's.

She was crouched under the dashboard, her knuckles sliced by little glass fragments. She was grabbing her face, shaking, near the edge of hysterics. Her mind could only take so much. First, Laurie disappeared, then she was held with a sharp object at her throat, and now she was involved in a serious crash.

"What happened?" she said.

"You alright?" Tyler asked.

"*What* happened?!"

"How the hell should I know?" Tyler got out of the car. He gazed down at the weird rope. It had broken off into several thin strands that stretched as they clung to the vehicle. They were white in color. Staring at it, he no longer thought of it as a rope. Rather, like an enormous piece of silk. Across the driveway was a tree which had been used as a post for this thick wire. It looped around the trunk in a thick blob of white.

On their side of the driveway, the stuff had been strung tightly around another tree, and tightened like a cable across the driveway, as though deliberately designed to trap unsuspecting drivers. And there was no doubt that it had been designed. Whatever it was, there was some sort of chemical composition to it. The way it stretched and stuck to the vehicle and debris meant that it was made from some kind of adhesive.

Tyler leaned to the left, looking past the nearest tree for a better view into the woods. Beyond the tree where the rope had been strung was what initially appeared to be a large white cloud. When walking around the car for a closer view, the illusion went from a cloud to a wall. Then from a wall to a net. A huge web had been weaved between several trees. And Tyler's eyes didn't betray him: this thing *was* a spider web. It stretched at least twenty feet high and maybe thirty feet in width.

The web comprising the huge net was the same material as that threading the huge strand in the driveway. No spider could possibly have threaded this...

His mind flashed to Chris' explanation of last night's events.

"It was...some animal! It had huge legs that sprawled out like..." he held his hands out, *"like, I don't know, a spider or something!"*

Tyler turned around. Sue was out of the car now, still somewhat disoriented. She barely seemed to notice the webbing.

"Babe?"

"What?" she said.

"We need to head back."

"No shit. Kira's gonna be pissed."

"No... we NEED to get back now."

Branches crackled overhead. Leaves of various autumn shades rained down around them. A chill struck Tyler. There was no wind passing through the woods. Then he saw the shadow overtake him. Sue looked up above him, cupped her mouth, and screamed.

Tyler looked up. Huge legs danced above him, while two crab-like pincers lunged. The body was segmented and brown in color, with a white stinger protruding from the abdomen.

The beast dangled from a strand of webbing, closing in on its unsuspecting victim. When the human started to run, the creature cut the strand and allowed gravity to do the rest of the work.

Tyler gasped and tried to sprint, only to be driven down by an immense force. He clawed at the ground and kicked his legs, only to feel his left femur snap under the pressure of powerful pincers. It pulled him under its body then slammed its abdomen onto his back.

Sue screamed, watching her boyfriend arch backward. He stared out, eyes wide, his open mouth frothing. His arms were locked out, fingers half-bent, as though electricity was surging through his veins.

She screamed his name, but went unheard. Tyler was on the ground, motionless other than the involuntary muscular spasms.

The creature lifted itself, its stinger coated in red. Self-preservation took over. Sue sprinted down the driveway, screaming to wake up from this horrible dream.

The beast turned, seeing the human taking off down the open path. She was a fast one, already disappearing around the bend. It abandoned the immobilized prey under its body in favor of securing more prey. Once the hunt was complete, it would proceed to cocoon these victims and gorge itself on their fluids.

Dust sprayed the air as the creature raced to the bend. As it made the turn, it sensed further vibrations drawing near.

****

"I hear screaming. Is that Sue?" Kira asked.

"I think so," Marshall said. They ran up the driveway, then slowed. "There she is!" He pointed at the bend up ahead, where Sue emerged. She was in complete dismay, arms waving about, hair frizzled, screaming nonstop as she ran toward them. She didn't even appear to be looking where she was going.

"Sue!" Kira said. She took a few steps to close the distance. "Sue, it's us." She stopped, seeing the enormous shape that appeared behind her. Its leg-span surpassed the width of the driveway, bending at forty-five degree angles to allow itself to scurry through the gap. At first, they believed they were looking at a huge spider—except it had huge front arms armed with razor-edge pincers. But it wasn't a scorpion, as it did not have a coiled tail. It was some amalgamation. A damnation of nature.

Kira screamed, helpless to do anything but watch as the beast leapt. Sue's scream finally ended, as the air was driven from her lungs by the crushing impact. The beast seized her in its claws, spinning her along the dirt for a suitable position. She yelped one last time as the stinger came down on her lower back. Venom pumped into her bloodstream, beginning the painful process of paralysis.

Marshall raised his shotgun and fired at the beast. It leapt straight up, startled by the strange impact of buckshot against its exoskeleton. He pumped and fired again. The creature bounced backward, slashing its arms and forward legs at the air. Another shot drove it back again, yet, there was no clear damage.

Chris was the first one to turn and run. Marshall and Kira were right behind him.

"Go through the trees!" Marshall said. They cut through the woods, zigzagging between the various obstacles between them and the cottage. They could hear the ravaging of nature behind them. The creature was only a dozen meters back, ripping vegetation from their roots as it pursued them.

Marshall glanced over his shoulder. He could see a blur of legs between the trees. The arachnoid teetered itself, teetering through tight spaces to catch up. And catching up it was. Despite its enormous mass, the arachnoid was agile and able to weave through the woods with ease.

It needed to be slowed down.

Marshall spun to his left, aimed the shotgun, and fired.

****

"Another shot," Bryce said. She pointed north. "Came from that way."

"Looks like your pet found some breakfast," Ethan said to Myles.

"They're close," Bryce said. "Up this way. Maybe seven hundred meters or so."

"Let's check it out," Myles said.

The small group ran north. As they closed in, another shotgun blast echoed through the woods.

****

The creature hissed and staggered backward. Green fluid spilled from its pedipalps. Marshall pumped his shotgun. He had only three shots left before the weapon ran empty. With the beast having moved back behind a group of trees, it'd be impossible to land a critical shot.

"Marshall?!" Kira shouted. Marshall sprinted into the clearing and found Kira and Chris standing near the RV.

"Did you kill it?" Chris said.

"No. It's still back there. Get into the cottage," Marshall said.

"What the hell is that thing?" Kira said.

"I warned you about it! You didn't believe me!" Chris yelled.

"Not now, Chris," Marshall said. The sound of crackling branches drew their attention back to the woods. At first, they saw nothing but trees. The raining of branches and leaves gave away the arachnoid's presence in the canopy. Legs arched over branches, then coiled as it got into position to leap at its prey.

Chris backed up. For a moment, he felt frozen. In this strange realm where time seemingly halted, his brain weighed a series of options. In this state, self-preservation took precedence. All consideration for others abruptly ceased. At this point, nothing else mattered than his own safety. It was the way of life, the means to survive. It didn't matter how the situation came about, or his role in preventing it. The here and now were the only things considered, and the only outcome that mattered was his own.

It didn't matter how the stealing affected Laurie and the others he stole from. He needed his drug fix, no matter the cost.

It didn't matter about the bank guard. When the uniformed officer reached for his sidearm, all considerations dissolved to dust. The fact that Chris and his friends had put themselves in that situation had no bearings on the issue. It was Chris or him, and when push came to shove, Chris put himself over the other. Nobody could prove that it was him who did it. His story worked out well for him, overall. And in his mind, he did what was necessary to survive.

Just as he was doing now.

The momentary freeze in time ceased. Chris faced the firepit, seeing the empty beer bottles propped up near the cooler. He snatched one of them up, turned to his left, and chucked it like a baseball into the back of Marshall's head.

Marshall's world flashed before his eyes. He fell forward, the shotgun skidding from his grip.

"Marshall!" Kira shouted. She glanced back at Chris, who was already sprinting into the cottage.

The arachnoid sprang, landing atop the RV. The vehicle shuddered, the roof indenting under its bulk. Cocking its legs, it reared its head down, poised to seize the fallen prey.

Kira dove for the shotgun. Landing on one knee, she scooped it up, raised it high, and fired. Buckshot struck the creature's face, rupturing one of its eyes. It flailed its arms and legs. Its violent motion doubled in ferocity as the next shot struck it. Kira fired a third and final blast, striking the creature's underside. Green blood spurted as one of the fragments struck the thin chitin at its joints. The arachnoid reeled backwards, landing on its back on the other side of the RV.

Kira grabbed Marshall by the shoulders. "Get up!"

His vision was fuzzy and his head throbbed. Her voice was like an echo, even though she was right next to his ear. Still, he had enough awareness to understand the danger.

He rose to his feet, nearly tumbling back down. Kira guided him to the cottage and grabbed the door handle. It was locked.

"Son of a bitch!" She banged on the door. "Chris! Goddamn you! Open this door!" There was no response. Marshall, with his bearings mostly regained, pounded on the door.

"Chris! Let us in!"

They heard the shattering of glass as the arachnoid climbed over the RV. It paused, still bleeding from its damaged eye. After gauging the potential threat these humans posed, it proceeded to climb over the vehicle.

Marshall and Kira backed toward the shore. When the arachnoid cleared the vehicle, it cocked its legs back, ready to scurry toward them with unmatched speed. It opened its claws, quivered its abdomen, pumping venom into its glands, then sprang. It cleared a dozen feet before suddenly jolting to the left. As though flung by a giant mallet, the creature flopped onto its back, kicking its legs into the air. It righted itself and turned toward the woods.

"You hit it!" a voice called out. "It needs more sedative! Bryce! Hurry! Get it now!"

A man and a woman, dressed in hunting attire, sprinted from the south tree line. Both of them were armed with crossbows. The woman positioned herself near the RV and aimed her crossbow, while the male loaded a fresh arrow into his.

She squeezed the trigger, plunging the projectile along the creature's shoulder joint. The beast flailed again, triggered by sudden pain. Legs whipped about, only to slow down. It stood high on its legs, tilting its abdomen high and cocking its claws back in a menacing pose. It advanced toward the human, only to stagger.

The man raised his freshly loaded crossbow and fired an arrow into its abdomen. The creature jolted again. It turned, ready to attack him instead. Its legs began to fold against its will. It teetered forward, bracing itself with its claws, only to lean back instead. Its claws snapped at the air, each 'attack' slower than the last. The creature staggered to its left and rolled onto its back. Its legs coiled over its body, settling in a deathly pose.

Marshall and Kira simultaneously breathed a sigh of relief. They watched as the two hunters circled the creature. The woman looked to the man and gave him a smile.

"We got it, baby!" She ran over to him and they embraced with a wet kiss. A third individual emerged from the woods. He was a shorter man, with dark hair, somewhat pale skin, and a high, straight-line nose. He carried a briefcase as he approached the creature.

"Yes!" he said. "Well done! Now we just need to get back to our truck and load it into the container."

"Yeah? What about them?" the woman said, pointing at Marshall and Kira. The short man turned around and saw them standing by the lake.

"Oh…"

'Oh'? Did this guy expect everyone to be dead? Marshall's heartrate slowed only a little. It was clear these people were aware of this creature's presence. And judging by the short man's expression, he didn't seem too pleased that there were survivors.

Marshall clutched Kira's hand. "Who the hell are you guys? And what the hell is that thing?"

CHAPTER 23

Chris pressed his hands over his ears and squeezed his eyes shut. If only he could shut out the horror taking place outside. Maybe, if that thing got Marshall and Kira, then it would be satisfied. It would go away. He repeated that hope to himself, partly to make himself feel safer, as well as to justify his recent actions.

They were going to die anyway.

He sat in the bathroom, figuring it'd be the safest place to hide. There were no windows, the area was dark, and he could hear what was going on around him in case the thing lingered. If it tried breaking in, he could make an escape through the front or back entrances, depending on where it would attack. Then again, to know it was trying to get in, he'd have to listen. Removing his hands from his ears seemed too daunting a task. Despite deliberately leaving Marshall and Kira to their fate, he didn't want to listen to their deathly screams. He'd never get it out of his mind. The sight of seeing the blood splattering across the wall when the guard was shot still haunted him, and that was someone he didn't even know. Kira and Marshall had at least shown him some kindness and didn't treat him like an animal.

Which he now realized he deserved.

They were going to die anyway, he reminded himself. The question was 'are they dead?'

Was it over? If so, was the thing gone? Chris opened his eyes. Not that it did much good; he was in a small room with the light off. His hands shook. It was like they had a willpower of their own and refused to leave his ears. After several seconds of resistance, he moved his hands, keeping them an inch from his head in case he needed to block out any horrible sound. There was no indication of struggle. There was no screaming, no sound of running or fighting. Yet, there was sound. Voices. Multiple voices, and not just Kira and Marshall's.

Who else was out there? And where was the monster?

Chris stood up, opened the door, and peeked into the hallway. Through the front window, he spotted movement. There were three people out there he didn't recognize. Two of them were wearing hunting gear and appeared to be armed to the teeth. The third only wore jeans and a sweater, yet, he seemed to be a part of this new group.

Several feet beyond them was the creature. It was on its back, immobilized. Chris leaned against the wall. The tension he felt had released all at once. The thing was dead. He would not suffer the fate of being impaled by its stinger and carried away to be eaten.

He could hear the hunters talking with Marshall and Kira. With the sound of their voices, the tension returned. The only reason they weren't kicking down the door to beat him to a pulp was because they were now busy with these new people, whoever they were. But that did not change the fact that they would be out for his blood.

Chris was breathing heavily again, near the point of hyperventilating. It dawned on him how badly he'd screwed up. He had just violently assaulted Marshall and left him and Kira to die to save his own skin. Marshall was a nice guy, but even nice people had a breaking point, and usually attempted homicide was that breaking point. And considering he still had the shotgun and some fresh shells around his belt, Chris wasn't eager to hang around to find out.

He considered his options. Right now, he wasn't budging from this cottage. Not yet, at least. As soon as he showed his face, Marshall and Kira would be all over him. He deserved it; he had that much self-awareness. Still, he wasn't going to subject himself to his punishment. *Especially* if it led to prison time.

I'm getting out of here.

The question was 'How?' Kira's car was destroyed, and the RV was badly damaged. He didn't know who these hunters were, but something in his gut sensed that they weren't people he wanted to mingle with. Maybe it was the guns, or the female's deliberately skimpy outfit, like she thought she was on some sort of Hollywood production. Who hunted in camo that shared a bare midriff and heavy cleavage? Maybe it was an *Instagram* thing. Then again, those people didn't carry dual pistols and a large Bowie knife. And there were plenty of scars to show these people weren't for show. The man had a brace on his left leg, after all. And somehow, they managed to show up right at the time a giant spider creature was lurking about? None of it made sense, and it all fed Chris' desire to get the hell out of here.

There was only one option he could think of: take Marshall's truck and head for the border. What he would do afterwards, he had no idea. Chris wasn't thinking that far ahead. All he wanted was to get out of dodge.

He took a moment to consider his plan. What would happen if he left Marshall and Kira with these strange people? Before he could ponder the possibilities, he forced it from his mind. Minutes ago, he left them as bait for the monster. Up until thirty-seconds ago, he thought they were dead anyway. What difference would it make now if these people meant no good? Whatever was left of his good conscience had been tossed aside in preference of his own survival.

Right now, it seemed they were distracted with the hunters. It was only a matter of time before they would come into the cottage. Chris needed to find those truck keys, assuming they weren't in Marshall's pockets. He searched around the table and the kitchen, then the guest bedroom where Marshall had set himself up to sleep. Those keys had to be here somewhere.

His life depended on it.

CHAPTER 24

"I don't get it. You guys *knew* this thing was out here?" Marshall said. His head continued to throb as he and Kira approached the strange trio. The beast was still on its back, its legs coiled like a half-clenched fist. The hunters stood on guard while the man in plain clothes approached it.

"You'd think we'd at least get a 'thank you' for saving your asses," the female hunter said.

"Thank you," Marshall said. "Now, who the hell are you, and what the hell is that thing?"

"It is a genetic miracle," the short man said.

"That thing is no miracle," Kira said. The man ignored her while he inspected the beast.

"Careful!" Marshall said. "That thing might not be dead!"

"It's not."

Marshall halted. "What?"

The man stood up and faced them. "Just taking a snooze."

"Then we'd better finish it off before it wakes up," Marshall said. He marched to his shotgun, only for the two hunters to step in his way.

"I'd back up if I were you," the man said.

"Get out of the way," Marshall said.

The man leaned forward slightly. "Don't take the leg brace for granted. Go toe-to-toe with me, and you'll be slurping meals through a straw."

Marshall weighed his options. Clearly, the scars all over the man's face and the discoloration in his eye indicated he had wrestled his fair share of foes. And Marshall's gut told him they weren't all human.

"Who the hell are you people?" Kira said.

The male hunter shrugged. "Nobody you need to worry about."

"That thing killed our friends," Marshall said.

The short man stood up from the arachnoid. "There were more of you?"

"Yes," Marshall said. He studied the doctor's body language. He wasn't surprised, or even shocked. Rather, he looked disappointed, as though this news was an inconvenience.

The male hunter laughed. "Your pet's really been getting around, Doc."

"Pet?" Marshall said. He looked at the doctor. "What's the story here?"

"Nothing you need to know," the doctor replied.

"I can put my imagination to work," Marshall replied. "I'm no wildlife expert, but I have common sense. That is not a normal creature. And you were proud, or dumb enough, to refer to it as a genetic miracle. Did you bio-engineer that thing?"

The scientist completed taking a few blood samples from the specimen and sealed them in his briefcase.

"I wouldn't expect you to appreciate the breakthroughs this specimen represents."

"You expect us to *appreciate* that thing?" Kira said. Her voice croaked, suppressed from screaming her fury at this crazy man. "It killed our friends. It tried to kill us."

"Which reminds me, Bower: it's probably built a nest near here. Since you're so keen on—"

"Don't use my name, you crazy fool!" the doctor snapped. The hunters chuckled, mocking his aggressive stance.

"Why? You not want *them* to know who you are? Dr. *Myles* Bower?" the female hunter said.

"I thought you were looking forward to being world famous," the man said.

"Unbelievable. I paid you top dollar—"

"To track down your pet. I never made any promises about keeping secrets and covering up whatever mess that thing left," the man said. He looked to his wife. "Right, babe?"

"That's right."

"By the way, what you paid was the children's rate."

Dr. Bower groaned, then looked at Marshall and Kira. "Where did you first encounter it?"

"It ambushed our friends down the driveway up that way. We heard a crash. By the time we got there—"

"It set a trap," Myles said to himself. "Not where its main nest would likely be. Still, let's check it out. You guys mind leading the way?"

Marshall glanced over at the hunters. *Do we really have a choice?*

They proceeded to walk up the driveway. It took about seven minutes to reach the bend where Sue was attacked. She was face-down in the dirt, her head cocked toward the group. Kira looked away and sucked in a deep breath, barely controlling the urge to regurgitate.

"Keep going," the male hunter said.

"Be nice to them, Ethan," the female said.

"Ethan," Marshall muttered. He then scoffed. Clearly, these people weren't too concerned with having their names revealed. Then again, what good were first names solely? He glanced back at the wife. "What do we call you?"

She smirked. "Bryce."

Myles glanced back from the front of the group. It was evident that he didn't like the exchange of information, but had little to no control over this duo.

They walked past the bend and arrived at the crash.

"Jesus," Marshall said, seeing the huge web in the woods. Extending from it was the thick strand that caused the crash.

"Just as I thought," Myles said.

"Shouldn't we be more concerned about the bug?" Marshall said. "What if it wakes up?"

"It won't," Myles assured him. "Not for several more hours."

They walked past Tyler's body. He was lying on his left side, bleeding from the small of his back. Marshall stopped, noticing a slight twitch in his fingers. Upon a closer look, he saw Tyler's lips quivering slightly.

"Wait!" he called out. Myles looked back.

"He's dead."

"I don't think so," Marshall said. Kira knelt beside him. She checked for a pulse.

"I felt one. It's barely there, but he's alive!"

"You *can't* help him," Myles said.

Marshall stood up. "Listen, you psycho. He has a pulse. We need to—" A heavy impact between his shoulder blades knocked him forward. Marshall looked back, seeing Ethan standing with his rifle unslung.

"Stop arguing. We need to check out the main nest."

"Why?" Kira said.

Ethan glanced over at Myles. "That's a good question. *Why?*"

Myles grimaced. He couldn't use 'erasing evidence' as his excuse—not in front of these two. With no weapons, he didn't have the means to eradicate loose ends himself. At least, not until he could convince Ethan and Bryce. Considering he was out of funds, he needed to stall for as long as possible until he could make them an offer they couldn't refuse.

Myles proceeded to inspect the web. As he predicted, there was a web trail which led further south. "This'll take us right to its lair. Come on. We don't have much time to waste."

With the hunters goading their backs, Marshall and Kira reluctantly followed the doctor into the woods.

CHAPTER 25

Chris threw the sheets onto the floor. His heart raced and his bowels threatened to spill. He couldn't find those keys. The suspicion that they might actually be in Marshall's jeans pocket began to sink in. Unfortunately, he didn't know how to hotwire a truck. In fact, most of today's computer-run vehicles weren't capable of being hotwired as shown in the movies.

No. I cannot stay here.

Now his bladder taunted him. He hadn't emptied it since he sat at the fireplace last night. Before he and Laurie went into the woods. Its fullness started making itself obvious during the standoff and had only got worse since. Even when huddled in the bathroom, Chris was too terrified to relieve himself. But now, with the adrenaline coursing through him, it was either do it, or soak himself in his own filth.

He went into the bathroom. The window was open a crack. The cool air hit him as he unloaded, both things having a soothing effect on his psyche. He was still bound on stealing the truck and getting the hell out of here, but the few moments of levity allowed him to focus his mind. After finishing, he allowed himself another moment to breathe the cool air. The jitters didn't go away, but they settled enough for him to focus. He glanced out to the trees and to the side yard. So far, no sign of Marshall, Kira, or the hunters.

Time to resume the search. Upon returning to the bedroom, he immediately noticed the nightstand on the far left corner. Had his mind not been in such a frenzy, he'd have easily noticed the wallet, pocketknife, and truck keys right away.

"Oh, yes. YES!" He hopped over the bed, grabbed the keys, then went for the door. He briefly glanced at the mess he made, debating whether to hide the evidence of ransacking. *Nah. They're gonna know it was me as soon as they realize the truck's gone—if they ever come out of the woods.*

Chris bolted down the stairs, while sorting out the vast collection of keys in search of the truck's. He arrived at the main entrance, then slowly peered outside. Nothing was out here, save for the arachnoid. It was still on its back, frozen in its coiled pose. Its underbelly was a lighter color than the rest of it. The exterior almost resembled a crab shell, except for the brownish color. The hairs on its body were like syringe needles, and even appeared rigid enough to pierce skin. With its legs locked in position, the small claws at the end of each foot were visible. But the feature that Chris found himself gazing at the most was that stinger protruding from its rear. That abdomen was such an odd shape. It wasn't perfectly rounded like a regular spider. Then again, spiders don't have crab-like pincers either. It was almost as though this thing was meant to be something else, but turned into a spider instead. With those claws tucked close to its head, he couldn't help but think of scorpions. Then again, those pedipalps and long legs were definitely spiderlike, as well as the way its body was segmented. He'd seen dead spiders die in such a way. He'd spray them off of buildings and watch them stumble about, then fall over.

Landscaping. It was the closest thing to normalcy that he'd ever gotten, and even *that* wasn't entirely normal, considering he was lucky to get a couple of properties in a week. Now, he'd be lucky to land a job shoveling French fries.

He was still set on Canada. Finally, the practical questions were starting to loom. Would he even get past customs? What would he do once he was there? He didn't know anybody. He'd never even been there before.

Chris shook his head. *Worry about that later. Just get the hell out of here. ALL of those problems are better than getting arrested.*

He started for the truck, only to stop again. He watched the supposedly dead thing.

Was that leg always like that? The rear appendage…he had sworn it was perfectly coiled to the point its foot was touching the abdomen. Now, it seemed only half-coiled. And the pincers…he was certain they were shut. Now, one of them was half open.

"It's dead," he reminded himself. "Your mind's just fucking with you." Despite saying it out loud, he still found himself glancing over at the shotgun. He almost went for it, only to remember at the last moment that Marshall had the shells. The thing served no purpose except as a club.

Besides, it was dead anyway.

Chris completed several more steps. This time, he saw the motion. Several legs partially extended, while a few more coiled further. Both pincers were open now. Chris gasped and sprinted back to the cottage, then crouched behind the couch. After several seconds, he peeked out the window. The thing remained in that pose.

"It's dead. Just a muscular spasm. That happens to all dead things."

The thing twitched again, causing Chris to duck. Several seconds passed and he peeked again. Several legs were no longer coiled, rather they were bent perfectly at a ninety-degree angle, as though the creature was 'standing' upside down.

Chris watched for any movement, while simultaneously glancing at the truck which was several meters past it. So close, yet so far. And despite his efforts to convince himself otherwise, Chris did not feel safe crossing the yard.

****

"So, who the hell are you exactly?" Marshall asked. He clutched Kira's hand as they trekked through the woods. Myles kept pace only a few feet ahead of them, while Ethan and Bryce favored the rear.

Myles sniffed, his eyes fixed on their surroundings.

"It's a long story," he replied.

Marshall chuckled. "Of course it is. Quite the cliché as well, I might add. Is this the part where I say 'we have time'?"

Myles stopped and looked back at him. "Not much, actually. Once we locate the specimen's lair, we have a lot of work to do."

"You call it a specimen," Kira said. "So, you *did* engineer that thing?"

Myles sighed. Clearly, he wasn't avoiding the argument with these civilians. No matter. What was the harm in telling them? If everything worked out in the doctor's favor, they wouldn't get around to telling anyone. And even if somehow they did, who'd believe a story about a giant killer spider anyway?

"With my research, we are on the verge of developing vaccines that were unprecedented even a few years ago. There's so many secrets to uncover by studying the world of insects and arachnids. By pumping its body full of venoms from varying species, then extracting blood samples and those of its own venom, we can produce new medicines and cure diseases. Muscular dystrophy. Huntington's Disease. The Avian Flu. Schizophrenia. Autoimmune disorders. As well as all the anti-venoms that we can produce, which can be provided to countries in South America, Asia, Australia, and others."

"Wow," Marshall said. "With all of that passion, you almost had me fooled. Except, I'm not sure how extracting the blood from an overgrown bug can help cure Schizophrenia. I'm no scientist, but—"

"You're right. You are not a scientist," Myles snapped.

"I'm not stupid, either," Marshall said.

"There is a thing called common sense," Kira said. "How does creating an oversized hybrid help conduct these cures?"

"We need blood samples. Can't produce them from normal-sized species."

"See? You'd have me fooled, if the damn thing didn't have fucking *claws*," Kira said. "I've seen the *Jurassic Park* movies. I know how this goes. Never thought I'd be discussing it in a serious sense."

"Ain't that the truth?" Marshall added.

"It's obvious you've gene-spliced a spider with something else. I'm guessing a scorpion. How exactly does *that* help the vaccine development process?"

"It doesn't," Marshall said. He noticed Myles tilt his head toward him. There was anger in his eyes. "Yeah-yeah, I know. I'm not a scientist. Go ahead and hide behind that. Next, I'll get to hear the whole 'you're too stupid and uneducated to understand' spiel. Right?"

Kira gazed back at the hunters, then back at Myles as they followed the web trail southwest.

"I'd say there's a lot of money in store for you. Hence, you're funding this operation yourself," she said. Myles didn't respond. "Obviously, whatever corporation or government entity—or both, is behind this, they either don't know your pet is loose, or they're willing to write it off. I'm suspecting the former. Maybe you're on thin ice with them. Maybe you're the type who causes more trouble than you're worth. But one thing's for sure; if your financers were funding this operation, there'd be a dozen, if not *dozens* of hunters out in these woods. Just these two Vikings? Clearly, they're taking money from your pocket."

This time, Myles looked back. Kira tapped her finger to her temple. "Like we said. Common sense."

"I like this chick," Ethan said. Bryce elbowed him in the ribs.

Marshall's stomach tightened. Common sense was abound between him and Kira alright. They shared a glance, reading each other's thoughts as though telepathically linked. Both of them realized the danger they were in. There was no logical reason this scientist wanted to track down the net other than to destroy the evidence. Hence the container of butane strapped to his belt alongside his pouch. With that likely being the case, what would this doctor do with these witnesses? Why was he so intent on them tagging along?

Then again, there was another question. If they were planning to dispose of them, why not do it right here? Not like the doctor needed them to find the lair, since they apparently had a trail to follow. If he wanted to dispose of them, he could've done it back at the cottage. Or right here. They were far enough in the woods that they could hide the bodies. Or, hell, even submerge them in the lake. It brought something else to mind— that these hunters, while clearly not the nicest of people, might not be on board with murdering civilians.

"What's the doctor paying you, if I may ask?" Marshall said.

"Enough," Bryce said.

"Yeah? *Enough*? As in, not a tremendous amount, but *enough* for you to take the job?"

"Not your concern," Ethan said.

"Just curious," Marshall said. "Clearly, you've been hired for a once-in-a-lifetime hunt. I imagine the paycheck was serious. Hell, he probably paid *millions,* considering what he's likely getting, or going to get, from whoever's funding this."

"Since that thing killed our friends, I imagine the company will want to bribe us with big bucks to keep us quiet," Kira said. "Oh, wait! IS the company funding this? I suppose Dr. Bower here is considering a proposition." Inside, she was cringing. She hated using her friends as leverage, and in no way would she ever accept money from this crazy loon. But, as Marshall was doing, she needed to gauge their intent. If these people were intending to execute them, she and Marshall may as well take their chances and run into the forest.

When glancing back, she noticed that Ethan's eyes were locked on Myles. There was bitterness in his expression. Marshall might have touched on something when he mentioned the supposed top-dollar rate these people were being paid. Bryce didn't seem to care. Perhaps she just enjoyed the sport of hunting. But Ethan clearly needed some sort of financial incentive. Whatever he got, she suspected it was beneath his skill-set.

"Up ahead," Myles said. All eyes followed his finger. The doctor stopped in his tracks, pointing slightly to the right. A few hundred feet into the woods was a sheet of white, similar to the net near the road.

From a distance, it resembled a typical spider web from any common species. Only when they approached did Kira and Marshall notice oddities. There were large bags strung against the web, mostly near the upper corners. Some were bigger than others. Fur patches protruded through some of the threads.

"Looks like he's found lunch," Ethan said.

They arrived at the foot of the huge web. Tucked under the branches was an enormous funnel, like the mouth of a cave. The outside was pure white, save for some leaves that fell on the casing. The inside was grimier due to dirt and other residue carried by the creature.

But Kira wasn't looking at the funnel. Her eyes were locked on the cocoons. They were spaced out a couple of yards. The first one was a fox or coyote, judging by the brown paw that protruded through the cocoon threads. Next was the dried husk of a cougar. Its face was shrunken, its teeth looking three times too big for the cat's skull. Its eyes were shriveled, as there was no sign of moisture left in the animal.

Then there was the third bag. It was wrapped fairly tight, its cargo secured and hidden from view. Only after taking a few steps to the left did she finally see strands of brunette hair sticking from the top.

"Laurie!"

"Nothing you can do for her," Myles said. Ignoring him, Kira stepped to the web and reached for it.

"Wait!" Marshall said. He grabbed her by the shoulders and pulled her back.

"Let me go! We need to get her down."

"Don't touch that stuff," Marshall said.

"He's right," Myles said. "You'll stick right to it. Believe me, getting out of this web is no small feat." He removed his butane cannister, sparked a blue flame, then held it to the web. The threads lit up easily, the fire quickly climbing up the net. The web shook as some of its supports burnt away, causing the lower right section to wave freely after separating from the ground.

Marshall watched as the flame climbed...right toward the cocooned victims.

"Whoa! Doc! We need to control this flame. You'll burn her alive."

"She's already dead."

"We don't know that."

"Accept it."

"Accept *this*." Marshall slammed a fist into the doctor's left eye, knocking him to the ground. Myles landed right next to the burning web, instantly feeling the heat inches from his face. Shrieking, he rolled to the left. As he got to his hands and knees, Marshall and Kira were grabbing handfuls of dirt and launching it into the web, with limited effect.

The doctor scowled at the two hunters, who just stood watching. "You gonna do something?"

"Like what?" Ethan said. "You hired us to hunt your bug. I'm not your henchman."

"He thinks he's *Dr. Evil*," Bryce said. They both chuckled.

Marshall and Kira proceeded to dig through nearby debris, until they found a fallen tree a few yards out. They found a large branch near the trunk and returned to the web. Using it as a giant rod, they tore at the weak spots in the net. The wood clung instantly, seized by the glue-like substance coating the web. Using this to their advantage, they pulled back on the branch like a rope. The net waved toward them, unwilling to budge from place. Meanwhile, the lower right side continued to burn. The flames approached the cocoons.

"She's going to burn alive," Kira said.

Marshall tugged as hard as he could, but the net would not give. "Shit! This stuff is fucking strong."

"You'll never rip through it," Myles said. "My specimen produces the finest webbing. It's a material that even the likes of NASA might want to get their hands on."

Marshall closed his eyes. Clearly, this scientist held delusions of grandeur. Why was he surprised?

He looked to the ground, seeing the butane torch in the grass. He snatched it up and moved to the other corner of the web.

"What are you doing?" Kira said as she watched him light the web on fire. The flame quickly climbed up along the tree it was strung along.

"We can't cut it down, so all we can do is weaken it as best we can," Marshall said. They watched as the flame steadily grew, quickly burning through the threads. The web rippled as each anchor was severed. As they waited, Marshall scraped his boot along the ground, loosening as much soil as he could.

More anchors broke free on each side, leaving the web mainly attached at the upper points.

"Alright, pull now," he said. He and Kira tugged as hard as they could against the branch. The web stretched further and further, threatening to pull them back. Finally, something snapped. It wasn't the web, but the bark it was attached to. The whole right side came free, except for the funnel, which was now beginning to burn.

The burning web waved toward them, like a flag seized by enemy forces. As the fire on the left side continued to weaken the anchors, Marshall and Kira managed to pull it free, dropping the cocoons to the ground. They scooped up handfuls of the dirt Marshall had scraped up, extinguishing the flames nearest to Laurie.

Meanwhile, Myles watched. Might as well. These fools were making his work easier. The funnel was now a ball of fire, which was also beginning to consume the branches it was connected to.

"Careful. Don't touch her," Marshall said to Kira as they moved around to Laurie's face. Using a few twigs, he carefully pulled the threads away from her head, revealing a pale face, whose terrified expression revealed bared teeth and wide eyes.

"Laurie?" Kira said, tapping her friend's face. There was no response. Upon pulling more of the web free, Marshall noticed a red stain on her shirt near her collar bone. She had an injury there—some kind of puncture wound. He felt her skin. She was cold, somewhat dry.

"It was draining her blood," he said. He looked over at the shriveled cougar. Judging by the differences between the corpses, it seemed the arachnoid hadn't finished draining Laurie and was saving the leftovers for later. There was no pulse. Not even the slightest hint. The thing had drained too much, causing her to go into full cardiac arrest.

Kira welled up, then looked away. They jumped back as flaming pieces of the funnel began raining down around them. The creature's lair came apart, the flames dwindling over the scorched tree trunk and bark. The fire continued to burn, but showed no signs of spreading. The wood was somewhat moist thanks to a recent thunderstorm. When they looked back at the doctor, he was talking to the hunters. They were talking in low tones, as though not wanting to be heard. But Kira was good at listening, especially when she saw an amused expression, as well as signs of relief on the doctor's face. Myles clearly didn't want a forest fire—despite his idiotic methods of removing the nest. And by the way he was talking, he wanted something else removed. Rather, some*one* else.

Ethan was shaking his head. "You don't pay me enough for that, Doc."

"I can get the money," Myles whispered. Even Bryce was shaking her head.

"IF you can get the money, and that's a big 'if', Doc. We—" She stopped, realizing their conversation wasn't as discrete as intended.

It didn't take a genius to understand what the doctor was proposing. *Kill these witnesses and I'll give you a big bonus.* It didn't matter whether the hunters agreed to it. Kira wasn't going to wait around for them to be convinced. Nor was Marshall.

Together, they dashed north, back toward the property.

"Fuck! You see what you did?" Myles said. He started running after them. Ethan groaned. Whether he liked it or not, the situation had just got more complicated. If those people escaped and got the police involved, he and Bryce would be seen as an accessory to Dr. Bower's crimes. He never really considered that as a reality, probably due to his overwhelming desire to complete the job and go home.

They chased after the civilians. Running through thick woods was nothing these hunters weren't used to. It only took a few seconds for them to pass Myles. Marshall and Kira were a few dozen yards ahead. They were better conditioned for the chase than Myles, but not to the level as their pursuers. The fact that they looked back and changed course to the right indicated they were aware of this.

"Come on!" Marshall said. He held Kira's hand, leading her east toward the lake. If they could get to the dock, they could take the boat across the lake. They'd be on foot from that point on, but at least they'd have significant distance between themselves and the hunters.

"These people are insane," Kira said.

"This whole day is insane," Marshall said. He zipped to the left to avoid plowing into a tree. With the next step, his foot failed to lift off the ground. Marshall fell flat on his face like a domino, bouncing once off the ground.

Kira stopped and looked back. "Get up!" She rushed by his side and pulled on his shoulder. He tried standing up, but realized his foot would not move. It was as though it was bolted to the ground. He looked back and saw the white threads clinging to his boot. He had stepped onto a web trap set by the spider-thing. He pulled as hard as he could but to no avail.

"Kira, go. Get out of here."

"No. I'm not leaving without you."

It was too late anyway. Marshall saw the rifle muzzle pointing toward him. Ethan and Bryce had slowed to a walk. Both were chuckling at Marshall's predicament.

"Where do you think you're going?" Ethan said.

"Clearly nowhere," Bryce said. "Looks like a fly!"

A few moments later, Myles finally caught up to them.

"I could have warned you that this specimen likes to lay traps around its lair," he said with a laugh.

"Like you would've warned us of *anything*," Kira replied.

Myles tapped Ethan and Bryce on the shoulders, ready to continue their negotiations.

"Don't bother, Doc. I already told you—you don't pay me enough to do that."

"I'm not asking you to kill them," Myles said.

"Then what?" Bryce said.

"Subdue them. Hogtie them. I'll administer a non-lethal dose of sedative."

"And do *what* with them, exactly? Give them a memory wipe?" Bryce said.

"No."

"Toss them in the lake?" Ethan said. "If so. You do it yourself. I'm not paid—"

"Yes, yes, you're not paid enough. Blah, blah, blah," Myles said, rolling his eyes. "No, we'll take them with us to the lab. The specimen can take care of them. I'll cremate the remains. Nobody will even know."

Kira, seeing the slight change in the hunters' facial expressions, realized that the odds were getting worse in their favor. There was no getting this web off Marshall's foot by pure force.

Only thing that worked was fire. She dug into her pocket, pulled her cigarette lighter out, and slowly began burning away at the web. The threads coiled away like dead leaves, the silk turning black as the flame ate away at it.

"Hurry, Marshall whispered. He watched the conversation, which clearly was coming to an end.

Bryce and Ethan shared a glance, then looked back at the doc.

"It'll still cost you extra," Ethan said.

"I'll have to owe ya. Two-hundred grand?"

"Five."

"Done."

With the sudden swiftness of a praying mantis springing into action, Bryce threw herself at Kira, closing the distance in the span of a second. Kira landed a punch, but it seemed to skid off Bryce's jaw as she slammed her target to the ground. They were locked in combat for a brief moment, but Kira could not outmuscle the seasoned hunter.

Marshall leaned up, ready to spring at the huntress. A kick to the jaw by Ethan knocked him back to the ground.

Kira cried out as her arm was locked behind her back. Bryce rolled her to her stomach, pinning her arm back, while pressing her knee to her neck. Kira kicked and tossed, but could not free herself.

Bryce winked at Ethan, aroused by her triumph, regardless of the ease.

Marshall opened his eyes, having blacked out for a moment. He leaned up, his vision blurring. He could still hear Kira struggling. When his eyes cleared, he saw Myles kneeling down by his open briefcase. He reached in and pulled out a syringe.

"The hell are you doing?"

"Just relax," the doctor said. "You're about to feel as light as a feather. Soon, all of your problems will go away." He started toward Kira.

Marshall began to struggle, only to be flattened again. His chest felt as though it was compressing his heart as Ethan pressed his boot down on him.

"Don't fight it, son. This is my good leg."

"You're just gonna take a nap," Myles said. *Just don't be surprised if you're a little 'stiff' when you wake up.*

CHAPTER 26

It had been several minutes. So far, the creature hadn't moved at all. Chris started to wonder again if those movements were just muscular reflexes. If it was alive, it'd be moving a lot more. Right? He hated staring at the hideous thing, however it was the beacon of hope beyond it that kept his gaze. He had the keys. All he needed to do was hurry up, get out to that truck, and haul ass out of here.

It was calling to him like a spirit, tempting him to step out into the light. In that light was the shadow of death, which lay on its back, legs partly sprawled. Perhaps those were its last dying movements. Perhaps it was safe to go out.

Right then, it dawned on him that the hunters never returned with Marshall and Kira. Something about that raised the hairs on the back of his neck. Something was off about those people, and it scared him almost as much as the monstrosity in the yard.

He stood up. Just a few short yards, and he'd be free.

He opened the door. It didn't move. He cautiously took a step out. Still, it didn't more. A few more steps, and yet, it didn't move. He started finding his courage…for the most part. He still made sure to walk wide of the spider-thing. In doing so, he came near the prong he used to threaten Sue. Considering the insanity which occurred since, he had actually nearly forgotten that had taken place, despite how recent it was. Then again, he tried instantly to force it from his mind. The arachnoid's appearance only made that easier.

Chris picked up the prong and held it like a baseball bat. He had the common sense to know it wouldn't do him any good, but it made him feel better, nonetheless. He continued walking the semi-circle before finally reaching the front of the truck. He cleared the last few yards with a sprint.

Realizing he wouldn't get far with the trailer attached, he went around the bed. It took a minute of staring at the gooseneck connection for him to figure out how it all worked. First, he removed the electrical cable, then the chains from the hitch. He pulled a metal pin to remove the collar over the coupler. The rest was simple; crank the lever to lower the jack and lift the coupler off of the ball.

The lever creaked loudly. Chris suspected it needed some greasing. Or perhaps he was just cranking it too fast. He didn't think much of it regardless. Soon the jack would touch the ground and he would be out of here.

His eyes went back to the creature. He froze.

One of its legs was moving. It was slow—he had to stare for several seconds to make sure his eyes weren't playing tricks on him. It was the forward leg on the left side. It pawed at the air in an odd pulsating motion. Then he realized that the left arm had extended. The pedipalps were twitching.

Chris' hand, greased by his own sweat, nearly slipped off the lever. Nervous ticks rippled his neck, ribs, and left eyelid. The thing wasn't dead. It was alive—waking up from a slumber. He cranked the lever rapidly, lifting the coupler from the ball. With each cranking movement, the legs threshed more rapidly. The thing spun like a top, then extended all eight legs on its left side, pushing it over like a bottle cap.

Chris threw himself into the truck. In his hastiness, he tried flooring the accelerator before starting the ignition. He dug into his pocket. The damn keyring had caught on something. He pulled harder, ripping the fabric of his inner pocket, then plunged the newly freed key into the ignition.

All the familiar lights came on, only to vanish right away. Only the seatbelt sign flashed, concurrent to an aggravating *beep*. There was fifteen feet of space between Chris and the bug, with a couple of yards to his left for him to swing to make a wide U-turn. Turning the wheel to the left, he drove toward the trees, then turned back to make the maneuver. The creature stood in place, arms tucked beneath its pedipalps. It leaned back, its abdomen nearly touching the ground.

Chris lifted his middle finger to the window as he faced the truck to the driveway. "Too slow, motherfucker."

In the next instant, right as he began to apply pressure to floor the accelerator, the arachnoid sprang. To the human eye, it looked as though the creature simply teleported from the mid-yard to the hood of the truck. It landed with a mighty crash that shattered the windshield.

Chris yelled, his hands still clutching the steering wheel. Pincers tore at the windshield frames, easily bending the metal out.

Echoes of impact traveled through the trees as the truck smashed into the RV.

****

Myles jumped at the sound. He and the hunters turned to the north. That was clearly a vehicle crash and it was nearby.

"What the hell?"

"That came from the property," Ethan said.

Marshall watched the trio. In that moment, all three of them were looking to the north. He gauged the position and distances of all three, then turned his gaze toward the brute standing over him. That brace on his left leg—to require that kind of support had to result from some kind of painful injury.

No time to think about it.

Marshall raised his right knee to his chest, cocking his foot back like the arrow in a bow, then plowed it into Ethan's knee. The hunter let out a yelp and fell backward, hitting the ground like a sack of potatoes.

Marshall leapt to his feet and rushed toward the doctor. Myles turned in time to see him coming, but was too flabbergasted to react. A swat from Marshall's hand knocked the syringe from his grasp. A right hook broke his nose and a left loosened a crown.

As the doctor fell backward, Marshall spun toward Bryce. She stared wide-eyed, as she was in a tricky position. Let go of Kira, which would undoubtedly result in her joining the fight, or try to hang on to her while fending off the man.

Marshall made the decision for her. He threw a kick into her jaw, which launched her backward into a bed of bushes.

Bryce spat blood, flailing her arms to grab ahold of anything to pull herself up with. "You bastard! You prick!"

Marshall helped Kira to her feet. He didn't waste time with questions of 'are you okay?' It was time to run.

They fled to the north toward the cottage. The plan was the same: get to the boat and take it to the other end of the lake.

Ethan limped to his wife and pulled her to her feet.

"Let's go after them!" she said, spitting blood with each word. She rubbed her jaw. The bastard had struck her as though punting a football. NOW Myles would have had no trouble negotiating the extra deed of disposing of these witnesses.

"Wait! We need to check the specimen," Myles said. He stood up, bleeding from the mouth and nose.

"I thought you said your sedatives would have it out for several hours," Ethan said.

"I know, but—" They heard screams coming from the property. "Something's going on up there."

Ethan and Bryce couldn't deny that fact. The husband tightened one of the nylon straps to his brace, then loaded an arrow into his crossbow.

"Alright, let's go."

Bryce shouldered her crossbow in favor of her rifle. Ethan noticed her sneer. Before he could say anything, she darted north.

"Wait!"

She didn't listen. And even with his brace, Ethan would not be able to catch up with her. In her rage and overwhelming ego, she didn't care so much about the job as she did about getting even.

Cursing under his breath, Ethan ran after her. Marshall had hit him good, however. He hadn't limped this bad in several months.

****

"No! NO! NOOOOO!" Chris threw his hands over his face, his screams continuing until all the breath left his lungs. The claws cut through the top of the frame like scissors then pulled it apart. In a springing motion, they came through the widened space. Razor edged clamps seized Chris and pulled him out into the open.

Marshall and Kira ran into the yard, only to pause in utter shock as they watched the creature standing aboard the crumpled hood of the truck. In its grasp was Chris Kalb, who kicked and screamed while it raised him over its head. The beast scurried onto the ground, then lowered him under its belly.

Kira gasped as the abdomen folded, then winced at the sickening groan Chris made as the stinger entered his body.

"Come on," Marshall said. He took her hand and they ran to the dock.

The whistle of a bullet whizzing by made them stop in their tracks. Marshall looked to the right. Out of the woods came a maddened Bryce, hellbent on catching them.

They continued running to the boat.

Bryce, her jaw throbbing and her adrenaline pulsing, fired another shot. She was off her game, as the bullet once again whizzed by Marshall's head. However, there was an unmoving target she would easily hit which would prevent their escape. She rotated to the right, lined her sights with the outboard motor, and fired another shot. Lead struck metal, instantly resulting in the smell of gasoline.

Marshall and Kira stopped, having seen the sparks that spat from the motor. They stood at the shore. With woods to the north and south, water to the east, and a killer arachnoid on the west, they had nowhere to go.

"Your mother should've taught you to never hit a girl," Bryce said.

"She did, but she was referring to humans," Marshall replied.

Bryce smirked, then aimed her rifle. In the corner of her eye, she spotted movement. The thing WAS awake…and staring right at her. Finally, her ego subsided, and she reached for her crossbow.

As her hand touched the metal frame, the arachnoid sprang like a cricket. Bryce screamed. A wall of force drove her to the ground. For the second time in five minutes, she was flattened, only now it was by an overwhelming presence that she couldn't outmuscle. She saw pedipalps twitching over her face. They were both fleshy and hairy, covering an array of inner mouth parts that carried an odd stench.

Like hot breath, but worse.

She thrust the crossbow to fire it point blank. As soon as she did, it was yanked from her grasp, crushed in the pincers of the beast. It crumpled the weapon and tossed it to the side, then threw its claws over the human. Intense pressure closed over her upper arms, snapping the bones.

Ethan could hear his wife's agonizing screams as he neared the tree line. Despite the pain in his leg, he pressed on. As he arrived at the clearing, those screams turned into strained grunts, as though she was being strangled. The cottage was between him and the creature, forcing him to go around the front.

He arrived just in time to see his wife's stiffening body under the arachnoid's pulsing abdomen. It lifted the stinger from her hip and spun toward him. He aimed the crossbow and fired.

The arrow plunged into one of the pincers. The arachnoid scurried back from the sudden nerve flare. With its other claw, it yanked the arrow free and tossed it to the side, the tip spraying the second half of the vial into the grass.

Ethan fumbled for another arrow, but the arachnoid was already coming toward him.

"Fuck!"

He ran to the side, followed closely by Myles. The arachnoid bumped into the corner, partially subdued by the portion of sedative that made it into its body. It staggered to the side, granting just enough time for the hunter and scientist to reach the back door.

Ethan continued around the front, intent on getting his wife. Myles, on the other hand, was quick to dive into the house and lock the door behind him. As Ethan came around to the main yard, he paused, finding himself face-to-face with Marshall and Kira.

In Marshall's hand was a twelve-gauge shotgun, which he scooped up off the ground. Whether it was loaded, the hunter couldn't be sure. Nor did it matter. At the moment, he wasn't interested in them. He hurried past them toward Bryce. She was lying flat on her back, eyes open, and skin pale.

"Bryce!"

The arachnoid emerged from around the corner. Immediately, it stood over her, deliberately guarding its prize. It hissed and held its claws out, forcing the hunter back. He tossed the crossbow to the side, shouldered his rifle, and fired several shots into its face.

Those hisses turned into horrifying screams, not from a creature in pain, but an insanely pissed off predator.

Ethan heard the cottage door open. Reality struck him. He had a split second to get inside, or end up like these other victims. Only because of the arachnoid's sluggishness did he have any chance at all—and that would wear off quickly.

Baring teeth, he ran for the cottage. Marshall stood there, begrudgingly holding the door open. His mind was caught in the battle between human decency and his personal wish to feed the hunter to the bug.

No sooner had they locked the door did the window explode into the room. Pincers reached inside, coming within inches of Kira, who fell out of reach. The beast pressed its seven remaining eyes to the four-foot window, gazing at the four humans inside.

Marshall pressed a shell into his shotgun and fired. Fluid burst as the pellets ruptured two of its eyes, driving the creature away. It flipped over its back, its legs clawing at the air above.

"Into the stairway," he said.

"We should keep hitting it," Ethan said.

"No. It won't do any good. You'll never hit a central nerve," Myles said. He was the first to head up into the stairs. Ethan aimed his rifle defiantly. He was not about to let that thing get his wife.

The arachnoid righted itself, then scurried to the left out of view. A moment later, the west wall was shaking. Ethan looked to the kitchen window just in time to see the sun get blotted out by its bulk. By the time it passed over, he saw nothing but white. The shaking continued to the north wall. The creature passed over the broken window, a long strand of web stretching behind it. A thick white line remained dead center in the opening.

The entire building shook as it darted around the sides, passing by the window a second time. Now, two thick web lines blocked their way, soon to be joined by a third, fourth, fifth, tenth, hundredth, maybe even a thousandth.

Ethan snarled at the others. "We just gonna let it trap us in here?"

Marshall pointed at the window. "You wanna take your chance? Be my guest."

Ethan took a step toward the window, intent on doing just that. Common sense returned at the last second. He remembered how that web worked like instant glue. Even vehicles moving at full speed couldn't outdo its grasp. There was no way he'd get through that window now without getting caught.

"Either go for it, or get away from the windows," Marshall said. He loaded the remaining shells into the shotgun.

Ethan sneered, then marched to the stairway, his eyes looking possessed. Marshall nearly raised the shotgun, only to realize he was going for the doctor rather than him.

Myles backed up the steps, holding his hands up. "Mr. Fekete, I warned you of the risks—" He squealed as Ethan took him by the collar.

"You little weasel! You said that tranquilizer was good for *hours*!"

"I may have misjudged—" Ethan plowed a fist into his gut, doubling him over. He lifted him to his feet and slammed him against the wall. Myles was near the point of tears. "I thought it would work…" Ethan punched him again.

Kira clutched Marshall's hand. It was a seeking of comfort, while also a way of asking if he would intervene. Marshall wasn't sure if he should. A small, evil part of him enjoyed watching the doctor get what he deserved.

God, I hate being a good person.

He did, however, hesitate long enough to allow Ethan to plant a few more blows before stepping in.

"Alright, that's enough."

Ethan, still holding Myles by the collar, rammed a knee into his stomach for good measure, then let him drop onto the stairs. He looked at Marshall, seeing the muzzle of the shotgun pointed at him.

"You even have it in you?"

"Want to find out?"

Normally, Ethan would snigger at such a comment, but right now, his mind was on his wife. That fact was made painfully obvious by the way his eyes kept going to the broken window…which was now obscured by four strands of web.

"Looks like we're gonna be stuck here with each other," Kira said. "We gonna work together to get out of this, or should we have a shootout right here?"

Ethan inhaled deeply. He took that opportunity to kick Myles in the ribs. He looked back at Marshall then scoffed.

"Like you're gonna trust me."

"Damn right I won't," he said. "Unfortunately, though, I'm no murderer either. But don't think I won't blow your head off if you try any bullshit."

Ethan scoffed again, then nudged the doctor with his boot. "Why don't we send him out as an offering, seeing as he got us all in this mess?"

Marshall lowered the shotgun. "As tempting as it is…"

The four of them moved to the upper floor and huddled at the top steps, out of reach from any of the windows. All they could do for now was listen to the thing move all over the cottage, and imagine the white funnel of web that coated the outside.

CHAPTER 27

The ticking of the wall clock seemed louder than ever. Over two hours had passed, and not for one second did the thing outside not move. Most of the vibrations were now on the west side of the cottage. The arachnoid was still active, and judging by those movements, it was still weaving.

The bruises were finally starting to turn shades of purple, giving Myles' face a racoon appearance. He remained on the top step, leaning against the wall. Marshall and Kira stood above him, the former keeping his shotgun at the ready. He was feeling a bit easier than before; not once in the two-plus hours did Ethan give any indication of turning on them. It was clear that the hunter was more focused on their current predicament, and the condition of his wife, rather than neutralizing any witnesses.

Ethan spent the majority of the time pacing up and down the steps. The broken window was covered in white now. He stopped to feel the vibrations of movement. The creature was still on the west side, which granted him an opportunity to try peering out through the north window. Except, all he saw was white silk. It was so thick, he couldn't see outside. It was as though they were in some kind of tomb.

He groaned. When he last saw her, Bryce was somewhere to the right. Thanks to the blockage, he had no way of knowing whether she was still there or not.

Succumbing to emotion, he reached out to push the web aside, only for his fingertips to get caught in the web.

"Fuck!"

He tried pulling back, only to stretch the sheet of web into the house. Suddenly, he realized there were no more vibrations on the west. He froze. It wasn't coming toward him, but his mind's eye was quick to picture the arachnoid poised, watching the window, intent on striking at the trapped prey. No doubt *it* would be able to tear through the web.

"What's going on down there?" Marshall said.

"Nothing," Ethan replied. Marshall came down and saw the hunter caught in both a lie and a web. Ethan exhaled slowly. His first instinct was to tell Marshall to go fuck himself. *Not the time.*

"Nothing, huh?"

That first instinct nearly broke through. Again, Ethan held back.

"Shh!" He nudged his head to the left, signaling that the arachnoid may be aware of his presence. Marshall went to the fireplace, grabbed a box of matches, and sparked a flame. The match singed Ethan's fingertips, though it was nothing he couldn't handle. He pulled his hand free of the web then slowly backed away from the window.

He licked his fingertips then reached into his vest pocket for a cigar. "Hope you don't mind if I light one up, because I'm doing it." He chewed the end off and lit the tip. The smell of tobacco triggered Kira's need to smoke. Typically, she wasn't for filling her cottage with smoke, but considering her lost desire to ever return here, it didn't seem to matter. She lit one up, filling the upper floor with smoke.

"Too bad the booze is all outside," she said.

Ethan removed a flask from his side pocket. He took a whiff of the whiskey inside. Whiskey and cigars; typically, he'd used these as celebration, or for general relaxation at home. He never thought he'd actually need them to quell his nerves.

They could hear the thing moving again. It was still on the west side. What it was doing, the group had no way of knowing. Ethan was tempted to take his lighter and burn all this web down. Of course, that would result in the cottage going up in flames with them in it. Still, it took every ounce of self-control not to follow through on that. He *needed* to know what was happening outside. Where was Bryce?

Myles' phone went off. Ethan spun on his heel and saw the doctor glance at his screen.

"Third time that thing's gone off since we've been in here," Ethan said. "Seems like Jedlinsky's quite eager to get ahold of you." Myles silenced the phone and tucked it back into his pocket. He was still hunched forward, his ribs feeling as though they'd been hit with a sledgehammer.

"Who's Jedlinsky?" Kira asked. "Those the guys who hired you?"

"*He* hired me," Ethan said, pointing at Myles. "He works for some bullshit corporation. For now, at least."

"So, there *is* someone else behind this," Marshall said. "And clearly, they're willing to do anything necessary to get it into their lab."

"Including killing us," Kira added.

"At least these two are," Marshall said.

"Oh, we're doing this now, I see," Ethan said.

"Seriously, dude?" Marshall said. "You think I'm gonna just forget what happened out there in the woods? How you were about to kill us?"

Ethan shrugged. "I wasn't about to kill anyone. As far as I know, you were about to be given a sedative. Whatever would occur afterwards is beyond my control."

"Give me a break, you know *exactly* what he was going to do. You guys think that when you whisper to each other right in front of us that we don't know what you're talking about?"

"He just doesn't care," Kira said. "He's focused on the technicalities. *He* wasn't going to be the one to kill us, so he figures his conscience is clear."

"It is," Ethan said. He puffed on his cigar. Myles' phone rang again, bringing the conversation to a halt. "You gonna answer that, Doc?"

Myles simply silenced it again.

"Maybe he should. Perhaps they'll send someone," Kira said.

Marshall sniggered. "You really want them *sending* people here? You see what their contractors are capable of."

"Doesn't change the fact that we're stuck here," Kira said.

Marshall shook his head. "No. It's bad enough that we have to deal with the spider. We barely got away from these guys. If we get this Jedlinsky Corporation, or whatever it's called, involved, we might as well blow our own brains out. And judging by his expression," he pointed at an uneasy looking Ethan, "he doesn't want them involved either. They probably don't even know you're out here hunting the thing, do they?"

"They don't even know it's loose," Ethan said. "Though, they might start having their suspicions by now. Who knows what the lab security has reported to them?"

Kira checked the windows along the upper floors. "This thing has cocooned this whole cottage." She stood over Myles. "What's its plan? Trap us in here and hope we eventually come out?"

"Yes," Myles said. "While it's capable of quick bursts of speed, it prefers to lay traps, such as the one your man found himself in. It was probably stalking your group since yesterday. During the night, it blocked the driveway and laid various pieces of webbing along the ground in case any of you would wander off."

"You almost seem proud of it," Marshall said.

Myles shrugged. "I created it. Surely, I can't help but find it remarkable how it's learned to adapt to this environment."

"How long has it been since I kicked your ass, Doc?" Ethan said. Myles stood up, alarmed once again. "Good. I see I have your attention. Now answer me this: docs its venom wear off?"

Myles swallowed. "I believe that, once it enters the circulatory system, it shuts down all major organs…"

"You're lying, Doc. You think I don't know what you did to that guy on the side of the road?"

Marshall and Kira glanced back and forth at the two strangers. *What guy? What did Myles do? Side of the road?*

"He was dead," Myles muttered.

"I felt a pulse. I know what you did. Apply a quick overdose of sedative and suddenly you have one less loose end," Ethan said. He marched up the steps. Myles backed up, only to trip on the last step. Ethan stood over him and grabbed him by the collar. For the second time, he lifted him up and slammed him hard against the wall. The red tip of the cigar touched the edge of Myles' nose, scorching him. "Tell me now: does that venom wear off?"

Myles looked over to Kira and Marshall. They weren't coming to his rescue this time, as they wanted to know as well.

Ethan reached for his Bowie knife, while pressing his entire left forearm to the doctor's collar, keeping him pinned to the wall. He pressed the tip to Myles' leg.

"Perhaps you should experience having a significant amount of tissue removed."

"Alright!" Myles said. Ethan dropped him. The doctor fell on his rear, then caught his breath. Ethan kept the blade inches from his face, deliberately keeping his threat relevant. "I can't say for sure. None of its victims survived long enough to experience withdrawal."

"But there have been signs," Ethan said.

"Yes. *Signs.* But the specimen fed on each subject before that could happen. And as far as I know, they'd be as good as dead anyway because of the germs and bacteria infecting the wound."

Ethan didn't hear anything beyond the word 'Yes'. He quickly marched down the steps and went to all of the windows as well as the back door. There *had* to be a way out.

Marshall entered the hallway, just in time to see Ethan clutching the backdoor handle.

"Don't open that!"

He did, and found a wall of web clinging to the door. It was several inches thick at least, granting no view to the outside. Ethan slammed the door shut and backed away.

The tapping of legs reverberated along the house.

Ethan gripped his rifle and looked up at the ceiling. "What's it doing?"

Before Marshall could think of an answer, the white curtain near the window stretched inward. One of the pincers broke through the treads. Like the head of a python, it reached inside and snapped.

"Mother of Christ!" Marshall said, backing into the hall. Kira rushed into the stairway, where Myles was already cowering.

The pincer snapped like crocodile jaws, seizing nothing but air. Ethan aimed his rifle, but refrained from squeezing the trigger. What good would wasting bullets on this appendage do, especially with the shell so durable?

The claw scraped the floor, dragging the rug toward the furniture. As it came up, it scraped one of the cushions, lifting it upward. With rapid speed, the other claw burst into the house, seizing what the arachnoid believed to be prey. It dragged the cushion out through the window, leaving a small gap between the threads.

They could hear the tearing of fabric. The beast quickly learned that the item was not food and tossed it away. The wall shuttered. Legs tapped the sidings as the creature began to scale the cottage.

Ethan peered through the tear in the webbing, focusing on the area where Bryce went down. "She's not there." He wanted to pound the wall. He looked up at the ceiling. "Come on back, you motherfucker. I've got something for you."

Marshall raised a hand. "Shh!"

"Give me a break. You might wanna stay here the rest of your life; not me, son."

"Don't call me your son. And shut up. You'll draw it back in."

"Good. Maybe we can set a trap of our own," Ethan said.

"We're more likely to get ourselves killed."

Ethan nearly spat his cigar. "Hate to break it to you, but we're gonna have to do *something*. It knows we're in here. It's just waiting to starve us out."

"Except we can't see it. We have no way of knowing its exact position. All we can do is listen for it, which only does so much good." Marshall's brow wrinkled. He listened intently. There was sound of movement outside, yet, it didn't seem the creature was on the building any longer. Yet, there was no sound of it climbing down to the ground. If it leapt, they definitely would've heard the landing.

"What's on your mind?" Kira asked.

"We need a visual," Marshall said. "We need to know what the conditions are outside. Fekete's right; we can't just sit here. But it won't do us any good to escape if we just run into whatever traps it has lain out there."

Ethan tried looking through the webbing again. "I can't see much through here. But from what I *can* see, the yard seems fairly normal."

"We won't outrun it," Myles said.

"No. And we don't have any more vehicles," Kira said. "Keep in mind, when we get out of here, we're gonna be on foot."

Marshall tried peering through the window. As Ethan stated, there wasn't much he could see.

"Let's go upstairs. There are smaller windows we can use. We'll try to cut a viewing hole through there. If it tries to come after us, it'll have less space to reach."

"You're wasting your time," Myles said. "That thing busted through steel-locked doors. It'll rip right through that wall if it wanted to. It just needs to *know* it can."

Ethan drew his Bowie knife and started up the steps. Myles remained crouched in the corner of the upstairs hallway, his arms wrapped around his stomach. Though he trembled, he didn't try to flee. Perhaps he was finally numb to the events taking place around him. Maybe he knew what his future held, and being shot or impaled by a Bowie knife was favorable. The hunter pointed the blade at his nose, warning him to keep quiet, then proceeded down the hall.

He entered the guest bedroom. The windows were blocked by thick webbing. He opened the inner window and cut through the screen on the other side, stopping every few moments to listen for movement. The web vibrated, as though receiving ripples from several meters away.

With the window open, he slowly stuck his blade out. Instantly the web clung. Still, he proceeded to saw away at it. With each thrust, the blade became more entangled.

"Fuck." He knew the web was strong, but he figured he'd at least manage to cut a small gap. He couldn't even get *that*.

The web wobbled. Suddenly, like the shoreline receding in the wake of a tsunami, the web tugged backward. A huge shadow overtook the window.

Ethan threw himself backward as one of the pincers punched through the opening he'd created. It snapped shut, nearly seizing his foot. Ethan scurried backwards on his elbows and heels until he collided with the nightstand. The claw splintered the frames as it reached further into the room. Like the head of a hydra, it whipped back and forth, snapping at the air.

Marshall and Kira rushed in and stopped inside the doorway. Ethan had his revolver drawn and was about to shoot. Before he could squeeze the trigger, the claw retracted, leaving a wobbling wall of web.

"Son of a bitch," Ethan said. He stood up, then shuddered from a pain in his injured leg.

"You alright?" Marshall said.

"Nothing I'm not used to." Ethan stood straight. "That bastard's not letting up." He approached the window with caution. The knife dangled inside the window, still caught by several silk strands. He tried to see through the webbing, but even after the ruckus, it was too thick. "I'd say the web's thickest over here."

Marshall looked. "It must've weaved a curtain between the trees near the corner. That's probably where it made its new funnel."

"Might also be where it's holding Bryce," Ethan said. His hand tightened around the knife handle. He drew his lighter and ran a flame along the blade, freeing it from the silk. "I swear, I'm gonna push this blade into its brain, then watch its body roast."

His foot bumped something as he stepped away from the window. He saw the step ladder, then looked up at the stained ceiling tile.

"Oh, shit," Marshall said.

Ethan scoffed. "All this shit happening now, and you're worried about *mold*?"

"No…the roof…" Marshall said. "There's almost nothing but tarp right above where you're standing. If that thing reaches through…"

Ethan was the first one out of the room. Only when he neared the door did he stop and look back at the window. He *needed* to know what was happening outside. It was as though the arachnoid was deliberately toying with his psyche. Not knowing Bryce's condition was worse than anything. His imagination was going nuts, especially after remembering those shriveled corpses in the webs.

"What the hell's it doing? Why isn't it coming after us? It knows we're in here," he said.

"Almost sounds like you *want* it to," Marshall said.

Ethan slipped the Bowie knife back into its sheath. "I kinda do, actually. Instead, it's fumbling around out there."

"It's preoccupied," Myles said.

This time, Ethan *did* spit his cigar. He moved along the hallway and stood over the scientist.

"If that thing harms one hair on my wife…"

Myles looked up at the hunter. "I informed you of what we were up against. You were well aware of the risks…"

A boot cracked his jaw. Myles sprawled onto the floor. He rolled to his left and spat blood and a crown onto the carpet. He moaned, watched the room spin, then slipped into unconsciousness.

Ethan looked back at Kira, who stood with an odd expression of bewilderment mixed with satisfaction. Mostly, though, it was bewilderment—as with most normal people, she wasn't used to such violence.

"Sorry 'bout the mess."

Kira shrugged. "Doesn't matter. I don't think I'll be keeping the place. If I walk out of here, that is."

"Ha! Way I see it, it's already no longer yours. That thing out there has already claimed it. A nice, warm spot where it can relax and… 'warm'…" He thought of the chamber Myles had built for it at the lab. The artificial hot springs, giving away heat and moisture.

Suddenly, he was very much aware of the furnace and the heat coming in through the vents.

"It's not just trapping us here. It's setting up house."

"Well, no shit. We burnt its other lair," Kira said.

"No, no...that's why it set up camp at that other guy's residence..." Now, Kira's expression was all bewilderment. "That was before my involvement in all of this. Point is, it attacked another house a little ways south of here. It made a nest there, and it totally makes sense why. It's the heat."

"Not much heat to get from a simple furnace. The bug's still outside," Kira said.

"Helps a little when you have busted windows letting the heat out," Ethan said. He looked down at Myles. "He was worried about the lower temperatures outside. Makes me wonder."

"Wonder about what?"

"About what details he 'forgot' to address regarding this thing."

CHAPTER 28

For the next hour, they remained huddled in the hallway, only leaving to use the downstairs restroom, which had no window. Myles was still unconscious. Kira and Marshall sat in the middle, the former keeping her lover's arm wrapped around her shoulder.

They kept a watchful eye on the hunter, who stood at the far wall. At this point, they weren't worried so much about him turning on them. It was clear that all he could think of was his wife. However, they were worried about him doing something rash, such as try to draw the creature in for some kind of last-stand.

The way Ethan kept his ear to the wall didn't help quell those concerns.

He'd spent most of the last hour listening for movement. The creature outside remained silent. There was no clicking on the walls, no shaking from its weight. And there was no vibration from the web that they could see. Was it asleep? Was it waiting and watching for them to try and make an escape?

Ethan's blood pressure was high. He kept glancing at the windows, furious that he couldn't see what was happening outside.

Does this thing understand psychological warfare? Is that what it's doing?

He heard Marshall stand up.

"Knees are starting to cramp," he said to Kira.

"Mine too," she said, standing up as well. They approached Ethan. "Any idea what it's doing?"

He shook its head. "The only way we're getting out of here is if we make the first move."

"I understand. But our options are limited," Marshall said. "We need to do something to drive the creature away if we're gonna escape."

"You said it's attracted by the heat. What if we turned it off?" Kira said.

Ethan shook his head. "I doubt that'll do anything at this point. It's already made its web. The only reason it'll leave is to set new traps."

"Can't stay, can't outrun it—kind of leaves us with no other choice. We have to *kill* it."

"Now you're speaking my language," Ethan said.

"Maybe not so much," she replied. "Bullets don't do much. We're out of those arrows you brought. And no way am I getting up close to stick a syringe from the doctor's briefcase into it."

"Wait..." Marshall said.

Kira chuckled. "Hey, if you want to try, be my guest."

"Obviously, I'm not gonna put on my rubber gloves and ask it to pull up its sleeve," Marshall replied. "But what if we tried something else? Like make a spear? We have broom handles in the storage room. We could use duct tape and strap a syringe to the end. That'll give us a little extra reach if it makes a move."

Kira nodded. "Still sounds a bit risky to me. BUT...if it works, and we manage to stick the syringe in a joint or in its mouth parts, we might be able to slow it down. Or hell, maybe even knock it out entirely. Won't last long, but it'll grant enough time for us to kill it for good."

"I'm sure it burns just as well as its web," Ethan said. Obviously, he approved.

Kira took a breath. "I can't believe I'm suggesting this, but...we know it'll attack if we disturb the web. We could try to draw it near and have it reach inside like it's been doing. One of us could act as the bait and use noise to give it something to snap at, while you guys try to stick the syringes."

"That's a tough call," Marshall said. "I doubt those needles will pierce the shell. We'll have to go for the joints. Chitin, I think it's called. The needles should penetrate that. Still won't be easy. We've seen how those arms lash about."

"So, we give it something to grab ahold to," Ethan said. He glanced over at the doctor.

"As tempting as that is, no," Marshall said. "That said, the overall idea is right. We need something that the bug will *think* is food. It thought it had something when it yanked the cushion from the sofa."

"We'll need something a little more convincing than a cushion or a pillow," Ethan said.

"I got spare boat oars in the storage room," Kira said. "I could get its attention with one of those. Let it clamp down on it. I can probably play tug-of-war long enough to keep its arm outstretched and allow you guys to stick the needles."

"Kira, that's risky," Marshall said.

"If it overpowers me, I'll just let go. Simple as that," she said.

"What if it grabs the oar and realizes it's not food? It's not like the thing has a texture like flesh," Marshall said.

"If it's moving, the bastard will think it's food," Ethan said. Marshall sighed. He hated the thought of deliberately putting themselves, especially Kira, in harm's way. But there was no escaping the reality of their predicament. Waiting for the thing to go away was no option.

"Fine by me. Let's get started." Kira hurried down the steps and went to the storage room. Marshall and Ethan were right behind her, keeping their weapons pointed at the windows.

"Don't make too much noise there," Marshall said. "Don't want to draw it in too soon."

"Stop worrying, babe," she replied. She handed one of the boat oars to Marshall, who slung his shotgun over his shoulder and took it. As she handed him the second, her foot tapped the gas can.

"Holy shit. You've had this in here the whole time?"

"What did you expect us to do with it?"

"Oh, I don't know. Spray the thing with it and light it on fire, maybe?" Ethan said.

"And burn the whole cottage down in the process? Besides, it's not like we have a flare gun to shoot it with," Marshall said.

"Fair enough. Still, it'll come in handy if we manage to knock that sucker out," Ethan said. "How much gas is in there?"

"About a gallon-and-a-half," Kira said.

"Good enough for me," Ethan said. He took the can and went back upstairs. Kira and Marshall followed, making sure to grab the doctor's briefcase along the way.

They began setting up their operation in the guest bedroom. Marshall strapped the syringes to a couple of broom handles, turning them into syringe spears. With several layers of duct tape, the syringes were tightly secured, ready to plunge into their target.

"With a little luck, it might put its face to the window and we can stick it in the eye," Marshall said.

"Whatever happens, make sure you're on target. I don't want to fuck with this thing any longer than I have to," Kira said. She was starting to feel wobbly. Her mind was starting to grasp the intensity of what they were going to attempt. The last-second urge to abort started to seep in.

She closed her eyes, took a breath, then lifted one of the boat oars.

"You alright?" Marshall asked.

"Yes. I think—"

Marshall could sense the apprehension. "If you want us to try something else—"

"Oh, give me a break," Ethan said.

"Shut up, man. We're not big game hunters. Give her a break."

"I'm fine," Kira said. "I just don't want to be strung up in that web. Just looking at it fucks with the mind."

Marshall leaned toward her. "Let's do this right. Once we get out of here, we'll plan a trip somewhere a little different. Don't know about you, but I haven't been to the beach in forever."

Kira managed to smile. "I don't know. With our luck, we'll probably run into a giant shark."

"Then we'll try a ski resort," Marshall said.

Ethan was staring at the ceiling. "Is the lovey-dovey routine all done? If you haven't forgotten, I'd like to kill this thing and find *my* wife."

Regardless of his feelings about the hunters, Marshall couldn't deny the logic behind his vehemence. They both stepped by the window.

"Ready?" he asked Kira. She nodded. He looked at Ethan, who also nodded and held his spear poised at the shoulder. "Alright. Go for the window. Be ready to back off right away."

Kira inched toward the window. One hand gripped the oar by the back handle, with another gripping the midsection. She held it like a lance, ready to jab it through the web. Apprehension seized her. Images of Laurie's dead, white face flashed in her mind. Her imagination took hold, envisioning Tyler and Sue cocooned in its web.

She stopped, the oar wiggling in her grip. She could see Ethan scowling in her peripheral vision.

"As soon as that web moves, just back away," Marshall said. "We'll take it from there."

Gritting teeth, Kira extended the oar through the window. The web wiggled. It was caught on the edge of the oar, just enough to secure the object, but lightly enough to grant her range of motion. She pulled it back into the room. The web shook.

She paused, waiting for any signs of the creature's advancement. The web was still. Perhaps she wasn't creating enough vibration. She thrust the oar out again, then pulled back. The web rippled.

"Come on! Where are you?"

Marshall, too, felt the anticipation. He could feel his palms sweating, threatening his grip on the broom handle. Across from him, Ethan stood motionless as a statue. Despite his confident demeanor, he was quickly losing patience. He thrust his elbow into the wall.

"Come on, *Charlotte*. We've got something for ya."

The doctor awoke with a splitting headache and a swollen jaw. The first thing he felt, other than the pain, was the taste of dried blood in his mouth. It took a few moments for him to remember where he was. The floor was hardwood, the walls lined with fishing and hunting memorabilia.

All the recent memories returned in one huge flash. After realizing that he was still stuck in a cocooned cottage, he noticed that the others were not in the hallway with him anymore.

An odd drumming sound reverberated from one of the other rooms. The doctor stood up on wobbly legs and moved down the hall. He turned the bend with caution then approached the guest bedroom. He peered inside. Through hazy vision, he saw his three companions at the window with broom handles and boat oars. They weren't using their firearms. In fact, Ethan's rifle was strung over his shoulder, and Marshall didn't have his at all.

The hunter was thumping the window, while the woman was thrashing an oar against the web outside. They were trying to attract the specimen. Their attention was so heavily fixed on the window, they didn't even notice him watching. Knowing Ethan, that would change in a few seconds.

As the haziness subsided, he examined the rest of the room. His briefcase was on the floor near the door. Just beyond that was Marshall's shotgun, propped on the wall near the bed. At the rear of the bed was a gas can.

Immediately, he saw an opportunity. He could get rid of these witnesses and disguise it as a simple fire accident, which would burn all traces of the spider web.

Looking back at the case, he realized a couple of syringes were missing. Only then did it finally register what they were trying to attempt.

Interesting. A longshot, but a good idea nonetheless under the circumstances.

If only they had their damn crossbows. Hell, even just the arrows. It would at least improve their odds.

"I feel something," Kira announced.

"The bug?" Ethan asked.

"No, the *Force*. OF COURSE the fucking bug!"

The web was wobbling intensely and stretching outward. The side of the siding creaked as the web tugged against it. A large mass was nearing the window.

"Get ready. Kira, as soon as it reaches, pull back as hard as you can. If you feel it overpowering you, let go," Marshall said.

A shadow overtook the white background. Like a bolt of lightning, the pincer lunged through the window and clamped down on the oar. Kira screamed, nearly losing her grasp due to sheer fright. Still, she managed to hold on. She pulled back as hard as she could. The bug, not anticipating the motion, slipped its arm further into the room.

Marshall went to the pincer. He could barely see the chitin joints connecting the claw. They were so narrow, it was hard to line the needle with them, especially with the claw whipping back and forth to free the oar. They needed the elbow joint.

"Bring it in more!"

Kira pulled, but couldn't outmuscle the beast. The arm pulled back. She dug her heels into the floor, only to feel them skid against the carpet.

"I can't!"

Marshall felt as though his heart was about to sink through his ribcage. They were so close to success, yet, were even closer to failure. He had to act fast.

"Ethan!" He tossed his spear to the hunter then ran to Kira's aid. Together, they tugged on the oar. Man and beast were at a standstill, the object of possession trembling from their tug-of-war. Without good leverage, the arachnoid began to slip further into the room.

Ethan couldn't believe it. He could almost see its elbow. This absurd plan might actually work. He leaned in, syringe raised back, the other leaning against the wall, ready to be snatched.

He noticed movement in his peripheral vision. The doctor was standing there by the doorway, watching. Not only watching, but nudging closer to the bed.

Not the bed...

The *shotgun*!

"Ethan! What are you doing?" Marshall said.

The hunter looked down at the arm. The elbow was exposed, revealing three inches of chitin. He brought the syringe down on the target. The syringe pierced the arachnoid, immediately injecting several milliliters of sedative into its system.

He grabbed the other spear and raised it high. Before he could strike, the arm retracted, scraping the syringe from its elbow. The web shook and the shadow disappeared.

"Ah, damn it to hell!" Ethan said. He checked the syringe. "Goddamnit. It only got about two-thirds. Not enough."

"Then we need to try again," Marshall said. They noticed Ethan dropping the spear and suddenly going for his revolver.

"Ah-ah!"

All eyes turned to the doctor, who was now pointing the shotgun across the bed at Kira.

"You son of a bitch!" Marshall said.

Myles grinned. "Ethan, knock them out and tie them up."

Ethan cocked an eyebrow. "Doc? Did I hit you a little *too* hard? What makes you think our arrangement is still valid?"

"You accepted the money..."

"Proof that a doctorate doesn't make you smart, *right here*, ladies and gentlemen."

The shotgun muzzle was starting to tremble in the doctor's hands. His eyes went off the civilians to the hunter. "You're up to your shoulders in this, right along with me. You think these people will simply forget you chased them down and were willing to feed them to the specimen?"

Ethan shrugged. "That was then. This is now. Situation has changed."

"Not really," Myles said. "One way or another, we have to catch that thing. If we can tranq it, we can still resolve the issue, AND you'll get paid that bonus I promised."

"After all of this, I'm getting paid that regardless, Doc," Ethan said. "Consider it hazard pay. And believe me, if we make it out alive, I'll BEAT the money out of you."

Myles froze. "You're seriously doing this? You know they'll report you."

"Let them," Ethan said.

"They know who you are. They know your NAME. *Ethan Fekete*."

"Not my real name, genius. What? You think I'm *that* stupid?"

Myles' attempt to hide his dismay failed. For a split second, he considered turning the gun on Ethan. Common sense vetoed that idea. Myles knew that Ethan's draw would beat him to the punch. Still, he didn't want to lower the weapon and lose his leverage.

"We don't have much time. Let's lure it back and tranq it," Myles said.

"Stop negotiating, Doc," Ethan said. "Ironically, the people you're pointing that thing at refused to let me use *you* as bait. They might have a change of heart if you don't put that down."

"I need that specimen. *Alive*," Myles said.

Ethan scoffed. "Trapped in a cocooned building, on the verge of getting eaten alive, and you're STILL more scared of Jedlinsky. How many calls did you miss while you were napping?" The muzzle wavered more. Ethan smiled. "Hell, he's probably got people out looking for you right now."

"I'll do it," Myles said. "I'll blow their heads off."

"No you won't."

"You wanna test me?"

"That's cute," Ethan said. "You squeeze that trigger, two things will happen: I'll put a bullet in each of your kneecaps and use you as bait for that thing out there. But before that happens, and more hilariously, by the way you're aiming that shotgun from the hip, it'll go flying out of your hands as soon as you squeeze the trigger. Clearly, you've watched too many old movies."

Myles tucked his chin, just enough to eye the way he held the weapon. In that moment, Ethan drew his revolver and pointed it at his head. Myles shuddered, watching the muzzle with wide eyes. Once again, he had lost.

The four of them stood motionless.

"What's it gonna be?" Ethan said.

Myles' teeth were chattering. His whole body was jittering. It was like he was caught in an earthquake. He even thought he could hear creaking down the halls, which added to the illusion.

Then he noticed Ethan's expression. He wasn't looking at the doctor, but *past* him. Same with Marshall and Kira.

That creaking… it wasn't creaking, but tapping, like pencils drumming on a workbench. They could hear it all along the walls and floor.

Myles turned around. A shadow overtook the doorway, then broke apart, as it was not cast by one figure, but many. He shrieked and stumbled backward as the first of many spiderlings entered the room.

They were just like their mother, only two-feet in length with a meter-long leg-span. One became two. Two became four. In seconds, they were crowding the door.

Myles fired blindly.

As predicted by Ethan, the shotgun flung out of his grasp, the muzzle striking him in the mouth. He fell over the bed, spitting blood from a second loosened tooth.

The blast miraculously caught one of the spiderlings dead center, exploding its legs and arms from the center-right frame where it climbed. The others scurried in. The first was struck by a .357 caliber round from Ethan's revolver. He aimed high and shot another, dropping it from the ceiling.

As he fired a third, Marshall leaped over the bed, grabbing the shotgun from the doctor. He pumped it, then fired into the doorway. Pieces of arachnoid splattered across the floor and wall. They could hear the drumming of little legs in the hallway.

"Christ!" Ethan exclaimed. He fired his remaining rounds, then unslung his rifle. With only a three-shot capacity, he had to aim with precision.

Loud *cracks* rang their ears. Kira squinted, her head pounding from the deafening gunfire. Cupping her hands over her ears, she was helpless to do anything but stand back.

The spiderlings were small, but fast. Only due to the narrowness of the doorway were Marshall and Ethan able to successfully land so many shots. But ammo was limited and dwindling fast. Already, Ethan was down to his last round, and Marshall's shotgun had a couple at most.

Still, the bastards kept coming.

Fear gripped Kira. She clutched the mattress, wrinkling the bedsheet. The room was hot, smelling of burnt gunpowder and bug innards.

Heat…

Kira looked down at the sheets, then stood up on her toes to see the gas can at the rear of the bed. Ethan stood right beside it, firing his last round into the crowd of invaders. He dropped the weapon and began loading his revolver.

Right behind him were the broom handles.

Kira lunged for the nearest one, snatching it off the floor, then grabbed the gas can. She brought them to the far end of the room, then proceeded to wrap the newly torn strip of mattress sheet around the duct tape, carefully avoiding the needle.

She poured gas over it then dug through her pockets for her lighter. She struck a flame, lit the torch, then started to move around the bed, only to stop at the sudden shaking of the web outside the window.

The spiderling's legs coiled around the bottom frame, pulling it through. It turned, pointing its eight eyes at Ethan's back.

"Look out!"

He turned around. "Shit!"

The thing sprang. Legs clawed his face and neck. Pedipalps twitched inches from his eyes. A pincer closed over his right cheek.

Ethan spun back, dropping the revolver in favor of his Bowie knife. "Fuck you! Motherfucker! Get the fuck off me!" He hacked at the bug, lacerating its abdomen and severing multiple legs. Still, it held on.

The stinger protruded from its abdomen, which tilted inward like a bee. The spiderling plunged, drawing a scream from the hunter. Pain and adrenaline multiplied his strength. He pried the thing off of him, the closed claw peeling a ribbon of flesh from his cheek. He threw it to the floor, pinned its abdomen with his boot, then rammed the knife through its head. He twisted and turned, drawing green watery fluid.

His increased physicality disappeared as quickly as it arrived. He could feel his chest and shoulders tightening, as though all the moisture had been drained from him in an instant. It was a feeling similar to dehydration combined with the stiffness of a strenuous workout, only much worse.

Kira watched him fall to his knees. Immediately, another spiderling arrived at the window. She rushed toward it and thrust the torch at it. The flame struck its forelegs, igniting the small hairs. Flailing its limbs, the arachnoid fell backward, getting tangled in its own mother's web.

Fighting against the stiffness, Ethan grabbed the revolver then pulled himself to his feet. He fell against the window, pointed the revolver, and blasted a round through the spiderling's abdomen.

Immediately after, he vomited.

She heard Marshall fire his last shotgun blast. She turned to the doorway, seeing severed legs fly from the exploded body and strike the wall. More spiderlings started scurrying in through the doorway. Once again, Kira felt the natural pullback from fear. The first step was the hardest. It was as though she had to break through a wall to finally charge the spiders.

She struck the nearest one with the torch, the gas-soaked end singeing it. The burning arachnoid scurried back into the hall, causing a frenzy among the four surviving brethren.

They hissed and clawed at her as she drove them back with the torch. Waving it back and forth, she kept them at bay, providing Marshall enough time to tear one of the pillowcases free and soak half of it with gas. He lit it on fire then, holding it by the good end, shook it like a rug at the arachnoids. The flame struck two of them at once, singeing them. With their faces smoldering, they backed away, while the others proceeded to retreat.

Kira brought her torch down like a spear, plunging the needle through the eye of one of the already burning arachnoids. The sedative took instant effect, allowing the bug to slumber through its slow-burning death. Swinging the torch like a gulf club, she knocked the other down the hall. The strip of fabric burnt away, leaving behind a simple broom handle.

The burning spider rolled on its back, its legs curling over its body. Two others remained by the stairs, unwilling to abandon their blood supplies. Kira spun on her heel, seeing Ethan crouched by the window. Myles was standing up off the bed, still dazed from being hit. On the floor between them was the revolver. She rushed back into the room and with a wild swing, she broke the already-cracked handle over the doctor's forehead, knocking him back down. She grabbed the revolver then ran back into the hallway.

It had been a while since she had fired a handgun of this caliber. She checked the cylinder. Three rounds. She closed it, took aim at an arachnoid on the ceiling, then fired. The kickback nearly sent the weapon spiraling up into the ceiling, but she maintained her grip. Better yet, she hit her target, which dropped from the ceiling. She cocked the hammer and fired at the second one. Young and inexperienced, it thought it was safe simply due to distance. The bullet struck it dead center, nearly splitting its body down the middle.

The two of them rushed the stairway, stopping briefly to check around the corner. There were two more waiting. Marshall waved the burning sheet, driving them back. He followed them all the way down the steps.

The nearest one attempted to stand its ground and claw at the strange source of heat. Marshall took a giant step forward, winding his foot back, then kicked it like a soccer ball. The creature landed on its back. Before it could right itself, Kira planted a round through its abdomen. Marshall chased the survivor, which was making its way through the broken window where it had initially come through. He brought the sheet down over its body, encasing it with flame. The arachnoid leapt like a grasshopper, plowing through the web and landing in the yard. It scurried back and forth, only to tumble over and burn alive.

They checked the kitchen and downstairs hallway, confirming the offspring were gone.

"Let's get this table over the window," Marshall said. They pulled the couch out of the way and flipped the living room table onto its side. Marshall pressed it to the window. There was a little bit of open space along the corners, but it covered the bulk of it. With a little bit of ingenuity, they would manage to cover it up with other supplies.

"Get my tool bag. There's nails and a hammer."

Kira ran into the bedroom, found Marshall's stuff, then came back down.

It was all starting to hit her at once. "What the fuck was that?! It hatched *babies*?!"

Marshall took the nails from her. "Looks like the doctor 'forgot' to mention that little detail."

Kira was still looking around, afraid that a crab-shaped creature would spring at her at any second. The creepy crawlies were at their worst. Her hair and neck itched. Worst of all, her stomach cramped. She couldn't bear the thought of getting stung by those things, let alone their mother.

"We really can't stay here," she said. "If there's more, they'll keep coming in."

"I know," Marshall said. He proceeded to hammer the nails into place, keeping the table over the window. As he did, Kira ripped cabinet doors free and searched the cottage for anything else they could use, including a med kit she kept in the bathroom.

For the next several seconds, they covered up the opening, then hurried upstairs to secure the broken guest bedroom window.

They found Ethan still crouched. At first glance, they were sure he was either dead, or at least completely immobilized by the spiderling's venom. Then he turned his head. His face was sickly, bleeding from the gash where the pincer had grabbed him. His right hand was cupped over the sting wound in his abdomen. The venom was circulating through his system, causing his veins to become pronounced and discolored.

But he was alive.

"Oh, Jesus," Kira said. She rushed to his side and checked his vitals. Never in a million years did she think she'd be so concerned for somebody who'd chased her down a few hours earlier. "Can you move?"

"Yes... sort of. Feels like my insides are being squeezed, though," he said. He coughed. His arms were curled by his chest. "Goddamn bugs."

Marshall began hammering nails. "They're babies. I guess their venom isn't quite as potent at this age. Maybe if you were the size of a beagle or something."

"You get them all out of here?" Ethan said.

"Yes. We barricaded the broken window with some wood."

"You think it'll be enough?" Kira asked.

"I hope so," Marshall said. "Unless the big one decides to come knocking. No way they'll withstand her." He looked up at the ceiling. "Gosh, it's only a matter of time before they figure out they can come in through that tarp."

"That's it, then. We can't stay here. We *have* to make a run for it," Kira said.

"How? Ethan can barely move. We can't even get through the door. Web's blocking it," Marshall replied. "Ethan's knife can't cut through it. It's almost as though this stuff was made by NASA." He looked over at the doctor. "Maybe that's another organization with stock in this project. Who knows?"

Ethan looked away as Kira taped a bandage over his puncture wound. He winced as she started packing some gauze against his lacerated cheek.

"I'm gonna have to stitch this," she said. She retreated to the master bedroom, then returned with a sewing needle and thread. "Hold still."

Ethan exhaled, not even wincing as the tip entered his skin. *What idiots. They don't realize if the shoe was on the other foot, I'd not waste a second thought leaving them behind.* At least, that's what he tried to tell himself. He never dedicated much time looking out for others, unless they were paying him, of course. Yet, they still looked out for him. Cautious but compassionate. Maybe they thought he was on their side after the recent standoff. Of course, he figured the natural instinct to protect them was simply out of his hate for the doctor. Also, they were a little handier with developing an escape solution. He forced the thought from his mind. Right now, he had bigger fish to fry.

The doctor, who was sprawled over the bed, was starting to get his wits back. It took him as long to sit up as it did for Kira to complete the stitching.

Ethan groaned. With Kira's help, he stood to his feet. He sheathed his knife then turned to face the doctor. He was conscious and very much aware of the hunter's bloodthirsty gaze.

Myles groaned. He sat up and rubbed his forehead, then was suddenly very aware of his loosened front tooth. Blood trickled from his lip.

"Loose tooth, huh? Let me help you with that," Ethan said. Using every ounce of strength, he stepped toward the doctor, hands outstretched to grab him. Myles backed up, hitting the dresser behind him.

"Listen!" He pointed a finger, which Ethan grabbed and bent back, sparking a high-pitched yelp.

"I should've known," Ethan growled, spitting thick foam. His knees wobbled, but he remained upright. Spurred by pride, he would not collapse in front of Myles Bower. "Just like the damn snake you had me chase after. That thing was carrying babies, you little shit! Now we know why you were so concerned about the lower temperature."

Now, Kira was fuming. She picked up one of the broom pieces and held it at the doctor's nose. "Is it true? Did you know it was carrying babies?"

Myles winced as his knuckle threatened to snap. "I had to impregnate it. Growing these things from artificial wombs is extremely expensive. It was easier to synthesize spermatozoa, sedate the specimen, and have her develop an egg sack."

"I didn't see it on her," Marshall said. "I thought spiders had their eggs on the outside."

"There's always anomalies in splicing genes. Sometimes it results in brand new traits. She stored her eggs inside her abdomen," Myles said.

"How many did she produce?" Ethan said. He swallowed, fighting back the urge to vomit and collapse.

"I have no way of knowing," Myles said. Ethan applied more pressure. Myles yelled. "I fucking swear!"

"You think that was all of them?" Kira said.

Myles hesitated, fearing they wouldn't like the answer. The added pressure on his knuckle forced it out of him. "I doubt it. She probably has a couple of other batches of eggs in the nest. Judging by what we've seen, each one probably contains about eighteen or so."

He was right. Ethan didn't like the answer. Myles screamed at the snapping of his finger.

The hunter staggered toward the window then fell again. Kira and Marshall rushed to his side. He was struggling for breath.

"Let's hope this shit wears off soon," he said.

"Absolutely. In the meantime, let's get you off the floor," Marshall said.

"What about him?" Kira said, tilting her head toward Myles.

"I say we throw him into the web," Ethan said. This time, they hesitated to object. Marshall even looked at the doctor as though considering following through on the suggestion. The guy was clearly nothing but trouble, and if recent events proved anything, it was that he would stab them in the back at any given opportunity. Unfortunately, that stupid nature of decency would not let him go through with it.

"No. But we will tie him up. We still have plenty of duct tape left."

Ethan groaned. The pain of letting Myles live was worse than the partial paralysis.

CHAPTER 29

Like a perimeter guard on an Army base, Marshall paced around the house, checking each window constantly. Each one had been boarded up with whatever wood they could salvage from dresser drawers, cabinet doors, and other miscellaneous pieces of junk.

It had nearly been an hour since the invasion, and still, nerves were on edge. He checked the storage room for the hundredth time, once again hoping he'd find something of use. An axe, radio, firewood, anything. Unfortunately, there wasn't much more in there other than a lawn mower and some general supplies, none of which would do him any good.

When he stepped out into the kitchen, he passed Myles Bower, who was seated on one of the chairs. His hands were cuffed together with duct tape, his chin red with his blood, giving the appearance of an undead fiend. Kira had just stepped away from him after letting him sip water through a straw. They considered taping his mouth shut...and still were. Luckily, Myles at least had the sense to not speak. Marshall suspected it was because the asshole was planning another scheme.

Let him. He's lucky I haven't thrown him outside already. Hell, I'm probably stupid for not having done so.

Marshall proceeded into the living room area and saw Ethan seated on the couch, which was now positioned in front of the fireplace. His arms were tucked close to his chest. By the strain in his face, it was evident that the venom was doing its worst. He was slouching to the side, straining to breathe through clenched teeth. Fatigue wore on him, the pain and stiffness were so bad he could barely grip his sidearm. Still, probably due to ego, he kept his weapons close. The rifle was on his lap, pointed at the window for easy aim. Through the spaces between barricade and frame, he could see bits of web. It was like a white background to a *Word* document, except it would occasionally wiggle in the wind.

"Need some water?" Marshall asked. Ethan shook his head. He looked past him at the Doc, then partially unsheathed his knife. The rising eyebrows on Myles' forehead gave him a weak chuckle.

In time. In due time.

He looked back to the window. He saw another wiggle in the webbing. Then another. Groaning, he leaned over for a better look. Marshall saw it too. It was evident that movement somewhere along the nest was causing it, but it was weak enough to suggest the source was further away.

Ethan's hand squeezed around the rifle. "You coming, you big bitch?"

Kira came running down the stairs, her face alive with dread. "You guys hear that?"

The room went silent. Marshall approached the window, cautiously watching through the cracks in case any spiderlings were on approach. He put his ear to the gap and listened.

She was right—there was a sound. Almost like a low growl. No...not a growl. A moan. A voice. A *human* voice, but in severe pain. Ethan could hear it too.

He stood up, only to fall back on the sofa. His injured leg could barely move. The venom was putting the nerves down there into overdrive. Even with the brace, it hurt to put any weight on it.

"Hold on a sec," Marshall said.

"To hell with that," Ethan replied. The moan intensified. It was lower than before. So much so, he didn't even think it was the same voice. He forced himself to his feet, and using his rifle as a crutch, he moved to the window. As usual, he couldn't see past the web, but it was clear that whatever was happening was taking place on the west side of the cottage, opposite the lake.

Each step played havoc on his body. His muscles felt like rubber bands stretched to the point of snapping. Even so, he made his way to the stairs. Marshall knew better than to try and stop him. He checked on the doctor. The bindings had him secured to the chair. He wasn't going anywhere.

The hunter was already halfway up the steps, though the strain was making him gasp for breath. He bared teeth like a wild animal, hissing every time his left leg completed a step. He completed the ascent and stumbled through the hallway, eventually ending up in the guest room.

Kira was already there. The moaning intensified.

"Something's happening."

"Move," Ethan said. He pushed her out of the way before she could respond. He pressed his eyes to the small gaps between the barrier and window frame. Nothing but web. But he recognized the voice. It was his wife. She was in agony, and for her, that was saying something. She was no stranger to pain, and it would take a cruel act of the devil himself to make her cry out.

"There's no way we can see what's going on," Marshall said. Ethan looked up into the ceiling.

"Didn't you say there's only a tarp up there?"

"Yes…" Marshall realized what Ethan was thinking. "Wait. DON'T!" Ethan pushed him back, nearly falling over in the process. Marshall's knees hit the bedframe, causing him to fall backward. As he did, Ethan fell to his knees—the only way he could get low enough to pick up the step ladder and extend it. It stretched to its maximum six-foot limit.

"Ethan, if there's little ones out there, you'll let them in!" Kira said. He ignored her and made the ascent. He nearly quit at the top step, as his muscles refused to move. His head bobbed, though he didn't feel like he was performing that action willingly. His body was squeezing tight, as though his chest plate was trying to escape through his shoulder blades.

Another intense moan from outside gave him the willpower to move despite the agony. He climbed into the rafters, propped himself up on one of the beams, then used his Bowie knife to cut a slit in the tarp.

Sunlight beamed into the room.

Marshall was back on his feet. He looked up and saw Ethan slipping through the tarp. "Fuck!" He climbed up the ladder and through the ceiling. He found something to prop himself up on next to Ethan and stuck his head through the tarp. He winced as the sunlight assaulted his eyes. "Come on, you fool. You're gonna get us k—"

Shivers ran up his spine as he beheld the sight of the arachnoid's nest. It was a world of white, stretching from the RV, to the nearby trees, and up and around the cottage. Tucked near a thick wall of web along the southwest corner was a huge funnel. And in the center of the huge sheet were seven cocoons. Antlers protruding from one of them confirmed the presence of a buck. The two next to it were some other animals, likely snagged in the various traps the arachnoid had laid.

And there it was, crouched in the dead center of the web, leaning down over the four cocoons strung up near the RV.

"Holy Christ."

Extending from between its pedipalps was a long, hose-like appendage, pink in color. It arched downward, like one of its legs, right into the cocoon. And in that cocoon was Tyler Paul.

His mouth was agape like an undead ghoul, his face paling and wrinkled. Veins swelled in his neck and face. That moan was coming from his throat.

He was alive and conscious, though mostly paralyzed by venom, and bound by webbing. The arachnoid rocked back and forth as it vacuumed the fluid from his body.

Other movement caught his eye. To the left were webbed formations. At first, Ethan and Marshall assumed it to be another funnel, until they noticed the pulsing, round objects under the web. Egg sacks, at least two of them. A few spiderlings already emerged, while their brethren hadn't deemed themselves ready. Some had crowded the animals, draining their blood. Others, however, decided to go toward the human cocoons.

One of those cocoons shivered. Fingers protruded through the silk threads. In the opening up top, a face was angled upward. As she fed, the mother shifted her weight, causing the cocoon to angle toward the cottage.

Ethan's fingers dug into the roof as he beheld the sight of his wife. Her jaw was locked open, slightly crooked. One of the arachnoid's legs brushed against her face as it adjusted. She was conscious, though frozen by venom. Her skin tone was mostly normal, indicating that she had not yet been fed on.

Tyler let out a dull shriek as the feeding tube retracted. The arachnoid lifted herself from her meal, quickly turning towards her offspring as they converged on the other three humans. Intent on keeping the freshest blood bags for herself, she maintained her pose, causing the spiderlings to divert toward the half-drained one she had just abandoned. Panicked groans filled the air as little arachnoids climbed over Tyler. Those groans became shrieks when multiple mouthparts entered his body.

The mother hovered over the other three. Sue, Chris, and Bryce were strung up in a straight line, separated by four or five feet. Chris was breathing heavily. There was no sign of struggle. The paralysis maintained its deadly grip, but his mind was working, as was Bryce and Sue's. The arachnoid finally lowered itself. The tube extended from its mouth. At its end was a spear-like tip.

No amount of paralysis could prevent the scream that escaped Bryce's lungs. The tube entered her flesh behind her left collarbone. Bryce convulsed in her cocoon as the suctioning began. That scream became a gag. She shifted in the confines of her restraints, her eyes and tongue bulging from place.

His heartrate surged, pushing his strained respiratory system beyond its limits, along with his psyche. Terror and desperation gripped Ethan. His face withered with rage.

"No!" Powered by will, he grabbed at the rooftop to haul himself over. Two hands grabbed him by the shoulder.

"Stop!" Marshall said. He tried his best to keep his voice down, despite the horror in front of him and the physical strain of restraining the hunter. Ethan elbowed him in the chest, momentarily weakening his grip. Marshall wrapped his arm around Ethan's neck, securing a chokehold. "Don't! You'll bring them down on us!"

"Get the hell off of me!" Ethan struck him again. Even in his weakened state, his strikes blew the wind out of Marshall. Realizing that he couldn't win against sheer willpower, Marshall relied on the only other technique he could muster. He allowed himself to slip from the support beam, still holding to Ethan. Gravity did the rest of the work.

The two men crashed through the ceiling tiles and landed on the floor. Kira cupped her mouth, then knelt by Marshall, who arched his back in pain.

"My God! You alright? What's happening?"

Marshall pushed himself to his feet then stepped away from Ethan. The hunter was on his elbows and knees, reaching for the stepladder. The heavy impact combined with the other ailments finally killed his ability to act further. He rolled over on his side.

The moans got louder. Bryce's were nearly rhythmic, as though her fluids were extracted in repeated slurps. Tyler's were almost gurgles at this point. Those offspring were taking their time with the leftovers. There was intense gasping from Chris and Sue, followed by stifled sounds of panic.

"What's happening to them?" a teary-eyed Kira asked. Marshall shook his head. *You don't want to know.*

But she did. She rushed to the other side of the bed, grabbed one of the oars, then yanked the barricade off the window.

"Kira, don't!"

She rammed the oar through the window, and with all of her might and no consideration as to what might be attracted by her motions, she shifted it to the right. The gap ripped in the layers of web was small, but it was enough for her to see the horror of what was happening outside. Marshall moved in to pull her back, but found himself unable to take his eyes off the terror.

Several spiderlings were crowding Chris and Sue and impaling them with their jaws, while their mother proceeded to feed on Bryce. The moans became saliva spitting gasps.

Kira staggered back. She felt lightheaded, as though her own blood was being syphoned out along with her friends'. Marshall caught her before she could collapse, then eased her onto the bed. She was conscious, but barely functioning. Marshall quickly resecured the barricade, then climbed onto the ladder to replace the ceiling tiles. Hopefully, those little ones wouldn't try to explore the roof.

Seeing Ethan roll onto his hands and knees again, Marshall stepped back. There was no telling what the hunter would attempt. Would he draw that revolver on him? Or slice him with that Bowie knife? Was their supposed alliance hanging by a thread? If it even existed at all?

To his slight surprise, Ethan simply sat against the wall. For the first time in his life, the hunter was truly defeated. All signs of the confident, poised, self-reliant hunter was gone. All that was left was the husk of a man, restricted by partial paralysis, forced to listen to the agonizing groans of his wife as she was eaten alive.

CHAPTER 30

"No. No..."

The voice was ghastly, like something Marshall thought he would hear from a haunted house. Even now, after an hour of continuous feeding, the victims—at least one or two of them, were still alive.

"N—no..."

He sat on the bottom stair next to Kira. Both of them cupped their hands to their ears. They couldn't even tell whose voice it was. Was the creature alternating between victims? Would it ever be satiated?

Across the living room sat Ethan. He was on his knees, his skin having turned a bizarre shade of purple. His eyes were red and veiny. He was still as stiff as before, though with enough effort, he could move around. But the pain was just as bad as ever, especially in his leg.

But nothing beat the agony of listening to the moans. He couldn't bear the sounds, yet, he couldn't bring himself to cup his ears and ignore them. He couldn't write off his wife. She was still alive and he needed to do something about it.

He stood up, fell back to his knees, then, using the window frame, tried again. With most of his weight on his left leg, and his arms still oddly bent, he stared at the doctor, who was still strapped to his kitchen chair. One of those hands started reaching for his Bowie knife.

"Ethan. Stop," Marshall said. The hunter ignored him. With the knife half-drawn, he started toward the doctor. "Ethan!"

Myles panicked in his chair, ultimately falling backwards, his feet kicking high in the air.

Marshall sprang from his feet, grabbed Ethan by the vest, and pulled him back. The hunter's leg buckled and he fell backward, right onto Marshall. Both of them hit the floor. Marshall rolled away and got to his feet, ready to grab anything he could use against the hunter should the attack be redirected at *him*.

Instead, Ethan got up on his right knee and glared at him. "All that do-good nonsense won't get you far, kid."

"As though murdering someone *will*?"

"Guys?" Kira said. She pointed at the windows. They could hear the tapping on the walls and glass, which reverberated from all corners of the cottage. They saw a crab-shaped body pass over the kitchen window. It stopped briefly, its leg protruding through the web, scraping the glass before moving out of sight. Arachnoid feet tapped the barricade. Tiny pincers reached through the gaps, only to retract.

Ethan drew his knife then stood up. He watched the window then raised the weapon high. When a spider leg protruded through the upper left corner, he slammed the blade down like a butcher. The leg flew off, its owner zipping off into the web maze. He pointed the knife at the doctor, who couldn't see it through the chair and his own feet.

"Doc, after all this is done, and there's no *Dudley Do-Right* here to protect you, I'm gonna burn you and your whole operation to the ground." Myles moaned under the duct tape, unable to voice his reply. Ethan looked back at Kira and Marshall. "I'll say it again: we should toss him out there and feed him to his own pet. Might give us an opportunity to get out."

Marshall shook his head.

They froze as legs tapped on the front door. The spiderlings were moving about, intently searching for a way in.

"Looks like more eggs are hatching. It's only a matter of time before they get in here," Ethan said. "I only have so many bullets."

"How would we get out anyway?" Kira said. "There's too much web. It sticks to you at the slightest touch. All the exits are blocked."

Marshall shook his head. "Not all."

"What do you mean?"

Marshall looked at Ethan, who concurred with a nod. "The roof."

"Isn't the roof covered with web?" Kira said.

"Yeah, but there's the tarp," Marshall said. "It's covering several feet of space around the hole we cut. The decking itself is untouched. We just need to remove the tarp and the web covering it. We can get out through there and not get stuck in the web."

"Doesn't change the fact that we have web surrounding the place and a big bug waiting for us to show our faces," Ethan said.

Marshall nodded. "Then we go with what you said before. We burn the doctor's operation. Literally. We set the web on fire and drive them away. With a little luck, the big bitch and the little ones will get caught in the flame and be reduced to burnt crust."

"But what about—" Kira's voice trailed off. She pointed in the direction of the cocoons.

Marshall shook his head. "We can't help them at this point."

"Whoa! Whoa! Whoa! Let me get this right," Ethan said. "You're not willing to let me kill this piece of shit, but you're willing to burn your own friends *alive*?"

"Shut up, man," Marshall said. "Don't twist it like that. You saw what I saw." He looked at Kira. "So did you. They're practically dead already. You've heard the—what's going on out there."

"So, you're writing them off, huh?" Ethan said.

"What did I just say?" Marshall said. "What would you have us do otherwise? Go out and cut them down? Oh, right—nothing can cut that web except fire."

Kira closed her eyes and faced the facts. Marshall was right. Their friends were dead one way or another. If any were still alive, a death, even one by flame, would be merciful in comparison to what they were going through.

"There's only so much gas left in that can," she said. "We can start a fire, but I'm not sure about burning this whole nest. At the very least, I don't see how we can set a flame that'll spread fast enough to kill the hive."

Marshall took a minute to think. "We might, actually."

Kira's eye widened. "The propane tank?"

"Mm-hmm."

"We're just as likely to fry ourselves as much as we are the bugs," Kira said.

"Alright then. Of course, we could take our chances. Maybe we won't get stung and cocooned "

Kira glanced over at Ethan. For somebody clearly no stranger to pain, he was barely keeping it together. A sting from one of those babies would have her in the fetal position at best. Then there was the thought of being eaten alive.

"There's no choice. Let's light these up."

"Not fucking happening," Ethan said.

"Yes it is," Marshall said. He started up the stairs. Ethan staggered after them.

"No it's not." Marshall didn't stop to listen. "Bryce is still out there. You're not burning her alive!"

This time, Marshall stopped. "She's not alive. Nor will we be if we wait."

"He's right," Kira said. She ascended the steps after him. Ethan tried to grab her but was too slow in his crippled state. Snarling, he made his way to the upper floor.

By the time he finally made it into the guest room, Marshall and Kira were in the process of tearing bedsheets to soak in gasoline. Marshall studied the window to make sure no spiderlings were nearby. He loosened the corner for a better peek. With the oar, Kira had made a gap in the web, just wide enough for a sharpshooter to shoot through. Better yet, he could see the propane tank. It wasn't too far away from the cocoons. He felt slight hesitation. Even though he had acknowledged it, the emotional part of his mind was tugging at him. If that tank blew, there would be absolutely no chance that anyone out there would survive.

However, that feeling ended when he looked at the cocoons. He swallowed. The urge to vomit was building fast. He moved away from the window and leaned against the wall to regain control.

"Marshall?" Kira said.

He opened his eyes to see Ethan standing at the doorway with his rifle pointed at them. His aim was wobbly, his stance relying on the door frame for support, but at this range, those obstacles were only a minor nuisance.

"Alright, Ethan. What's your plan? Shoot me and her and use *us* for bait? Divert the attention of the arachnids while you make an escape?"

"I ought to," Ethan said. "I *really* ought to. Be the easiest thing in the world, really, now that you don't have a weapon to defend yourself with."

Their eyes went to the discarded shotgun on the floor.

"Yet, you won't," Kira said.

Ethan wrinkled his nose. The cramps, the headaches, fever, shakiness, and general pain took some of his quick wit away. He had basically admitted he had no intention of shooting them.

"This is our only chance," Marshall said.

"You're not blowing that tank near my wife," Ethan replied. "I WILL shoot you to prevent that."

"Even if it means the rest of us getting killed?" Kira said.

"You're actually asking me to choose between you two or my wife?" Ethan said.

"There's no choice," Marshall said. "She's dead."

The weapon wavered. Ethan snarled. "I ought to shoot you for trying to bullshit me. About *this* of all things."

"It's not bullshit. Just take a look out there. You'll see for yourself."

"Nice try," Ethan said.

Marshall shrugged. Paranoia. The hunter thought they'd try to disarm him as soon as he took his eyes off the iron sights.

"So, you're not going to budge?"

"Whatever keeps you from doing what you plan to do," Ethan said. "I'll blow your head off if necessary."

Marshall raised his hands. "Alright. Shoot me." He noticed the subtle shift in Ethan's eyes. "Yeah, you heard me right. Squeeze the trigger and put an end to it. If we can't follow through on this plan, then frankly, I'd rather die like this. Go ahead. Do it."

Kira inhaled deeply. Her first instinct was to throw herself in the path of the bullet, only for rationality to kick in—she'd just be delaying the inevitable. With a few seconds of critical thought, she realized Marshall was right. Their doom was around the corner. It was only a matter of 'how' at this point. A quick death from a high-powered rifle sounded better than being drained of all fluids.

"Do it," she said. "Come on. Get it over with."

Ethan's eyes panned between the two lovers. His finger rested on the trigger, applying a minute amount of pressure. *I should do it. I REALLY should.* But that final squeeze could not be made. Not like this. If only these idiots would just make their move to explode the propane tank. *Then* he'd do it, no problem. Honor. He didn't think he had any.

Ethan thought he knew himself. He thought.

"What the hell are you waiting for?" Marshall said.

The barrel shook. The hunter growled, panned the muzzle to the right about six inches, then squeezed the trigger. Marshall cringed, expecting the wall of blackness to consume his consciousness, and whatever lay beyond that. Instead, there was no nothingness. He was alive and perfectly unharmed, aside from his ringing ears. He looked to the window at the remains of the spiderling that was prying through the barricade.

When his eyes faced Ethan again, the hunter had crossed the room.

"Get out of the way." Marshall didn't have to, as he was shoved. Ethan checked the window for any threat, hesitated, then gazed out at the cocoons. The white bags were blood-soaked. The one named Tyler was reduced to a dried husk, his jaw outstretched and losing teeth, skin grey and cracked.

The other female wasn't moving, though the spiderlings continued to feed on her. Either she was dead or had lost consciousness. Then there was the one they called Chris. He was still alive and moaning loudly.

"H—eelllp."

Ethan ignored him, as he finally braved looking at the fourth cocoon. Bryce was slouched to the left. Her eyes were open, but there was no movement. Her skin was somewhat wrinkly, though not as much as Tyler's. Still, it was pasty white. With the contrast of the bright red blood on her chin, she resembled a slumbering vampire. Except, she wasn't slumbering. She was dead.

As though waiting for him to watch, the mother arachnoid crawled from its funnel and made its way to Bryce. The mouth part protruded and plunged into the back of her neck, ready to drain whatever was left.

Ethan slammed the barricade and collapsed along the wall. Now, his heart was gripped by failure. Then, the pain subsided, replaced by intense thirst. Not for water, but for revenge.

He looked up at Marshall and Kira. "You win. But we're not only escaping. We're gonna *kill* that bitch."

Kira nodded. "Works for me."

ARACHNOID

CHAPTER 31

Kira tore the sheets from her bedroom mattress and went to work slicing away large ribbons. On her nightstand were the two halves of the broomstick that she had broken over Myles' head. She tied the ribbons around one end of each stick, which would be soaked in gas to be used as a torch.

When she brought them back to the guest room, Ethan was giving Marshall a quick tutorial of his rifle. The hunter's left arm was completely tucked against his ribs, and not by choice. He seemed to have more use of his other side, though it was still incredibly stiff.

"You comfortable with it?" he asked.

"Yep," Marshall said. He finished loading the weapon and cocked the lever.

"Just be careful. It's not a 30.06. That bad boy's got a real kick to the untrained shoulder."

"As long as it puts a hole in that tank," Marshall said. He slung the weapon over his shoulder. He took a deep breath and looked at the window. He couldn't see anything with the barricade secure, but his imagination had no problem envisioning what waited for them out there.

"Well, looks like we're about ready to get started. Everyone on the same page regarding the plan?" Ethan asked.

"Light the torches, shoot the tank, throw the torches. Boom. Fire burns bugs. We climb up out, jump, and run away. Sounds simple enough," Marshall said.

"We sure that tank won't blow when we shoot it?" Kira said.

"There's a chance if the bullet produces a spark when it penetrates, but it's usually so brief that the gas won't ignite," Ethan said. "Don't believe all that stuff you see in the movies."

"Fair enough."

Ethan gazed up at the ceiling. "I'd like to make one amendment to the plan."

"That is?"

"When that thing blows, we're literally gonna be surrounded by an inferno. That fire will spread damn fast. We're gonna have to move damn fast, and I'd rather not be delayed because of that damn tarp. I'd say we remove that first."

Marshall nodded. "Sounds good enough to me. Let's get the doctor up here and we can get started."

He and Kira went downstairs and found Myles hunched over in his seat. There was a stench suggesting he was holding in a nervous bowel movement. At least, they preferred to think he was holding it in.

Marshall kept the muzzle on him while Kira cut the binding at his feet and his waist, keeping his wrists tightly wrapped.

"Alright, Doc, we're about to make our getaway," Marshall said. "No tricks, no shenanigans, and don't attempt to run away. Try any of those things, and I won't get in Ethan's way when he decides to gut you."

The doctor's jaw wobbled as he tried to speak. Kira ripped the duct tape from his mouth. "What's that?"

Myles spat, ridding himself of the weird taste of the tape, then took a deep breath. "You can't do this. You don't understand what you're doing."

"We understand it just fine, Doc," Kira said. She pushed him forward. Marshall goaded him with the muzzle of the rifle. He hated doing so. It made him feel like an imperial soldier forcing a prisoner to march. But Myles was no innocent peasant being oppressed by a tyrannical government. All the misery he experienced, he brought on himself. And *them.* Suddenly, Marshall felt the guilt lift away. A lesser man would have squeezed the trigger.

"This is insane. You're destroying something that could hold the cure to countless diseases. Maybe even cancer!"

"Give us a break, Doc," Marshall said. "We know all you see are dollar signs."

"People who are so willing to sacrifice others for personal gain don't usually care about such things as cancer and health," Kira added.

"Yet, you align with the hunter, who was ready to turn you over?"

Marshall prodded him until he finally got to the top step. "At least he doesn't pretend to be so virtuous. And he seems to hate you now, so that's a plus."

That sentiment was reinforced with a piercing stare by Ethan as they entered the room.

"Stand over there," he said, gesturing to the wall near the nightstand.

"One million dollars," Myles said. Kira, seeing the not-so-subtle shift in Ethan's hand, which was now resting on the knife hilt, stuck the duct tape back over the doctor's mouth and shoved him to the desired location.

Marshall spilled some gas over one of the torches. Before climbing the ladder, he pulled back part of the barricade for a quick glance outside. There were more spiderlings crawling about, many of them converged on Chris now. He was dead, or close to it. Either way, he was beyond saving.

With the torch in one hand, and the lighter in another, he climbed the ladder into the ceiling. After removing the panel, he proceeded into the roof. Propped up on a board, he positioned himself under the slit that Ethan sliced earlier. He pushed it open slightly, making sure no spiderlings were waiting for him. He couldn't see any, but he did see the thick webbing over the tarp and roof. He tried pushing it off, but as he surmised, it was stuck to the roof thanks to the web. It would have to be burnt.

He lit the torch. An orange flame ignited with a growl, as though it was a demonic lifeform he held in his hand. He pushed the slit apart and touched the flame to the web on the outside. The fire clung to the silky substance. He ran the torch in a circle, slowly spreading the flame. Soon, he was surrounded by intense heat.

Confident that the fire would do the rest of the work, he slipped back down. By the time he lowered himself back down into the room, they could hear scurrying legs. The flame was agitating the arachnoid and her spiderlings.

He unshouldered the rifle and moved toward the window. "You guys ready?" Kira shrugged. Who would ever be *ready* for something like this?

"Doesn't matter. We're committed now," Ethan replied. He pushed himself off the wall he leaned on. Perhaps it was the adrenaline, but he was feeling a tad less pain in his left leg. Still, he was slow. He limped across the room and drew his revolver.

Kira went to the window and began to remove the barricades. She screamed and reeled backwards. Already, the spiderlings were starting to attack.

"Holy SHIT!" Marshall ran to the window and batted the first one away with the butt of the rifle. He struck another, crushing its head against the flame, then jumped back as several more began to flood into the room.

Christ! How did we not think to plan for this part?! Simple, he had assumed they'd at least have a few moments to shoot the propane tank and throw the torch.

Kira grabbed the barricade and rammed it against the window, stopping only to kick some of the critters in her path. Two gunshots shook the room.

Ethan had to grip his revolver with both hands in order to aim, but both shots were on the mark. Marshall fired a round from the rifle, splattering a bug that scurried across the ceiling.

Meanwhile, Myles made a run for the door, only to find the muzzle of Ethan's revolver pointing at his face.

"One more step, Doc. Do it."

Myles looked back at the others for protection, only to remember Marshall's recent threat. Before he could move, he was knocked backward by Ethan, who instantly regretted headbutting him, as it intensified his already brutal headache. Despite this, he fired his revolver at another spiderling, exploding its abdomen. Legs flailed from the half-body, only to coil into a stiff pose.

Kira was holding the barricade against the window, while Marshall used the oar to bash the remaining arachnoid.

"They're still trying to get in!" Kira said. She shook as the offspring began to converge on the window.

"Give me just a sec," Marshall said. With the torch having burnt out, he grabbed the other one and poured gas over it. "Here, take this," he said to Ethan, who quickly snatched the torch from his grip. Marshall then soaked a pillowcase in gas then went to the window.

Understanding the plan, Ethan lit the torch, then nodded.

Marshall nudged Kira. "Alright...three...two...one...MOVE!" She jumped back. Marshall threw the gas-soaked pillowcase over the window frame, then leapt back as Ethan charged with the torch. The flame ignited immediately. A ball of flame climbed, driving the spiderlings back.

Two more shots from Ethan killed the duo that made it inside. He reloaded his revolver, then limped back from the window.

"You're up, *Marshal Dillon*," he said.

"Intriguing sense of humor," Marshall replied. He stepped up to the window then shouldered the rifle. The mother arachnoid was stepping out of her funnel. Pincers were already extended, implying agitation. He rested the weapon on the ridge and teetered the weapon down toward the propane tank. "Give me the torch. The rest of you, take cover in the other room. Put as much house between you and the blast as possible."

Ethan had no problem with that. He placed the torch at Marshall's feet, then went for the doctor. With the revolver muzzle against his back, Myles stepped out into the hall, followed by Ethan and Kira.

Marshall took aim. There was so much movement all over the web, it almost made him nauseous. The web around the window had burnt away entirely, the heat impeding on his focus. He could see thin trails of smoke overhead. The fire above was dying out. He could only hope that enough of the tarp had burned. Then again, whatever didn't burn would likely ignite once that propane tank went.

He centered the northern end of the tank in his sights. He squeezed the trigger...right as the arachnoid sprang from her funnel. He saw a display of blood as the bullet struck her in one of the pedipalps.

"Fuck!" he shouted.

Legs and arms were thrashing. By now, she understood the connection between the loud bangs and the sudden sensation of stinging impact. Being an instinct driven beast, she would never understand she actually impeded the enemy's plan by blocking the bullet with her body. All she knew was survival, for herself, and her young.

Hissing vehemently, she advanced toward the window.

"Shit! Shit! Shit!" Marshall said. He cocked the lever. She was coming, and fast. Even her offspring cleared the way, as if they knew their mother was pissed off.

By the time Marshall took aim, the arachnoid was completely in the way. Panic took hold, causing him to fire the last remaining round. The shot brought a momentary pause to her advance—just enough for Marshall to dash from the window.

The flaming pillowcase had burnt to ash, the fire around it quickly dying into candlewick-sized flames, which were quickly extinguished by eight rampaging feet.

Marshall pulled some bullets from his pocket, cocked the lever, then started to reload. A thunderous impact shook the cottage, causing him to drop the cartridges.

"Fuck!"

"What's happening?" Kira asked. She ran back into the room. "Marshall, are you—" She screamed when she saw the pincers tearing away at the wall. Huge chunks of building came away, each strip larger than the next.

The arachnoid finally learned she was capable of tearing through this hideout. The torch below her did little to spur her. They had killed her young, thus, they were a threat to the propagation of her 'species'.

Ethan stepped through the doorway. "Holy shit."

"She got in the way. I couldn't blow the tank," Marshall said. Ethan fired his revolver at the beast. Most of the rounds skidded off her shell. She proceeded to enlarge the wall, making enough space for her entire face to peer inside. Ethan greeted her with a shot through the pedipalps. Blood spattered the floor. The arachnoid reeled backward. With the shift in her weight, the web under her rear legs, weakened by the fire, gave way. The arachnoid fell to the ground, momentarily tangled in her own web.

"Alright, this is our chance," Ethan said. He reloaded his revolver, then picked up the rounds dropped by Marshall. "Hurry up. Blow the tank and we can finally—" He noticed a shadow on the wall behind him. Before he could turn around, Myles drove his foot into the back of his injured knee. With a scream of pain, Ethan dropped to the floor, the revolver bouncing from his grip.

Myles, empowered by desperation, threw himself at Marshall, swinging his tapped hands as though holding a baseball bat. The combined fists clubbed Marshall across the jaw, knocking him against the nightstand.

In any other occasion, Ethan would've been back on his feet holding the perpetrator in a suffocating chokehold. But he could barely move his left arm and it still hurt to breathe. With his right hand, he pushed himself to his knees, only to catch a kick to the ribs.

Myles proceeded to stomp on the hunter's midsection as he rolled to his back. He turned around, just in time to receive a haymaker from Kira. Before he could retaliate, Marshall closed in with a blow to the temple.

Perhaps it was all the abuse that he had suffered through the last few hours. Perhaps it was his determination to keep his creation alive at all cost. Perhaps he wanted to avoid Jedlinsky's wrath. Or possibly a combination of all three. Whichever it was,

Myles Bower absorbed the blows like a professional boxer. There was pain, but this time he was able to endure it.

Still, it was two on one, and his enemies were almost equally as desperate. Almost. However, they had a distraction that he didn't have…

The wall shuttered. Through the large breach, the pincers emerged, followed by the first set of legs. It was climbing back up.

Myles threw himself at Kira. He absorbed an elbow with his forehead as he ducked down. He struck her with his shoulder, then cocked his body to the right. With all of his might, he swung his wrists, knocking her toward the breach. Her knee hit the corner of the bed, causing her to stagger and fall.

Marshall saw his girlfriend on the floor, mere feet from the rising pincers. Aborting his next attack on Myles, he rushed to her side. He grabbed her by the shoulders and started lifting her up. They both shrieked as the creature's blood-soaked face emerged.

Its pincer, serrated and bone-hard, lashed at its prey. Kira screamed as she felt the appendage close around her ankle. Her boot tightened against her flesh, barely cushioning the vice-like grip enough to keep it from snapping her bone right there. But that didn't change the fact that she was caught in an unbreakable grip.

Marshall pulled her back as hard as he could. Man and beast were locked in a tug-of-war. The opposite pulls resulted in Kira being completely lifted off the ground by shoulder and foot.

"Marshall!" she cried. He understood the unspoken words. *Don't let it take me. I don't want to end up a shriveled corpse.*

His broken finger was throbbing under the duct tape. His jaw was pulsing and bleeding once again from his loosened teeth. But Myles didn't care. He had foiled their plans. He had outsmarted them all—with the help of his precious creation, of course. Now, all he needed to do was take one of the discarded arrows lying in the yard, refill the vial with sedative, find Ethan's discarded crossbow, and tranq the arachnoid himself. And with it preoccupied with cocooning these lovers, it would be an easy shot even for an amateur like him.

He turned around, expecting a clear path to the door. He was surprised to see Ethan standing up. And frightened.

The hunter thrust his hand out and clutched the doctor by the throat. Myles writhed, feeling his airway closing off. He struck the hunter's face with his clubbed hands, but that grip only tightened. It was then he realized that Ethan was energized by the one thing stronger than desperation—hate. No amount of venom, tissue loss, or pain would avert his wrath.

Ethan choke-slammed Myles into the floor. He rose up, only to slam an elbow in the doctor's ribs. Myles let out a muffled cry as two of his ribs snapped. Ethan lifted himself again, intent on continuing the punishment. Only the scream from the window halted the bombardment.

He looked to the window. The thing had Kira and was pulling her closer. It was only a matter of seconds before she'd be fully in its grasp.

Near the corner of the bed was the revolver.

Ethan glanced down at Myles. Yet again, he'd have to postpone his execution. Still, he didn't hold back one last blow. He plowed a fist into Myles' groin, amplifying his muffled shriek, then dove for the weapon. Landing on his belly, he gripped the gun, pointed it, and fired.

Once again, the bullets ravaged the soft pedipalp tissue. The creature released its grip and slid a few feet down the wall.

Kira and Marshall both fell to the floor, gasping for breath. Ethan was on his feet and limping toward the now-enlarged window. He could see the tank.

There was still time. Even if the bastard wasn't caught in the explosion, the fire would at least drive it off long enough for them to get out. He didn't bother going for the rifle. He could make the shot with his revolver. All he needed was a few seconds to steady his aim.

Another vibration shook the earth. If not for the loud truck engines, he would've assumed it was from the arachnoid climbing the walls. Marshall and Kira could hear it too.

Marshall and Kira went to the far wall. From there, they saw movement coming from the driveway. There were multiple vehicles: two company pickup trucks and one semi-truck.

Men dressed in black tactical gear raced from the pickup trucks.

"There it is!" one of them shouted.

"You've got a clear shot. Shoot it now!" another said. They held crossbows, similar to what Ethan and Bryce carried. The first arrow skidded off the arachnoid's back. Still, it was enough to get the creature's attention. Still on the wall, it turned to face the new threat.

The next arrow struck it in the leg, immediately injecting sedative. Another hit it along the underside. It had only recently overcome the sluggishness of the last dose, and already, its strength was fading again. Despite this, it lunged for an attack, only to trip over its own web. It plummeted in a spiraling motion, tearing down a large sheet of webbing. It landed on its back, its legs clawing at the air above it. More arrows penetrated its shell.

"We've got it! It's slowing down!" someone shouted.

Over the next several seconds, the thrashing movements slowed to a stop.

"It's got offspring!" another screamed.

"Back the container up. Use the bait!"

The semi-truck driver was already in the process. Within a few seconds, the rear of the vehicle was facing the yard, the edge scraping Marshall's smashed pickup truck.

The rear compartment opened. Immediately, a man rushed inside. The loud *beeps* of a forklift coming to life pierced the air. The vehicle backed out of the ramp, carrying a large clear container. It was eight-foot wide at least, and appeared as though made of glass, with a steel platform on the bottom with two slots for the forklift. Inside that container were two pigs.

A figure, dressed in a suit and tie, stepped to the middle of the yard. "Alright. Take it up to the nest." The driver complied and gently set the container down. With the press of a remote button, the top split into two doors which yawned apart.

The men raced back to the trucks. Some geared up with net launchers, while one of them put on a harness connected with some kind of air tank. That man ran around the back of the nest, then aimed the nozzle like a World War Two soldier about to spit flame at a Japanese bunker. Instead of flame, it was an aerosol spray that sprayed from the nozzle. Whatever the chemical mixture was, the spiderlings didn't like it.

"Alright, they're coming into the yard now. Most will go for the bait. Net only the stragglers," the man in the suit said.

The men fanned out and waited as the twenty-or-so spiderlings raced from the web. As predicted by the man in the suit, most went straight for the vulnerable blood supply in the glass container. The pigs squealed as a dozen stingers pierced them at once. Spiderlings fought over the flesh, snapping their pincers at one another, only to settle their differences by plunging their mouthparts into different areas of the paralyzed pigs.

The overhead doors closed, sealing them in. With the press of a button, a second set of doors opened on the side.

As Marshall, Kira, and Ethan watched, they realized the end of the container had two walls, allowing for controlled access. The inner wall had a sliding door in the middle, controlled by a mechanical railing system, which would only open when the exterior was shut. From the outside looking in, the wires and frames looked like veins in a human body.

The few stragglers that raced about the yard were quickly seized by nets, fired at bullet-speed from the muzzles of those guns. The creatures thrashed violently as they were picked up by poles and taken to the container. One-by-one, they were fed into the compartment. As soon as the doors shut, another pole would enter through a port, carefully cutting through the net and freeing the spiderling, which would then enter the main compartment.

"Like clockwork," one of the men said. They proceeded to high-five each other. Meanwhile, the man in the suit approached the cottage. He could see the spectators inside, watching from above.

He smiled. "Ethan Fekete. Been a long time since I've seen you, sir."

"I suppose," Ethan replied.

Marshall and Kira looked at him, the latter asking, "You know this guy?"

He nodded. "That's Jedlinsky. Looks like those security guys got in touch with him. My guess is he decided to come to town a little early. Once he realized what the Doc was up to, he decided to take matters into his own hands."

"How'd they know to look here?" Marshall said.

"They were probably out looking. Saw the smoke, heard the gunshots—probably wasn't hard to piece together what was going on," Ethan said.

They looked back at the company CEO. The way Myles spoke about him, they expected an old, grisly looking man with balding hair, a sagging gut, and a wrinkled tie. To their surprise, he almost looked like any other guy dressed in a suit. He was maybe fifty, though he could've passed for early-forties. He was a dark-skinned man with thin black hair. He spoke in a calm, yet commanding voice. Either he had some kind of military background, or was simply used to being in charge of others. Marshall suspected the latter, as managing a company with enough resources to create genetic specimens was no small matter.

"Is Doctor Bower in the cottage with you?" Jedlinsky asked.

Ethan looked over at the doctor, who was still in the fetal position clutching his crotch. He looked as though on the brink of tears, and not from the pain.

"Yeah, he's in here," Ethan replied.

"Excellent. Is he well?"

Ethan shrugged. "He's a little roughed up."

"I suppose he hired you directly," Jedlinsky said.

"That would be logical."

"I'm surprised you would take such a job, considering how your last endeavor resulted. Not to mention the insufficient funds that Dr. Bower has at his disposal."

Ethan sighed. "I suppose I was in need of a good hunt."

Jedlinsky nodded. "That puts it into better perspective. Did your wife come along?" Ethan didn't answer, which in *itself* was an answer. The silence caused Jedlinsky to study the cocoons. He didn't recognize Bryce at first...and still didn't even after a more careful look. Only because of the tactical gear did he know it was her wrapped in the web. "My most sincere condolences."

"Appreciate it."

"I assume those people standing with you are the owners of this property?"

"They are."

"How unfortunate," Jedlinsky said. He looked at the various vehicles. There was the car they passed in the driveway, the RV, and the truck. Yet, only two people stood with Ethan. "Very unfortunate, indeed."

Marshall swallowed. He initially wanted to warn them about the sedative, but now felt it was best to say nothing.

"Dr. Bower?" Jedlinsky said. "Please come out. Right now." Myles didn't want to move.

He looked up at Marshall and Kira. "Tell him I'm dead," he tried to say through the tape, forgetting that Ethan had already confirmed his presence.

"Dr. Bower, my patience is running thin," Jedlinsky said.

Ethan walked over to the doctor. With his Bowie knife, he freed his hands. "Go. Your boss wants to see you."

"No…" Myles said. Ethan held the blade to his crotch, touching the tip to the fabric. Myles jumped back, then slowly moved downstairs. He could hear some of the men outside, cutting the web away from the door. When he opened it, they had enough of it removed so he could push the door wide enough to squeeze out. He paused, seeing Jedlinsky waiting for him, hands tucked behind his back.

Myles hoped for the best. Maybe Jedlinsky would see the merit in his attempt to fix his wrongs.

"Mr. Jedlinsky," he said, trying to sound formal. The shaky voice betrayed his lack of confidence.

"Dr. Bower." Jedlinsky's voice was as steady as ever. "Explain to me what happened?"

"It escaped during transit," he explained.

"And?"

"I was afraid for its health. The temperatures are lower than what it's used to. I had to act fast and recapture it."

"Is that so? Yet, you didn't confide in me."

"I thought it would be a simple matter to hunt it down," Myles said. "I paid for the fee with my own pocket. I wanted to show I was reliable."

Jedlinsky smirked. "Reliable? You mean loyal?"

Myles nodded hastily. "Y-yes!"

"So, you tried to catch the creature and haul it to the lab in time before my arrival? I would have shown up and never known it was missing in the first place?"

The words cut deep. Myles tried to speak, but all that came out was a stammer. He felt like a kid who'd tried to replace a broken heirloom without his parents finding out that it was missing in the first place.

"You know what I value most in my associates, right?"

"Loyalty," Myles said. "I'm loyal."

"You're loyal, you say?" Jedlinsky nodded. "It's like a wannabe king declaring "I'm King!" without displaying the qualities. You know one of the most valuable aspects of loyal members of my organization?"

Myles thought hard for a strong response. "Results?"

"Transparency."

Myles felt the muzzle of a pistol press into his abdomen. His ears rang simultaneously to the sensation of sudden heat and piercing pain in his intestines. He stumbled backward, bobbing his head as though holding back vomit. What ultimately came out was more of a belch full of blood droplets. He looked down at himself, seeing a red stain rapidly expanding along his midsection. The heat was so intense, he was surprised he didn't see smoke coming out of the gunshot.

"I—" He fell to his knees. "I'm loyal…"

Jedlinsky couldn't suppress his chuckle. Even on the brink of death, this idiot was still trying to appeal to him.

"I no longer require your services, Doctor. Frankly, you've proven to be more trouble than you're worth. Now that we have the genetic breakthrough, I can have my scientists duplicate the DNA. I have people at your labs right now. They're going through your computers, taking every bit of information, regardless of how insignificant it is."

Myles' jaw dropped. Jedlinsky's words were having the desired effect. They actually *added* to the pain. He tried to speak, but could only groan. His insides were on fire, and at the same time, his guts felt as though in a blender. He was no expert on firearms, thus, he didn't understand that he was struck with a hollow point.

"Now, Doctor, if you would excuse me. I have other business I must attend to." Jedlinsky nodded at the two men standing behind Myles. They picked him up by the arms and led him to the glass container. Myles gazed at the spiderlings jampacked in the compartment, then back at Jedlinsky. "Consider this your last contribution to science." He snapped his fingers at the guards, who opened the exterior doors and shoved Myles inside. Blood stained the glass as he got back on his knees and pressed his hands to the doors. He tried to speak, but went unheard. One of the guards took a cattle prod and pushed it through one of the ports. The electrified tip zapped Myles, knocking him backward into the main compartment.

The spiderlings wasted no time crowding the new blood source. Myles writhed as a half dozen stingers punctured his leg, groin, neck, and ribs. He jerked, rapidly becoming more rigid. His joints hyperextended near breaking point, including his already-broken finger.

Before paralysis took hold, the feeding had begun. The youngsters were growing, thus, an abundance of sustenance was required.

CHAPTER 32

"Oh my God," Kira said. As much as she hated Myles, it was still horrifying to see a man shot in the gut, let alone be thrown into the tank of baby arachnoids. She backed away from the breach. It wasn't strictly out of fear or disgust, rather *distrust*. A man who would execute a man right in front of them was likely not going to bother sweet-talking witnesses.

Marshall was thinking the same thing.

"Ethan?" he whispered. "We need to get out of here."

The hunter nodded. "Just play along."

"Play along? With what? He just killed the Doc. We're next."

"Yes."

"So, we should run for it."

"Use your eyes, kid. There are six guys down there with automatic weapons, who clearly have no qualms about killing. If we tried to run, we wouldn't even make it to the trees before they cut us down. Especially not me." He arched his back slightly, trying to overcome the stiffness. "They won't even have to aim; just spray. One of those bullets would find its way into our backs."

"So, your solution is to simply stay *here*?!"

"We just need to last a few more minutes," Ethan said.

"That's saying an awful lot," Kira said. "We don't have much to fight back with."

"We might have more than you think," Ethan whispered. He tilted his head downward. Though she couldn't see it, Kira realized what he was gesturing towards. Marshall understood too. Best not to say anything and risk being overheard by the commandos.

Like Ethan had instructed, he wanted to drag this out as long as possible. Fleeing further into the cottage might spur the commandos into opening fire. No, it was better to stay right here in plain sight...as long as he kept a watchful eye on their body language.

Ethan turned back to face Kira. "Psst!" He tilted his head down at the rifle. She had seen the loading process, which wasn't complicated, and there were several cartridges on the floor. She went to work loading the weapon, while simultaneously declaring that the next property she would own would contain at least ten firearms.

Never again would she make fun of preppers.

Ethan holstered his revolver, though he kept his hand close to it. The commandos maintained their formation. Their rifles were pointed at the ground...for now. Jedlinsky was a man of professionalism. Sure, he'd waste people he saw as in the way, but there was an odd quality about him. It was as though he needed to *explain* the situation to the people he disposed of. Maybe it eased what conscience he had left. Ethan would never know. But what he did know was that the men were not getting to work right away on loading the arachnoid into the container, which was a red flag in his eyes.

As he predicted, Jedlinsky stepped forward to speak.

"Ethan Fekete. Did the doctor pay you in advance?"

"That he did," Ethan said.

"Did he make any arrangements with any other clients?"

"My understanding is that he came directly to me."

"I see. Once again, my condolences for your loss. Are there any next of kin?"

"Would it make any difference if there was?" Ethan said.

Jedlinsky shook his head. Interestingly enough, he seemed reluctant to give the men the order. Ethan Fekete was a reliable man, after all. He wasn't one to spill the beans, so long as the proper funds were given.

"Why's he waiting so long?" Kira whispered.

"You're complaining?" Marshall said.

"Almost...because something's off about this. Maybe he'll actually let us go."

"No. Not you guys," Ethan whispered.

"Wait...just us?" Kira said.

Jedlinsky's next announcement provided the answer. "Mr. Fekete, your reputation precedes you. There's a reason companies pay you top dollar. I'm willing to compensate you for your loss and services, and of course, for your silence. Because of that aforementioned reputation, there is trust that *you* will not disclose the events that unfolded here today."

Marshall felt his throat tighten. *I'm suspecting Kira and I aren't getting such a deal. After all, we have no reputation to guarantee we'd be quiet.* It made sense that Ethan would be offered a deal. Even someone as powerful as Jedlinsky couldn't go around killing all of his contractors. If too many people associated with his organization started disappearing, then everyone else would avoid business.

"I'm sensing there's something you're leaving out," Ethan said.

"I saw two people in that cottage with you. Are there any others?"

"None that are alive."

"I see. That's unfortunate." Jedlinsky shook his head again. "Well, sir, the last remaining part of the deal is to 'handle' them."

"I don't get paid enough for that," Ethan said.

"Oh, right. Forgive me, I should have remembered. You're often very clear on such details," Jedlinsky said. He looked down a moment, then back up at them. "Four million dollars. All you have to do is bring them out. Nothing else. Then, of course, never speak of this day. Ever."

Ethan stood silent.

Marshall grew even more nervous. He watched the hunter's expression. Here it was—a clean shot at survival AND a hefty paycheck. And, technically, he wouldn't have to betray his principles. Hours ago, he was ready to do the same thing for much less.

"He doesn't mean it," Kira said.

"Yes he does," Ethan replied.

"You can't trust him," Marshall said.

"Stop talking about things you know nothing about," Ethan said. "Jedlinsky is many things, but as he demonstrated, he appreciates transparency."

The CEO cleared his throat. "Mr. Fekete, I'd appreciate it if you came to a decision quickly. We have things we need to take care of."

Marshall tensed. *Things to take care of—like burning down any evidence of this thing's existence.*

He looked at Ethan. He considered tackling him and taking his revolver. Except, the hunter's palm was already resting on the grip. He'd have a hole blown in him by the second step. Kira had the rifle, but the lever was not cocked. The sound of it cocking back would alert Ethan to her intentions. Even with his injuries, the hunter would have the faster draw. It wasn't his first rodeo.

Marshall didn't waste his breath. One way or another, they were screwed.

Then, a realization hit. Ethan was taking his sweet time coming to a decision…as though he was deliberately running out the clock.

Jedlinsky's patience was finally running thin. "Mr. Fekete…"

"Relax," the hunter said. He pulled the revolver from his holster, then started to turn as though to face Marshall. "That is a tempting offer." He gave each of them a glance, then looked back at the CEO. "Unfortunately, I'll have to turn you down." He aimed the revolver and fired.

Jedlinsky ducked, then ran back around the truck while the commandos spread out. Automatic rifles ravaged the cottage, splintering the walls and roof.

Kira and Marshall hit the floor. They army-crawled into the hallway, as the room behind them was shredded by bullets. Holes exploded through the hallway wall. The commandos were simply cutting through the cottage at this point.

"Jesus, Mary, FUCK!" Kira cried.

"Give me the rifle," Ethan said. She slid it back to him. A bullet whizzed between her and Marshall, causing both of them to shudder, then check themselves for injuries. More bullets whizzed around them. Any second now, they were bound to get hit.

Ethan made his way to the guest bathroom. He stopped as several bullets cut through the floor and into the upper left wall. More holes appeared, sending tile flying into his face. It was as though they KNEW he was going in there. Rather, these guys weren't stupid, and knew a good sniping position when they saw one.

Another bullet cut through the floor. It whistled across his face, causing him to roll backward into the hallway.

"Son of a bitch!" He looked over at Marshall and Kira. "Next time, I'm taking the fucking money." He forced a smile, then looked at his watch. *Any fucking second now…*

****

It was surrounded by intense thunder. Ear-shattering sounds that it had never experienced in such abundance. It was like the sound of the human-held weapons that ravaged a few of its eyes and bloodied its mandibles. Only, these were rapid, and so thunderous that even the deepest of sleep couldn't drown it out.

The sluggishness it experienced was vaporized by an adrenaline-like surge. The creature was very much aware of the hostile humans surrounding it. They were assaulting its nest, the rapid noise rife with menace. It could feel the faint vibrations of its young.

A shift in its body directed its eyes at the enclosure that trapped them. It was a trap set by these new invaders. It didn't bother speculating motive. Its instinct made its judgement—and that was that these humans were hostile. They were not food, they were *enemies*. Predators, like ants slaying a tarantula. Their stings had worn off, allowing the arachnoid to right itself with a single springing motion.

The nearest commando was in the process of reloading when he heard the sound of heavy impact behind him. He spun on his heel, then screamed as the mighty leviathan lunged at him. Claws seized him, one by the shoulder, the other by the leg.

All eyes turned toward the beast as it lifted their companion into the air then slammed him face first into the grass like a toy plane. The impact snapped the man's neck, his head flopping backward between his shoulders.

"Christ! It's still alive!" one shouted. The five remaining commandos directed their aim at the arachnoid. Impact of bullets against its shell sparked further rage. The arachnoid leapt at the nearest target in a blur of motion.

Pincers plunged into his abdomen like spears, then quickly pulled apart. There was an agonizing sound of ripping fabric along with a brief cry. Entrails unraveled over the grass.

From the front of the truck, Jedlinsky watched as the arachnoid proceeded to shred the man. Limbs separated in multiple pieces. The claws repeatedly hacked the body like butcher's knives, stopping only when the remaining gunman resumed fire.

The CEO was astonished. How could this be? How was this creature awake? Had it adapted to metabolize the sedative faster? He mentally shoved these questions to the side in favor of solutions. The creature was loose again and needed to be stopped.

Despite how eager he was to get it to the lab, it was clear that this beast could not be controlled outside of a lab chamber. They had the spiderlings, which would grow up into over twenty giant arachnoids. There was no real loss, aside from a slight delay. Still, it was nothing his shareholders wouldn't understand, so long as they personally saw the specimens.

"Just kill it!" he shouted to the men. "Put everything you have into it."

The arachnoid scurried toward its next target, absorbing numerous bullets in the process. Some penetrated its armor, antagonizing it to the point of mass rage. It would kill anything and everything that moved.

The commando, unable to halt the creature's advance, spun on his heel and ran toward the lake. The rapid stomping of feet behind him continued to intensify, until he felt a sudden pressure on his right knee. In the blink of an eye, that pressure intensified into an imploding *crack!*

He hit the ground. Before he could recover, he could feel himself being dragged backward by the broken limb. That pressure continued into a burning, slicing sensation. He looked back then screamed, witnessing the bloody spectacle of the pincer removing his leg. The arachnoid tossed it to the side and proceeded to further ravage its victim. The commando was flipped onto his back. The creature, as if it had an expertise in human anatomy, reached for the soft abdominal tissue. Pincers cut like surgical instruments, though not with the same care as an OR physician. This was a medieval disembowelment. Intestines were violently ripped from place, followed by rib bone and stomach tissue.

The remaining commandos were in disarray. There seemed to be no stopping the beast.

"Keep hitting it!" one shouted. "Go for the eyes!"

The creature turned around. It stood high on its legs. Its abdomen rose, as did its two arms, forming a terrifying stance before darting to the next gunman.

The commando's rifle couldn't have run dry at a worse time. He repeatedly squeezed the trigger with no results, then tossed the weapon aside. Overcome by panic, he turned and ran…only to end up face-first in the web between the tree and RV. He thrashed about, completely glued to the substance.

He could feel the hybrid closing in, until finally, he was overtaken by its shadow.

"No! No! NOOOOO!"

Pincers closed over his neck and tightened until the serrated edges touched together. The severed head bobbed, still stuck to the web, while the rest of the body twitched.

****

The screaming and shouting were more than enough to indicate that his plan had worked. Ethan pushed himself to his feet then went to the nearest window. He could see the beast ravaging its latest victim.

There were two men left. One was in the process of barricading himself inside the truck container, while the other freshly reloaded his rifle with intent to stand his ground. The arachnoid decided to go for the coward, blocking the doors with its arms before they could close. For a moment, it was lodged, allowing the other to move closer for a better shot.

The side of the beast was heavily scarred from sustaining repeated gunshots. Believing the exoskeleton to be weakened, the commando concentrated his aim on that point.

Bullets pounded its abdomen, penetrating its shell and spraying blood over the yard.

In a savage motion the arachnoid tore itself free from the container and spun toward its enemy. It wasted no time closing in. The commando regretted his gallantry, and in that moment realized that his companion was the smart one. Unfortunately, it was too late to turn and run.

The beast seized him in its claws, splintering his ribs and slicing flesh. The pedipalps expended, revealing the two fangs whose purpose was about to be revealed. They weren't for stunning prey, as the abdominal stinger served that purpose. They were simply weapons for impalement for rival arachnoids, among other enemies.

The commando let out a final scream, only to spasm uncontrollably as the fangs pierced his eye sockets.

"Goddamn!" Ethan said. He looked at the other gunman. He was still trying to close the container doors, but appeared to be having some sort of trouble. Then there was Jedlinsky, who was crouched near one of the pickup trucks. He watched the CEO slowly move toward the driver's seat. "Where the hell do you think you're going?"

He heard the truck engine come to life. The CEO was making a run for it. To hell with wiping away the evidence. To hell with the specimens. To hell with his man whom he was leaving behind for the slaughter. All Jedlinsky cared about now was saving his own skin.

"Get the gas can. Hurry!" he said to Marshall. No time was wasted asking questions. Marshall dashed to the guest room, grabbed the can, and brought it to Ethan, who then doused the webbing outside the window with gas, then lit it on fire.

It took a moment for the fire to open up a space wide enough for him to take aim out of. During that time, Jedlinsky had begun circling around the yard. Ethan stuck his rifle through the window. The truck was now pointed to the driveway and accelerating. He only had a split second before the target was out of sight.

He aimed low and to the left, then squeezed the trigger.

****

Escape was right there, just a dozen yards or so in front of his face. Already, Jedlinsky was working on his contingency plan. As soon as he was out on Dray Street he would get on the horn to his associates and get an entire crew out here, properly equipped to handle the specimen and evidence. With the creature preoccupied with the remaining gunman, he had a clear avenue for escape.

Then came the crack of a high-powered rifle coinciding with a heavy tremor in the forward left tire. Pieces of rubber blasted along his window like mulch. The truck dipped to the left, away from the driveway, right into a tree.

The airbag went off, knocking Jedlinsky back against his headrest. Disoriented and bleeding from his nose, he stumbled out of the vehicle. The engine was smashed and billowing smoke. He was standing near the front of the semi, unable to see the beast. However, he could hear it, as well as the screams of the one remaining commando.

There was a squealing sound of metal being stretched, followed by a loud *ping* of the door hinges giving way. He then saw the container shake as the creature made its way into the vehicle. The tremors only lasted a moment, after which the creature stepped back out, holding a writhing victim in its pincers. After pinning him to the ground, the arachnoid proceeded to tear off his right arm. Next was his right leg, from the knee down. The pincers then raked down the gunman's center, slicing through flesh and bone like soft bread.

The beast could sense other movement nearby. When the final gasps left its current victim, it rose up and turned to the right, spotting the man who funded its creation. Such details meant nothing to the arachnoid. It only understood survival, which meant eliminating all threats. This human arrived with the others, thus, he was part of the swarm that sought to destroy its nest.

Jedlinsky glanced briefly at the semi-truck. Common sense dictated that he would never get that thing through the driveway fast enough to escape the creature. His only chance was to run through the trees and hope the woods would provide enough obstacles to slow the beast down.

He took off with a sprint, leaping over bushes and hills. Not since his youth had he run so fast. In the few instances in his adult life, he was winded very quickly. But this was not casual exercise; this was survival.

He could hear the creature somewhere behind him. He didn't bother to look back. What was the point? He just needed to keep going. If he got far enough, maybe it would give up in favor of Ethan and the two civilians.

Just a little further. Just need to get out of—

His thoughts ended as swiftly as his retreat. His last step hit the ground, only to never lift off. He fell forward with a heavy thud. Immediately, he could feel the bruising along his ribs.

The drumming of legs grew louder. He had to move. Yet, he couldn't. There was a wetness underneath him. The ground was covered in a white silky substance. It was essentially a classic spider web design, just stretched along the forest floor.

Memories of video conferences with Myles Bower flashed in his mind. He remembered being told of the creature's instinct to lay traps for unsuspecting prey. He shook with desperation, but each attempt to pull free of the web only resulted in him getting stuck more firmly. He would need a crane to lift him off.

This couldn't be! He was in charge of an empire! He was worth BILLIONS! None of this should be happening to *him*. This is what pawns are for. Scientists, security professionals, contractors, everyone deemed beneath him. But not Jedlinsky!

His delusion of grandeur ceased, along with his life, as the arachnoid hovered over its next victim. It spun like a top, expanding its stinger to the maximum eighteen-inch length, then slammed it down…right through the back of Jedlinsky's skull.

CHAPTER 33

"Come on. Put your back into it," Ethan said as Marshall and Kira slammed against the front door. The web was still holding it tight, despite the cutting Jedlinsky's men had done to allow Myles to get out. They shouldered it together, creating just enough space for them to squeeze through.

Kira almost did not recognize her yard. Body parts were strung about. The air had a foul stench that she would never forget. It was a horrific sight that made her double down on her decision to never return.

The arachnoid was gone for the moment. The spiderlings were grouped inside the glass container. Most were motionless, as they were busy feeding off the corpses inside.

Ethan followed them outside and immediately pointed to the remaining company pickup truck. "We can use that to get out of here."

"What about those things?" Kira said.

Ethan groaned. "They're trapped in there."

"Unless their mother breaks them free," Kira said.

"If she does, and they get out and grow…only to spawn more and more…we could be looking at a real problem here," Marshall added.

"Tell the authorities, then," Ethan said.

"Ha! Like they'll do anything!" Marshall said. "I figured a guy as smart as you would be lecturing *us* about that."

Ethan limped toward the company truck. "I'm also smart enough to know that thing's coming back." He took a few more steps, then stopped. Slowly, he turned around and looked at the cocoons in the web. The sight of Bryce's contorted face rekindled his inner rage. Had he not already known it was her, he would never be able to identify who it was in that cocoon.

His survival instincts faded in favor of vengeance.

"Like I said: it's coming back. And the agreement was to kill it. I wouldn't mind pissing it off first." He looked at the gas can hanging from Kira's grip. "Let's put the rest of that to use."

They moved to the container. Along the way, Marshall scooped up one of the automatic rifles from the dead gunmen. He found the ejector, detached the old magazine, then slammed a fresh one in.

"Pull back on the cocking lever," Ethan said. Marshall did as instructed. He was more familiar with shotguns, bolt-action hunting rifles, and pistols. This was his first time with a military-grade weapon. Still, it was common sense what the symbols meant by the firing lever. He set it for three-round bursts, then made sure the red dot was visible. The weapon was ready to fire.

"What are we going to do? Pour the gas into the container and light it?" Kira asked.

"I've got a better idea," Ethan said. "Marshall, can you handle a forklift?"

"With my eyes shut," Marshall replied.

"Good. Get in. Use it to put those ugly bastards next to the propane tank. The blast will be more than enough to kill them."

"You got it. I'm assuming the rest of the plan is the same as before?"

"Once that thing is in place, we'll soak the area around the tank with gas. Then we'll draw Mommy in close. Once she's near, we'll light the gas, shoot the tank. Boom. Then we can ride off into the sunset."

"Assuming we don't get fried." Kira said.

"Better get cracking then," Marshall said. He hopped into the forklift and started it up. He lowered the forks then approached the container. The spiderlings broke away from their meal and scurried about in panic as their world suddenly began to shake. Marshall maneuvered around the east yard, circling around to the propane tank. He set the container down next to it, then backed away.

Kira ran to the container with the gas can. She unscrewed the lid, tossed it aside, and began soaking the web with gasoline. Her stomach started to churn. She could hear a squelching noise above her. Looking high into the nest, she could see the egg sacks pulsing.

"Oh, no…"

Little legs protruded, light grey in color. Pincers tore away at the thin casing, unveiling the world that the creatures would occupy. Three of them scurried out of the web, momentarily halting, as though blinded by the sun. They then scurried to the cocoons, only to find the hosts void of blood.

More legs flailed through the egg sacks. Three became six. Six became nine. And the egg sacks were still pulsing. In mere minutes, nine would become fifty.

"Oh, shit. If they could only have waited two more fucking minutes…" Ethan said.

Marshall could see it too. "Kira…get away from there. Hurry!"

She dropped the gas can and dashed around the back of the nest. Triggered by motion, the creatures turned. There was no training to be had. There was no nursing to be needed, no training to endure. The arachnoids were pre-programmed to kill, should their mother fail to supply adequate sustenance.

Marshall unslung his rifle and burst through the cab door. He centered his aim at the three initial hatchlings and squeezed the trigger. The three-round burst surprisingly didn't have as much recoil as he expected. One of the spiderlings exploded into a fountain of guts. He fired again, ravaging another.

Before he could hit the third, it leapt.

Kira had been watching it in the corner of her eye. Wincing, she batted her arms, knocking it away. Legs and pincers scratched her wrists as they tried to secure a hold, only to claw the air as the arachnoid landed on its back. The disoriented newborn flailed, unused to taking such a blow. It began to right itself, only to explode into a dozen fragments.

Marshall watched his third kill spray its innards like a ruptured soda bottle. The satisfaction was momentary, and turned to pure fright as he saw the swarm high above racing toward his girlfriend. Two more sprang from the edge of the web, their limbs briefly outstretched like flying squirrels, then coiling to absorb the landing.

Kira looked over her shoulder and saw the critters scurrying less than three yards behind her. She ran to the fireplace, out of Ethan's way.

"Hey," he said. He tossed her his rifle, which she caught by the stock. Before she could turn, he was already firing his revolver. Both spiderlings splattered, their legs bending repeatedly at the knuckles.

More were coming, and more were hatching from the egg sacks. Marshall cut down a few as they emerged. Guts soaked the web, the body parts mixing in with the fallen leaves and other residue that added to the filthy texture. Marshall put another spiderling in his sights and squeezed the trigger. *Click.*

"Shit!"

With a dry magazine, he had no other weapons.

He stared at the forklift controls, then at the spiderlings springing to the ground. He cocked a smile, then shut the door. He started the vehicle up again and pushed it to the max, right into the swarm. Little fountains of blood sprayed from the tracks as he crushed several spiderlings to mulch. He proceeded to circle about, catching a couple more.

There were only a few left. Just a few tight circles, and he'd have them all squished. Only a small handful were emerging from the egg sacks that he could see, and they were nothing he wouldn't be able to handle.

"Yeah, that's right, you little fuckers." He reversed the forklift, catching a couple more as they leapt to the ground. He could hear the cracking of exoskeleton and the squishing of organs as he ground them into the earth. Then he heard something else. Thunder…

No, not thunder…

He looked behind him. "Jesus!"

Like a raging bull, the arachnoid mother charged out of the woods and slammed into the forklift. Pincers raked the cab, cracking the glass and bending the frames. Marshall strapped himself in. The vehicle was shaking violently. He tried to accelerate, but the beast had him in a firm grasp. The wheels kicked up dirt and body parts as they spun in place.

Ethan and Kira didn't have time to stand and watch, as the remaining spiderlings were quickly approaching. Kira steadied her aim and fired. To her surprise, she hit the target dead center. She cocked the lever and aimed again. The nearest arachnoid was fifteen feet away and closing fast. Yet, it traveled in a straight line, making aim fairly simple.

She pointed the muzzle about six inches ahead of its path. By the time she squeezed the trigger, the bullet and target were perfectly lined up, resulting in a spectacular dance as the creature flipped backward, with a perfect hole in its abdomen.

Her kill did not foil the sense of terror. There were seven babies swarming toward her and she had only one shot. Worse yet, the love of her life was being attacked by the adult.

Ethan shot his remaining rounds in rapid succession, eliminating four of the little bastards. He had one remaining speed loader, but no time to grab it. He holstered the revolver in favor of his Bowie knife. Like a grasshopper, one of the spiderlings jumped at him. He slashed the knife, catching the creature in midair. It flailed to the left, landing belly up. It flailed its five remaining legs, gushing blood from all three stubs and the laceration in its abdomen.

The next one came at Kira. She stepped back and took aim, only to fall backward as her foot never touched ground. She fell into the firepit, smothering herself in ash and dirt. The arachnoid pinched her swollen ankle. Shrieking, she thrust the butt of the rifle into it, knocking it backward.

Kira rolled to her side, ending up on her hands and knees. The arachnoid was already righting itself. Her first instinct was to go at it with the rifle. Then she felt the cooking prong between her palm and the grass. Without hesitation, she rose to her feet, pinned the creature under her boot, and plunged the metal prong through its head, pinning it to the ground.

As she looked up, Ethan had already disposed of the last one, slicing it mid-leap with his Bowie knife. For an injured man with a limp and partial paralysis, his aim was impeccable.

Her admiration gave way to concern. The arachnoid was still tearing away at the forklift. The glass windows had shattered, along with the windshield. She could hear Marshall screaming as it began to reach into the cab with its pincer.

After cocking the rifle lever, she took aim. Its head was barely visible over the top of the cab. She aimed for the sensitive pedipalps and squeezed off her last round.

The arachnoid hissed and withdrew, scratching its claws over its injured mandibles. Marshall breathed a sigh of relief. A millisecond ago, its pincer was within inches of his face.

He drove the vehicle forward, putting distance between him and the predator. He performed a tight U-turn while raising the forks midway. At the end of the turn, he was lined up perfectly with the arachnoid. He put the vehicle in forward gear, ready to charge head-on with the beast.

Only, it didn't go for him. It darted to his left—right for Kira.

Kira gasped. Instinctively, she squeezed the trigger, only to remember it was empty. She raised the rifle by the barrel and threw it like a tomahawk, smashing it over the arachnoid's face. It didn't slow. It closed in, cocking its arms back, ready to snip her head clean off her shoulders.

Loud *cracks* concurrent to sudden pain in its abdomen made the creature spin to its right.

Ethan's shots were, as usual, well placed, landing right into the open wound in its abdomen. Despite the immense injuries it endured, the damn thing still wouldn't die!

He had three rounds left—the *last* three. He fired one, popping another of the arachnoid's eyes. The pain only served to enrage the beast further. Eight enormous legs lacerated the earth, propelling the beast at its target.

Gritting teeth from pain and anger, Ethan fired again, hitting it in the pedipalps. It slowed momentarily, only to close in in a singular leap. Claws reached in toward him. Ethan staggered backwards, only to fall on his rear. He scampered back from its reach, but he couldn't outpace the pincers.

One closed over his left leg, sparking pain that only medieval torture could rival. The claw tightened, slicing through the brace. He could feel his bones on the verge of snapping.

All he had was his last bullet, and knowledge of where the bitch hurt the most. He pointed the revolver and fired a shot into its pedipalps. The arachnoid let go and staggered back. Its right pedipalp was nothing more than mangled flesh. The creature staggered, bleeding from its jaws and eyes.

Ethan glanced at his leg. The brace was completely destroyed, leaving nothing but mangled muscle underneath. Between that and the venom flaring up the little bit of muscle still there, he wasn't going anywhere.

He drew his knife again and pointed it at the arachnoid.

"Come on, you fat-ass cunt. Bring it!"

The beast poised, ready to come at him again. It took a few steps, only to stop. There was the sound of a large object rapidly moving in. The beast turned around, then raised its body high as it saw the forklift speeding towards it.

Marshall raised the forks a little higher, just in time to plunge them into the creature's abdomen. Blood sprayed the cab, drenching his clothes and face. Blinded, he could only hook to the right to avoid running over Ethan. The forklift angled toward the cottage, carrying the flailing arachnoid in its lift.

They struck the building with a thunderous *boom,* caving in the section of wall.

The creature flailed in agony. Behind that agony was a desire to kill the one responsible. It snapped its pincers at the cockpit, the tips closing shut within centimeters of their target.

Marshall pushed the machine forward, keeping the creature pinned.

"Go!" he shouted.

"Marshall!" Kira cried.

Ethan turned over onto his left side. At first, he assumed Kira was protesting Marshall's self-sacrifice. While that was true, he realized there was something else triggering her fear for him.

There was movement in his peripheral vision.

"You've got to be fucking kidding," he muttered. The baby arachnoid, lacking three of its legs, and still gushing blood from the laceration in its abdomen, was righting itself. It didn't move as fast as it did before, but its motive was still the same. Feed.

And it was going straight for the man inside the metal body.

"Oh no you don't." Ethan threw the useless revolver at it, knocking the spiderling over. This time, it moved faster, hissing at its attacker. Ethan didn't anticipate its sudden increase in speed. Despite its injuries, it was able to dart right for him.

He tried scurrying back, but his injured leg failed him completely. With the bug nearly closed in, he leaned forward and slashed his knife.

But the arachnoid stopped short, dodging his slash. It wasn't a defensive tactic, rather an offensive one that brought it luck. It was merely stopping to cock its legs for a jump.

It crossed the air like a bullet, tackling Ethan to his back. A thousand curses and phrases crossed his mind, ready to escape his tongue. Instead, all he could do was yell as he felt its stinger plunge into his abdomen.

He rolled to the left, pinning the arachnoid like a wrestler, then forced his Bowie knife through its head.

Already, he could feel the venom taking effect. He was starting to shake. There was a strange tightening in his throat. His muscles burned. There was the same sensation of them stretching like rubber bands, only twice as bad. With the venom from the previous sting still in his system, he knew he only had moments before suffering total paralysis.

Frothing at the mouth, he used all of his energy to crawl to the forklift. He grabbed the handle, pulled himself up, then opened it.

"Get out of here!" He grabbed Marshall by the shirt and threw him onto the lawn, then took his seat. It took everything to even get his hands to reach the controls. Straining hard, he put the vehicle in reverse, carrying the angry arachnoid on the forks.

He angled it toward the nest, then gave one last glance to Marshall. "Go! It's about to get hot!"

Before Marshall could protest, Ethan accelerated at full speed, plowing straight through the nest. The web folded then collapsed around them. The forklift's path came to a sudden stop as it rammed into the propane tank. The left fork, protruding from the creature's rear, impaled the steel hull. Tons of propane gas escaped into the air.

Marshall ran to Kira. "Come on!" Together, they dashed to the company pickup truck. With the engine left running, it was a simple matter of turning the truck around in the yard and racing out through the driveway.

But not without giving one last glance to Ethan Fekete. Marshall didn't take his actions for granted. The hunter, who nearly killed him earlier that day, had saved his life.

Ethan could feel his veins popping. His jaw was crooked, his eyes bulging. He reached for his vest pocket, managing to find his lighter despite barely being able to move his fingers. He hesitated long enough to see the young couple make their escape.

His eyes went back to the arachnoid. She was peering into the cab. He could see anger in those black eyes. It was as if she knew what was coming. To the right were the spiderlings, scurrying about in their entrapment. The crash has struck the end, creating a large crack in the glass.

Propane gas filled the cab.

His last ounce of energy was divided between smiling at his mortal enemy and the spinning of the flint wheel. The little flame expanded into an enormous fireball rivaling hellfire missiles. A tidal wave of fire consumed the property in the blink of an eye, the explosive force throwing a volley of smoking body parts and property fragments in all directions.

CHAPTER 34

Never in her life did Kira love the sight of Dray Street more than this very moment. She and Marshall could feel the heat of the explosion on their backs as they raced onto the road. Marshall turned the vehicle to the left and stomped on the brakes.

They stepped out, frozen in awe at the enormous fireball that rose above the trees. A huge tornado of smoke twisted high in the air. It was a sight that would be seen for miles. At the very least, it would be enough to attract the attention of the Fire Department, freeing the lovers of the burden of trying to find out how to alert them without a phone.

It was all done. The arachnoid was dead, along with its creators. The truth about Jedlinsky's Corporation would be exposed. The knowledge brought mild comfort to Kira. At least her friends would get the retribution they deserved. She did not look forward to the inevitable explanations she would have to present to their families. But, with the inevitable arrival of police, she would have a little assistance in that matter.

She leaned against Marshall as he put his hand over her shoulder. Together, they watched the fire continue to climb. He put his head against hers.

"You alright?"

"I will be."

He shrugged. "Sorry about the setback in repairs."

She didn't think she could smile in this moment, but somehow, Marshall had performed a miracle. She faced him, cupped his face in her hands, and pressed her lips to his.

"So, what now?" she said, leaning her head against his chest.

"Well, once all this investigative stuff is done, I saw we should get a place together."

"Yeah? Where?"

"Somewhere where's there's a lot of water. I saw a place on Lake Huron for sale."

"A cottage?"

Marshall shook his head. "A house. Enough for at least two. Well, four, really. I'd hate to live there all by myself—"

She cupped his face again. "Count me in." Their lips met again, as they would endlessly for the years to come.

The End

Made in the USA
Middletown, DE
30 May 2021